THE
ULTRA
BETRAYAL

A CONOR THORN NOVEL

D1202596

THE
TORCH
BETRAYAL

A CONOR THORN NOVEL

GLENN DYER

TMR PRESS, LLC

ALSO BY THE AUTHOR

The Torch Betrayal

TMR PRESS, LLC
2057 MAHRE DRIVE
PARK CITY, UTAH 84098

THE ULTRA BETRAYAL A Conor Thorn Novel (Book 2)

www.glenndyer.net

First Edition

ISBN 978-0-9991173-5-4 (ebook)
978-0-9991173-4-7 (paperback)
978-0-9991173-6-1 (hardback)

Printed in the United States of America

Cover and Interior Design: JD Smith Design
Author Photo By Terry Moffitt

The OSS logo is a registered trademark of The OSS Society, Inc. and is used with its permission.

You can grab a free short story that pits Britain's Winston Churchill against the leader of the Soviet Union, Joseph Stalin, when you join my newsletter. You'll also get the Prologue and Chapter One of *The Torch Betrayal*, the first book in the Conor Thorn Series, and notice of upcoming releases, promotions, and personal updates.

Sign up today at:

WWW.GLENNDYER.NET/SUBSCRIBE

For my children, Thomas, Michael, and Riley

Though those that are betray'd do feel treason,
yet the traitor stands in worse case of woe.
—William Shakespeare, *The Tragedie of Cymbeline*

He that has eyes to see and ears to hear may convince himself
that no mortal can keep a secret. If his lips are silent he chatters
with his fingertips; betrayal oozes out of him at every pore.
—Sigmund Freud

There is room for a sweeping statement:
ULTRA was essential to victory in the Battles of
Britain and the Atlantic, the war in Africa, and the
landing in Sicily and Normandy. Without ULTRA, victory
in the spring of 1945 would have been unthinkable.
—Dr. Harold C. Deutsch,
Parameters: Journal of the U.S. Army War College

PROLOGUE

2245 Hours, Saturday, October 17, 1942
The Crown Inn, Fenny Stratford, Buckinghamshire

Eve Lind scrubbed her hands with a stiff bristle brush and lye soap. Already chapped and cracked, they were soon spotted with beads of blood. She stopped herself and dropped the brush into the sink, raising her hands to her face and drawing in a deep breath. There was no remaining scent.

She picked up the small packet of bacon fat and poison, which she had wrapped into a three-inch square of brown wax paper, put on her wool waistcoat, and took a seat in Gunnar's favorite chair. She knew she would not have to wait long.

If the Crown Inn's landlady continued her tedious routine, she would emerge at the top of the hour from her flat across the hall, she and her dog, a brown cocker spaniel that expressed her dislike for Eve at every turn. The dog, Winny, would nearly drag Mrs. Buckmaster to the stairs that led down to the inn's front door. Tonight, though, the routine would be altered. Eve's husband wouldn't be sitting in his favorite chair near the stout coal-burning stove, and he wouldn't announce to Eve the moment he heard Mrs. Buckmaster and Winny embarking on their nightly walk. Because Gunnar Lind was gone.

Eve would give the woman and her fiendish dog enough time to make their way to the woods behind the inn before she set out into the chilly night to join them. Eve had been angry that, ever

1

since she and Gunnar had had their worst argument several weeks prior, Gunnar had spent a lot of time with Mrs. Buckmaster in the downstairs pub in the evenings. When she had asked him about it, he would only say that the woman, a widow in her late sixties, was lonely. Her two sons were in North Africa with the British Army, and she hadn't heard from them in quite a while. Eve didn't believe him. Since their evening chats had begun, she could feel the once warm and friendly landlady had turned cold toward her—which meant the woman was a threat.

Eve looked at the clock on the mantel. It was time.

She quickly descended the flight of stairs. None of the sparsely numbered pub patrons took notice of her, and once outside, she picked up her pace and closed the distance to the woman and her dog. The gravel crunched under her shoes, echoing under the leafy roof that covered the path, but that was fine. She didn't need to sneak up on the woman.

When she was twenty yards away, Mrs. Buckmaster stopped and turned around. Eve couldn't see her face clearly, but when the woman took two steps back, she realized that the landlady was frightened.

"Who is that?" she said.

Winny began her own questioning with a sharp series of barks.

"It's just me, Mrs. Buckmaster. Eve Lind. I didn't mean to startle you. Please excuse me."

"Well, you did just that ... startled me, that is. What do you want? Shush, Winny."

"I've been meaning to knock on your door. For a visit. I wanted to ask you about Gunnar," Eve said as she bent over to pat the dog. But Winny was having none of it as she backpedaled, stopping behind Mrs. Buckmaster's legs.

"What about him?" Mrs. Buckmaster said.

"He never came home last night, and I haven't heard from him all day. I know you two have been spending time together in the evenings lately. Did he say anything to you?" Eve said, taking a step closer.

Mrs. Buckmaster didn't answer. She retreated a step and stepped on Winny's paw. The high-pitched yelp startled both women.

"I'm worried. I'm sure you can understand that," Eve said, adding a noticeable quaver in her voice.

"Maybe you should ask those people he works with. They should know. Not me."

The lie came to Eve easily. "I already have. They were no help."

Mrs. Buckmaster shook her head. "I can't help you."

Eve inched closer. "You can't or won't, Mrs. Buckmaster?"

"Actually, Mrs. Lind, if you must know, I won't."

"I see. And why is that?" Eve said, drawing out the small wax paper packet from her pocket.

"I heard enough from your husband, you could say."

"And what was that? What did he say?"

"I'm done talking to you. Now leave us alone."

"Did he ever mention anything about a letter or letters?"

Again, Mrs. Buckmaster didn't answer. But when she flinched at the mention of letters, Eve pulled the bacon fat from the packet and tossed it at the woman's feet.

"What is that? What are you doing?"

Winny wasted no time lapping up the lard. Eve tossed the wax paper on the ground for good measure.

"Stop, Winny," Mrs. Buckmaster yelled as she pulled at the dog's leash.

"It seems that Winny was hungry. You must not be feeding her enough."

Mrs. Buckmaster pulled at the leash, and Winny choked several times. With another tug, Mrs. Buckmaster began dragging Winny away.

Eve didn't want to kill the dog. It was just a necessary step. She had debated whether to do it before or after. It had depended on the way Mrs. Buckmaster answered her, and her cold and uninformative replies had made the decision for Eve. Killing the dog in front of the meddlesome landlady suited Eve just fine.

Winny sprawled on her side in the gravel and started convulsing. Her paws spasmodically sprayed the gravel across the path.

"What have you done, you witch?" Mrs. Buckmaster bent down to tend to the dog.

Eve reached inside her coat pocket and pulled out the sock filled with stones the size of chestnuts. It was one of Gunnar's socks. She had bought the pair for him last Christmas. She whipped it around in a tight circle, and it landed on the back of

Mrs. Buckmaster's head. The crunching sound would be hard to forget. Blood spattered on the back of Mrs. Buckmaster's coat and Eve's bare legs.

Eve rolled over Mrs. Buckmaster's body and placed her index finger under her nostrils. The woman's breathing was evident but labored. Eve had a cure for that. After all, she was a doctor. She squeezed the woman's nose shut and placed her other hand over Mrs. Buckmaster's mouth. Five seconds later, Mrs. Buckmaster began to struggle, her legs kicking and her hands tugging on Eve's coat. Eve brought her weight down on the old woman. The struggle was short-lived.

Breathing rapidly herself, Eve rose to her feet and ran to a nearby stand of trees to retrieve the shovel she had left there the night before. The rush of adrenaline was liberating. Problem solved.

CHAPTER ONE

1400 Hours, Monday, October 19, 1942
Government Code & Cypher School (GC&CS),
Bletchley Park, Buckinghamshire

The paper-thin walls of Hut 8 failed miserably at keeping the dampness brought on by the steady rains at bay. Alan Turing had his scarf wrapped tightly around his neck, and his gloved hands coiled around a tepid cup of tea. He stared across the office at Gunnar Lind's desk. Its surface was a complete mess, just like his. The only difference was that Turing had shown up for work, whereas Lind had not. Turing was not exactly sure how long it had been since Lind, his Swedish cryptologist associate, was last at his desk. Turing had been so deep down the rabbit hole in his own work for the past several days that he had lost all sense of his surroundings. Yet he knew that it would be one of the first questions Travis would ask him. He better have an answer.

Turing turned to a calendar pinned to a corkboard near his desk and saw that it hadn't been flipped to the new month. He pulled it down, changed the page, and studied October. Turing remembered a conversation he'd had with Lind after enlisting in the infantry section of the home guards. Lind had asked him why he would do such a thing, and Turing had answered that he wanted to learn to shoot a rifle. Lind had laughed, which puzzled Turing. His reason seemed to be perfectly logical. It was the next day, after that conversation, that he'd first noticed Lind didn't appear in Hut 8.

That would make it 15 October. Four days ago. Turing padlocked his mug to the radiator and picked up his phone.

#

Edward Travis, head of the Government Code & Cypher School, sat behind his desk, which was marked by a wooden inbox overflowing with paperwork. A desk lamp was switched on to combat the gloomy skies outside the unsightly Victorian country mansion that housed the main offices of the GC&CS. When Alan Turing, one of his leading cryptologists, was shown in, Travis saw a drenched, dark-haired man in his thirties who looked like he hadn't changed clothes for days on end.

"You know, Turing, there must be hundreds of brollies in Bletchley Park. You seem to not have noticed."

Turing ran his hands through his soaked hair and flicked them free of the rain. "Of course, sir. But it's such a short walk from the hut, and I didn't want to waste any time."

"What's so—"

"Gunnar Lind has not shown up for work for four days," Turing said. "He also hasn't been seen at the Crown Inn, where he was billeted. I know this because it is the same place where I live."

Travis turned his palms upward and shrugged. "Under the weather possibly? That would certainly be understandable given—"

"I placed a call to Mrs. Buckmaster, our landlady, who is quite a headstrong woman. She believes, by the way, I have contributed nothing to the war effort." Turing paused. "Do you think someday she will know? That would be some comfort."

"And?"

Turing cocked his head. "And what?"

"What did the landlady say, Turing?" Travis said, not hiding his annoyance.

"Oh, well ... the strange thing is that no one knows where Mrs. Buckmaster is. She hasn't been seen since late Saturday night, I'm told. Her daughter, Maisie, reported her absence to the local police."

Travis sat up straight. "That's a strange coincidence. What was Lind working on?"

Turing sucked in his breath. "I work best alone, but Gunnar knows when to pose the right question at the right time. He's very much a muse, so to speak. I need my muse."

Travis stood quickly, startling Turing. "Again, Turing, what was he working on?"

"He was refining the hand code-breaking methods that I devised for the cryptanalysis of the Lorenz cipher produced by the SZ40 and SZ42 teleprinters." Turing sucked in a quick breath. "Tunny. He was working on Tunny."

At the word "Tunny," Travis gasped and plopped back into this chair. The Germans used the Lorenz teleprinters to send enciphered messages wirelessly to German High Command and army group commanders in the field. *Fish* was the British code name for any German teleprinter–generated ciphers. It was inspired by the German name for one of their wireless transmission systems— *Sägefisch*, or sawfish. *Tunny* was the name given to the wireless traffic enciphered by the Lorenz SZ machines. Worse, Tunny was a major part of Ultra—British military intelligence's designation for signals intel that came from high-level Nazi cipher traffic—as was breaking the German Enigma machine codes. Lind's knowledge of Fish and Enigma code-breaking efforts, should it be passed on to the Germans, would be catastrophic to upcoming Allied operations in French North Africa and General Montgomery's El Alamein offensive. "Why in God's name didn't you mention this sooner? Four days? Four bloody days, Turing?"

"Ahh, ahhh, ahhh, ahhh …" Travis knew this was Turing's habit to keep people from interrupting him while he was thinking of a response. "I was lost … in my work. I try not to pay attention to my surroundings. Except when I need something."

Travis was stunned when Turing spun on his heel and left his office.

That was all he needed: a missing cryptologist with intimate knowledge of Ultra. Travis reached for his phone. "Headley, ring up Winterbotham at MI6 straightaway. Then have my car brought around. I am sure they'll want to take their pound of flesh in person."

CHAPTER TWO

1800 Hours, Monday, October 19, 1942
Savoy Hotel, Victoria Embankment, London

The lanes of Savoy Court were jammed with cars spewing a cloud of exhaust smoke that was slow to escape the narrow, canyon-like street in front of the famous London hotel. Conor Thorn, OSS agent and former lieutenant in the US Navy, had just returned from a mission with beautiful MI6 agent Emily Bright. He pulled the Buick Roadmaster to the curb and turned to his driver, Hollis. Conor always insisted on driving, so she was sitting comfortably in the backseat, reading the *Daily Mirror*. Its headline blared news of a new German attack on Stalingrad.

"Miss Hollis, we'll jump out here. We won't need you any further tonight," Conor said, seeing Emily raising an eyebrow in his direction. He reached over and opened Emily's door. They darted across the Strand, and a doorman well into his seventies saw them approach. He was dressed in a black three-piece suit with a top hat. The ensemble, Conor noticed, was a size too small; the lower vest buttons looked very distressed. The doorman opened the door, which let the chatter from the lobby drift into the court.

Conor and Emily stopped in the expansive lobby and took in the sight. The black-and-white-checkered marble floor gleamed, as did the dark wood of the reception area. A bellboy rushed past them carrying a tray with an envelope on it as Conor watched Emily survey the scene. Her light-brown shoulder-length hair glistened, and her eyes sparkled.

"Don't you think that we deserve a little spoiling after our mad dash across the Mediterranean, tracking down those who would do us harm?" he said.

Emily turned to Conor and cracked a smile. "What do you have in mind, Mr. Thorn?"

Conor leaned in and got a whiff of lavender. "Actually, I was thinking of getting a room key."

"Whatever for?" Emily said in faux shock.

"Well, for one thing, I hear the Savoy decor is something to marvel at."

"Then we'll have to experience that, won't we?"

A wide-eyed Conor nodded, pleased by this response. "Wait here a minute," he said and headed toward the reception desk.

A tall man with slumping shoulders and a burgeoning waistline was coming down a side staircase. He was wearing the dress whites of a US Navy officer, the rank of a captain. He passed Conor, then stopped and turned back.

"Thorn?"

Conor stopped and saw Captain Bivens, the last captain he'd served under—the man who had forced Conor out of the US Navy. Conor's shock was quickly eclipsed by his anger at seeing his old commanding officer. Emily joined Conor as the man spoke.

"I almost didn't recognize you, Thorn."

"I'm not wearing a uniform, Captain."

Bivens nodded but didn't reply.

"This is Emily Bright. Emily, this is Captain Bivens."

Emily shook Bivens's extended hand. "Hello, Captain. Nice to meet you."

Bivens gave Emily a quick nod.

"Still on sea duty, Captain?" Conor asked.

"No, no. Too old. I'm the assistant naval attaché here in London." Bivens stammered. "L-l-listen, Thorn. My wife left me for some desk-bound lifer from the State Department that she was cheating on me with."

Emily looked at Conor, who made no attempt to respond.

"So I did you and the navy a major disservice when I told you to resign your commission. She eventually told me that you didn't … assault her. She was just trying to get my attention. But by then it was too late. You had already tendered your resignation. I'm sorry. If there's anything I—"

"Captain," Conor said, and then stopped for a beat. "There's nothing I could ever want from you. So stop."

Bivens nodded and carefully placed his combination cap on his head, wheeled around, and walked out of the lobby into the chaos of Savoy Court.

"That's a story you never told me," Emily said.

"I was in a bad place back then. It was probably for the best." Conor took her elbow and headed upstairs to the American Bar, passing the reception desk without getting a key.

#

Immediately upon entering, Conor saw his father, Jack, at the bar, chatting with Ed Murrow from CBS Radio. He felt Emily tugging at his sleeve, then saw her motion to a woman several feet away, sitting at a small cocktail table and writing rapidly on a sheet of paper. It was his sister Maggie. She also worked for CBS Radio after leaving Republic Broadcasting Service, run by their father, Jack. A letter was lying to the side, and tears were streaming down her face. "Emily, I can see Dad at the bar. Can you join him? I need to see who or what made my little sister cry."

"Sure. Let me know if I can help."

Maggie was so focused on her writing that she was unaware of Conor's presence as he approached. "So, can I buy you a drink, young lady?"

A startled Maggie looked up at Conor and dabbed her eyes with a handkerchief. She picked up the letter and handed it to him. "I received this today. It's from Sue Ryan."

Conor knew Sue Ryan well. She was with Grace, Conor's late wife, when they first met at a Sunday afternoon tea dance at the Naval Academy during his plebe year. Sue and Grace were so close that Grace had asked Sue to be her maid of honor. Conor took the letter. "Is she okay?"

"Just read it."

October 5, 1942
Dear Maggie,

I do hope this letter finds you safe and sound. I heard from your old college roommate at Villanova, Joan Fitzgerald, that you had been transferred to the RBS London office. It must be exciting, and some-what dangerous, to be in London, is it not?

I have gone back and forth for days about whether I should write this letter to you. It concerns Conor and Grace. Mostly Grace, unfortunately. I have no idea where Conor is these days. I lost track of him after he left the navy. Forgive me, but I will leave it to you to decide if Conor should be told what I'm about to tell you.

I have kept a secret of Grace's for a long time. It is one that I can no longer keep to myself, as I have recently been diagnosed with heart disease and do not have long to live. I apologize for burdening you with this.

Grace came to me in late March of 1941 and revealed that she had been raped.

Conor looked up from the letter, his lips pressed together. A buzzing in his ears blocked out all other sounds. Maggie was staring at him, fresh tears slowly making their way down her cheeks.

"Keep reading."

Conor looked around at the steady stream of patrons filling the bar and took a deep breath.

She said it occurred at a dinner held at her father's house in Oyster Bay. A dinner she said you were also at. Grace said she was feeling low and was missing Conor. She regretted an argument about her desire to get pregnant that they'd had just before he left to rejoin the Reuben James *for convoy duty. She said she begged him to get her pregnant before he left. But Conor insisted that she needed to heed her doctor's advice that it was too danger-ous, given her past bout of rheumatic fever. She said there was too much drinking at the dinner and that she didn't want to tell me who assaulted her. After they finished eating, he said he just wanted to talk and walked her to the library, but then he pushed her against the wall and covered her mouth.*

"Son of a bitch," Conor said, prompting a few stares.

> *She told me she can't stand the smell of aftershave and hair cream to this day because it reminded her of him. She struggled to fight him, but he was too strong. When it was over, he just left her there.*
>
> *I realize that I am betraying Grace's confidence, but I won't take this to my grave. I loved her too much to do that, and seeing Grace suffer so deeply in the weeks after, I couldn't help but think that the rape changed her deeply. She withdrew from all of her friends and family. She stopped returning my calls and letters. Whoever it was, he should pay for what he did. I only wish she would have told me who it was. But she was afraid that Conor would do something stupid. Maggie, you always struck me as someone with a level head, and you always seemed to know the right thing to do. I'll leave this with you.*
> *Good luck,*
> *Sue*

Conor's eyes welled with tears, but he quickly blinked them away. How did he not notice the pain she was in? Was he so consumed by his own career that he couldn't see she was troubled? But Grace was right. He wouldn't have stopped until he'd found the bastard that violated his wife. But maybe it wasn't too late for that. *I'm sorry, Grace. I know this is not what you wanted, but I just can't let this slide.* He carefully folded the letter, placed it back into the envelope, then put it into his breast pocket. Maggie handed him the sheet of paper she had been writing on. The Savoy Hotel stationery was tear-stained. On it, Maggie had written several names in a bold script.

"What's this?"

"Names of the men that were at the dinner. The ones I remember."

There was a short note after each name. Conor recognized several of the names as old friends of the Maxwell family. One name was already crossed out by Maggie—*Bill Maxwell*, Grace's father. A name jumped out at Conor—*Preston Simms*, Grace's stepbrother. Next to his name was a note—*USAAF Public Affairs officer at RAF Daws Hill*. On the bottom of the list were two question marks. Conor looked up at Maggie.

"I'm so sorry, but I just never got their names. I was drinking too. I think one was a friend of Preston, who was a jerk, and the other guy arrived late. I wish I knew more."

"That's okay, Maggie. Thanks for letting me see the letter. And thanks for the list." Conor began folding the paper.

"I loved Grace, Conor. She was the best of us."

Conor cleared his throat. A moment passed. "She sure was that."

They both rose and headed toward the bar, Maggie taking the lead, when a hand grabbed Conor's shoulder. Already tense, he spun around, ready to pounce.

"Hey, buddy. Didn't think I'd see you so soon." The moment Conor saw his old friend Bobby Heugle, the tension drained from his body. "Hello, Maggie. How's things?"

Conor gave Bobby, also an OSS agent, a handshake and a soft chest bump.

Maggie hugged her old boyfriend and gave him a gentle kiss on the cheek. "I'll leave you two boys alone," Maggie said as she headed toward the bar, which was now three deep.

"So, you got thrown out of Lisbon too? How long were you there? Three days?" Conor asked, referring to both of them being reassigned from Tangier two weeks prior.

"Ha. About that long. After that shit storm you triggered at Portela Airport, the Portuguese government ordered the United States and Germany to expel five staff members each. I was the fifth." Bobby had aptly described the skirmish at the airport between Conor, Emily, and elements of the NKVD and Abwehr—it was a shitty mess that went from bad to worse in an eye blink. With a big human toll. And nothing to count for it. No missing plans for the Torch invasion nor the man who betrayed the Allies. Luckily, Conor and Emily had eventually caught up to both the missing invasion directives and the man who wanted to place those directives in the hands of the Nazis.

"What about the Soviets? Or did they get a pass?"

"Not sure about that. Hey, I've got a tickle in my throat. How about you?"

The rest of the evening was a blur. He listened mostly, said little. Heugle held the floor, like he usually did. And Conor was grateful for it. Emily kept by his side, her arm intertwined with his, and seemed to enjoy herself for the first time since they'd met in the basement pub at MI6 Headquarters. But the seismic emotional shift from feeling like a giddy schoolboy with his dream date on his arm to being a sullen hulk of a man with rage building up inside him was too enormous for him to grasp. When Conor told Emily he had to leave to take care of something, she looked hurt. And that just killed him to see.

CHAPTER THREE

1100 Hours, Tuesday, October 20, 1942
No. 10 Downing Street, London

Stewart Menzies was entirely embarrassed. In all the years he had met with Prime Minister Winston Churchill, never once had the head of Britain's Secret Intelligence Service, also known as MI6, been summoned and then asked to deliver his report through a bathroom door.

David Inches, a proud Scot who was Churchill's butler, knocked lightly to announce him. Menzies could hear water sloshing and Churchill clearing his throat. "Prime Minister, Mr. Menzies is here. He says it's rather important."

"Thank you, Inches." A Pause. "Yes, Stewart," Churchill said, "what do you have for me today?"

Menzies looked at Inches. "It is extremely sensitive, Mr. Prime Minister."

"Yes, yes, of course. Inches … leave us. I can fend for myself for a few minutes."

Inches hurried down the hallway out of earshot. More water sloshing was followed by a sizable sneeze. "Bless you."

Menzies heard a grunt of recognition. "So, Stewart, get on with it."

"Sir, it seems that an important member of our team at Bletchley Park has turned up missing. He was deeply involved in Ultra matters." The sloshing about of bathwater ceased.

"Just what are you telling me?"

Menzies paused. "I'll not sugarcoat this ... Ultra could be at risk." The secret of Ultra was his to protect. If the Germans became aware that their ciphers were being read, a new system of communication with units in the field could prove to be harder to break than the Enigma system. Worse, Churchill would be forced to take control of Ultra away from him. "But we have launched a massive search for this man. Ports, train stations, airports, hospitals, hotels. Given the fact that he had been arguing with his wife, we have even checked ... houses of ill repute."

Menzies could hear more splashing followed by multiple grunts. Then the door opened. Churchill stood in a robe, cinching the belt around his ample waist. His slippers were embroidered with Asian dragons. The cigar in his mouth was unlit. His face, flushed from the bath, was frozen with the look of a man who had just witnessed a horrific crime.

"This is devastating news. Just who is this man?"

"Gunnar Lind. A Swedish mathematician and cryptologist we brought over from France in 1940. He's been at Bletchley since then, working closely with Alan Turing. He once worked at a factory in Berlin that manufactured Enigma machines. In 1938, he built a replica of the Enigma machine for us for ten thousand pounds, British passports for him and his wife, and a resident's permit for France."

"And we put this scoundrel to work at Bletchley? Someone with an allegiance to money above England?"

"Mr. Prime Minister, he's a brilliant man. And as you are well aware, we have struggled mightily to recruit experts to Bletchley since the war broke out. He has vast experience that many of our own recruits from Cambridge and Oxford and elsewhere did not have."

Churchill grumbled as he walked past Menzies and down the hallway. Menzies wasn't sure whether he should follow. This was a new experience. He was debating his next move when Churchill ducked into a room off the hallway and called out, "Stewart!"

Menzies hurried down the hallway after him. Churchill was sitting in a wingback leather chair in the robe, his legs spread wide.

"Have you told our American friends? Have you told Donovan?"

The question startled Menzies. Churchill knew that Menzies was not impressed with Bill Donovan or his OSS. They were careless with information and extremely arrogant. Why would he bring them into this? "Sir, this is our problem. I hardly think—"

"Stewart! You need all the help you can muster. Tell Donovan," Churchill said, his voice rising with each word, "and find this ... this Lind."

#

Conor arrived at No. 10 early for the meeting with the prime minister. As he was the first to arrive, he was asked to wait in the Porter's Room, just off the inner hall. He was thinking about a visit he and Colonel "Wild Bill" Donovan, head of the OSS, had made earlier that morning to a motor gun boat demonstration off Canvey Island, about forty miles east of London. MGB 622, a Fairmile D model, 115-foot, 91-ton vessel powered by four Packard supercharged engines, had a top speed of 31 knots. Fairmile D boats were called "Dog Boats." MGB 622 had been stripped of its deck-mounted armament. Sir George Binney, a noted arctic explorer and a Royal Navy Reserve officer, explained that the boat's speed was increased when engine exhausts were fitted underwater. Binney went on to describe his plan for a mission that would send the modified MGB 622 to Sweden to pick up ball bearings, which were in great demand. If Binney could prove that such a mission—which would have to transit the heavily mined Skagerrak Strait, the body of water between Norway and Denmark—was successful, more vessels and crews would be found to add more missions.

Conor's appetite for the open sea would be more than satisfied by a ride in such a swift boat—feeling the salt breeze on his face, waves flung up by the bow ...

He suddenly realized it was sweltering in the narrow room. He opened the door and as he tried to open the window, he heard a woman's voice over his shoulder. "Save your strength, Conor," Emily said, standing just inside the doorway. "None of the windows on the street side open."

"Emily ... you snuck up on me." *Conor, you owe her an apology for being so morose last night.* "Listen—"

"Why did you leave the Savoy without saying anything to me? Did you not want to—"

"No, no, no, it wasn't that at all, trust me."

Emily took two quick steps toward him. She was two feet away. Her eyes narrowed, then softened. "Listen to me, Conor. I don't think that I've exactly hidden that I am ... attracted to you," she said in a tenor that said she wasn't concerned if she was overheard. "Yes, I realize that you had a life before we met. Grace died. I am so saddened by that. And then your son. My heart truly breaks for you. But I don't know how to deal with your swings in temperament."

Conor shoved his hands into his pockets. "I owe you an apology. I had just learned something from Maggie. I needed some time to process it. It had nothing to do with you."

"What was she so emotional about?"

Conor could have recited Sue Ryan's letter verbatim at this point but decided to keep the lurid details to himself. "The letter Maggie got was from a friend of Grace's." Conor took a deep breath, lowered his voice, and continued. "She said that Grace was raped in March of last year. Just after I left for another convoy escort mission."

Emily's face was a study in revulsion, but that moment passed quickly as her whole body then seemed to sag under the weight of the news. "I am so so sorry. Did the letter—"

A woman knocked on the doorframe and said that the prime minister and guests were assembled in the Blue Room. "Please follow me."

A moment later, Conor and Emily were shaking hands with Bill Donovan and General Dwight D. Eisenhower. Prime Minister Churchill and Stewart Menzies were huddled near a window on the other side of the room. Churchill was doing all the talking. Menzies looked like he was getting an ass chewing.

General Eisenhower approached, and Conor's spine stiffened just like it had ever since his days at the academy when a superior officer approached. "Conor, Emily, I can't properly express how indebted I am—hell, how indebted all British and Americans are—to you for your outstanding work in helping keep critical information about Operation Torch out of the wrong hands." He shook both Conor's and Emily's hands.

Churchill approached with Menzies in tow. "Couldn't agree more, General. Outstanding, indeed. No doubt these two are a most effective team. Wouldn't you say, Stewart, Bill?"

Both men nodded.

"And, General, speaking of Torch, what news have you?"

Eisenhower did a quick survey of the room before answering. "Well, Prime Minister, in two days, the Western Task Force sets sail from the States, and the day after, the Eastern and Central Task Forces will slip out of the Firth of Clyde, headed to their assigned targets."

"Excellent news, General. The beginning of the end, shall we say? The cabinet will be very happy indeed to hear your report," Churchill said, smiling broadly.

A woman who Conor recognized as Elizabeth Nel, Churchill's secretary, from a meeting he and Emily had had with Churchill just a week prior, entered the Blue Room. "Prime Minister, your cabinet has taken their seats."

Minus Henry Longworth, the traitor, thought Conor.

"Yes, of course, Elizabeth. I'll be there in a minute." Churchill's mood shifted, and a stern look came over his face. "Stewart will fill you all in on a quite serious situation that has come up. I must say that it is even more serious than the situation you all dealt with regarding Operation Torch. Emily, Conor, I don't know what your next assignments *were* going to be, but I know what they *will* be. The OSS and MI6 will have you focus on this next mission. The outcome of the war depends on it." Churchill pulled a cigar from his suit coat breast pocket and waved it at the group. "Carry on," he said, and glided out of the room, followed by General Eisenhower.

"Stewart, what was that all about?" Donovan asked.

Menzies cleared his throat and, making little eye contact with the group, ran through the details of the missing Swedish cryptologist, Gunnar Lind, and the threat he posed to an operation called "Ultra."

Conor saw the blood rush from Donovan's face. "What exactly is Ultra?" Conor asked, knowing it had something to do with codes if a cryptologist was involved.

"A detailed explanation of Ultra will not be forthcoming. But you heard what the prime minister said. The outcome of the war hangs in the balance."

"Stewart, maybe you can bring me up to speed with more details," Donovan said.

"Certainly. I'm told we need all the help we can get," Menzies said. Donovan and Menzies moved to a corner of the room, out of Conor's and Emily's earshot.

Conor looked at Emily. Her face was as ashen as Donovan's a few moments before. "Do you know anything about Ultra?" Conor asked.

"Very little, actually," Emily said while Donovan and Menzies left the room, heading deeper inside No. 10. "But I do know Gunnar Lind, and the man I know would never have done what Menzies fears he has."

"And you know this how?"

Emily turned to Conor. "Because Gunnar Lind owes his life to the British."

CHAPTER FOUR

1400 Hours, Wednesday, October 21, 1942
Claridge's, Brook Street, London

Conor was sitting in what could only be called a closet at OSS headquarters, reading a short bio on Gunnar Lind, when an out-of-breath Duncan Lee, Donovan's assistant, barged through the door.

"The colonel wants to see you right away. He sounded pretty agitated." Conor had been waiting for the summons since yesterday. He was surprised it took this long, given Churchill's ominous explanation of the mission.

Eight minutes later, Conor was walking through the lobby of Claridge's. Head down, he started to ascend the hotel's grand staircase to the second floor. Halfway up, he heard a young woman's slightly accented voice.

"Step aside, please."

Conor looked up and caught sight of a woman somewhere in her sixties walking down the staircase in an orange flannel dressing gown, followed by several young women wearing black calf-length dresses. Conor stepped aside. "Who the heck is that?"

One young woman stopped. "Queen Wilhelmina of the Netherlands. Please, show some respect."

"Respect? She's dressed in her pajamas."

The woman huffed and rejoined what looked like a procession. Conor shook his head and took the rest of the staircase two steps at a time.

When he entered the suite, he found Donovan's head buried in a file stamped with bold red letters: TOP SECRET. Without looking up, Donovan pointed at one of the club chairs in front of his desk. Conor knew to be quiet until his boss had pulled his head out of the file. Two minutes later, Donovan came up for air.

"All right. Stewart brought me up to speed, as I asked. What we have is equal parts mess and mystery. We and MI6 will do the best we can, given our responsibilities with Torch." Donovan leaned forward, resting his elbows on the desk. "It's obvious the prime minister thinks highly of you and Emily."

"Good to have friends in high places, Colonel."

"Sometimes it does work that way. Sometimes you get handed a mess like this."

Conor chuckled but saw that Donovan wasn't playing for laughs.

"You and Emily will work this together for a day or so. Then, she's going to be sent on another mission, or so Stewart tells me. They're delaying her departure as long as they can because she knows this Gunnar Lind. So ask all the questions you can come up with while she's still in England."

The news of Emily's looming departure jolted Conor. His desire to watch out for and protect her had grown as he'd gotten to know her better. "Where is she headed, Colonel?"

"Norway, but I know nothing more."

Conor nodded. *Norway, in German hands since mid-1940. A damn bit more dangerous than Lisbon and Rome, two stops on their last mission. But why didn't Emily tell him she was going behind enemy lines?*

"So what are the details about this … mess, Colonel?"

Donovan opened the file and read from it. "Gunnar Lind is a Swedish mathematician and cryptologist assigned to Bletchley Park. In 1940, MI6 flew him and his wife out of France just ahead of the advancing Germans. He is highly skilled and has sold top secret information in the past." Donovan put the file down. "To the British."

Conor cocked his head and sat back. That fit with what Emily had said and what he read earlier.

Donovan handed the file to Conor, who opened it and saw a

picture of a lanky man in his late twenties, with light wavy hair and a prominent nose on a thin face. He was standing next to an attractive blond who was at least a foot shorter than him.

Donovan walked to a window behind his desk. "He built a replica of a German Enigma machine and sold it to the Brits in 1938. Well, you can read the file."

Conor scanned the pages and learned that the Enigma machine was a critical piece of equipment used by the Germans to communicate with field units and U-boat wolf packs. *Ten thousand pounds sterling. That is a lot of money.*

Donovan put in, "It doesn't have to be said, but none of this can ever be disclosed." He pointed at a small leather jeweler's box on his desk. "Open it."

Conor did and saw two rather large capsules. He looked up at his boss.

"Cyanide capsules. Given what I have already told you, if you ever get captured, you pop one of these between your teeth and bite. Any … questions … or concerns before I go further?"

Conor closed the box. The loud, crisp sound of the spring-loaded cover closing filled the room. He dropped the box into his coat pocket.

Donovan nodded. "Good." He turned back toward the window, which looked over a quiet Brook Street. "Lind is a treasure trove of information about British efforts at breaking German military and naval codes. Their successes have saved thousands of lives. The Germans still think their codes are unbreakable, so they've done nothing to protect their communications. If news of their success reaches the Nazis, codes will be changed and Allied efforts will be set back months, if not years. The loss of life will be unthinkable."

Holy shit. The last mission was about one offensive. This … this is the whole damn war. "What else do we know?" he asked.

"He has an estranged brother and a wife. That's it as far as family goes. Eve Lind is also Swedish and has family back in Stockholm. She's a doctor but has been working as a nurse in a clinic outside Bletchley. She's not qualified to practice in England. She hasn't been back to Sweden since their wedding in early thirty-eight. No children. Reports have it that they have been arguing of late."

"About?"

"Not clear."

"Who reported him missing?"

"One of the other cryptologists who works closely with him: Alan Turing. You should meet with him."

"What was he working on?"

"That is something that has not been made clear to me. And if it was, I may not be able to share it with you. Suffice to say, Lind's disappearance set off some loud alarm bells inside the British military."

"Search-wise, what has been done so far?"

"The Brits have looked all over England. They widened the search radius to include Scotland and Wales. They're even starting to look around in Northern Ireland and Eire."

"How the hell could someone get off the island?"

"Good question. It wouldn't be easy. Actually it's nearly impossible, I'm told, without some very hard-to-get paperwork from pretty high up in the government."

"Has extortion been ruled out?"

"There's been no outreach from Lind. Doesn't mean there won't be. I'm told that MI5 is questioning Lind's wife tomorrow morning up near Bletchley. That's your next stop, along with Emily."

Donovan came around his desk, signaling that they were done. Conor closed the file and rose.

"I know you're not a trained detective, but you're quick on the uptake. Trust your gut on this." Donovan extended his hand.

"What if we never turn up this Lind? What next?"

"Let's hope he's six feet under somewhere on this island."

CHAPTER FIVE

1400 Hours, Wednesday, October 21, 1942
Regents Park, London

The wind that blew through the park was chilled. It rattled the newspaper the man seated on the gravel path was reading. Its headline, in bold black letters, blared news of an Allied commission to investigate Nazi war crimes. Kim Philby chuckled at the perfect example of positive Allied thinking. Victory over the Nazis was not guaranteed, and many people were going to die before that commission ever convened.

Philby smoked a cigarette while he waited for his handler, Shapak. A woman's shouts captured his attention. They came from a victory garden about thirty yards behind him. He turned and saw a middle-aged woman sticking her finger in the face of an older man. It seemed that the woman was not impressed with the amount of tilling and weeding the old man was doing. The old man leaned on the handle of his hoe and scanned the darkening sky, which only resulted in the woman shouting louder.

"Let us find a more quiet place."

Shapak's arrival startled Philby. Before he could say anything, Shapak was already headed down the path toward a vacant bench. Philby tossed his cigarette, grabbed his umbrella, and took a seat when he'd caught up with Shapak. Shapak wore a waist-length wool coat and a wide-brimmed hat pulled down snugly over his ears.

"It seems the invasion of North Africa proceeds."

Philby was not surprised at Shapak's opening. If the roles were reversed, he would have gone there too.

"Your grand plan failed," Shapak said, staring at the ground with his hands buried in his pockets. "Give the Germans the invasion plans, and the operation would be abandoned, leading to the revival of plans for a cross-channel attack on France." Shapak turned to look at Philby. "What happened?"

Philby lit another cigarette and blew out a long stream of blue smoke. "Canaris happened. We both know he is a friend of Menzies and a foe of Hitler. He dreams of Nazi setbacks wherever they can occur. His presence in Rome was a surprise."

A light rain began to fall.

"Unfortunate," Shapak said. "Very unfortunate. This outcome will do nothing to quell fears that Moscow has about you."

"Well, it didn't take long for the 'he's a triple agent' fairy tale to come up."

"For Moscow, it is not a fairy tale. It is reality. A reality you should take more seriously."

"Oh, I can assure you, I do. But you must understand that given all the risks that I take to provide high-quality intelligence, it is insulting and annoying that Moscow Center questions its veracity."

"It is the cross you bear, Philby. But be warned, you should be careful about expressing any annoyance with Moscow Center. Their patience is a shallow well," Shapak said, looking at the ground again.

Philby fidgeted and rubbed the back of his neck. "I, too, have a limited supply of patience. The intelligence that I am passing along, intelligence derived from Ultra, must be heeded. Too often it is not, which only leads to the loss of Soviet lives and matériel. The battles of Voronezh and the second battle of Kharkov ... we both know my intelligence was ignored."

Shapak's head bobbed up and down slowly, giving Philby the confidence to carry on.

"In the case of the battle of Kharkov, ignored intelligence coupled with critical errors on the part of commanding officers resulted in 250,000 men being slaughtered by the Nazis. Why am I risking everything if I am not believed?" Philby fell silent, smoking his cigarette.

Shapak didn't move.

"What if ..." Philby said, then paused for a beat. "What if a third party, someone else who works deep inside the Secret Intelligence Service, could convince Moscow that the intelligence they receive from me is genuine and comes from massive code-breaking efforts, an operation called Ultra. If they don't believe me, maybe they'd believe a deeply involved third party."

Shapak gave no signs that what Philby proposed was being positively or negatively considered.

"Shapak, when Moscow Center doubts me, how do they not doubt you?"

Shapak snorted and, head tilted forward, resumed his stare at the ground.

It began to rain harder. Philby opened his umbrella, but it was only large enough to shield one person. The rain rolled off the wide brim of Shapak's hat onto the ground, where it puddled. Philby watched the man from earlier run past holding a newspaper over his head.

"Who is this third party?"

"A cryptologist from Bletchley Park has gone missing, a Swede. A search has been launched but with no results. There is great concern that his deep knowledge of our code-breaking efforts may be up for sale."

"Why do they suspect that?"

"Apparently, he has asked for ... compensation in the past in exchange for his knowledge and has gotten it. He might be able to convince Moscow that my intelligence can be trusted and that the intelligence they receive directly from Churchill is not from a 'most reliable source,' as he calls it, but from painstaking code breaking."

"Say this makes sense. What next?"

"That's simple: find this Swede. His name is Gunnar Lind."

CHAPTER SIX

1000 Hours, Thursday, October 22, 1942
Office of Benjamin Andersson, BI Maskineri Företag,
Östermalm, Stockholm

Gunnar Lind didn't know what was more irritating: the tightness of his old, faded suit or his sweaty palms. Both made him uncomfortable and both signaled something he didn't want communicated: that he was a nervous man of little means. Standing in the outer office, he ran his palms down the sides of his legs as the matronly secretary announced his arrival to his father-in-law, Benjamin Andersson. Gunnar could hear Andersson's shocked reaction to the spontaneous visit.

The secretary returned. "Mr. Andersson will see you now, Mr. Lind."

Gunnar dabbed his forehead with his handkerchief and then, with weak knees, stepped into the office.

The chamber was massive. Art deco–style furniture occupied three of the four corners with a large oak desk in the remaining corner. Andersson, in his midfifties, was tall with a slight build. His mostly gray mustache was neat and trimmed, as was a set of long sideburns. He held an unlit pipe. Gunnar tried not to stare at the man's lazy eye that seemed to roam around the room, searching for something.

"Gunnar ... I'm ... utterly astonished to see you. Especially without my daughter. Where is Eve?"

Gunnar stood beside a low-back club chair. His knees were quaking. He hoped that Andersson would ask him to sit soon. "Ah, Eve. She will be joining me soon. If all goes according to plan."

"Plan? What plan?" Andersson asked, placing his pipe in a pewter ashtray the size of a dinner plate. "And how did you travel here from England?"

"Well, to your last question, that is a long story." Gunnar clutched the top of the chair and squeezed. "As for your first question, that is what I have come to discuss."

Andersson motioned for him to take a seat. Gunnar sighed with relief as he almost fell into the chair. He pulled his handkerchief from his breast pocket and dabbed his forehead.

The office was quiet except for a desk clock that ticked away. Andersson studied Gunnar as he squirmed in his seat. "It has been quite some time since we last saw you both."

Gunnar nodded, worried what direction the conversation was going to go in.

"That wouldn't be the case if you had accepted the position I offered you when you married. Eve's mother and I were very disappointed with your decision."

Gunnar hesitated. "Yes. I knew of your disappointment. But at the time, I had an important position in Germany, designing and overseeing the manufacturing of … critical equipment for the military. There were promises of a promotion and more money."

Andersson picked up his pipe and began stuffing it with tobacco, while he resumed his silent study of Gunnar. The desk clock ticked on. "So you said. In the last letter I received from Eve, she seemed quite depressed. She went on about being miserable in England. Why didn't you stay in Paris? She was very happy there."

"There were reasons to fear the Germans as they approached the city. I had …" Gunnar paused and reviewed the answer he'd rehearsed during the past two days. "How shall I put it? I made certain decisions that put me on the wrong side of the Germans. They would have found a reason to put me in prison. I could not let that happen to Eve."

Andersson nodded, seemingly satisfied with Gunnar's response.

"And given the absolute chaos that enveloped Paris, we had few options but to flee the city before it fell. I had a relationship with some important people in the British government, and I accepted their offer of safe passage to England."

"I see," Andersson said, squinting through a gray haze of tobacco smoke. "What sort of relationship?"

The tobacco smelled like burnt twigs. Gunnar paused. "I assisted British intelligence in … sensitive matters. They were appreciative and wanted to continue the relationship."

Andersson nodded once more. "Hence, your issues with the Germans."

"Exactly."

"So why are you here … without my daughter?"

"Ah, yes," Gunnar said. "I have a proposal to make to the Germans, one I cannot make to them personally for fear of my, and possibly Eve's, safety."

"What do you mean, Eve's safety?"

Gunnar leaned forward. "As you've pointed out, Eve is miserable in England. She and I wish to relocate to Stockholm to raise a family."

Andersson's eyes widened, and he returned his pipe to the ashtray.

"And my proposal would, if accepted by the Germans, provide the funds to make that happen."

"It makes no sense for you to do business with the Germans if they already … think you are working against them."

"That is why I am here to ask you to represent me in the negotiations. They dare not cross the line with you for fear of jeopardizing future shipments of ball bearings and other materials your company manufactures. Is that not right?"

"Yes. Most likely. Just what is this proposal?"

Gunnar leaned back, pleased that he had been able to answer the more troubling questions thus far. "I have certain information that I acquired while working for British intelligence that the Germans would find very interesting—so interesting that they would pay dearly for it."

"And the nature of this information?"

"To not place you in … a sensitive position, I cannot fully explain." Gunnar knew that revealing the nature of his information—namely the details of the British's successful efforts to break high-level encrypted German radio and teleprinter communication traffic—could easily be pried out of someone like Andersson.

"And in return, what are you asking for?"

"The information , classified human intelligence, is worth much more than I am asking. But I'll accept one million krona."

Andersson snapped his head back; his lazy eye spasmed and darted about the office. "That is quite a sum. You are sure of its value?"

"Completely."

"What are your terms?"

Gunnar wiped his palms on his thighs. "Before I give them my information, the money should be deposited into a local bank by an agreed-upon date, possibly a bank that you have a relationship with. It should be counted and verified as noncounterfeit. Once that is accomplished, instructions will be given as to where the documentation can be found."

Andersson mulled over Gunnar's instructions. "While the Germans will be careful not to hurt our relationship, they are not foolish. You offer no proof that the information has any value. Why would they pay anything?"

Gunnar reached inside his suit coat and pulled out an envelope. He stood and handed it to Andersson. He felt the sweaty seat of his pants sticking to his rear as he rose. "This should convince them that I have access to valuable information."

Andersson reached for a pair of glasses and opened the envelope. Gunnar had memorized the text.

MOST SECRET

MPO/PD/1002
13.10.42

TO: MD
FROM: MPO
COPY: S

BE ADVISED … ITALIAN GOVERNMENT
SCHEDULING A MAJOR RECEPTION IN
HONOR OF REICHSFUHRER—SS HEINRICH
HIMMLER AT HOTEL AMBASSADORE. DATE
9.11.42.

ATTENDING … ALL FASCIST PARTY
LEADERS AND ALL MEMBERS OF ITALIAN
GOVERNMENT.

SUGGEST THOROUGH APPRAISAL OF
OPPORTUNITY FOR TERMINATION BY
PARTISANS WITH ASSIST FROM MPO.

Andersson put the document down and removed his glasses. He rubbed his lazy eye as if he were calming it down after the reading exercise. "You're confident that this will convince the Germans that what you are promising is of value?"

"Yes. I am. Once they confirm Himmler's travel schedule, they will be assured."

Andersson nodded slowly as he put the document back in the envelope.

"For your assistance, twenty-five thousand krona is yours."

Andersson chuckled. "I am a rich man and do not require a share. But given my relationship with the German government and, of course, my love for my daughter, I will present your proposal."

Gunnar sighed audibly, and the tension that had gripped his body released. "I am most grateful."

Andersson instructed Gunnar to open an account at his bank—Svenska Bank. "I will contact the bank manager, Nils Berg, and instruct him to assist you in opening a joint account in both our names. He will have you sign some papers, but do not worry. He will not ask questions. He is a longtime family friend." Andersson came around his desk.

Gunnar rose, still somewhat weak-kneed.

"When will Eve be arriving?"

"If all happens as we have planned, in a manner of days."

Andersson smiled and extended his hand.

Gunnar took it, all the while staring at Andersson's roving eye.

"Where are you staying, Gunnar?"

"I have taken a room at a hotel. Small but comfortable."

"Nonsense. I'd have you stay with Edith and I, except I have painters coming today, and the house will be in too much chaos. But take our summer house. It is not far from here. I bought it recently and plan to surprise Edith with it as an anniversary gift once some modifications have been completed. You can avail yourself of a car in the barn." Andersson began to walk Gunnar to the door.

"You are very generous. I accept."

"You look as if you have put on some weight, Gunnar. And lost some of your hair."

Gunnar hesitated, then nodded in agreement.

#

Andersson watched Gunnar walk past his secretary's desk and out into the hallway. He was not impressed with Gunnar's scuffed shoes and ill-fitting suit. When his son-in-law was gone, he asked his secretary to ring the German minister and then returned to his office. He headed to the credenza behind his desk and picked up a heavy gold-plated picture frame, studying the black-and-white photo from Eve's wedding four years earlier. Eve and Gunnar were flanked by Andersson and his wife. It was shot from a slight distance. The man in front of him was much changed. The war had certainly taken its toll on his son-in-law. His secretary interrupted his reverie with the announcement that the minister was on the line.

Andersson placed his hand on the phone and paused for several seconds before picking it up. "Minister Kleist, I have a proposal that you and your government will find quite intriguing."

CHAPTER SEVEN

1100 Hours, Thursday, October 22, 1942
Milton Keynes Police Station, Buckinghamshire

Few people were getting on and off the train, which allowed them to make good time to Bletchley Park. Conor and Emily had the compartment to themselves. Emily was sitting directly opposite him, staring out the window, her shapely legs crossed.

The intelligence that Ian Fleming, Emily's close friend who was assigned to the Naval Intelligence Division, shared with him late yesterday about an upcoming mission in Norway called Operation Freshman rattled around in his head. The target was a hydrochemical plant. Fleming wouldn't give him all the details, but what he did say was enough to keep Conor awake for most of the night. Emily was to be sent in before the operation to coordinate with the local resistance—alone.

"How much longer until we arrive?" Conor asked as he looked at his watch. He tried to mask his irritation, but he knew he didn't try hard enough. Emily had already pointed out his foul mood before they'd even boarded the train at Victoria Station.

"About ten minutes. Are you going to tell me what's bothering you?"

"Sure. Why not? It's you."

"Me?"

"Why haven't you mentioned Norway?"

Emily straightened in suspicion. "Who told you?"

"Doesn't really matter, does it? What does is that you didn't mention it to me. It's not like I'm going to spill it to the editor of the *Daily Mirror*."

"My, you are in a mood."

Conor didn't respond. He just locked his gaze on her, waiting for her to answer his question.

Emily calmly stared back at him. "I am not allowed to share such information. With anyone. You, of all people, can understand that."

"I would have told you." *Possibly*, Conor thought. He'd hate to have her so worried about him, but he might not tell her. But that didn't mean it didn't hurt that she hadn't shared it with him. They weren't just colleagues. They were more.

"And you would have been wrong to do so." She uncrossed her legs and leaned forward, putting her elbows on her knees. "What is this about?"

"Wow. You are a bit dense."

Emily cracked a smile but let it fade. "Conor, the war will be over one day. Then we can share everything. But now we both have jobs to do. Sometimes they're dangerous. And they're vital to the war effort, whether we think so or not."

"When do you leave?"

"Tomorrow night."

Conor blew out a hot breath. "You could have told me so I could have said that I ... am worried about you. Norway is occupied."

That provoked a mocking look complete with raised eyebrows. "You just did."

"Did what?"

"Told me that you're worried about me."

Conor let that hang in the air.

"I know you feel like you didn't protect Grace ... and I also know that you want to protect me. And I love you for it." Emily sat back and recrossed her legs. "But I have a job to do. And so do you." Emily thankfully left unsaid, *So snap out of it, Conor.* But she was right. Deep down, he was still dealing with his failure at seeing what Grace was going through. It was something he'd have to live with for the rest of his life

#

The back room of the station was as cramped as the rest of the place. The space apparently doubled as an interrogation room and a storeroom, given the boxes of files in the corner. A small table with four chairs took up most of the remaining space. The bulletin board on one wall had two propaganda posters pinned on it, one extolling the RAF in the Battle of Britain with bold white letters over a blue sky: "Never was so much owed by so many to so few." Another poster urged the women of Britain to "Come into the factories" and featured a smiling woman who held her arms wide open in a welcoming pose. Conor hadn't seen that many smiling faces during his time in England. It definitely was not an accurate picture of reality, but then again, no propaganda really was.

Conor had reviewed the brief that Emily gave him about Gunnar Lind on their way north. She had been sent to meet him and his wife when they arrived from Paris, just ahead of the blitzkrieging Wehrmacht. Over their first two weeks in England, Emily had helped them both settle in and had been struck by Gunnar's kindness and gratitude as equally as she was by his wife's curtness and surly behavior. Eve was unhappy; he was thankful. Eve wanted nothing to do with the British; he wanted to help in any way he could. Regardless, Emily had been impressed by Gunnar's devotion to his wife. It had seemed as though a large portion of his relief had been because he had gotten her out of harm's way.

While Conor and Emily waited for Jack Wallace, an MI5 agent, to bring in Eve Lind for questioning, Conor looked over the list of dinner guests that Maggie had given him for at least the tenth time, zeroing in on the line she scribbled next to one of the two entries with a question mark: *I didn't catch his name. He sat on the other side at the far end of the table. Arrived late. He was not in a uniform and was already half in the bag.* Not much to go on. He was desperate to start ruling out some of the names on the list.

"What are you reading?" Emily asked.

Conor had known pulling the list out would prompt her to ask. He wanted her to. He wanted to share what he was feeling. Maybe she could explain why he was so sad and ashamed one minute and seconds away from harming someone the next. He wanted her to comfort him. "A list Maggie gave me of the people at the dinner the night Grace was raped."

"You're here. What good does it do to focus on that? There's nothing you could do anyway about a crime that took place over two years ago on the other side of the ocean. Don't torture yourself, Conor."

"I can't just let it go. It was my job to protect her. It was—"

"It was your job to go where you were ordered. To be with your crew. Grace knew that. She knew you were married both to her and the navy. Just like my father and brother. My mother and I knew that."

Conor heard heavy footsteps coming down the hall. An instant later, the door flew open and Wallace ushered in Eve Lind. She looked angry. At the sight of Emily's familiar face, Eve stopped dead in her tracks. Her look of anger vanished.

"Hello, Eve. Nice to see you again," Emily said, her tone soft and welcoming.

Lind was about five feet eight inches. Her hair was shoulder length, straight, and blond. She wore a royal blue beret and a matching coat. A small olive-colored cloth bag hung from her shoulder. She wore no makeup, but that was true for almost all women since the outbreak of the war. It did not detract from her beauty.

"You're … Emily Bright." Eve stared at Emily and ignored Conor completely. "You met us when we came from Paris. What are you …"

"This is Conor Thorn, my associate. Please, have a seat. We have some questions about your husband."

Eve slid out a chair and sat. "Have you found him? Have you found that worthless bastard?"

Wallace nodded at Emily and shrugged his shoulders in a *Not my fault she's a handful* gesture, then took the chair next to Emily.

Conor held up his hands. "Whoa. Slow it down a bit." Her accent was prominent. Due, Conor assumed, to Eve's lack of interest in assimilating with her English hosts. He waited while Eve sat back, her lips pursed, turning white from the pressure. "If we found him alive, we would want to talk to you to make sure you weren't a part of whatever he was up to. If we found him … dead, we'd still want to talk to you."

Eve recoiled.

"Which we haven't. Found him dead or alive, that is." Conor added.

"Eve, tell me why Gunnar is a bastard. I never found him to be anything other than nice," Emily said, her voice soft and sweet.

Eve waited a beat. Then another. "He betrayed me." She looked at Emily's left hand. "I see there's no ring on your finger, so you wouldn't understand that."

Conor thought it was a cheap shot, but all it did was make Emily smile. It was an interesting comment given that Conor didn't see a wedding ring on her finger either. "And where's your ring, Eve?" Conor asked.

"I sold it. And I wasted no time doing it. I needed to eat."

"I understand." Conor paused for a moment. "Why does Gunnar hate you so much?"

Wallace, smoking a cigarette, choked.

"He … he …" Eve was off balance.

They waited for her to recover. After all, they needed some information to fill in the blanks.

"He doesn't hate me. How dare you say that. I have devoted my life to him, following him wherever he said we should go, leaving behind a growing medical practice each time. I hate him. Now. But I did love him. Quite deeply. Up until a few weeks ago. Until I found these." Eve reached into her cloth bag and pulled out a short stack of letters bound by twine.

"What are these?" Conor asked as he reached for the stack.

"Love letters. From his whore," Eve hissed.

Conor untied the twine and opened one of the envelopes. Emily and Wallace both took one as well. The one Conor read offered no surprises: *I love you. I miss you. I wish we be together forever.* Emily Dickinson didn't need to worry about the "whore's" emotive styling. Eve sat back, clearly enjoying the show.

"Not dated," Emily pointed out.

"No return addresses," Conor said.

Wallace chimed in, his cigarette dangling from his mouth, ash falling to the table. "Poor grammar too. Shameful."

Conor noted that they were signed with a flourish: *Your love, Rubie.*

"How long has this been going on?" Emily asked.

"I don't know. Maybe a month or so."

"Do you know who this Rubie is?" asked Conor.

"No. No, I don't. But if I did ..."

"You'd ... what, Eve?" Emily asked.

Eve hesitated, then turned to Emily, maybe looking for a gender ally. "He took all of the money. Our money. Every last pence."

"How much?" Wallace asked.

"Several thousand pounds."

Left over from Lind's deal with the British in '38. "How often did you argue?" Conor asked.

Eve snapped her attention back to Conor. "Who said we argued?"

"Every husband and wife argue," Conor said.

Wallace shot Conor a look and nodded.

"Are you married, Mr. Thorn?" Eve asked.

Conor paused. "No. Not anymore. Marriage didn't agree with me."

That answer provoked a noticeable response from Emily, which Conor worked hard to ignore. He needed Eve to spill her guts, and she needed encouragement.

"We did argue. But only recently. I told him I hated living in England. He ignored me. He was always working on something. And he never paid attention to me. We stopped ..." Eve paused. She was hyperventilating.

"Eve, take a minute," Emily said.

Eve's chin fell to her chest, and Emily looked at Conor and signaled *slow down* with her ringless left hand.

"His head was always buried in his blasted work, even after spending hour after hour at that wretched place," Eve said, her voice cracking.

Wallace looked at Conor and ran his hand across his throat.

Conor nodded, yet it felt as if he were watching a cheerless stage play of a scorned, suffering, neglected wife, helpless to defend herself.

Eve's sobbing abruptly stopped, and she lurched halfway across the table at Conor and grabbed his shirt with her right hand. It was shaking. The move caught Emily and Wallace off guard, but Conor didn't budge.

"He's ruined me. Ruined us. Let me help you find him. Maybe I can get the money back. Maybe I can rebuild my life ... or what's left of it." She pounded the table. Her cheeks were dry, her eyes bulging with rage. "I want to find him more than you do." Her voice was hoarse. "Do you hear me?"

Conor wasn't sure what he'd just witnessed: a performance or someone wallowing in raw pain and anger. If it was a performance, that would lead to quite a few questions about Eve Lind.

CHAPTER EIGHT

1215 Hours, Thursday, October 22, 1942
MI6 Headquarters, No. 54 Broadway, London

The heavy royal-blue brocade curtains drawn across the windows in Stewart Menzies's office did little to block the sound of a hard rain as it pelted the glass. The claps of thunder would make speaking momentarily futile. Menzies, his head buried in the morning edition of the *Daily Mirror*, didn't hear MI6 Deputy Chief Frederick Winterbotham enter his office and only noticed him when he laid a file on his desk.

"A recent decrypt from Station X," Winterbotham said. Given his primary responsibility for the security of Ultra, Winterbotham rarely, if ever, referred to Bletchley Park by its actual name, instead using its code name. "I brought it in because it will be of particular interest to the prime minister, in my opinion."

Menzies opened the file and read the decrypt. He stopped halfway through and looked up at Winterbotham. "Are you surprised?"

"That Hitler wants to slaughter commandos whether they are in uniforms or not? No, not at all."

Menzies nodded and closed the file. "Of course, the prime minister will not welcome this news, since the Special Operations Executive is his brainchild." The SOE was responsible for espionage, sabotage, and reconnaissance in occupied territories. A sheet of rain lashed at the windows as his secretary knocked on the open door. "Yes, what is it, Miss Pettigrew?"

His secretary approached in long strides. "Sir, Mr. Travis is here and says it's quite urgent. Shall—"

Travis rushed past the formidable woman before she could stop him. "C, I have something. I think we might have found Lind." He passed a file to Menzies.

"That will be all, Miss Pettigrew," Menzies said, sending the woman out of the room.

"We intercepted a wireless transmission sent from the German minister in Stockholm to the German Foreign Office in Berlin."

"Stockholm?" Winterbotham asked.

"Yes. As you can see, it mentions a meeting with an industrialist who is representing someone from British intelligence who has information to sell."

Menzies shook his head. "Well, he is Swedish. That makes some sense. But it's not possible. This can't be Lind. How in God's good name could Lind get to Sweden?"

Travis shrugged in reply. "Travel to Stockholm is tightly controlled," he said. "It doesn't seem possible that he could secure the proper paperwork and permissions."

"But ... if this isn't Lind, then we have another problem to deal with," Menzies said as he slumped in his chair. The sound of heavy rainfall and the rumble of thunder filled the room for several seconds. Menzies stood, walked over to the coat stand, and grabbed his bowler hat and walking stick. He turned back to Travis. "Despite how highly unlikely it is, send someone from our embassy over to keep an eye on the comings and goings at the German Legation. Make sure he has a detailed description of Lind." Menzies nestled the handle of the walking stick in the crook of his left arm and put on his bowler. "I truly believe that our man is still somewhere on the island." Menzies made for the door.

The news that he was about to pass along to the prime minister might be the last straw, causing him to be stripped of oversight of the most secret and critical operation in any British intelligence organization.

A black eye of epic proportions.

And the end to his career.

CHAPTER NINE

1615 Hours, Thursday, October 22, 1942
German Legation, Södra Blasieholmshammer 2, Stockholm

Lina Stuben, the Reich Main Security Office (RSHA) lead Sicherheitsdienst (SD) agent in Sweden, had the handset of her desk phone tucked between her ear and her shoulder while she frantically took notes. The German minister was excited, which caused him to speak rapidly and, at times, nonsensically. She asked Minister Kleist to slow down several times, which he did, but only for a moment.

When she replaced the handset, she ran her fingers through her cropped blond hair and looked over her notes. The Ausland-SD was the Foreign Intelligence Service of the SS, and the ambassador had just communicated to her that a windfall of invaluable intelligence could end up in their hands very soon.

"So what did the nincompoop have to say today?" asked Kurt Eklof. "Is his gout keeping him awake again?"

Eklof, Stuben's second, was a former Luftwaffe pilot who was wounded under, what Stuben was told were, questionable circumstances in the North African campaign. He was tall, over six feet, stout, and had wide shoulders, a slim waist, and a face anchored by a square jaw. His silver hair gleamed. But it was his brown leather eye patch, in the shape of a shield, that caused others to stare—that and his one sky-blue eye.

"We may have an important development to address," Stuben

said as Eklof gazed out the window that overlooked the plaza below her third-floor office. Stuben went on to relate the details of a British intelligence defector offering to sell Allied secrets. "Kleist has already contacted the Foreign Office with details, seeking guidance. I will also reach out to ..." Eklof was seemingly not paying attention, and she growled, "What are you looking at?"

"We have a new friend who seems to be very interested in us."

Stuben joined him at the window.

"Do you see the older man in the gray overcoat? He's smoking and pacing across the plaza. He's been there for thirty minutes."

Stuben spied a burly man in his late fifties, his collar pulled up to shield against a steady rain. "Who is he?"

"I've seen him before. He's English. Works at their legation. Probably MI6." Eklof hadn't moved an inch in the past half hour. "It may have something to do with this new development that you speak of. Maybe he's looking for the defector." Eklof turned to Stuben. "What do you think?" Eklof, a foot away from Stuben, loomed over her five-foot-three-inch form.

She was close enough to get a musky whiff of leather. "It is possible. It would be advantageous for us to learn more about this defector. Would you agree?"

"I agree," Eklof said as he made his way to the door. He passed a portrait of Hitler hanging slightly askew. He stopped and straightened it with his index finger, then turned back to Stuben, smiling. "I will invite our friend in for a cup of tea. We will gather in the special room in the basement if you care to join us."

#

Stuben had been down in the basement once before to question a Norwegian thought to have ties with his country's underground. He eventually admitted to seeking financial assistance and supplies for the partisans; he broke quickly. Just as well, as Stuben disliked their special room. It housed the building's incinerator, which emitted the overpowering stench of garbage ash, and a massive boiler, which provided the building's heat. The maze of pipes and ducts that ran in multiple directions just below the ceiling banged and knocked incessantly, muffling most other sounds.

Stuben took a seat in a dimly lit corner of the room next to a stack of boxes that contained pictures of Hitler and hundreds of small Nazi flags to be passed out at community events. Eklof sat directly in front of the MI6 agent, who was tied to an armless wooden chair. A legation security guard stood in another corner. The agent was heavier than he looked from a distance; a flabby chin crowned his thick neck. Eklof held the agent's billfold.

"Where's my tea? Your goons promised me a hot cuppa," the agent said.

"Another cocky Englishman," said Eklof.

"You realize that you've violated several diplomatic protocols by bringing me here against my will?"

Eklof's face was the picture of impassiveness. "As you can see, I'm terrified." He opened the billfold. "Roger McInnis, just why have you taken such an interest in our legation on this soggy day?"

"I'm a fan of Swedish architecture. I was making the rounds of the city."

Eklof nodded slowly, then stood; his tall frame missed the maze of pipes by only a few inches. He started pacing. "You are an MI6 agent. You work out of the British Legation. You are spying on us. What or whom are you looking for?"

"Like I said, I'm really just a tourist. Getting to know Stockholm. I'm told that I have some Swedish blood in the family. Who is the pretty lady over there? She wouldn't be your boss, would she?" McInnis smiled, then quickly stopped. "And I'm dying to know: Where did you lose the eye? Was it a dustup in some whorehouse after you decided you weren't going to pay because you couldn't cut the mustard?"

Eklof took one long step toward McInnis. His momentum fueled a staggering backhanded slap across McInnis's face that sent him and the chair toppling. The guard rushed over and pulled the chair and McInnis upright. A red-faced Eklof rubbed the back of his hand.

Stuben smirked. She thought back to when she was working at Gestapo headquarters in Paris and she was allowed to be in the room when suspected members of the French resistance were questioned. Those agents took pride in their methods and results. She had attempted to acquire some of their tools when she arrived in Stockholm: a small vise to crush testicles, an iron ring to tighten around a person's head, electrodes, a car battery for an acid drip. Her only successes were a soldering iron and rubber hoses. But a physical beating was usually most effective.

Eklof bent over, his face just inches from McInnis's face. "Why were you sent here?" The right side of McInnis's face began to swell. "Who are you looking for?" Eklof asked, his voice becoming louder with each word. A loud bang from a pipe directly above sounded like a starter's pistol. McInnis snapped his head forward, looking to land a head-butt to Eklof's nose, but Eklof just as quickly shifted away, McInnis's forehead landing uselessly on Eklof's upper chest. Eklof grabbed the Brit by his hair with one hand and sent an uppercut deep into his gut. A rush of air left his body, and McInnis started choking.

Eklof took a step back, surprised by the unusual reaction. McInnis's face twisted as if a knife had been planted deep in his back. Gasping, he struggled for air, and then, just as suddenly, his head slumped forward and he stopped.

Alarmed, Stuben rose and walked over to Eklof. "What is wrong with him?"

Eklof gripped McInnis's hair and pulled his head up. The man's eyes had rolled back. At that moment, the boiler fired up and several pipes began knocking loudly. Eklof said something that Stuben couldn't hear.

"What did you say?"

Eklof released the head, which fell forward, the chin bouncing twice on the man's chest. He turned to face her. "He's dead," he shouted. "The fat bastard is dead."

CHAPTER TEN

0930 Hours, Friday, October 23, 1942
Government Code & Cypher School (GC&CS),
Bletchley Park, Buckinghamshire

The morning was chilly, quite the contrast with the previous day's unseasonably warm temperatures. On their walk from the main gate, Conor saw steam rise from the surface of a nearby pond as well as from Emily's breath.

"She described someone I didn't know. A stranger."

"In what way?" Conor said.

"The Gunnar Lind I knew—now, mind you, I only had a limited exposure to him and Eve—but the man I knew cared little for money. He said it was Eve's idea, not his, to ask for money from MI6 for his Enigma replica. He would have given it to MI6, no strings attached. But Eve thought him foolish ... stupid, he said she called him. She insisted."

"Men can change, sometimes for the worse." Conor stopped and asked a passing couple where Hut 8 was.

"Straight ahead, then bear to the right."

Conor thanked them, and they resumed their walk.

"I understand people can change, but ... I don't know. It struck me that two things governed Gunnar's life: his studies of cryptology and his wife. It was never money. The idea that he's selling secrets is unfathomable to me," Emily said.

"You haven't said much about Eve. How did you find her two years later?"

"It seems that her anger has hardened. If it's true that he has a mistress, I can certainly understand."

Hut 8 was a simply constructed long building with a peaked roof. A small covered shelter brimming with bicycles adjoined the building. On either side of the door were four windows, all of which had dark drapes drawn across them.

Conor knocked on the door and went in, followed by Emily. A dark-haired man in a tweed sports jacket was bent over, going through the drawers of a desk along the far wall. Startled, he straightened and spun around. "Who ... who are you? What are you doing here?" he asked, pushing back hair that had fallen across his face during his search.

Conor thought he looked like a young boy caught looking at women modeling bras in a Ward's catalog. "Conor Thorn. I was told I could find Alan Turing here."

"He's not in yet, as you can see." The man slammed closed the drawers he had opened. "You're an American. Who are you with?"

"The Office of Strategic Services. And you are?"

"Office of Strategic Services. What a silly name. It could cover any amount of activities."

"I didn't catch your name."

"I didn't throw it."

"Well, I suggest you try."

The man started to respond but hesitated. "Cairncross. John Cairncross. I work with Alan. Who should be in soon. You can wait here. I have work to get back to."

Conor watched the man leave. "The nervous type, wouldn't you say?"

"I would. Sure seemed to be looking for something."

Conor walked over to the desk Cairncross had been searching. He didn't see anything out of the ordinary: a small ink blotter, a desk pad with a large black ink spill, a wire basket that was empty. An Imperial typewriter had a blank sheet of paper in the carriage. Conor was leaning over to pick up a small photo of Eve Lind in a cardboard frame when the door behind him opened.

Conor turned, and what he saw startled him.

A man in a rumpled suit, a satchel in his hand, stood in the doorway, wearing a gas mask. He said something, but the gas mask muffled his words.

Conor pointed to his ears and shrugged.

The man removed the gas mask, revealing a round face with a ruddy complexion that featured a day's growth of beard. "I said, who the devil are you?"

"Are you Alan Turing?" Conor asked, handing the photo to Emily.

"Yes. I answered your question, now please answer mine."

"Conor Thorn, and this is Emily Bright. We've been sent from London to ask you a few questions about Gunnar Lind."

Turing headed to the desk in the corner and put his satchel and gas mask down. He turned to the radiator below the window behind his desk and opened a padlock that secured a mug. "I'll be back in a moment. Do you want some tea?"

Conor and Emily both shook their heads.

Turing walked past them and through the same door Cairncross had used.

"Not sure what to make of that," Conor said.

"You'd be in good company."

A few minutes later, Turing returned with a steaming mug and sat behind his desk. Conor dragged over a chair for Emily, while he remained standing.

Turing had his head buried in his satchel, eventually pulling a small red tin from it. "Shortbread biscuits. Interested?"

They both declined.

He was about to ask his first question when Turing spoke again. "I'm curious. Why didn't you ask me about my gas mask?"

Conor chuckled. "Two reasons. One, I am sure you have a good reason to wear it. Two, it's not why we're here."

Turing laughed. A few crumbs fell in his lap. "Score one for you." He took a sip. "Pollen. Ragweed, to be precise. I wear it to tame my allergies."

"You see, that makes perfect sense, but it doesn't look good on you. I'm sure you know that. You'll scare all the ladies away," Emily said.

Conor heard her soft, sweet tone again.

Turing coughed into his hand, blushing—not the reaction Conor expected. "Lind. That's why you're here." After a pause he said, "He is dearly missed." The abrupt pivot caught Conor off guard. "He's a great listener and was never afraid to call me out for the silly things that I proposed."

"Did he ever take time away from his work?" Conor said.

"I never once remember him taking time away from here. He was dedicated to his work. So much so that when we struggled in our mission, he felt it cost people their lives. Each failure took something out of him. I did try to cheer him up, but ..." Turing took another sip of his tea. "Each success buoyed his spirits dramatically, each failure the opposite. He was like a pendulum."

"What was his marriage like?" Emily asked.

"I can't tell you much. I do know they argued."

"He told you that?" Conor said.

"No. It was widely known at the Crown Inn. He and his wife were billeted there. As am I."

"What did they argue about? Money, Gunnar's long hours?" Emily said.

"I have no direct knowledge. Mrs. Buckmaster—she's the landlady—she gets slightly miffed with me. She often bemoans that I, a healthy young man, am not 'doing my bit for the war effort.' It forces me to sometimes work behind the bar to mitigate her laments. Oh, did I mention that she's been missing herself for the past week?"

"Two days after Lind is last seen, she disappears?" Conor shot a look at Emily. "Were they—"

"No, no, no. She is a lot older than Gunnar. Besides, she was quite sweet on a local farmer, or so she told me one evening while I was behind the bar."

"What did Lind and his wife argue about?" Emily asked again.

"Well, Mrs. Buckmaster once said that Eve hated living in England. She felt like a prisoner."

"Was Lind ... a ladies' man? Did he have a roving eye, so to speak?" Conor said.

Turing seemed amused by the suggestion. "No, no. That was not in his character. He adored Eve."

Out of the corner of his eye, Conor saw Emily nodding her head.

"He often said he was lucky he found her. She's beautiful, you know."

Conor nodded. "Did he ever say anything about someday going to a place he always wanted to go to?"

"No. You must understand, most of us have put off any thoughts like that for until after the war is over."

"Alan … can I call you Alan?" Emily asked.

"Please do, Emily."

"Gunnar has a brother. Could he have gone to visit him? Or another relative?"

"I asked about his family once when he first arrived. He mentioned a deceased mother. And when he mentioned a brother, he gave no characterization as to their relationship, but it was clear to me it wasn't a good one. I know of no other relatives."

"I understand. Alan, who is John Cairncross?" Emily said.

"Why do you ask?"

"When we arrived, he was going through that desk," Conor said, pointing with his thumb.

"Really? Well, that is Gunnar's desk. It was cleared out of anything critical the day I reported him missing. John—he's a cryptologist here—knows that."

Emily rose. "Anything else you can tell us?"

"Well … Gunnar, he liked silly jokes. Wasn't always in the best of health, but the hours did that to him. And during our lunch breaks, he wrote in a journal. Poems. I didn't find them very good. I told him that once. He was quite taken aback. My mother says that I should curb my tongue more."

Conor looked over at the desk. "Could Cairncross have been looking for the journal?"

"I don't know why. John and Gunnar hardly spoke. For some reason, they were rather suspicious of each other."

"Suspicious of what?" Emily asked.

"Neither one would ever say. It seems that they had their secrets."

CHAPTER ELEVEN

0900 Hours, Saturday, October 24, 1942
MI6 Headquarters, No. 54 Broadway, London

Philby stood in front of Menzies's desk while he read the intercept. He had just finished the part that reported General Stumme had died of a heart attack after coming under assault in the opening stages of the second battle for El Alamein.

Philby raised his eyebrows and looked at Menzies. "Yes. They're going to drag the old Desert Fox out of his sickbed to replace him. If that's not a sign that their officer ranks are thinning, I don't know what is," Menzies said.

"It's good timing," Philby said as he handed the intercept back. "It will take Rommel some time to get in place. Meanwhile, Montgomery presses on. I'm sure the Afrika Korps will be in disarray without their commanding general. Stumme's officers loved him."

"My heart bleeds for them," Menzies said, his right hand perched over his heart.

Both men turned sharply at a loud double knock at the door.

Frederick Winterbotham hurried across the blue-and-gold Persian rug, a file in his hand, and looked at Philby.

"It's all right, Frederick. Nothing Kim can't hear. What is it?"

"Our embassy in Stockholm was notified by the local police that our agent, the one we sent to keep watch of the German Legation, turned up floating in the harbor."

Menzies greeted the news stone-faced.

"The body ... Roger McInnis is in the city morgue. They won't release it until their investigation is finished." Winterbotham handed the file to Menzies.

"Surely the Germans can't be this stupid. Can they?" Menzies asked.

"Apparently so," said Winterbotham.

"Someone panicked, it seems. Too inexperienced. Maybe too anxious to protect something ... or someone," said Philby.

Winterbotham looked annoyed by Philby's observation.

"McInnis ... did I know him?" Menzies asked, putting the file down.

"I'm not sure. He'd been with us since thirty-six," Winterbotham said.

Menzies shook his head, not recognizing the name.

"A former Royal Marine. That's why the Stockholm police reached out to us. He had a Royal Marine tattoo on his upper arm," Winterbotham said.

"This is getting out of hand," said Menzies. He picked up the file and bit his lower lip.

Philby saw that Menzies was rattled.

Still looking at the intercept, Menzies asked, "When was the last time we heard from Bright?"

"Ahhh, well ... last night. We had to move the flight up several hours because of weather around the drop zone," Winterbotham said. "But she reported that she arrived safely in Norway and that she had already set up a meeting with the partisans operating near the Vemonk hydroelectric plant."

"Yes ... heavy water," Menzies mumbled. He shut the file and sat back in his chair. "I want three agents—I don't care who—on a plane to Stockholm right away. We need to know what's going on there. And pull Bright out of Norway and send her there too. This problem is more critical, at this point at least."

"This can't be Lind," Winterbotham said.

The mention of Lind's name caused Philby to snap his head up.

"It's not like he can board a BOAC flight out of Leuchars. Hell, the king himself would have trouble getting papers to make that trip," Philby said, aware that British Overseas Airways initiated service from Leuchars, Scotland to Stockholm in 1941 with planes owned by the Norwegian Purchasing Commission and flown by Norwegian crews.

"Well, someone is causing trouble there," Menzies said. "And as we have had no luck finding him on our soil, we'll throw some assets at it and see what we come up with. Have Bright check in at the embassy first to get fully briefed."

Winterbotham nodded.

"Tell her to find out if this someone from British intelligence is Lind. If it is, bring him back before he causes massive damage. If he refuses, eliminate him. And if he's not Lind, eliminate him too, whoever it is." Menzies dismissed both men with a wave of his hand.

Just outside Menzies's office Philby said, "Quite a mess, Frederick."

"You don't know the half of it," Winterbotham said, racing ahead of him.

Philby knew more than Winterbotham was aware, but since that was clearly classified, he simply nodded as the man disappeared down the corridor.

16 Jun 20

CHAPTER TWELVE

1000 Hours, Saturday, October 24, 1942
The Crown Inn, Fenny Stratford, Buckinghamshire

The small patch of grass in front of the Crown Inn still lay in shadow when Conor drove up. The early morning frost hadn't yet melted. Before entering, something caught Conor's ear, and he looked up at the partly cloudy sky. Along the edge of the inn's slate roof, a line of pink-gray doves were perched, emitting a monotonous cooing. A hearty laugh from inside the inn startled the birds, and they scattered.

Once inside, Conor heard indiscriminate chatter from a small group of patrons having a late breakfast with mugs of steaming liquid. Conor asked a young woman bussing a table if Maisie Buckmaster was around.

"She is. What do you want with her?" the woman said, not looking up as she stacked dishes scraped clean into a small wooden tub. A lock of her dark hair dangled in front of her face, obscuring Conor's view.

"I want to talk to her about her mother."

The young woman stopped and looked up at Conor. Her eyes showed the effects of a good cry, but despite the redness and swelling, the woman was very attractive. "Are you from the police?" she asked, brushing away the lock of hair with the back of her hand.

"Not exactly. Do you know where I can find her?" Conor asked, knowing the right question was, *Are you Maisie Buckmaster?*

"What can I do for you, Mister … ?"

"Conor Thorn, ma'am." He extended his hand. Hers was warm and moist. "Alan Turing suggested that I track you down and ask some questions about one of your boarders and …"

"My mother, who's been missing for a week. It's okay, Mr. Thorn. I'm … I'm told by the police that she must have needed to get away. Running this place isn't easy on her, even with my help. She does have a wild streak in her. A bit spontaneous. It was the drink that made her so. It drove me crazy." She paused for a moment. "Are you a friend of Alan's?"

"Can't say as I am. I met him only once."

"Hmm," Maisie said, very slowly nodding her head, sizing up Conor. "What boarder is it you're interested in?"

"Gunnar Lind. He works with Turing."

"Doing what exactly? I could never even get an inkling what those two men do."

"That's not clear to me either. What can you tell me about Lind?"

"Listen, Mr. Thorn," Maisie said, blowing strands of hair off her forehead. "With my mother out on a lark, I am busier than a cat covering poop on a concrete floor. Can you be more specific?"

Conor chuckled. He detected a soft Irish accent coming through. "It seems Lind has also gone missing. There are no clues as to his whereabouts."

"Just like in my mother's case."

"Yes, as far as I know, that's right. His wife is completely in the dark as to where he might be. Can you tell me when you last saw him?"

"You're a Yank. Who did you say you're with?"

"I didn't. Let's just say someone very important in London wants me to help find Lind. And I'm not having much luck."

"So you're not looking for my mother?" Maisie asked, cocking her head.

"I believe the local police are handling that. My main focus is Lind. But if there were any … connections between the two disappearances, I'd surely communicate that to the police."

Maisie nodded slowly, looked down, and fiddled with some dishes in her tub. "They talked. They liked each other," she said.

"She was twenty years older than him. And he was a devoted husband. I don't see any … connections between them."

"I didn't mean to imply—"

"No worries, Mr. Thorn. The police asked the question outright."

"So you were aware that Lind was missing also?"

"Yes. There's been talk. Among the villagers mostly."

Conor nodded. "She'll come back. To you. To this place."

Her turn to nod. "You're a handsome one. Anyone ever tell you that? Oh, of course they have. Let's sit. My feet are already aching," Maisie said, grabbing Conor's wrist and leading him to a table by the fireplace in the front room.

As they sat, Maisie got the attention of an older man behind the bar and held up two fingers. "I believe it was a week ago Wednesday. It was late. A rainy night. I was wiping down the tables. My mother had gone to bed. When he came downstairs, he said he was going for a walk, to post a letter."

The barman arrived with two mugs of hot tea.

"I said it was a nasty night for a walk, but he just shrugged his shoulders and pulled up his collar and left. My mum and he talked a lot, like I said. He took many walks in the woods behind the inn. He said it always helped clear his mind. She and Winny would join him often. Winny was her dog. You know the dog is missing too, don't you?"

"I didn't know that."

"She told me that Gunnar said that their long walks made Eve jealous." A beat passed. "I wish she hadn't taken Winny. It would be a good reason for her to come back," Maisie said, dabbing her eyes with the corner of her stained apron. "She loved that dog."

Conor took a sip from his mug to give Maisie a moment. "Did Lind have a good marriage? Any … ah …"

"You're cute. Hanky-panky, you mean?"

"Yes. Hanky-panky." Conor smiled. He liked this woman. "I came across some information about another woman."

"What?" Maisie shouted, then looked around to see if anyone had noticed. "Never heard that. But I will tell you that he and Eve, his wife, did argue. I don't know about what, but other boarders complained." She took a deep breath. "I told Eve that others were complaining, and she told me to mind my own business. The nerve.

I said, this *is* our business. And she just slammed the door in my face. She's Swedish, you know. I always thought they were more polite than that."

"Did you ever see him with another woman? Maybe someone he met here in the pub?"

"No. Never. He seemed devoted to her. Too shy anyway. But what I can say is that he's been lookin' a bit ... sad, you know? Like depressed about something. Maybe about the arguing."

Conor took another sip of the tea. "You've been very helpful. Do you mind if I come back if I have more questions?"

"That would be lovely, Mr. Thorn. Think of some more questions," she said, extending her hand. "And call me Maisie."

Conor took it and said, "Call me Conor." He stood up. "Is there a church around here by any chance?"

"Are you Catholic?"

"Ahh ... yes." Conor realized the last time he was in a Catholic church was for Grace's funeral. She was a devoted Catholic and often chided him for being less so. When he lost her, his faith in the church, in God, weakened further. He could still smell the overpowering incense. But he needed to sort some things out—a talk with Grace on her turf might help.

"Well, you're out of luck. There's St. Mary's, not far from here. It's Anglican, but it's a church. They pray to the same God we do. But Mr. Lind and his wife don't go to any church."

"It's a personal matter."

"Looking for answers, are we?"

"No. Maybe a little forgiveness for something that I may have to do," Conor said as he softly patted Maggie's list in his breast pocket.

"It is wartime, Conor. Your actions may be covered."

Conor looked at her for a long moment. "Thanks for your time. And your help." He made for the door.

Three steps from reaching it, Eve Lind walked through carrying a cloth sack; the thin stalks of a few carrots fell over the sides. "Mr. Thorn, what a surprise." Eve looked past him to the table where Maisie still sat, now watching them. "Or on second thought, maybe not."

"Eve, do you have a minute? I have a question," he said.

"I do. If it can help you find my husband."

They sat in a booth near the door.

"Do you have any leads?"

"No. Or no strong leads. Maisie Buckmaster said the last time she saw your husband, he went to mail a letter. My question: Do you know who he was writing to?"

Eve looked over at Maisie, who was still watching them, drinking her tea. "I don't know for sure, but I'd have to guess it was Rubie, his whore."

Conor nodded. "From what I have been able to gather so far, it seems that your husband was very devoted to you. You were the love of his life. What do you say to that?"

Eve looked at Conor. "No one knows the whole story of what goes on behind closed doors, Mr. Thorn. That's what I have to say."

"Not even Gunnar's brother?" He had nothing and was going nowhere fast. The question was a Hail Mary pass.

No answer.

Conor only offered a thin smile.

They held each other's gaze. Even the sound of glassware crashing to the floor failed to break their focus.

Eve spoke first. "Gunnar never spoke of his brother but once, and that was to explain why he didn't invite him to our wedding."

"And why was that?"

"Because his brother threatened to kill him over Gunnar's handling of his ... *their* mother's estate."

"Where is his brother?"

Eve's eyes narrowed. "Why?"

"Gunnar's missing." Conor pulled off the kid gloves. "He could be dead. Maybe at the hand of his brother. Where is he?"

"That is preposterous. I have no idea where he is. The last Gunnar knew of his whereabouts, he was in Malmö."

A Swede in Sweden. No alarm bells going off with that news. "Doing what?"

"I don't know because Gunnar didn't know ... and didn't care. And I don't care, Mr. Thorn."

Conor noted the edge in her voice, which betrayed her annoyance at the line of questioning. "Thank you. I'll be in touch."

Eve started to rise but stopped and looked at Conor. "Mr.

Thorn, I wish I could be of more help to you." The edge in her voice was gone. "I will do my best to answer all your questions. I am desperate to find him and take back the money … my money that he stole from me." Eve slid out of the booth and raced up the stairs.

Conor walked over to Maisie. She said, "Such a lovely woman, isn't she?"

Conor ignored the catty comment but did appreciate the quality of the sarcasm. *One of the great linguistic qualities of all us Irish.* "Two questions, Maisie. Did the Linds have many visitors since they arrived here?"

"Not that I noticed. They would occasionally take supper with Alan Turing here in the pub. But that's all I ever noticed. My mum would have a better answer. She's nosier than me."

Conor nodded. "By the way, do you have any samples of Eve Lind's handwriting?"

CHAPTER THIRTEEN

0800 Hours, Sunday, October 25, 1942
Oslo Central Station, Oslo, Norway

The line to board the morning train to Stockholm snaked up and down the platform. The chirping of a small flock of birds echoed under the steel roof. Bird excrement ran down the sides of the roof girders. Emily's progress in the line was sporadic, the Gestapo ushering some people through quickly and questioning others. An older couple was directly in front of her, the man dressed in dark pants and a matching jacket with two columns of brass buttons running up each side of the jacket's opening. The woman's brown skirt was almost floor length and was topped off by a gold long-sleeve blouse and a black waistcoat.

Emily's focus shifted to the Gestapo agent ahead. As the line crept along, he would lift his gaze from travel documents to look at the people still to come. Only those with hard-to-attain paperwork from the Norwegian puppet government would be passed through—unless you knew some of the best forgers in Oslo, as MI6 did.

Emily detected a foul odor, and the older man in front of her turned to her and bowed his head. "I apologize. When I get nervous ... I get—"

His companion slapped his arm and said something Emily didn't understand.

The older man blushed.

Emily smiled and nodded. She understood better than anyone that Gestapo agents triggered an array of negative reactions, including her own nervous sweating.

Up ahead, some travelers were being pulled from the line and ushered into a waiting room adjacent to the platform, which increased the level of nervous chatter. It took Emily fifteen minutes to reach the head of the line. Her passport and travel papers, identifying her as Swiss citizen Mia Durs, were held tightly in one hand, her carpetbag in the other. Nerves in check, she handed over her papers with a steady hand.

"You are Swiss. I assume you speak German?"

"Yes." Emily knew that her proficiency with the German language, though somewhat unimpressive, was good enough to help her being accepted into MI6.

"The reason for your trip?" the stocky Gestapo agent asked, a cigarette dangling from the corner of his mouth, a crooked ash moments away from falling on his tunic. His head was bowed as he read Emily's papers.

"I am visiting a sick aunt."

The Gestapo agent jerked his head up. "I detect an accent. It sounds ..."

"My mother is British, but I was born in Geneva and raised in both countries."

The agent stared at Emily, then motioned for a guard to join them. "Search her bag."

While the guard searched, Emily directed her gaze at passengers that were getting settled inside the train.

"Where are you traveling from?"

The question caught Emily slightly off guard. After a long moment the agent started to ask the question again, but Emily spoke up. "Rjukan." As soon as she uttered the word, she realized her mistake. Rjukan was the site of the heavy water production facility that she had been sent to investigate. She was only slightly comforted that, as far as MI6 knew, what took place at the facility wasn't widely known.

The agent snatched his cigarette from his mouth, tossed it under the train car, and handed her papers back to her. Emily grabbed them, but the agent wouldn't let go. She smiled and tugged at the papers, the agent eventually gave her a thin smile and released his grip. The guard handed her bag back, and she was motioned to board.

Emily stepped up onto the nearest train car and took the first seat she found. Looking out the window, she saw the Gestapo agent walk over to a small podium with a phone located along a far wall. He picked up the handset and began talking. About her? Instead of just sitting and waiting, Emily decided to err on the side of caution. If she could alter her appearance, it might increase her chances of not being found or followed. Across the aisle, Emily eyed a woman who was fast asleep, her head leaning against the window, her gray wool coat draped over the seat back. A sky-blue, wide-brimmed felt hat sat on the seat. Emily looked up and down the train car, then moved into the aisle and leaned toward the coat. By the time the woman stirred, her eyes slowly opening, Emily was already two steps down the aisle, headed toward the far end of the train car. She ducked into the lavatory and locked the door, her heart racing.

Taking a few deep breaths, Emily calmed herself and pulled a map from her bag. Her finger followed the route from Oslo eastward into Sweden, where it terminated one station short of Stockholm—her stop. From there, a bus would take her to her final destination.

Emily rested her head against the lavatory wall as the train began to pull out of the station. The wheels clacked over the rails, first slowly, then picking up speed. Her thoughts drifted back to 1940, when she'd met a plane at RAF Tempsford in the wee hours to help a young couple being flown from Paris. Gunnar Lind had been a gentle man, always lost in his own thoughts, who loved his wife deeply but was ashamed because he could not father children due to his sterility. A shame that was almost unbearable, he had confided to her.

#

0830 Hours, Monday, October 26, 1942
British Legation, Strandvägen 82, Stockholm

Emily feared she was riper than her own senses indicated. T. F. Masterman, the legation's military control officer / passport control officer, who provided cover for MI6's agents in Sweden, didn't give any signals that this was the case though, which gave her some comfort. But the sooner she could find a bath, the better off she and anyone around her would be.

Masterman's office was located on the third floor of a four-story redbrick building. When Emily was shown into his office, she caught him midyawn, which he fought off. Emily related the details of her trip from Oslo, including her suspicions that the Gestapo agent at the train station had his doubts about her. When Masterman was done asking questions, it was Emily's turn.

"So, who did we lose?"

"That would be Roger McInnis. He was a real character. His death has hit the legation staff hard. He was a Royal Marine. Served with them for over twenty years before joining the intelligence service. Lost his wife in the Blitz. No children."

"Should he have been sent out alone that day?"

Masterman shot Emily a sharp look and crossed his arms over his chest. "Couldn't be helped, Bright. We're doing the best we can with a thin staff."

She had just crossed over to his bad side. "I was told that three new agents were being sent to assist. Have you heard anything?"

"We're told that nasty weather has kept them on the ground since Saturday. Bad luck."

Bad luck, indeed, Emily thought. She was going to have to cover a lot of ground on her own. "Do you have anyone you can free up?"

"I will in a couple of days. I sent two men to Lysekil to check on a shipment of ball bearings and machine tools."

"Very well," Emily said. "So the assumption is that they took him inside the legation. But why did the appearance of one agent rattle them so much that they acted so aggressively?"

"Well, as for why they did what they did, my guess is they have something, someone they didn't want us to see or get close to. What or who that is, is anybody's guess."

Emily looked up at a portrait of King George VI holding a scepter and dressed in ceremonial uniform, complete with sword, medals, and epaulets; he returned Emily's gaze, as if waiting for her to do something. "Could the someone be Lind?"

"As I said, anybody's guess. But that's as good a guess as any."

"Where's McInnis's body?"

"Still at the city morgue. They won't release it to us until they finish their investigation."

Emily nodded. "Who's heading up the investigation for the local police?"

"That would be Inspector Tronstad. A good fellow; he is quite … deliberate."

"Could you call him and let him know I'll be dropping by later today? Say in a couple hours. I need to head over to Lind's father-in-law's office and see if he has heard from his son-in-law. I'll visit the morgue after that."

Masterman stood. The front of his pants were deeply creased, as if he had been sitting for days. "One thing, Bright. When you're out and about, be aware of your surroundings. Stockholm is getting as bad as Lisbon."

"I'll be careful. Oh, I almost forgot. Do you have the rest of my cover story?"

Masterman nodded and handed Emily an index card. "Name and address and biographical notes about your sick aunt."

CHAPTER FOURTEEN

1100 Hours, Monday, October 26, 1942
USAAF Eighth Bomber Command, RAF Daws Hill, High Wycombe

The last time Conor Thorn had been stood up was back in high school. A girl named Stephanie was a no-show at Seymour's Luncheonette. It had hurt. But this time, it pissed him off. John Cairncross, the inquisitive coworker of Lind's, couldn't be found when Conor arrived at the agreed-upon time at Bletchley Park. Conor left Cairncross a nasty note, which did nothing to diffuse his anger.

He had to get to another interview. As he drove from Bletchley to RAF Daws Hill, he thought about what he'd learned earlier in Bill Donovan's office: Emily had been sent to Stockholm.

"Stockholm?" Conor asked. "What happened in Norway?"

"Nothing. She wasn't there long enough. The operation was put on hold. Recent intercepts place someone associated with British intelligence there looking to sell top secret information to the Germans through their legation."

"Why did they send Emily alone?"

"They didn't. Three other agents were dispatched from London to join her," Bill Donovan said. "Menzies said the staff in Stockholm has been picked over. MI6 agents have been shifted from Stockholm, Geneva, and Bern and sent to Lisbon, Morocco, and Gibraltar. We've moved some agents also because of Torch."

That three agents were on the move to join Emily hadn't made

Conor feel any better, and even now, he stewed about the danger she was in, only stopping when he arrived at the airfield where Preston Simms, Grace's stepbrother, was assigned as a public affairs officer for the Eighth Bomber Command.

Conor and Simms had met only one time, at the wedding. Grace and Simms did not get along, though Conor never could get the exact reason for their frosty relationship out of Grace; she was too nice to speak ill of him.

Conor fought off pangs of apprehension. Maggie had called the day before, saying she had remembered what might be an important detail. "It's about one of the guys we don't have a name for. I overheard the one who got there late say he played football at the academy." Conor grimaced at the vagueness of the clue. *Could he have played alongside Grace's rapist?*

He and Simms had arranged to meet in the officers' mess, which was nearly empty save for a handful of officers. Conor, struggling to remember what Simms looked like, walked past a table with two lieutenants seated across from each other having a cup of coffee.

"Conor?"

He stopped and turned toward the voice behind him. A lieutenant, his face puffy and dark circles under his eyes, was looking at him. "Preston?"

"Yes," Simms said. He nodded to the other lieutenant, who picked up his mug and left, leaving the table to the virtual strangers.

Conor took the lieutenant's seat. "It's been a long time, Preston. Thanks for seeing me."

"No problem. I won't lie: I am more than curious as to why you want to see me. It's not like we were close."

Sitting across from Simms, Conor got a whiff of some strong aftershave. "Well, you're right. But I knew I was going to be in the area, and there are some questions I wanted to ask."

Simms nodded slowly and took a sip of coffee. "Let me guess … why didn't Grace and I get along?"

"Good place to start."

Simms chuckled. "What did she say?"

"Never did. She was too nice."

"Maybe. What does it matter … now? She's—"

"Dead. That's right." Conor looked around the mess hall. No one was within earshot. "Let me stop the dancing around. Back in March of last year, there was a dinner at Grace's father's house. Quite a few guests, including you, from what I've been told."

Simms's knitted eyebrows betrayed his confusion. "That was a long time ago, Conor."

"Do you remember who the male guests were?"

Simms flinched. "Listen, Conor, we're both busy, so why don't you tell me what this is all about?"

"The night of that dinner, someone raped Grace."

Simms's shoulders slumped. "Oh my God. How horrific." Then he sat upright. "Hey, wait a minute. I'll admit that when my mother got remarried, I was pissed. I acted like a shit, to Grace … to her father. But if you're accusing me of …" Simms was choking back a laugh.

"This isn't funny, Preston. Not in the least."

"It would never happen," Simms said, his eyes boring into Conor.

Conor didn't understand the logic of that. "What the hell does that mean?"

Simms leaned in close to Conor. "Do I really need to lay it out for you? I don't swim in that pool. Is that clear enough?"

Conor stiffened. The pool analogy threw him at first. He believed he understood what Simms meant. But he had to be certain. "Are you telling me that you don't—"

"I thought Grace told you, but I'm guessing from the look on your face, she didn't. Look, I'm sorry she died. She was a good person. As far as her being raped, I can't begin to tell you how sad that makes me. Please believe me."

Conor nodded at the sincerity in his words. "I believe you." He took a moment to let Simms's revelation sink in. *One less suspect. Progress, but not enough.* "What can you tell me about some of the other male guests?"

Simms mentioned that there were several older men, friends of his stepfather's. "Family friends that knew Grace well. There were two others. One who arrived late for cocktail hour. I never got his name because, a little after he arrived, he made it clear that he wasn't interested in me. He made that real clear. I must have insulted his masculinity by saying something stupid. I, like everyone else, was drinking. But I do remember that Grace was not pleased to see him. She said something about a part of her past spoiling her day."

"What did he look like?"

"Slicked-back hair. Expensive blue suit. Too much aftershave."

Conor raised an eyebrow.

"Yeah, I know. I get carried away sometimes when a shower isn't possible, but like I said, I'm on a different team."

CHAPTER FIFTEEN

1000 Hours, Monday, October 26, 1942
BI Maskineri Företag, Östermalm, Stockholm

Emily told her driver that she didn't think she'd be long. The building where Benjamin Andersson's manufacturing company was headquartered had a granite facade for the first two floors with red brick taking over for the top three. A brass plaque with the company name confirmed she was in the right place. The lone security guard told her to head to the third floor. When she stepped off the elevator, she found herself in a large room with three long lines of identical desks on one side. Each desk was occupied by a woman who was typing away, intensely focused on small easels that held sheets of paper. Directly in front of Emily was a dark-stained oak door. The nameplate identified it as the office of Benjamin Andersson.

"I'm sorry, but you do not have an appointment," a sixtyish, statuesque woman with thinning blue-tinted hair said. "And Mr. Andersson is in a very important meeting that will last for a while. What is your name?"

Emily hadn't thought about what name to use, hers or her cover name. The long trip from Norway had drained much of her energy. Her fatigue was spawning sloppiness. "I'll wait for introductions when we meet face-to-face. Tell Mr. Andersson that I will be back later."

The squat woman didn't look happy at not getting a name. "Can I at least tell him what it's about?"

Emily had an answer for that. "It's about his son-in-law, Gunnar."

#

Minister Hermann Kleist, the head of chancery of the German Legation, sank deeply into the leather club chair. His ample frame fit snugly between the arms. Benjamin Andersson sat directly opposite the minister in a matching chair, thinking he was the dealmaker of the group.

"Please introduce your ... friends, Minister Kleist."

"Ah, yes. These are members of my advisory team. We work closely together. A well-oiled machine, Mr. Andersson, like your factory," Kleist said, followed by a shrill cackle, drawing sour looks from his companions.

Kleist first introduced Lina Stuben, who was dressed in a tailored black pantsuit and black leather boots that came up to her knees, something Andersson had never seen a woman wear. Next, a brooding hulk of a man named Kurt Eklof was introduced; the eye patch Eklof wore drew Andersson's focus and held it for several moments. Stuben and Eklof shared a couch situated against the wall; a window directly behind them let in a dim backlight.

"Thank you for coming. I believe what you will hear will convince you that this will not be a waste of your time."

"We are ready to listen, Mr. Andersson," Kleist said.

"I have agreed to represent a relation of mine, someone who I trust completely."

Kleist leaned forward and nodded. Stuben and Eklof remained stoic.

"This relation is a former member of British intelligence, and when he left, he took sensitive information—information so valuable that he is being hunted as we speak. This is the main reason why I agreed to stand in for him."

"What might be the other reasons?" asked Stuben, her voice a low, menacing mutter, which gave Andersson pause.

"I love my family. I will do anything for them, Miss Stuben—or is it Mrs. Stuben?"

Stuben did not answer.

Andersson saw Eklof give Stuben a look from the corner of his eye. "As I was saying, this information, I have been told, could change the course of the war in Germany's favor."

"The course of the war is already in Germany's favor, wouldn't you agree, Minister Kleist?" Eklof asked.

"Yes, of course. But let us listen to this proposal. If our progress can be made swifter, then victory is even closer at hand."

Andersson detected a slight curl of Eklof's lip.

"What is the nature of this information?" Stuben asked.

"I have only been told that it involves communications."

"Mr. Andersson, please get to the point," Stuben said.

Andersson realized she was who he needed to deal with. He held her gaze before speaking again. "Yes … certainly. For this top secret intelligence, the asking price is one million krona—"

"Stop," Stuben said harshly, cutting him off. "That ridiculous sum for nothing but a hint of what this intelligence says? What do you take us for?"

"Please, calm down, Lina," Kleist said, but she shot him a withering glance, which made him sink deeper into his chair.

"I understand your position, Miss Stuben." Andersson took an envelope from his breast pocket. "My relation predicted your reluctance to agreeing to this proposal." Kleist reached out for the envelope, but Andersson offered it to Stuben. "My relation has experience with high-level human intelligence. In your hands is an example of the quality of his access."

Stuben opened the envelope and pulled out the message revealing Heinrich Himmler's upcoming meeting in Rome. Andersson was an expert at reading the reactions of those he negotiated with, and when Stuben bit her lower lip, he took it as a sign of concern and anxiety. It was a signal to him that the intelligence made an impression on her.

"I have been told that this example should convince you of the potential value of my relation's offer. Would you agree, Miss Stuben?"

She put the paper back in the envelope. "The information in this intercept will have to be confirmed. If … if it is accurate, we shall give further action consideration." She stood and marched for the door.

"Miss Stuben, I require an answer tomorrow."

She stopped and spun around. "If none is given?"

"Ah, well—"

"Don't insult me, Mr. Andersson. What other buyers would there be?" Stuben bolted from the office.

Eklof followed.

Andersson walked to the door with Kleist. "Minister Kleist, please accept my invitation to a dinner the city of Stockholm is having to, I am embarrassed to say, honor my contributions to the community." Honors never embarrassed the prideful Andersson, but he knew some humility was good. "Will you come?" As Andersson helped the minister on with his coat, he saw Stuben having an animated conversation with Eklof in the outer office.

CHAPTER SIXTEEN

1100 Hours, Monday, October 26, 1942
City Morgue, Kungsholmen, Stockholm

At first, Emily was glad she'd dismissed her legation driver and decided to walk the five blocks to the city morgue. The late-morning sun felt good on her face, and the walk gave her some time to think. Regrets started to form when she noticed two men in a light gray Volvo following sixty feet or so behind her. They made little effort to hide their agenda. They wanted to put Emily on notice.

Every inch of the morgue's interior was dreary. The walls were covered with battleship-gray paint; the floors, in a similarly colored linoleum, were marred with the black skid marks left by gurney wheels. Many empty stretchers lined the walls. Emily had been in morgues before and knew what to expect, but the smell in this one was nearly overpowering. The young attendant with thick, black-framed glasses was seemingly unfazed by the stench and smiled when he came from a back room to greet her. After showing him identification describing her as a member of the British Legation, the attendant took her through a set of double doors into a softly lit room populated by two dozen gurneys with white sheets covering their occupants. In the center of the room was one gurney with two large lights focused on its sheet-covered body.

"Here he is," the attendant said, his voice squeaky and pubescent. He solemnly pulled down the sheet until Roger McInnis's body was exposed from the waist up. The once-dark ink of the

Royal Marine tattoo on his upper left arm was faded. The body was bloated, the skin slightly lighter than the pearly luster of talc. His face was bruised. His left-hand ring finger was missing.

"What was the actual cause of death? Drowning?"

The attendant covered the body. "No definitive cause, as the British Legation did not approve an autopsy. But given his age and weight, it's probable that he suffered a heart attack due to some physical trauma."

"Were there any personal effects?"

"Yes." The attendant bent down and pulled a brown paper bag from a shelf below the body and handed it to Emily. She emptied the contents on top of the sheet still covering McInnis's legs. She sorted through an empty billfold, some silver and copper coins … and a small pin.

"What's this?" She held up a stickpin, no longer than a quarter of an inch, with a Nazi swastika over a black background.

"Yes, that was strange. We found it in his mouth. It looks like something someone would wear on the lapel of a suit coat."

Emily asked if she could take it.

"No. It's evidence. But I can give you a photograph of it. We have several photos of his belongings and the body." The attendant looked around the room nervously. "But I could get into trouble, you see."

Emily reached into her pocket, pulled out some bills, and handed them over. The attendant excused himself to collect the photos. While Emily waited, she thought of her new friends outside waiting for her.

The attendant returned a minute later with a file.

"I need two favors," Emily said. "Could you please mail the photos to the British Legation, to the attention of Captain Masterman?" Emily handed over two more bills. "And if anyone asks why I was here today, say I was here to see my old boyfriend."

The attendant folded the bills and stuffed them into the breast pocket of his lab coat. He was blushing.

#

Standing on the front steps, Emily scanned up and down the street. The Volvo was parked last in a line of cars on the opposite side of the street. It was pointed in the direction she planned to take to the main branch of the Stockholm police station. A squat man was leaning against the front fender of the car, smoking a cigarette. He was staring at her. She cursed herself for deciding to travel alone. She had learned some evasive tactics in her training, but most were designed for busy streets and various modes of transportation. The street before her was quiet, and she saw few people and fewer vehicles. She forced herself to remain calm and took several deep breaths. The driver of the Volvo sat inside, also smoking. He, too, was watching her intently. Emily headed in the direction of the police station, and the car pulled away from the curb, leaving the squat man behind.

CHAPTER SEVENTEEN

1200 Hours, Monday, October 26, 1942
German Legation, Södra Blasieholmshammer 2, Stockholm

Stuben's assistant was writing frantically, trying to keep up with her boss's rapid-fire dictation. When Stuben finished, she paused for a long moment to allow her assistant to catch up. Stuben glanced at the photo of Heinrich Himmler and herself standing shoulder to shoulder on a patio high up in the mountains. Scrawled across the bottom was *To Lina, your loyalty humbles me. HH.* "Read it back to me."

The assistant, her glasses perched on the tip of her nose, flipped some pages to get to the beginning of the message to Reichsführer Himmler. Stuben, paying particular attention to the part where she detailed the intelligence regarding the Reichsführer's visit to Rome, did not notice any mistakes or omissions.

"Read the last two sentences again," Stuben said, looking intently at a picture of Adolf Hitler that hung on the wall behind the assistant.

"I am convinced that this agent has access to high-value classified information that will be of use to the Reich in the war against our enemies. I am seeking your approval to immediately proceed with the acquisition of this intelligence." The assistant laid her notebook on her lap and placed her folded hands on top of it.

Stuben considered what might possibly sound wrong. "Change 'agent' to 'British traitor' and have it sent at once."

The assistant sprang from her chair and left the office. Stuben noticed the woman didn't go directly to the legation's communications room but instead sat at her desk and looked as if she was writing notes. Puzzled and annoyed, Stuben stepped outside her office and approached the woman's desk. "I clearly said to send the message at once," she said, specks of spittle landing on the desktop. "What could be more important than a critical message to Reichsführer Himmler? Go at once."

The assistant bolted from her desk.

Stuben ran the back of her hand across her mouth and was about to return to her office when Kurt Eklof appeared. "Well, what is it?"

"I just received a message from one of the men assigned to follow what we think is a newly arrived British agent. They followed her to the city morgue."

"And why does this concern us?"

"The morgue attendant said she examined the body of the old man and went through his belongings."

Stuben thought about that. "We removed anything that could identify him. Emptied his wallet, even took the ring finger because we couldn't get his ring off."

Eklof took a deep breath. "Yes, but we missed a tattoo."

She looked at him sharply. "What did you say?"

"He had a Royal Marine arm tattoo. And there's one more thing."

"Good God, what?"

"The attendant said that the old man had a Nazi Party lapel pin in his mouth when they found him. The agent saw it."

Stuben's jaw dropped. "A party—" She zeroed in on Eklof's suit coat lapel. "Are you telling me that he somehow took your ... your party pin?"

Eklof's sole response was a small nod.

"You fool. How could you not notice it was missing?" Stuben hissed through her clenched jaw. Not waiting for an answer, she began pacing. "This agent has now seen evidence that ties us to this dead man. That puts us at risk with the local authorities at a time when we are engaged in a matter of great importance to the Reich." Stuben stopped and turned to Eklof. "Where is this woman?"

"The man following her reported that she is at the police station. She's been there for the last fifteen minutes."

Stuben turned to the picture of Himmler on her desk. "We must rectify this ... misstep. When she leaves the station, take her."

CHAPTER EIGHTEEN

1300 Hours, Monday, October 26, 1942
Reich Main Security Office, Prinz-Albrecht-Strasse 9, Berlin

The street outside Prinz-Albrecht-Strasse 9 was nearly devoid of vehicles and pedestrians. Even Berliners knew to stay away from the headquarters of the RSHA.

Brigadeführer Walter Schellenberg, chief of the SD-Ausland, the organization assigned to gather foreign intelligence for Himmler's SS, drove up to the front entrance of the massive five-story granite building. Two SS guards flanking the entrance snapped to attention when he exited his car. Schellenberg dismissed his driver and tugged down the bottom of his gray service uniform tunic. Above the entrance hung a massive red banner with a large black swastika. Over time, the sun had bleached the deep-red hue to a lighter shade. Schellenberg entered the building and decided to take the stairs to the fifth-floor office of Heinrich Himmler. He needed to stretch his legs.

When he entered Himmler's outer office, he expected to be greeted by Rudolf Brandt, Himmler's personal administrative officer, but the office was vacant. He gently knocked on Himmler's office door and entered. Two enormous Nazi flags loomed over a desk heaped with several stacks of files. The spacious office was austere; besides the desk and two chairs that were placed in front of it, there was a couch and two club chairs in a corner of the office. A surprisingly small picture of Hitler hung on the wall behind the desk. The door to a small bathroom adjacent to the office was open. Schellenberg could see the back of Brandt, who was speaking to Himmler as he shaved.

Himmler saw Schellenberg in the mirror and stopped. "Walter, I won't be long. I just returned from Zhytomyr. I'm just cleaning up. Please sit."

The trip from Zhytomyr, Schellenberg knew, was a long and arduous one. Located southwest of Kiev in the Ukraine, Himmler had picked Zhytomyr as one of his headquarters because he wanted to be close to Hitler's eastern front headquarters at Vinnista and the German General Staff headquarters at Berdichev.

"Continue, Brandt." Schellenberg had witnessed this scene before. In the morning, Brandt would read the most important items that had arrived in the office while Himmler shaved. Fearing that bad news would lead to a flinch and possibly some blood, Brandt would give a quasi-warning, saying, "Pardon, Herr Reichsführer," a signal to Himmler to pause his shaving.

Brandt cleared his throat and delivered his warning followed by a pause. A shirtless Himmler stopped shaving, turned, and gave Schellenberg a brief look. "The last item is a message from Agent Lina Stuben." Himmler resumed shaving. Schellenberg was well aware of Stuben. He had recommended that she receive field agent training, followed by an assignment to Stockholm, after Himmler's wife, Margarete, had discovered her husband and Stuben's romantic relationship.

Brandt read a message regarding a defecting British intelligence agent and a proposal to sell classified information, then paused. "Pardon, Herr Reichsführer."

Himmler again stopped and turned to Brandt.

"'To prove that this Swede had access to top secret information, he revealed to me that he had knowledge of Herr Reichsführer's upcoming trip to Rome, where you will be honored by the Italian government. He supplied travel details and timetable information.'"

Himmler threw his razor into the sink and turned to Schellenberg. "This is unacceptable. Can we not keep anything secret?" His nostrils flaring, Himmler took a few breaths. "Lives can be lost. My life," Himmler said as he pounded his chest. Red-faced, he removed his glasses and returned to the sink and ran some water.

Brandt finished reading the message, which ended with a request for permission to negotiate for the intelligence.

A calmer Himmler dried his face, dismissed Brandt, and then disappeared from Schellenberg's view. "So, what are your thoughts, Walter?"

Schellenberg moved closer to the bathroom so he could be heard. "My first thought is to question any offering from someone associated with the SIS, especially one with such a high cost."

"I agree. But only a small number of people knew of this upcoming trip to Rome. You, Brandt, Dr. Kersten, and maybe two or three others. And I trust you all implicitly." Himmler emerged from the bathroom, buttoning his uniform tunic, then sat at his desk.

Schellenberg took his seat, not surprised that Himmler had told his physical therapist something he wanted to keep closely held. Kersten was Himmler's closest confidant.

"And the leak is not from the Italians. Mussolini hasn't even announced the tribute."

"Stuben sounds convinced that the information has high value. Maybe news of your trip does give credence to this. Do you trust her instincts?"

Himmler picked up a letter opener adorned with a spread eagle atop a wreath surrounding a swastika, then began slapping the blade into his palm. "I do. She wouldn't ask for such a large sum of money if she weren't sure. She knows that if she is wrong, she has no future back in Berlin. Or Stockholm, for that matter."

"So that's it, then? Give her permission to proceed?"

Himmler took off his glasses and cleaned them with a handkerchief. "Yes. Go tell Brandt to send a reply with instructions to proceed. And tell him to cancel the trip to Rome. Then come back. I want to discuss something more important than this matter."

"What would that be, Herr Reichsführer?" Schellenberg asked, knowing full well what the answer was.

"How to end this two-front war that we cannot win."

CHAPTER NINETEEN

1300 Hours, Monday, October 26, 1942
German Safe House, Stockholm

A dried crust made it difficult to open her eyes, so Emily used the tips of her index fingers to free her eyelids of detritus. When she opened them, what she saw confused her. For a moment, she thought she was in a cage. As she swiveled her head slowly to take in her surroundings, bolts of pain shot up and down her neck. She was lying on a thin mattress laid out on a concrete floor; steel bars surrounded her. She *was* in a cage. Two identical cells flanked hers. She propped herself up on her elbow and shifted onto her left side. Hip pain radiated down her leg and forced her to fall back onto the mattress.

She slowly closed her eyes as the memories came back. After she met with Tronstad and learned nothing, she stood on the steps of the police station. She had seen the Volvo parked across the street. The squat man had rejoined his friend, and she'd headed toward the same narrow street she'd come down fifteen minutes ago, this time in the direction of the British Legation. She remembered looking at the street name on the side of the building so she wouldn't get lost—Coldinutrapen. A sign just below noted that there was no outlet for vehicles, only a steep flight of stairs that led up to another narrow street that led back to the British Legation. She needed to reach those stairs.

She'd stopped twice to look at reflections in shop windows to determine the proximity of the Volvo. On the second stop, she stood next to a trash bin. She used her body to block the view of her car-bound followers as she deposited her legation identification into the bin. She was halfway down Coldinutrapen when she heard the roar of a car engine. She turned and saw the Volvo bearing down on her. It swerved at the last second, smashing its right front fender into her left side, slamming her to the pavement. And then nothing.

Emily tried to sit up again, this time on her right side. The mattress under her elbow was stiff with dried blood, but not hers as far as she could tell. The bucket in the corner of the cell reeked. The walls of the basement were built of large, smooth river rock. The concrete seams between the rocks were cracked and wept moisture. She became aware of a heavy musky smell, as if the basement was used to store vegetables that had turned rotten. On the far side of the basement were some wood crates stacked in a corner. A commode with dark cracks that spread like veins from its base was located in the other corner, a mop nearby.

The quiet was broken by the sound of heavy footsteps from above. Emily looked up and noticed places where light could be seen breaking through the floorboards, adding to the faint light provided by the one exposed light bulb suspended from the ceiling. The muffled sound of someone speaking, followed by two men laughing, filtered through the ceiling.

Emily lay back and closed her eyes, silently berating herself for walking around Stockholm alone. Not taking Masterman's claim as seriously as she should that Stockholm was as dangerous as Lisbon was a mistake she might not live long enough to remedy. Her hip and leg throbbed in time with her heartbeat as she became light-headed and began to drift to sleep.

CHAPTER TWENTY

1700 Hours, Monday, October 26, 1942
White's Club, No. 37–38 St. James Street, London

Bill Donovan handed his umbrella to the attendant and removed his raincoat, shedding an ample amount of rainwater on the marble floor, provoking a slight frown from the attendant.

"I'm here to see Stewart Menzies."

"Yes, sir. You'll find him in the Morning Room. He is with one other guest. This way," the attendant said, leading Donovan to a door off the main entrance hall.

Donovan took in his surroundings as they walked, portraits of former members lining the walls of the main hall. He had heard of White's Club, the oldest gentleman's club in London, but this was his first time inside. The attendant stopped in a doorway and pointed at two men seated opposite each other on leather couches that flanked a fireplace. Menzies faced Donovan, but Donovan couldn't make out whom his guest was. As he closed the distance to them, Donovan could see that Menzies was well past his first drink, his face flushed, his body leaning heavily against the couch's arm, a drink in hand. When Menzies noticed him, he did not rise, but his guest did. David Niven, in the uniform of a British Army lieutenant, greeted Donovan with a bright smile topped off by a neatly trimmed moustache.

"Colonel Donovan, Stewart here has been telling me all about you. It's an honor to meet you," Niven said, shaking Donovan's hand. "I note from the look on your face that I was the last person you expected to see. But it is me, in the flesh."

"You're right on that account," Donovan said. "I would be remiss if I didn't mention that President Roosevelt rather enjoyed your performance in *The First of the Few*."

Niven's mouth fell open.

"We watched the film in the White House back in September. It was recommended to him by the prime minister, and the president was quite taken by the story of Mitchell and the contribution his Spitfire made to the Battle of Britain."

"That film, Colonel, was a labor of pure patriotic love. It's a shame Mitchell is no longer with us." Donovan looked at Menzies, who had just drained his glass. Niven noticed it too and retrieved his officer's hat from the couch. "Well, I'm off. I'll let you two conspire in private. Colonel, do pass on my thanks to your president. It's nice to know that I have a fan in the White House."

"I will. He'll be tickled to hear of our meeting."

Niven nodded at Menzies and departed, taking long strides to the door.

When Donovan sunk into Niven's seat, a rush of air from the seat cushion welcomed him. "Are you all right? You look a bit ... haggard," Donovan said.

Menzies placed his glass on a side table. "Haggard, yes, I'd say that description fits. Do you want a drink? Oh, excuse me, I forgot you don't indulge."

Donovan was unsure if he detected a feigned apologetic tone but decided to press on. "What are the new developments regarding Lind?"

Menzies sat forward and rested his elbows on his knees. "I sent Bright to Stockholm when we heard chatter that someone is setting up a deal with the Germans. I have an exceptionally thin staff there because of Torch."

Donovan nodded.

"But she has disappeared also."

"Damn," Donovan said, leaning toward Menzies. "What else do you know?"

"She wasn't on the ground long. She said she was going to visit Lind's father-in-law, head to the morgue to examine the body of the first agent we sent to surveil the German Legation, and then go to the police station. We know she made all three stops, but she never reported back to the embassy."

"Are the police investigating?"

"Yes, but even with diplomatic pressure, they're moving slowly."

"Listen, Stewart, I can't do much. I just opened an office there. And I'm getting a lot of pushback from our State Department about agents infiltrating the country; some of the top people still think spying is immoral."

"Well, then I must be the devil in their eyes." Menzies sat back and smoothed his mustache with an index finger. "Colonel, I could use some help. I'd like to get Thorn to Stockholm as soon as possible. He knows how Bright thinks, and he's hardheaded and aggressive. That's what we need at the moment."

Donovan nodded. "When Conor hears that Emily is missing, I don't think I could keep him in England unless I locked him in the Tower of London."

"Right, then. Let's get him up to Leuchars as soon as possible. I have three other agents ready to make the trip to Stockholm, but they've been grounded for two days due to a massive weather front over the North Sea."

"This news is going to hit him hard."

Menzies looked at the dying embers in the fireplace. "Not as hard as it will hit us if we don't find Lind."

#

1700 Hours, Monday, October 26, 1942
Holy Trinity Church, Knightsbridge, London

The maple trees that lined the long driveway that stretched from Ennismore Gardens Mews and ended at Holy Trinity Church were losing their leaves. The temperature was dropping as the afternoon turned into evening. Philby turned up the collar on his suit coat and buried his hands in his pockets, seeking the warmth radiating from his thigh muscles due to the long walk. His plan for the day hadn't included a stop at the church, a popular dead-drop location used by Shapak, but he couldn't ignore the signal Shapak had left at the Broadway entrance to St. James Park Underground Station—a white chalk mark placed in the corner of a tattered poster calling for people to enlist as air-raid wardens.

When he reached the church, he headed into the gardens, which Philby found empty. Behind the statue of St. Francis of Assisi, at its base, he found a folded newspaper held down with a stone. He shoved it under his arm and headed into the church, locating a bank of votive candles set below an impressively sized stained glass window. It depicted an angel holding the baby Jesus with a young St. John the Baptist to one side. At that time of day, the fading sun filtering through the stained glass only managed to produce muted colors. Philby opened the broadsheet and found the financial section. The message was short. The newspaper back under his arm, he held the message in both hands, angling it toward the light of the bank of candles, and read. His grip tightened, his knuckles turning white as he read. His lips pursed tightly, and his breathing quickened.

"Damn them," Philby mumbled. He laid the message over the bank of candles and watched it burn. Some ashes fell to the marble floor, where Philby ground them under the sole of his shoe, then exited quickly.

He started his trek down the long driveway. The news that Moscow Center had chosen to ignore priceless intelligence he had provided angered him deeply. They were ignoring him. Their trust in Philby had taken a blow. But ignoring his recent Ultra intelligence regarding Hitler's order to suspend all activity on the eastern front except for Stalingrad and the Terek River in the Caucasus was foolhardy. The opportunity for an offensive strike while most of the German army stood down had now been lost—because Moscow Center doubted him.

Philby picked up his pace and elongated his stride, his heels pounding the asphalt of the long driveway. "Damn them."

CHAPTER TWENTY-ONE

Conor had been staring at the sheet of Claridge's stationery for several long minutes when the phone rang. He picked up the handset. "Thorn."

"Conor, David Bruce. Colonel Donovan needs to see you ASAP. We're upstairs in his suite."

"On my way." Conor capped his fountain pen and looked at the letter. He'd only gotten as far as *Dear Sue*.

When David Bruce opened the door to Donovan's suite, he greeted Conor with a flourish of his left hand. "Come on in and take a seat."

Conor walked through the small foyer of the suite and entered the main sitting room. Donovan, eyes puffy, was behind his massive art deco desk with his chin resting in his hand. Conor was surprised to also see Menzies sitting on a nearby couch. He looked out of sorts, his tie askew and his hair mussed. Both men looked dejected.

Donovan motioned for Conor to take a seat and waited until he sat down before saying, "Emily Bright is missing."

The news rang in his ears, and he stopped breathing for several seconds. "Operation Freshman," Conor mumbled. "What happened?" he asked.

Menzies snapped to. "What did you say?"

"She was in Norway, coordinating with local resistance in the lead up to Operation Freshman. What the hell happened?" Conor asked.

Menzies shot a look at Donovan and jumped to his feet. "Did you tell him?"

"Negative," Donovan said, then turned to Conor. "Where did you hear about that?"

"Someone high up who trusts me and cares about Emily. Just like you, Colonel." Donovan took a few seconds to settle back in his chair. Menzies followed his lead.

"She wasn't in Norway. She was pulled out and sent to Stockholm to track down leads on the Lind disappearance. She was supposed to report back to the British Legation a few hours ago," Menzies said.

"She's the second agent to disappear in the last few days," Menzies added.

Conor's head snapped toward him.

"The first one was found floating in the harbor," Donovan said.

Conor sprang forward, nearly out of his chair. "She was working these leads alone?"

Menzies folded his arms. The question seemed to touch a nerve. *He's not my boss.*

"Conor, she's an experienced agent. It was necessary to get her out in the field as soon as she arrived. We're both short on operatives in Stockholm," Donovan said. "That's one reason we're sending you there. You will take over for Emily. Find Lind. Then find Emily."

Conor wasn't so sure about the order. "How soon?"

"We'll get to that," Donovan said.

Conor sat back. "Colonel, you said it was nearly impossible to get out of England without approvals from people high up in the British government. Does that mean Lind had some help?"

David Bruce started to fidget in his chair.

"Listen here, Thorn," Menzies said, standing. "We don't know if this person in Stockholm is Lind. If it is, we'll get to the bottom of how he got there."

Touched another nerve there.

Menzies handed Conor a file, and he scanned the cover page. It listed background information on Lind and his wife, most of which he already knew. Some information was new: an appraisal of his health, work habits. Behind a series of photos of Lind was a brief on the German presence in Stockholm.

"Look over the file and commit it to memory," Menzies said, then turned to Donovan.

"Okay," Donovan said.

Bruce walked over to the door to the bedroom, opened it, and out came Eve Lind.

Conor's jaw dropped. "What the hell?"

"You two have met," Menzies said. "Mrs. Lind will be making the trip with you."

Conor started to protest, but Donovan held up a hand to cut him off. "She grew up in Stockholm, has family there. Her father is very well connected. She and her father could be a great help in finding her husband … if Lind is, indeed, there."

Menzies turned to Eve, who was dressed in the same attire as she was at the Milton Keynes Police Station except for the beret.

She shifted nervously from side to side.

"She could be useful in helping persuade her husband to abandon whatever he's about to do with the Germans," Menzies said.

"I must find my husband, Mr. Thorn. I told you that. I need to settle things. I can be of great assistance in helping you move in and about Stockholm. I won't hold you back."

"Thankfully, it's not Thorn's call," Menzies said, noticing the look on Conor's face. "The decision has been made. Mrs. Lind, please wait in the other room."

Bruce walked her back to the bedroom and closed the door. Conor recalled the tearless outburst he'd witnessed when he first met Eve Lind; the sense that she was acting bothered him now more than it did then.

"How do we get back to England?"

Bruce retook his chair. "By motor gun boat out of Lysekil, a port on the west coast. You'll take a legation car and travel west. It should take seven to eight hours."

"Conor, that demonstration we saw a few days ago—the boat that was designed to run ball bearings and machine tools from Stockholm to England?" Donovan said. "That's going to be your ride back. It's crewed by civilians. It will arrive Thursday and must depart no later than Friday, after nightfall. The Brits are desperate for ball bearings. If you don't make it in time, you'll have to wait for the next trip."

"If there is one. This is a trial run," Menzies pointed out.

"Wouldn't a submarine extraction make more sense?" Conor asked.

"It's a matter of resources. With the Torch landing just days away, all air and sea resources are aimed at the approaches to the western Med and French North Africa."

"What about by plane?"

"Too risky," Bruce said. "Airports attract spies like bears to honey. You know that from your unfortunate experience in Lisbon."

Conor couldn't argue that point. Portela Airport had been teeming with Abwehr and NKVD agents when he and Emily passed through on their chase to capture Henry Longworth.

"Stay in contact with us while you're in Stockholm. There's a flight to Leuchars leaving RAF Tempsford in two hours. At Leuchars, you'll meet up with three other MI6 agents. Two are desk people. They have no field training, except for the lead agent. It's the best we can do, I'm afraid. They've been stuck there since Saturday, waiting out a storm front. Reports predict a break in the bad weather over the North Sea. Don't be late," Menzies said, then strode out of the room.

"Colonel, I have a request, if I may. I understand that Bobby Heugle is here in London, waiting for a new assignment. Can he come along?" Conor went on to explain that Heugle's father was in the State Department before he retired and was posted to Stockholm when Heugle was a teenager. "He could be of help."

Donovan shrugged. "I don't see why not."

"Bill, I need Heugle back in Tangier after the landings," Bruce said.

"We have enough time. Heugle's experience in Stockholm could come in handy. I'll reach out to Menzies and make arrangements."

Conor got up to leave.

"There's one more thing," Donovan said. "I have communicated to the head of the Stockholm office that you and your mission are to be his number one priority. The head of our office there, Homer"—Donovan shook his head—"the jury is still out on him. But his chief of operations, Gus Karlson, is top notch. He'll get you what you need. Just keep him in the loop. Now, go and pack. David will reach out to Heugle and get him moving, and Hollis will pick you up in an hour. And let her drive this time. You've already got too much to think about," he added pointedly.

CHAPTER TWENTY-TWO

0930 Hours, Tuesday, October 27, 1942
BI Maskineri Företag, Östermalm Section of Stockholm

Benjamin Andersson sat at his desk, sipping a cup of coffee as he listened to a radio newscast. Most of the news focused on the war, which was of great interest to him. After all, war was good for his business. Every plane, tank, and truck that was destroyed in battle had to be replaced. The announcer started to report on a failed German attack launched days before on Sukho Island, located in Lake Ladoga, when the intercom on his desk buzzed. He flipped a toggle switch.

"Yes?"

"Mr. Andersson, your guests have arrived."

"Show them in, please."

Andersson strode over to the radio on the credenza as the office door opened and in marched Lina Stuben and Kurt Eklof. As they approached the desk, the announcer continued his report on the Sukho Island attack, citing the casualties stemming from the German Wehrmacht's failure to break a Soviet supply route to Leningrad. Andersson was slow to turn the radio off, and when he turned to greet his guests, it was obvious that the report annoyed both of them—not the way he wanted to resume negotiations.

"Please, sit," Andersson said, motioning to them. "Minister Kleist won't be joining us?"

"This is a matter of military intelligence. It is best dealt with by those who appreciate the importance of intelligence and can properly appraise its value," said Stuben.

"Very well." Andersson picked up his pipe and began stuffing tobacco into the bowl. "And your response to our proposal?"

Stuben took a deep breath and slowly released it. "We agree to your price." She smiled briefly, as did Andersson, but his smile was masking his surprise.

He had been fully prepared to hear a counterproposal and negotiate.

"But being such a large sum, we need some time to arrange for the funds."

"How much time?" Andersson lit his pipe and watched Stuben glance at Eklof.

"A week at the minimum," Eklof said.

Andersson tilted his head back and forcefully blew a cloud of smoke into the air. He waited several seconds before he replied, giving the impression that he was seriously considering their request. "Let's agree on three days, shall we? There are … special circumstances that need to be considered. Circumstances that I am not in complete control of."

"What circumstances?" Lina asked, her expression pinched. "Three days is very little time."

"I am not at liberty to discuss the circumstances. That said, I am sure the all-powerful German government will have little trouble making the proper arrangements."

Lina's lips pressed into a line as Andersson continued.

"Now, some specifics. The money will need to be deposited in the Svenska Bank by eleven o'clock Friday morning. Once the money has been verified as noncounterfeit"—Andersson noted the sneer that appeared on Stuben's face—"a call will be placed to the legation telling you where you can retrieve the intelligence."

Stuben slammed her hands on the arms of her chair and bolted upright so quickly that the chair almost toppled over.

Andersson remained calm. He had witnessed such outbursts before in negotiations, typically when he pushed too far.

"Mr. Andersson, my country and your company have enjoyed a very healthy relationship over the years," Stuben said. Eklof stood, as did Andersson. "But I must tell you that if the value of this so-called intelligence disappoints, I will personally hunt down this *relation* of yours and seek the retribution that is owed to us."

CHAPTER TWENTY-THREE

1830 Hours, Tuesday, October 27, 1942
Leuchars Airfield, Scotland

The hour-and-a-half flight from RAF Tempsford to Leuchars was, for the most part, uneventful until their approach to the airfield. The pilot of the Lockheed Hudson struggled with a stiff crosswind, ending with one of the worst landings Conor had ever experienced. It amazed Conor that the landing didn't seem to bother Bobby, Eve, or the RAF officer that accompanied them. Bobby had insisted on eating two Stilton cheese sandwiches during the flight; the strong-smelling cheese did nothing but antagonize Conor's abdominal issues, which had already kicked into gear due to his anxiety around flying.

During the flight, while Bobby ate and Eve slept, Conor tried to focus on the mission details. What concerned him most was the scant amount of time they had before the motor gun boat was scheduled to return to England. He had a lot of ground to cover in four days.

As they deplaned, Conor saw a Lockheed Lodestar parked nearby with British Overseas Airways markings, the ground crew in the process of refueling.

A man in a blue uniform with two stripes on the ends of his coat sleeves approached them with a flashlight in his hand. "I'm looking for Thorn. Conor Thorn."

"That'd be me."

"I'm Captain Hansen." Conor detected an accent but couldn't place it. "And these folks must be Heugle and Lind," he said as he shined the flashlight in Bobby's and Lind's faces. He left the light on Lind's face much longer.

Yep, she's pretty.

"Have we've met?" Hansen asked.

Lind averted her eyes and shielded them from the light with her hand. "No. I'm sure we haven't."

He directed the flashlight to the ground but continued to look at her. Eventually, he turned back to Bobby. "I've got bad news for you, Mr. Heugle. We've had a late addition to our passenger manifest. He's a higher priority, a US Navy commander, which means you get bumped."

"Captain, we've got important business in Stockholm," Conor said.

"You and everyone on that flight. I'm already overweight with the size of the diplomatic pouch they just delivered. Sorry, but I can't accommodate. He can catch the next flight." He turned to leave but said over his shoulder, "We take off as soon as they finish topping off our fuel tanks."

Conor looked at Heugle. "Sorry, Bobby."

"It's fine. Just don't do anything stupid until I get there. I don't want to pull your ass out of the wood chipper. Come on. I'll walk you over to the plane." Bobby picked up his bag and Lind's, and they headed for the Lodestar. A crowd was gathered near the rear door.

"Get to a phone and make sure the colonel knows you got bumped. Don't get bumped again. Even if they have to make something up, like you're the bastard child of the King of Sweden."

"Yeah. Or something like that," Bobby said. "I wish I had one hand free so I could deck you."

Conor's grin prompted Bobby to shake his head slowly in mock admonishment. He and Bobby had been close since the eighth grade. Though he'd just moved into town at the start of the school year, it hadn't taken long before Bobby could count nearly the entire class as a close friend. But Conor and Bobby had remained close, and having a close friend to watch his back while in Stockholm was a comfort—one that would have to be postponed for a while.

They approached the group waiting to board, dropped their bags along with all the others, and joined the group.

A man about Conor's height and age walked over; an unlit pipe dangled from his mouth. "You wouldn't be Thorn, would you?" he asked in a booming voice.

Conor nodded.

"Excellent. I'm James Roper-Hastings," he said, extending a hand. "One of the three people who had orders to get to Stockholm in a hurry. That was going on three days ago. Do you know what it's like—"

"Thorn?" A US naval officer, a commander, interrupted Roper-Hastings. The commander moved toward Conor, whose face slackened. "Holy smokes. Sam Seaker. Class of thirty-six."

Conor remembered the name—his teammates called him Buster—but the face was different: fuller, rounder … as was his waistline. "Buster Seaker? You played safety, right?"

Conor had replaced Seaker as safety when he was in his second year. Seaker had a bad ankle sprain, or so he remembered. But Seaker hadn't gotten his starting position back. Conor was that good. He did remember that Seaker came off as a blowhard in the locker room. Much more than other teammates. He elevated it to an artform.

"That's me. Should have been captain of the team my last year, but there were some shenanigans going on with the vote count. Couldn't prove it, but I'm pretty sure."

"More bullshit from Sam Seaker. You don't remember me, do you, Seaker?" asked Bobby.

Conor shot Bobby a look.

"No. Don't believe I do. Should I?" Seaker said in a halting voice.

"I think so. You got me thrown out of the academy."

Seaker took a long look at Bobby.

Bobby had never told Conor who was behind his expulsion, so this was a surprise to him. "For some chickenshit reason. Just to prove you're the biggest asshole in the brigade."

A light went off. "Bugle. You and that guy Simpson. You both lied about getting authorization for your tutoring. You both had no documentation."

"It's Heugle, and like I said: chickenshit. We were in the same squad. If one member of the squad was falling behind, we all were. Simpson needed help with his German. He said he got all the approvals. He lied. Not me. But you threw your weight around and got what you wanted."

"Which was?"

"Fear. You were an angry man. You wanted all the plebes to fear you." Bobby looked at Conor. "Actually quite understandable if you know your psychology, right, Conor?"

Seaker, his chest puffed out, took a step toward Bobby. "What the hell are you talking about?"

The two men bristled as they stood inches away from each other. The crowd picked up on the tension and a hush settled over them.

"Small dick. Gotta compensate."

The crowd loved that one. The laughter measured just south of the reaction to a Bob Hope joke. Seaker shoved his hand in Bobby's face, but Bobby recovered his balance quickly and was midpunch when Conor stepped between the men, facing Bobby. "Go call Donovan."

"Conor, Simpson told me a story about this guy. You gotta hear it. This guy is bad news. Whatever you do—"

"Bobby, go. Place the call."

#

Conor, along with Seaker, Eve, and Roper-Hastings were the last passengers to board. Conor and Roper-Hastings sat across from each other in the last row with Seaker sitting in front of Conor and Eve in front of Roper-Hastings.

It didn't take Seaker long to tee off on Bobby. He twisted rearward and cleared his throat. "Your friend is a hothead."

"Maybe. But it doesn't make him wrong."

The rear door was about to close when a member of the ground crew entered the cabin, his grease-stained coveralls reeking of aviation fuel. He held up an envelope. "Looking for C. Thorn."

"Right here, buddy." Conor took the envelope and noted the big greasy thumbprint when he opened it. "Thanks."

Coveralls jumped to the ground and shut the door.

```
Thorn:

Thought you should know: Mrs.
Buckmaster's body was found last
night in the woods behind the Crown
Inn. Preliminary cause of death is
suffocation. She also had a large
gash on the back of her head. Could
have been caused by a shovel that
was found nearby.

J. Wallace/MI5
```

Conor exhaled.

"Not bad news, I hope," Roper-Hastings said.

Conor folded the note. "It certainly is for someone."

He leaned into the aisle and handed the note to Eve. Sitting ahead of him and across the aisle, Conor couldn't clearly see Eve's reaction, but he thought he heard a slight gasp. She turned back to Conor and handed him the note.

She was touching a gold cross around her neck. "That is such horrible news. She was a lovely woman. Some people will miss her dearly, I am sure."

Some people? Conor pocketed the note. "That include you, Eve?"

Eve pursed her lips, then turned back and settled into her seat.

#

Most of the passengers, minus Conor and his seatmate along with Eve, decided to grab some sleep, which surprised Conor given that the closer they got to the Norwegian coast, the odds that they'd get attacked by the Luftwaffe spiked. But apparently, after three years of war, the possibility that death might come knocking was taken in stride. Conor mulled over the mission details.

Conor and Roper-Hastings discussed Gunnar Lind, Conor

doing most of the talking. He noticed Eve constantly fidgeting in her seat.

"Thanks for the briefing. Being stuck up here for the past few days, we didn't hear much from Broadway," Roper-Hastings said.

"I get it."

"I hope you don't mind my asking: Why is an OSS agent attached to this mission?"

"Well, for one, I was available. That and I've worked with Emily before."

"That so. Where?"

"Mostly London, but we've operated in Lisbon and Rome."

Roper-Hastings eyes widened. "Dangerous places. And you lived to tell the tale. So tell me what's the situation with ..." Roper-Hastings pointed at Eve.

"She wants to help us find her husband ... and gut him if we let her. Or so she says." Conor shook his head. "Your boss and my boss think she's an asset. As each day passes, I believe it less and less."

Roper-Hastings nodded. "Good to know. Well, I think I'll grab some sleep."

Just as Conor settled back and closed his eyes, Seaker turned around in his seat.

"I'm dying to know why you're not in uniform. The navy get tired of you?"

Conor was surprised it had taken this long for the question to come up. "Let's say it was mutual."

"But if you're on this flight, you must be doing something pretty important."

Conor hesitated. He knew Seaker was waiting for him to fill in the blanks. He decided to just nod. After a short pause, he asked, "What about you? No US naval bases where we're going."

Seaker smiled. "Headed back to my assignment at the legation: assistant military air attaché." He puffed out his chest, probably waiting for a pat on the back.

You had to have aviation experience to be an air attaché. Conor didn't know that Seaker had opted for flight school at Pensacola.

"I was back in London acting as a liaison between our navy and the Royal Navy on the lead up to a really big op. Can't tell you much. You'll hear about it soon enough."

"I'm sure I will." Conor sent the signal that he was done by folding his arms and closing his eyes.

"Say, Conor, aren't you married to Grace Maxwell?"

He opened his eyes and locked his gaze on Seaker. "Not anymore."

CHAPTER TWENTY-FOUR

1500 Hours, Tuesday, October 27, 1942
German Safe House, Stockholm

Ten minutes had passed since Emily'd had any sensation in her hands. When the guard, an unshaven older man, had closed the handcuffs around her wrists, he had stared at her to see if she'd reacted as he tightened the fit. She hadn't given him the satisfaction. Another much younger guard hoisted her up roughly and slipped the handcuffs over a large hook that was screwed into a wooden support column. She could touch the floor with her bare toes, relieving only slightly the strain on her wrists and arm sockets. Neither guard uttered a word as they stood back and admired their handiwork. Then they left.

Emily rested her chin on her chest and waited for what was sure to be an interrogation. She didn't have to wait long. A well-built man wearing an eye patch came down the stairs along with a woman with short hair, wearing a black leather coat that came to midcalf, where it met a pair of black leather boots. She walked up to Emily, locking her gaze on her while she took off her gloves and handed them to the man before beginning to pace.

"There was a man, a member of the French underground, whose name was Pierre Brossier. During his interrogation, he realized that he was getting close to giving up the identities of his fellow members of the resistance," the woman said. She stopped directly in front of Emily. "Do you understand me?"

Emily struggled with what the fast-talking woman was saying, but she nodded slowly.

Stuben continued. "Instead of confessing, he jumped out of a window and fell four floors to his death. You have noticed that there are no windows here, Mia Durs."

"Why are you holding me here? I have done nothing," Emily said deliberately.

"Oh, on the contrary. You have been interfering in matters that are of no concern to you."

"What matters?" Emily said.

"Your visit to the morgue. We know why you were there. The attendant was very talkative. He remembered seeing your British Legation identity card. And don't tell me you were visiting an old boyfriend. We are not fools."

The realization that she had few options other than to stick to her cover story, a weak one at best, sickened Emily. They had already killed one agent. Another killing wasn't out of the question. "You searched me. I only have identification as Mia Durs. And that boy ... he's lying to save his skin. I am just visiting a sick aunt."

The woman glared at Emily. "What were you doing at the police station?"

"I was reporting a theft. Someone stole a gift that I brought for my aunt."

The woman took a short step to Emily and slapped her with such force that Emily's head snapped back and hit the wood column, producing a flash of sparks in her vision.

"Stop wasting my time. Why are you here? What has MI6 asked you to do?"

"I've told you. My aunt is gravely ill. I wanted to see her before she dies."

The woman's jaw clenched. She nodded to the tall man, who raced up the stairs two steps at a time. "While I worked with the Gestapo, I started out as a mere secretary," she said as she began pacing once more. "When I expressed interest in watching an interrogation, my superiors were surprised. They didn't believe a woman would have the nerve or the stomach for the process. But I was a good student. I learned much." The woman approached Emily. They were nose to nose when she continued. "I learned that most effective interrogation techniques were designed for men. Like electrodes that sent a current from the man's penis to his anus."

Emily could see the blood vessels that serpentined across the whites of the woman's eyes. The idea of head-butting her came and went. It would do nothing but cause Emily greater harm. Her only real strategy was to confound her.

"Or a vise to crush the testicles. I told my superiors that techniques must be developed for women. And do you know what they said? They said, 'Lina, that is your next project.'" She turned her back to Emily. "Unfortunately, I didn't get the opportunity to work on a live subject." She turned around quickly. "Until now. Who are you looking for?"

"I've told you. I'm here to see a sick aunt," Emily said, her words clipped and tinged with anger. Her arm sockets throbbed with pain. She felt something running down her arms and saw a trickle of blood coming from the skin around her wrists. She heard heavy footsteps and saw the man was returning, a metal rod in one hand. Wrapped around the end he was holding was a thick pad. He gingerly handed it to the woman.

"I told my superiors that for a woman, her beauty is a cherished thing. As, I am sure, it is for you. You are quite beautiful. You must have many men at your beck and call." Lina took hold of Emily's dress between her index finger and thumb and pulled it up until it reached midthigh.

Emily began hyperventilating as she felt heat radiating from the rod. She clenched her teeth. It was all she could do to ready herself for the horror about to fall on her.

Lina raised the rod and spit on it. It hissed. She looked up at Emily. "Who. Are. You. Looking. For?"

Emily felt blood dribble into her armpits. "I've told you. My aunt."

Lina took the rod and pressed it to the sensitive flesh of Emily's inner thigh.

Pain roared through her, and Emily screamed. Her eyes shut tight; tears ran down her cheeks. Her skin sizzled for three torturous seconds before Lina pulled the rod back. The smell of burning skin easily overpowered the basement's habitual odor of rotten produce.

Emily opened her eyes.

Lina was smiling.

Emily stared at her through her tears. The stark fear that the next touch of the rod would break her washed over her. Could she ever do this to another woman in the name of her country? *Of course not*, she thought. But that thought provided little solace at that moment.

"Now, any man that will have you will have a greeting waiting for him—one that will only provoke questions as to your past."

Emily ground her teeth and groaned. "My aunt is Helga Bjorn. Her address is number fifty-three Slottsbacken."

"I told you. We are not fools," Lina said as she raised the rod and took a step toward Emily again.

Not willing to submit, Emily suddenly raised her legs, putting immeasurable strain on her wrists, and launched both feet into Lina's chest. The move sent Lina crashing to the floor, the rod clanging as it hit the concrete. The man landed a punch to Emily's face a mere second later. Then, everything went dark.

CHAPTER TWENTY-FIVE

1530 Hours, Tuesday, October 27, 1942
MI6 Headquarters, No. 54 Broadway, London

The red light above the door to Menzies's office was lit when Philby arrived.

"So sorry, Mr. Philby," Miss Pettigrew said. "He just took a call from the prime minister. I don't know how long he'll be. And Colonel Tordeaux was scheduled to go before you. We are a little backed up, sorry to say."

Philby looked across the outer office and saw Tordeaux sitting with a sheaf of papers in his lap; he was tapping his foot and looked a little antsy. "No apologies necessary. I'll just chat with the colonel for a few minutes." When he approached Tordeaux, the foot tapping stopped. "Hello, Colonel. I hear congratulations are in order," Philby said.

"Not sure what you mean, Kim." Tordeaux said, fiddling with his tie knot.

"Oh, come now. You know it's nearly impossible to keep a secret inside Broadway. Your pending assignment as the controller for the northern area had the boys talking downstairs in the bar." Tordeaux's new G Section assignment covered Holland, Norway, Sweden, Denmark, and Finland.

"I see. Well, there's nothing official yet." He adjusted his tie again. "C has asked that I keep an eye on things in the meantime."

"Everything all right, Colonel? You look a bit anxious."

"Never fond of delivering bad news to C."

"I understand. We've all been there."

"You've been here longer than I. Any advice?"

Philby sat across from Tordeaux. "Well, I'd deliver the news right off the top. Not too much detail. Would you like me to look over your notes?"

"Would you? I may have packed too much into the report." Tordeaux pulled the top two pages from the sheaf of papers in his lap and handed them over.

Philby glanced at the first typed page. At the top, Tordeaux had initialed where it noted whom the report was coming from. "Well, first off, don't use green ink. Only the chief uses green ink."

"Good to know. A little too late for today."

Philby started to read the details of an extraction plan for OSS agent C. Thorn, along with others, from Sweden. "Others? Would that include our Bletchley escapee?"

"We can only hope it's him. Along with Agent Bright."

"Yes, of course, Bright." Philby continued reading. "Ah, I see the bad news. Engine trouble for the motor gun boat."

"Not to mention a lead motor mechanic laid up in hospital due to an appendectomy."

"So your main concern is that Thorn and these others may be stuck ... How do you pronounce this name?"

"It's spelled L-y-s-e-k-i-l but pronounced Lisa-sheel."

"So they may be stuck there for some time due to mechanical problems?"

Tordeaux tugged again at his tie knot. "That and the cargo of ball bearings. We're desperate for them."

"Right, well, as I said, don't try to beat about the bush when you get in there," Philby said as he handed back the papers. "No telling what mood he might be in after talking to the prime minister. Just—"

"Colonel, he's ready for you," Miss Pettigrew said.

Both men turned and saw the green light above C's office door blinking.

"Well, off you go," Philby said with a flick of his hand.

Tordeaux straightened his tie and walked through the open door held by Miss Pettigrew.

Philby rose and walked over to Miss Pettigrew as she closed the office door. The green light stopped blinking, and the red light switched on. "I just realized that there's something urgent that I need to deal with. Tell the chief I won't be long."

CHAPTER TWENTY-SIX

1530 Hours, Tuesday, October 27, 1942
German Legation, Södra Blasieholmshammer 2, Stockholm

"Helga Bjorn is dead. The funeral is tomorrow." Kurt Eklof stood in the doorway, breathing hard. Lina Stuben looked up from reading the contents of a file. "Aren't you going to let her go?"

"You are stupid to ask that given what we know to be true."

"But her story checks out. We're just wasting time with her."

"No. She's no innocent niece. Not the way she withstood that interrogation. She did not cry or beg. She has been trained. We can't let her go. She will break. I just need more time for some new … tools to arrive."

Stuben's secretary poked her head in the office and Eklof moved aside. "A message from Herr Himmler," she said as she handed the message to Stuben with a shaky hand.

Stuben took the message. "What's wrong with you?"

"Nothing, Fraulein Stuben," the secretary said as she scurried from the office.

Stuben shook her head and read the message. It was short. She was ordered to Berlin in two days to pick up the money for the exchange. "Ah, things are progressing nicely. I am to report to Reichsführer Himmler to collect the necessary funds. In the meantime, we have orders to spare nothing in the search for this man. We must put more pressure on Andersson."

Eklof nodded.

Stuben's eyes dropped to the photo on her desk of her with Himmler. A smile betrayed her delight with the news that she was to see him again—maybe only briefly, but she would cherish every second. She realized that Eklof was staring at her, and she felt her cheeks flush.

She tossed the message onto the desk, and her lip curled. "Dismissed."

CHAPTER TWENTY-SEVEN

2300 Hours, Tuesday, October 27, 1942
Bromma Airport, Stockholm

The Lockheed Lodestar bounced several times before it settled on its landing gear, but the long taxi to the terminal allowed Conor's stomach acids to calm. The propellers had hardly stopped when Seaker jumped out of his seat and stood in the aisle.

"Will you be working out of the legation?" he asked.

Conor, still seated, unbuckled his belt. "Some of the time. Not sure how much."

"Whatever I can do for a fellow teammate, let me know. I have friends in town and access to some people that may be of some help."

Eve rose to her feet as well, holding her black medical bag tightly.

"Hello there. We've not met. I'm Buster Seaker."

Eve quickly departed without responding.

Seaker looked at Conor and shrugged. "Pretty but cold." He winked at Conor and deplaned.

Conor's feelings of dislike of Seaker were starting to catch up to his mounting qualms about Eve's true intentions.

Outside the aircraft, passengers were milling about in pools of light from the several tugs waiting for their bags to be unloaded. Eve stood apart from the group. Conor convened with Roper-Hastings, who had slept during the latter part of the flight.

"I didn't mention earlier that, first thing in the morning, I'm headed over to the Swedish Secret Intelligence Service to visit its chief, Carl Tolberg," Roper-Hastings said. "I don't think I'll get much out of him. We hear he leans toward the Nazi side of the ledger."

"Maybe news of what's happening to the Germans on the eastern front has made him reconsider."

"Ha, I like your thinking, Thorn. What about you?"

Conor tilted his head in the direction of Eve Lind. "She has family here—her parents. That's the first stop. Let's keep each other posted. I'll make sure to drop by the legation to exchange information."

Roper-Hastings started to speak but stopped. He was looking over Conor's shoulder. Conor turned and found Eve standing right behind him, suitcase and medical bag in hand.

"Are you done?" Eve asked. "We're wasting time."

#

2350 Hours, Tuesday, October 27, 1942
Grand Hôtel, Södra Blasieholmshammer 8, Stockholm

During the cab ride to the hotel, no one spoke. Eve was slumped deep in the seat with her coat collar pulled up to her ears as if to signal, *Stay away.* Conor decided he'd put off pressing Eve on the Buckmaster murder till morning.

The lobby of the Grand Hotel was opulent, as expected, and quite busy, not as expected, given the hour. Couples in fine attire were gathered in groups of four or more, chatting away excitedly, possibly rehashing the evening's highs and lows, some in Swedish, but others in English. Swedish wasn't a language Conor had experience with, but he knew many in positions of power and authority had adopted English as a second language, so he was hoping it wouldn't be a problem.

After a quick check-in at the desk, Conor and Eve went up

to the fourth floor and entered their suite. Eve's surliness was beginning to grate on Conor.

"I'm starving. Do you want some food?" Conor said.

Eve sat on a chaise longue still wearing her coat, her medical bag at her feet. "No, my stomach is upset."

"Maybe you should get some sleep."

Eve stared at him.

"Okay, then." Conor dialed room service and ordered a ham and cheese sandwich, a custard pudding, and a bottle of beer. "I'm going to clean up a bit. Sit tight."

Eve didn't move, and Conor headed into the bathroom, leaving the door open a crack, so he could see the door to the hallway.

He washed the travel grime off his face and lathered up for a shave. Halfway through, there was a knock at the door. "Eve, will you get that?"

No response. But Conor saw her, still wearing her coat, answer the door. The attendant rolled a cart past the bathroom door and quickly exited. Conor finished his shave and toweled off. He left the bathroom still buttoning his shirt.

The cart had been placed before the chaise longue, and Eve's suitcase and medical bag were now at the foot of the bed, which she was lying on top of, her eyes closed. "You'd be more comfortable if you took off your coat and got under the covers."

Eve didn't respond.

Asleep. Fine by me.

Conor downed the sandwich quickly and dug into the pudding. He hadn't eaten anything in close to twenty-four hours. After finishing the pudding, he grabbed the bottle of beer and sat back. He was thinking about how he'd start in on Eve about the Buckmaster murder when he felt his stomach flip. His abdominal muscles contracted, then released and contracted once again. Bile was crawling up his throat, and his bowels began to rumble. *Bad ham? Bad cheese? Did anything taste funny?*

He looked over at Eve. He could hear a faint snore. His bowels told him he'd better run. He lunged for the bathroom and made it just in time. But just as he was recovering from his bowel problems, his stomach took over, and in a flash, Conor was on his knees, retching violently. His head bobbed inside the toilet for what seemed like five minutes. While he was retching, his head pounding, he couldn't hear anything—including the door to the hallway as it opened and closed.

CHAPTER TWENTY-EIGHT

0100 Hours, Wednesday, October 28, 1942
Home of Benjamin Andersson, Norrmalm, Stockholm

Eve Lind sat on the bed she'd slept in as a child. The bedroom had changed little. There was not a speck of dust anywhere. Two framed photos were on her dresser, just where she had last placed them: one of Eve with her parents on her wedding day and the other of Eve and Gunnar, which she now took and put in her dresser drawer. Coming home was not as comforting as she had thought it would be. She checked her pulse. Her heart was still racing from escaping the watchful eye of Conor Thorn. She looked at her watch. By now he would be starting to recover and possibly start looking for her.

Eve heard the dog before she saw him. He ran down the hallway outside her bedroom, scampered through the open door, and jumped on the bed. The dog, a Swedish Vallhund named Blix, settled at the near end of the bed after a few cursory sniffs of the new guest. He had been a birthday gift from her mother to her father. Before long, Blix was asleep, and Eve heard her father coming down the hall.

Benjamin Andersson, dressed in his nightclothes and long royal-blue robe, entered carrying Eve's suitcase and medical bag. He was out of breath. "Eve, you look drained," he said, placing her bags on the bench seat at the base of her bed. "You must get some rest."

"I know, but I'm too anxious to sleep."

"Tell me again how you managed to travel here. Something about the British," Andersson said, taking a seat between Eve and Blix.

"The British are searching for Gunnar. I told them I could help them find him."

"But surely you don't want the British to find him. He's your husband."

"Of course not. But it was the only way I could reunite with him. It has always been my goal to raise our children in my home country."

"As you've said in your letters."

"Yes. After we went to England, Gunnar was too committed to his work for the British, but I convinced him that we needed to ... take action. He finally agreed."

"Because he loves you."

"Yes. I told him that if we could somehow reach out to the Germans with information about his work, maybe we could have more financial stability to properly raise a family."

"But ..." Her father didn't finish. His position on giving her, or Gunnar, any money after she was married was clear; he had always been adamant that she earn her own way through life as he had, not taking anything from anyone, especially family. He was keen on building strong character, even for his daughter.

"Don't worry, Father. I will never take money from you. I must do this on my own. Like you did." She detected a sigh of relief. "Have you agreed to help us?"

"Yes, of course. I have already contacted the Germans, and they have agreed to our terms."

Eve smiled and reached out, placing her hand on his shoulder. "Thank you, Father. Gunnar and I owe you so much." She pulled her hand away. "Speaking of Gunnar, where is he?"

Andersson began petting Blix, who rolled over on his side. "He is staying at a summer home I recently bought for your mother on Skeppsholmen. I plan to refurbish it and give it to her for our anniversary. He is safe."

Eve had visited the island just east of Stockholm's old town, Gamla Stan, as a child for boating excursions. "I must see him."

"He will be overjoyed that you have made it to Stockholm."

119

Eve imagined Conor Thorn, bent over a commode, his body convulsing as he vomited. "Father, Conor Thorn, an American agent, he will be calling on you. He and others are looking for Gunnar. You must not cooperate with them in any way. Once they realize Gunnar cannot be found, they will stop their search and move on to other matters."

"I understand. Leave that to me, my darling."

Eve took her father's hand. "I have news." She teared up. "I am with child."

"No," Andersson nearly shouted. "Finally, a grandchild. That is wonderful news." He stood and kissed Eve on the cheek. "And given your long trip, you must see the best doctor in Stockholm, our family doctor. I will arrange a visit first thing in the morning, then you can see your husband."

Eve wiped away tears with the back of her hand. "But I—"

"No. I insist. As will your mother when she hears the wonderful news. Now, get some sleep."

Andersson left the door open slightly when he left, and Eve listened as his footsteps faded. She looked at the dog sleeping at the foot of the bed, raised her left leg, and kicked it. The dog yelped as it fell to the floor.

CHAPTER TWENTY-NINE

0900 Hours, Wednesday, October 28, 1942
BI Maskineri Företag, Östermalm Section of Stockholm

Conor's head still pounded, not letting him forget his intimate relationship with the hotel's toilet the previous night. It had kept him from getting any sleep, which put a sharp edge on his already grumpy mood. It didn't help that he had been waiting for over thirty minutes for Benjamin Andersson to arrive at the office. So much for the boss setting the tone by being the first guy in.

His secretary, an older, long-limbed woman, wasn't happy when he told her that he'd wait for her boss. She signaled her displeasure every ten seconds by looking at Conor and following up with an audible exhale. Conor would respond with a look at his watch, which always produced another heavy exhale. It was their little dance.

A few minutes after the top of the hour, a lanky man in a double-breasted gray pinstripe suit entered the outer office. Without stopping, he glanced at Conor, then at his secretary, and continued on into his office with her a step behind.

Conor stood and was about to knock on the door when she emerged.

"Mr. Andersson will see you in a few minutes. Please take a seat, Mr. Thorn."

Conor didn't take anything. A couple minutes later, an intercom box on her desk buzzed, and he made for the door before Miss

Long Limbs could stop him. He was impressed with the size of the office. The academy's football team could have held a practice there without bumping into one another.

Andersson was at his desk, reading a newspaper, a smile on his face. He looked up as Conor approached the massive piece of furniture and laid the newspaper down. The man's long, bushy sideburns reminded him of the impressive set sported by John Quincy Adams. But his attention was quickly captured by Andersson's lazy eye.

Just look at his mouth. Or his normal eye.

Andersson stretched over the desk and extended his hand. "Mr. Thorn. A pleasure. Please sit."

Conor shook hands and took a seat.

"And what is the reason for your visit?"

"Well, you can tell me if you've seen your daughter."

Andersson cocked his head, and his roaming eye shot up toward the ceiling. "And please tell me why the interest in my daughter."

"We traveled here together. She offered her assistance in locating her husband. Instead of assisting, she has disappeared, just like her husband. Speaking of, when did you last see him?"

"You're an American, I take it. You must work for your government. Would that be accurate?"

Andersson's evasive tactic was a strong signal that Conor wasn't going to get much useful information out of him. "Close enough. But you haven't answered my question," he said with a raised voice.

"Well, my daughter phoned me late last night. She sounded distraught about her husband. I thought she would be better off at her home than some hotel. That, and I wanted to see her. It had been too long."

Conor leaned forward. "Where is she now?"

"She is visiting a doctor with her mother. Eve looked ... unwell."

"What about Gunnar?"

Andersson leaned forward and steepled his hands, which obscured part of his face. He took his time before replying—another signal to Conor that there was some subterfuge happening. "I haven't seen Gunnar since the wedding. He was insistent on taking Eve to Germany after they were married. Against my wishes." Andersson picked up a pipe and began scraping its bowl with a silver tool.

Conor's eyes narrowed and he leaned back. He reached into his breast pocket, pulled out two photos, and held one up. "Have you ever seen this woman?"

Andersson leaned forward and squinted. "No, I have not. Who is she?" The photo of Emily was from her MI6 file. Her hair was parted down the middle, her green eyes open wide and complemented by a slightly wry smile.

"She's someone looking for your son-in-law." Conor returned the photo to his breast pocket. "And she seems to have turned up missing also. Two missing people. A daughter on the loose. I wonder how they're all connected."

"*If* they are connected, Mr. Thorn."

Convinced he was wasting his time, Conor stood. "Tell your daughter to call me at the British Legation when she returns. She needs to deliver on what she promised she'd do."

"I am sure she will. She comes from an honorable family."

"Good day, Mr. Andersson."

Conor paused at the secretary's desk. He pulled the other photo from his coat pocket. "Have you ever seen this man?"

Her posture turned rigid. She shook her head, but as far as Conor was concerned, Miss Long Limb's physical reaction loudly confirmed she had.

Her phone rang, and she reached for it, fumbling to pick it up. As she recovered and answered, he thought maybe he should have started with her instead of Andersson. It would have saved some time.

#

Andersson put his pipe down as soon as he heard the door close. He considered his encounter with Thorn. He hadn't met many Americans, but they were known for their brashness. Thorn seemed to possess his share and then some. He picked up the handset of his phone and dialed. After three rings, he heard a male voice.

"Who is this?"

"Gunnar, it's your father-in-law. Is everything all right?"

"Yes. Why do you ask?"

"Do you know a Conor Thorn?"

There was a moment of silence. "No, I don't. Who is he?"

"He's looking for you. And apparently, he's not the only one. There's a woman also looking for you. Be sure to stay where you are. Do not take chances."

"Have you heard anything from the Germans?"

"Not today. But I don't regard that as a concern. They have money to collect."

"Yes. Of course."

"And, Gunnar. Eve has arrived. Just as you said she would."

Silence.

"Gunnar?"

CHAPTER THIRTY

0900 Hours, Wednesday, October 28, 1942
Reich Main Security Office, Prinz-Albrecht-Strasse 9, Berlin

Walter Schellenberg sat quietly in the private room adjacent to Himmler's office while Himmler was being worked on by his masseur and physical therapist, Felix Kersten, a Finnish national with Baltic German heritage. According to Himmler, Kersten had saved his life. For years, Himmler was tormented by colic and intestinal cramps so overwhelming that they would restrict his activities for hours—until he met Kersten. Himmler had even convinced Schellenberg to partake of Kersten's treatments for similar issues.

Schellenberg knew Kersten, a man of average height with a stocky frame that supported over two hundred and fifty pounds, was a bit of a magician when it came to relieving pain and discomfort, including his, with his arduous massages. He also knew he was a cunning manipulator of Reichsführer Himmler.

Kersten was dressed in wool pants and braces, the sleeves of his white shirt rolled up to reveal forearms that could have belonged to a stevedore. Himmler was on his back, his eyes closed, and a towel draped across his waist. He held his glasses in his hand. Kersten was dripping rubbing alcohol into his hands. The disinfectant-like odor from the alcohol mingled with that of ointments in the small room.

"I have been thinking. This trip to Stockholm by Dr. Kersten and Langbehn—I am having second thoughts," Himmler said.

"The risks are high should our intentions somehow leak. Bormann and Ribbentrop will pounce."

Kersten's jaw dropped, and he shot a look at Schellenberg, who held up his hand to keep the man from overreacting. Schellenberg and Kersten had conspired since August to pressure—no, that's not the word; one could not pressure the reichsführer to do anything. But he could be manipulated. And Schellenberg was as effective a manipulator as Kersten. Over the past several weeks, they had made progress. Some days, Himmler was an extremely willing participant. Then there were days like today.

Schellenberg motioned for Kersten to begin his treatment and spoke. "Reichsführer, what has caused this change in your thinking?"

Himmler flinched when Kersten first placed his hands on his abdomen. "I just said why: Ribbentrop and Bormann. They seek every avenue to work against me. They are close to the führer. They have come between the führer and myself. Winning them over or outright replacing them is an impossible task."

"Reichsführer, you yourself have said many times that you are convinced the führer is ill and consumed by neuroses, unfit to lead Germany," Kersten said.

Himmler flicked his hand. "Stop! Stop! You must stop throwing words back in my face."

Kersten backed away.

Himmler, his face pinched in pain, held his breath and then emptied his lungs as the pain passed.

Kersten went back to work. "It is the stress, Reichsführer," Kersten said. "If you put ten amps on a circuit—"

"Yes, yes … made for six, you are bound to blow a fuse. Again with the silly fuse saying. Just give me some relief."

Schellenberg needed to do just what Himmler accused Kersten of doing: throw Himmler's words back in his face. But he needed a deft touch to keep Himmler from giving up their plan and seeking a peace deal with the Western Allies. "Mein Herr, you have stated clearly that our great leader is losing the war. Your dossier on his health proves he is no longer fit to lead Germany."

Himmler put on his glasses and turned to Schellenberg, who, speaking softly, clenched his fists as if to accent his words. "It is you who must assume the leadership role, proving to the Allies that change has come."

This talk of high treason gave Schellenberg an adrenaline rush, raising the hair on the back of his neck. "Only then will your plan to shift forces from the west and focus our efforts on the eastern front come to fruition," Schellenberg continued. "They will listen to you. They respect your power and influence. We can take advantage of the British and American growing distrust of their supposed Soviet ally."

Himmler stared stonily at Schellenberg.

Receiving no verbal negative reaction, Schellenberg decided to take a bold step. "I am convinced that, in such a situation, King Henry would do this for his countrymen."

Himmler jumped off the table, catching the towel before it fell to the floor. "Who told you of King Henry?" He whipped around. "Kersten, did you tell him?"

A fuse had just blown. Schellenberg's mention of Henry the Fowler, who became king in 919 of East Francia, a medieval German state, was risky—Himmler had convinced himself that he was the king's reincarnation and held this belief close.

"Reichsführer, the time has come. I received word today that sixty thousand German troops and two tank divisions launched a new attack on Stalingrad."

Himmler puffed out his chest at the news.

"They have advanced fifty yards."

Himmler groaned and slumped against the massage table. Was it the result of intestinal pain or the spasms of defeatism?

Schellenberg hoped it was the latter. "Your people need you, Reichsführer."

Kersten put in, "Reichsführer, please, let me bring you some relief. I can see that you are in pain."

Himmler remounted the table, lay on his back, and removed his glasses. "You have my permission to carry on with the meeting in Stockholm. Schellenberg, I will hold you responsible if news of this secret agenda is revealed to those who don't understand how dire our situation is." Himmler closed his eyes. "And, Schellenberg—" Himmler's abdomen contracted and his fists clenched.

Schellenberg could hear a low groan.

Kersten waved Schellenberg away with both hands, like he would a rat searching for food.

CHAPTER THIRTY-ONE

1015 Hours, Wednesday, October 28, 1942
British Legation, Strandvägen 82, Stockholm

Conor's stomach periodically rumbled loud enough for people near him to take notice. He was hungry but didn't dare feed the thing that had turned on him in the early morning hours. It had to have been the hotel food, but the timing of it and the exit of Eve Lind was too coincidental and very troubling. He regretted not searching her medical bag. His stomach called out again.

"Are you feeling all right, Thorn?" Captain Masterman asked.

"Yeah. Better with every minute," he replied as he sat across from Masterman. When he walked in, he'd interrupted Masterman's morning meal: a steaming cup of what smelled like coffee and a golden brown pastry shaped like an S.

Masterman pushed the pastry aside. "As I was saying, we've asked for more assistance from the local police and from the Swedish Secret Intelligence Service—the C Bureau, as it's called by most. Roper-Hastings should be on his way back by now. We're even checking hospitals and the city morgue."

Masterman gave voice to thoughts Conor had been trying to choke the life out of for days. In his mind, he had been running from facing the reality that Emily wasn't just missing but possibly wounded and suffering. Dead was another concrete prospect. One that Conor couldn't run from any longer.

"Thorn? Did you hear me?"

"I did. Hospitals and the morgue. Anything come from that?"

"No. No sign of her." Masterman took a sip from his mug and made a face. He put the cup down, spilling some of the liquid. "Lovely girl, that Bright. Just bloody awful that she's missing."

And I'm here to find her. Conor asked what Emily's cover story was.

After Masterman finished explaining her "visiting a sick aunt" cover, he looked past Masterman at a framed picture of Churchill on the wall. Emily was a favorite of Churchill's, who by now was probably aware that she was missing—more bad news for the prime minister to bear. But could that mean more resources would be put behind the search for her? Conor asked himself.

"So, listen to me for a minute," Conor said, returning his gaze to Masterman. "Through intercepts, we hear about a guy with connections to British intelligence who has approached the German Legation here. You guys are put on alert and send someone to watch their legation. He goes missing, then turns up dead as a doornail floating in the harbor."

Masterman's eyes widened.

"Sorry. Was he a friend?" Conor asked.

"Yes. Yes he was." Masterman sucked in a deep breath. "So you were saying?"

"Right. So, then Bright shows up, also snoops around. Probably followed, right?"

"Certainly. They follow us; we follow them."

"Okay. So the Nazis panic, maybe worry that Bright has discovered something. They need to keep something quiet, or maybe they're protecting someone. Maybe this someone is—"

"This guy, as you call him, with SIS connections: Gunnar Lind."

"Makes some sense, right?"

"Yes. It matches our thinking."

"So who runs the show for the … is it the Abwehr?"

"There is an Abwehr office here, but it's very small. Much smaller than their operations in Spain, Switzerland, and Lisbon. They used to be housed at the German Legation, but they moved just about a week ago. No, you need to be on the lookout for the SD. The Reich Security Office's intelligence-gathering outfit. They're based at the legation."

"Who's in charge?"

Masterman pulled out a bottom drawer in his desk, removed a brown accordion file, and rummaged for something inside it. "This is who runs the office." He handed over a somewhat grainy photo.

"You're kidding … a woman?"

"Yes. But don't make the mistake of underestimating her."

Thorn studied the photo. Graininess aside, the woman's beauty still shone through. She had short, light-colored hair; the lines of her jaw were sharply defined. The picture in his hand clearly depicted a determined woman, her brow intensely furrowed. Her long stride said she was also in a hurry. "There's a rumor that she was Himmler's mistress. He broke it off and sent her here. She's been looking to get reassigned to Berlin since the minute she arrived."

"Is she smart?"

"Smart enough. Has a reputation for nasty interrogations."

"Lovely. Sounds like a good Nazi."

"There's also a goon who hardly ever leaves her side. Name is Kurt Eklof." Masterman pulled out two more photos and handed them to Conor.

One was another grainy photo, this one of a good-size man in a long dark coat and a black hat with a wide brim. Conor couldn't make out much. The other photo was a color photo of a silver-haired man in a Luftwaffe uniform; his face was turned to the camera, but his eyes looked to his left. He seemed angry, as if someone had called him a name. His eyes were a piercing blue.

"Eklof was a fighter pilot. A good one too. He was wounded in a Special Air Service attack on his base in Libya in December last year."

Conor had heard about the SAS—units using small, light-weight vehicles that were heavily armed. They would hit hard and fast. He had read of one raid in which sixty aircraft were destroyed on the ground.

"When the raid started, Eklof got caught raping a young Libyan girl by one of our boys, who barged in. Eklof took a round in the groin while the girl took a spoon to his eye—nearly scooped it out. He wears an eye patch now and …" Masterman's face sprouted a smile.

"And?"

"Eklof hasn't seen the inside of any of Stockholm's knocking shops."

"Well, if I put 'groin shot' together with 'knocking shops' I think I get the picture," Conor said with a slight grin.

Masterman laughed.

There was a soft rap on the door, and Roper-Hastings poked his head in. "I hate to interrupt. It seems you are having a rip-roaring time."

"Come in, Jim. I was just filling Thorn in on our SD friends over at the legation. What do you have for us?"

"Hate to disappoint, but my meeting with Tolberg did not go well. He seemed to have a chip on his shoulder about the 'illegal'—a term he used several times—activity the warring nations were conducting in his country. And given the absence of anyone from the German Legation, we took the brunt of his ravings."

"What about Andersson?" Conor asked. "Did you ask if he was involved with the Germans in any … illegal activity?"

"Yes, that was when he threw me out of his office. Let's just say he scoffed at the possibility."

Conor was taking in a ton of information, but none of it was getting him closer to finding Lind or Emily.

Masterman's phone rang, and after answering, he handed it to Conor.

"Thorn."

"It's Eve."

"Where the hell have you been?"

Eve cleared her throat. "I was visiting my grandmother. She's ill. I went with my mother." Conor noted the lie. "I just couldn't stay in that room. I get sick when I see or hear someone vomiting. I can't control my reaction. I'm sorry I left."

Conor decided that lying ran in the Andersson family. Something he shouldn't forget moving forward. "Tell me this: Are there any family members, yours or your husband's, who he would reach out to when he arrived in Stockholm?"

A long pause.

"A cousin of Gunnar's visited us when we lived in Paris. She lived north of here … in Solna."

"Where are you now?"

"At my father's home."

"Stay there. I'll be there in ten minutes. We're going to Solna." Conor hung up. "Captain, do you have the address of the German Legation?"

Masterman's eyes darted from Thorn to Roper-Hastings, then back to Thorn. "Listen, showing your face there will accomplish nothing except getting you thrown in a back room while they try to figure out just who the hell you are and why you're asking questions about missing persons."

Conor had gotten nowhere with Andersson, and so far, teaming up with Eve Lind had produced few leads. *Why not tap your number one suspect on the shoulder and ask some questions?* It's what his Uncle Mickey, a twenty-year veteran of the New York Police Department, would do. "Just trying to size up the competition, that's all, Captain."

"Heed my advice: stay away. We've already lost at least one agent, maybe two."

He stood, realizing that Masterman wasn't going to give him the address.

"Have you checked in with Gus Karlson yet?" Masterman asked.

Karlson. Head of Operations. Donovan's guy he was supposed to keep in the loop. "No. Not yet. But I will after I get back from Solna."

"Maybe before you go to Solna. Might be a good idea."

Conor headed for the door, thinking that Masterman would be dialing up the American Legation and Gus Karlson before his shoes hit the stairs.

CHAPTER THIRTY-TWO

1230 Hours, Wednesday, October 28, 1942
Return Trip from Solna

Gunnar's cousin hadn't heard from him. Thorn had known a phone call could have yielded that information, but people lie. While Eve and the cousin talked, Conor managed a quick trip to the bathroom and took the opportunity to look around, to see if Cousin Gunnar had decided to hide out in Solna. Another swing and a miss. Conor asked the cousin, a fortyish tall blond with some streaks of gray, if Gunnar would have contacted any other family or friends.

"No. The Gunnar I knew kept to himself. A bit shy. His own family fell apart after his father left them for another woman."

Eve turned to Conor. "Like father, like son. Isn't that how the saying goes, Mr. Thorn?"

"Something like that. Some fathers can be counted on; some can't," Conor said.

Eve began to finger the gold cross around her neck, just as she had when reacting to the news of Mrs. Buckmaster's murder. *A tell?* Conor made a note to watch for it again. He thanked the cousin, and he and Eve took their leave.

Back in the car, Conor decided to explore the father-daughter relationship. Maybe he'd learn just how far Andersson would go to protect or help his daughter. "Your father seems to be a devoted man."

"Yes, he is. I love my father."

Conor noted that Eve wasn't surprised he had met her father. "Devoted enough to lie for you?"

Eve recoiled. "My father doesn't lie. He is an honorable man. Why would you ask such a thing?"

"Well, he may not be lying, but I don't think he's been … fully forthcoming about your husband."

"He wants Gunnar found as much as I do. As much as you do."

"I want to believe that, Eve. I really do."

Conor silently bemoaned Eve's manipulation skills. She'd clearly oversold her claim that she would be an asset in the search for Gunnar, something that he'd make sure to point out to Colonel Donovan and Menzies. Conor couldn't shake the feeling that all Eve was doing was waiting for Conor to give up.

The woman squirmed in her seat, looking like she wanted to be anywhere but in the 1942 Ford DeLuxe Fordor sedan. "Where are we going?"

"*We* are going nowhere. *You* are going back to your father's home. And you need to stay there until I come and get you. I'm headed over to the German Legation to see some people. Better that they don't know about you."

Eve's squirming ceased and she slumped down in her seat.

CHAPTER THIRTY-THREE

1315 Hours, Wednesday, October 28, 1942
Home of Benjamin Andersson, Norrmalm, Stockholm

Five minutes later, Conor turned up the gravel driveway of a stately Victorian home. Two men dressed in white overalls were on ladders, painting the window trim a bright sky blue. To say Eve was eager to get out of the car was understating it; her door was open before Conor brought the sedan to a stop.

"Eve, stay"—the door slammed shut—"put," Conor said.

\#

1335 Hours, Wednesday, October 28, 1942
Andersson Summer Home, Skeppsholmen, Stockholm

When her father's car pulled up to the front door twenty minutes later, Eve hopped into the back seat. She noticed her rapid breathing, took her pulse, and realized she was experiencing an adrenaline rush. The feeling was becoming familiar, except this time, she wasn't feeling any sensation of increased strength. Not like she'd felt three days before when she confronted her nosy landlady.

As the car approached her father's summer house, Eve saw the choppy water of the Ladugårdslandsviken, the bay east of the island, through the trees. The driver got out to open her door, but Eve had already jumped out. She ran up the front steps and pounded on the door. Seconds later, a tall, long-limbed man with receding, wavy hair stood in the open doorway. His mouth fell open as Eve leaped toward him, wrapping her arms around his neck and kissing him deeply.

"I told you this would work," Eve said. "You didn't believe me."

He shut the door with Eve still draped around his neck. "I didn't. The plan was so … so outlandish."

Eve released her hold, and they walked into a library off the foyer. It was strewn with newspapers. Eve spotted several dirty dishes here and there.

"How did you convince them to bring you to Stockholm?"

"We can discuss that later. Where's the bedroom?"

"Eve. The baby."

Eve shook her head. "Such a silly man."

Half an hour later, he returned to the bedroom wearing a white robe and carrying two wineglasses in one hand and a bottle of wine in the other. Eve, lying naked on the bed, sat up and took one glass. A sheen of sweat covered her body. He filled her glass and sat down next to her. "I took a call from your father earlier today. He asked if I knew a Conor Thorn."

Eve nodded. "He's an American. Works with MI6. He's one of the people looking for you. Don't worry. Leave him to me."

"He also mentioned a woman. Didn't mention her name. Someone he said was also looking for me. Who is that?"

"Hmm, I'm not sure." The news that someone else was looking for Gunnar didn't really surprise her. Could it be the Bright woman, she wondered. But why didn't they send her with Thorn? She didn't want to alarm anyone too greatly. "Father says there is a woman in the German Legation he is dealing with. I would not be surprised if she was looking for you."

He put his glass down on the nightstand, cinched the robe's sash, and started pacing. Eve pulled a bed sheet up to her neck. "I know you said they would come looking for me, but now that it is happening, I'm getting …"

"Scared?"

"Yes. I don't mind admitting it. They could put us both away for a long time."

"We must stick to our plan. It will work. We have my father to protect us. He is very powerful—the city of Stockholm is honoring him tonight."

"Yes. I read about it in the newspaper today."

"He has invited me to attend."

He stopped pacing. "Eve, don't go. You need to keep out of sight. The newspaper said that people from the diplomatic corps will be there. That means Germans. It's too dangerous. We're almost at the end of this."

Eve finished her wine and leaned over to place her glass on the nightstand. The sheet fell to her waist. "Listen to me. Do not weaken. Our plan will work. Trust me."

He took a step toward the bed. "Why are you so sure?"

Eve wasn't sure at all. Her sense that Thorn was growing suspicious of her was concerning. "The most challenging elements to our plan are behind us. We just need to wait for the Germans to deposit the money. Then we both disappear." Eve smiled. "This is our last time together until we complete our plan." She reached out, grabbed the robe's sash, untied it and pulled him toward her. He let the robe fall to the floor.

#

1345 Hours, Wednesday, October 28, 1942
Brompton Oratory, Knightsbridge, London

Kim Philby, as instructed, had arrived early at the Church of the Immaculate Heart of Mary, also known as Brompton Oratory. It mystified Philby why Shapak, who claimed to be an atheist like all good Communists, insisted on using churches for dead drops and meetings. He'd pressed him on this several months ago but received no reply, just a shrug of the shoulders. As for himself, churches in general made him uncomfortable; statuary, gold-leaf cupolas, stained glass windows, and ornate metal and wood carvings left him cold. His religion was Communism.

When he arrived, Philby saw a custodian mopping near the

altar. Another person was walking through the pews, methodically putting missals in place. Philby walked down the center aisle, headed for the eighteenth row, as per his instructions, and moved to the center of the pew. He sat and took the missal from the small wooden rack on the back of the pew in front. He placed a folded sheet of paper inside, on page eighteen, where the lyrics for "Ave Maria" were found. The paper contained his tight ink scrawl laying out the extraction plans he had learned the day before from Tordeaux outside Menzies's office. He replaced the missal and moved back a row. He knelt in the middle of the pew and bowed his head over folded hands.

And waited.

And waited.

Shapak had no respect for his time. Not like Otto, his previous handler, who willingly went back to the Soviet Union when summoned by Moscow Center, knowing it would not end well. It still left Philby mystified as to why he returned.

Philby's knees began to throb. He entertained the thought of leaving, but just then, Shapak ambled up the center aisle, genuflected, and entered the eighteenth row. He shuffled down the pew and sat. He was five feet from the still-kneeling Philby.

"Did you just genuflect?" Philby asked, his head still bowed.

Shapak nodded slowly. "I am a good spy. I play the part I must play."

"Well, don't get carried away. Moscow Center will get suspicious of you, just like they are of me."

"What do you have for me?" Shapak did not want to hear more of Philby's complaints.

"The day, time, and method for extracting Thorn and Bright, along with our Swedish cryptologist back to England, if or when they find him."

Shapak took a position on the kneeler in front of him. He did not reach for the missal. Instead, he bowed his head. "You still believe that seizing this cryptologist will help your standing with Moscow?"

"Yes. If they have difficulty believing my information, maybe they'll believe the Swede when he tells them of Ultra."

Shapak coughed several times, then pulled a wrinkled

handkerchief from his pants pocket. The honking sound of him blowing his nose made the custodian stop his mopping. "We have discovered from our agent in the German Legation that the Nazis are arranging to buy some high-level intelligence from an industrialist. We do not know if there is a connection between this man and the cryptologist you speak of." Shapak fell silent.

"And?"

"And we will make a counteroffer tonight for the intelligence and the source of the intelligence. If that turns out to be this cryptologist … this will make you happy, no?"

"I believe it will."

"And if it's not the man you seek?"

"Well then, MI6 has a bigger problem than it thinks it has." Philby stood. His right knee made a cracking sound. He moved slowly down the pew to the center aisle. When he passed Shapak, he saw the man reach for the missal to his right. As Philby walked toward the back of the church, he began to hum the tune of "Ave Maria."

CHAPTER THIRTY-FOUR

1330 Hours, Wednesday, October 28, 1942
German Legation, Södra Blasieholmshammer 2, Stockholm

Conor pulled the Ford into a parking stall just behind a waiting taxi and noted the proximity of the legation to the Grand Hotel—only a block away. Maybe he should get his room changed to one overlooking the legation and ask the front desk to lay their hands on some binoculars. He got out of the sedan and pulled his trench coat collar up to fend off the steady drizzle. Pausing in a small courtyard outside the main entrance, he surveyed the building's five stories, saw some interior lights on in the upper floors and a massive Nazi flag snapping in the breeze on a roof-mounted pole. Maybe one day, it would fly at half-mast when Hitler kicked the bucket. The thought made him smile. He headed for the front entrance, thinking about Masterman's prediction that he might wind up in a back room in the next few minutes.

Just inside the entrance, Conor shook the rain from his coat and smoothed down his hair. Two wide, sweeping staircases framed the lobby, leading to a mezzanine generously adorned with Nazi flags and banners. Several people sat in armchairs that flanked a central desk that faced the entrance. What appeared to be a husband and wife both sat leaning forward, ready to jump when called. Nearby, three men in tailored suits sat with briefcases resting in their laps—Swedes looking to do business with the Reich, Conor supposed.

He headed straight for the reception desk, where a staunch-looking woman in her thirties sat, her blond hair pulled back in a bun. Glasses rested on the tip of her nose while she typed away furiously with oversized, bony hands. Above and slightly behind her head was an impressively large portrait of Hitler that was suspended from the ceiling below the mezzanine with two gold chains. It swayed side to side ever so slightly.

"Who are you here to see?" the lady asked without looking up. Her German was crisp and stern.

Conor knew that his heavily accented German would give him away, no matter how proper his grammar was, but he didn't really care. "I'm here to see Lina Stuben."

She stopped typing and looked up at Conor, her fingers still resting on the keys. "What is your business with her?"

"I'm sorry, but that would be between me and her. I'm sure you understand."

"I do not understand." Her right hand fell below desktop level for several seconds, then reappeared. "Who are you and what is your business here?" she said in a raised voice, attracting the attention of those waiting nearby.

"I have questions for her. I hope she has answers for me." Conor had expected the cold shoulder.

The flinty woman stood and smoothed her dress with those large hands. She was at least six feet, her head level with Conor's. "Are you going to tell me who you are? You are an American, are you not?"

"That's not important. What is important is that I have some questions for Stuben. Tell her that I'm not leaving until I get some answers."

Not pleased with Conor's stubbornness, she blew a short breath out through her nostrils. "As I said—"

"What is it that you want answers to, Mister … ?" A woman's voice from just above them.

Conor craned his neck and saw Lina Stuben standing on the mezzanine, her arms folded across her chest, giving Conor the clear impression she wasn't coming any closer. She wore a white blouse and dark-gray trousers. A pair of gleaming black boots stopped just below her knees.

"Ah, Miss Stuben. A simple question really. I have lost track of a dear friend. He might have contacted you. You see, he supposedly has information to sell, and it seems that you might be a willing buyer. Or so I have heard."

Stuben didn't move or change her expression.

"Might I come up and continue this conversation in private?"

"Stay where you are," Stuben said. She unfolded her arms and leaned on the wrought iron railing. "What is this man's name?"

"Gunnar Lind." Conor pulled a photo from his breast pocket and held it above his head. "Have you seen him?"

Stuben motioned to the receptionist, who snatched the photo from Conor's hand and raced up the staircase. While she ascended the stairs, Conor saw that the visitors in the lobby were rapt by the drama unfolding before them. Conor nodded in their direction. Stuben took the photo and mumbled something to the receptionist, who responded briefly, then quickly disappeared.

She called the cavalry. Not much time left.

Stuben studied the photo. "I have never seen this man."

"I thought you would say that." Conor reached into his breast pocket again and produced another photo. "What about this man? Roger McInnis. He worked at the British Legation, disappeared after being taken inside this legation, but he was found later, floating in the harbor, dead." Conor showed the photo to the lobby audience. His voice grew louder. "Are you sure that you want to deal with these people? You may not survive the encounter."

The husband and wife bolted from their chairs and rushed past Conor.

Conor saw three men coming down the staircase. Not one looked like he weighed less than two fifty. "I have questions, and I demand answers."

Conor, his arms raised above his head, kept turning, making sure his remaining audience saw the photo. Just as he was about to make his exit, before the herd of security was on top of him, he felt a forceful tug on the belt of his trench coat, pulling him backward. He regained his balance and turned to see a fiftyish man with graying hair below the rim of a brown felt hat still holding the coat's belt.

"Thanks for checking in with me, Thorn. Now let's take our leave from these nice people."

Karlson. Masterman made a call after all. Karlson still tightly held Conor's trench coat belt as he bum-rushed Conor out of the lobby. The three security men were less than twenty feet away when Conor and Karlson passed through the front door and were greeted on the sidewalk by three men of equal size. A red-faced Karlson led Conor past the men, who stood shoulder to shoulder. When the three pursuers tried to push their way past, Karlson's men gave no ground, but they also did not throw a single punch. Neither did the legation's guards.

No international incident today, Conor thought. *Just a standoff. But there's always tomorrow.*

#

Lina Stuben watched from her perch on the mezzanine as security rushed toward the American. With the photo of Gunnar Lind in hand, she returned to her office, closing the door with a bang, startling the already jumpy Benjamin Andersson. She dropped into her chair, shielding the photo so Andersson couldn't see it. She stared at Andersson. The clock on her desk was the only sound as it ticked off ten seconds.

"Who is Gunnar Lind?"

Andersson flinched like a hatpin had stuck him. "Excuse me?"

"Is this Gunnar Lind?" Stuben asked, shoving the photo across her desk.

Andersson glanced at it. Stuben had the name thanks to the American. He picked up the photo, glimpsed at it front and back, then placed it on the desk. "Yes."

"He is the relation that you are representing?"

"Yes."

"What is he to you?"

Andersson shifted in his chair as Stuben heard footsteps outside her door. She rose, quietly stepped to the door, and in one swift move, opened it. The secretary was seated but breathing rapidly as she brushed her hair off her forehead.

"What are you doing?"

Her secretary turned to Stuben, eyes wide. "Nothing, miss. I just finished the filing of today's message traffic."

Stuben sneered. "Go find Eklof. Tell him to report to me immediately." Stuben communicated her displeasure with the sharp crack of the door slamming shut.

Andersson jerked in his seat again.

"Well?" she demanded.

"He's a relation. Just as I said."

Stuben rested against the front of her desk, inches from the old man. She noticed that he wouldn't look at her directly, which, given his one lazy eye, was preferable. She leaned over to get closer. She was sure he could feel her breath float across his face. "It seems that he is being hunted by his former employers. Why don't you tell me where he is so we can help protect him?" A slight pause. "And the information he is so willing to sell."

"That is not possible. I don't even know where he is. He telephones me when he needs to talk."

She took a deep breath and exhaled; her upper lip curled scornfully.

"He calls at least once a day."

Stuben backed off. "Now you have something to tell him. He is a hunted man. I am sure the Allies wouldn't think twice about putting a bullet between his eyes."

"I shall communicate that. It will not surprise him."

"And, Mr. Andersson ... be sure to tell him that *I* will put a bullet between his eyes, and yours, if either of you deceive me."

Andersson simply shrugged, which caused her blood to boil. He knew killing him would do much harm to their war production; they needed his ball bearings.

"I have one question. Who is Mia Durs?" Andersson asked.

Stuben slid off the edge of her desk and stood over Andersson. "What are you talking about? Where did you get that name?"

Andersson reached for the photo and showed her the backside. In black block letters was written, WHERE IS MIA DURS?

#

Conor wasn't surprised that Karlson hadn't responded when he'd said thanks for the intervention. The clenched jaw told him that

Karlson was pissed off. That and the fact that he hadn't let go of Conor's coat until they were half a block away from the legation.

"So tell me"—Karlson removed his hat and ran his fingers through his hair—"what did that accomplish other than saying that Conor Thorn was in town?"

"Look, the chances are very good that the man I'm looking for—we're looking for—is dealing with the Germans. And most likely with German intelligence. The SD. I just wanted to make them look over their shoulder, think twice before acting. Shake them up a bit. Maybe that leads to them making a mistake." Conor thought it was a convincing argument.

A stiff breeze kicked up as Karlson said flatly, "Colonel Donovan speaks very highly of you. Says you're smart, brash, and unconventional in your approach. I saw that for myself today— well, the unconventional and brash side." Karlson paused a beat. "Don't pull that kind of shit again. This isn't Tangier."

Conor jerked his head back.

"Yeah, the colonel filled me in about your run-in with some Gestapo agents and you cutting their spark plug wires. You almost let an informant fall into their hands."

"I saved his ass," Conor said. "If it wasn't—"

Karlson held up his hand to stop Conor. "The Swedes don't need a lot of reasons to deport someone like you. And Colonel Donovan wouldn't want to see that happen. Any questions?"

That was a pretty good ass chewing. I deserved it. "No, I understand."

"Good. So it seems your German is pretty good," Karlson said, lighting a cigarette.

"I had a strict teacher in high school. Can't shake my accent though."

Karlson nodded. "I just arrived here a few weeks ago. My German is rusty. Bob Homer—he's head of the office here—needs to see you."

"Anything important? I've got to—"

"It seems that he has some visitors from Germany, and his German skills are nonexistent. He doesn't want to screw up the meeting by not fully grasping what they have to say."

"Why not just get an interpreter from the staff?"

Karlson shook his head. "No. This is too high-level. The only ones on the staff now that speak German are Swedes. And they're playing their cards close to their vest. They want to back a winner, and right now, many think the Germans have the upper hand. The only other German speakers are two of our agents, and they were sent to Norway a week ago to assist the resistance with their sabotage efforts."

"What's so important about this meeting?"

"Heinrich Himmler wants a peace deal with the Allies. That important enough for you?"

CHAPTER THIRTY-FIVE

1600 Hours, Wednesday, October 28, 1942
United States Legation, Strandvägen 7A, Stockholm

Conor and Karlson pulled past a towering iron gate into the courtyard of the U-shaped art nouveau building that housed the American Legation, including the offices of the OSS. Conor parked at the base of a statue of a naked woman, a hand cupped around her ear as if she were straining to hear what was being said inside the walls. Karlson had just finished telling Conor that the American military attaché office was located at the back of the courtyard—Buster Seaker's neighborhood.

"And believe it or not, the German military attaché office is right next door," Karlson said as they got out of the Ford, pointing to the part of the building on the right side of the courtyard.

"Pretty cozy. Do they say gesundheit when someone at the American Legation sneezes?"

"Only in the summertime when the windows are open," Karlson said, poker-faced. "There's a barbershop not far from here where you could be seated between someone from the German Legation and someone from the local Abwehr shop. So be careful."

Not too different than Tangier.

The seven-story structure, its walls made of limestone and plaster, overlooked the quays along a bay called Nybroviken. Conor saw that the building's ornately designed towers and balconies fit in with the surrounding buildings along the wide boulevard. This was definitely the high-rent district. A single-stack ferry was tied up along the quay with a line of passengers disembarking.

Conor and Karlson entered an ostentatiously styled elevator replete with mirrors and brass fittings to get to the legation's chancery, its main office, and, when they stepped off, were met by a young woman wringing her hands and biting her lower lip.

"He wants to see you right away," she said before the elevator gate closed behind them.

"Who, Helga? Homer?"

"No. Minister Ramsay. He's a bit agitated. He's been meeting with Mr. Homer." Karlson had said that he was a deputy to Homer but that his cover was serving as special assistant to William Ramsay, the lead US diplomat in Stockholm, appointed five days after Pearl Harbor.

The young woman left them, and Conor turned to Karlson. "I'll wait here while you deal with your other boss."

"No. He'll want to meet you. Homer told him that Colonel Donovan was sending you over. But he didn't know why. Ramsay is not a big fan of the OSS. He thinks spying is ungentlemanly, but he keeps a close eye on our activities. He's told us many times to not get caught."

Conor slowly shook his head and gave Karlson a bemused look. "Yeah, I know. So come up with something as to why you're here. And one thing: don't say anything about the painting of George Washington that hangs behind his desk."

"What are you talking about?"

"It's a famous Gilbert Stuart. Called the *Athenaeum Portrait*. It's unfinished. He gets upset when people point it out. So don't."

Just what the hell am I walking into?

Karlson headed down the hallway, with Conor following, thinking up a story about why Donovan sent him to Stockholm.

As they reached the door, Conor could hear a raised voice. Clearly, someone was getting reprimanded. A secretary immediately rose and knocked on the office door. The upbraiding stopped. She poked her head in and announced Karlson's arrival.

When they entered the office, a fortyish man with gray hair sat in a leather armchair in front of a desk that clearly belonged to the husky man wearing a dark single-breasted suit coat and vest seated behind it. The desk was flanked by American flags, and sure enough, there was a painting of the first president. The lower half and a good portion of the left side of the painting was blank. Washington's dour expression said that he was a little peeved. Ramsay's scowl said the same thing.

"Karlson, who is this?"

"Conor Thorn, Minister. I believe Mr. Homer mentioned his pending arrival."

"He did. Did you just arrive, Mr. Thorn?"

"No, sir. I had a few matters to attend to."

Ramsay's face became pinched. "Like what, for example?"

Conor wasn't really ready for the question. *Here goes.* "Colonel Donovan wanted me to deliver a personal message to Major Carl Tolberg, head of—"

"Yes, yes. I know, head of the Swedish Secret Intelligence Service. What was the message?"

"Sorry, sir, it was personal."

"He sent you over just for that? That's hard to believe."

"He also thought that Mr. Homer could use a little help … with … keeping tabs on the German intelligence staff."

Homer and Karlson both turned from Ramsay to Conor. Homer was nodding.

"He's aware that there's quite a large contingent of operatives stationed here, and he wanted a couple more eyes and ears on the ground."

Ramsay rose and leaned over his desk, fingers digging into the surface, turning his fingernails white. "You listen to me, Thorn … all of you, listen. If your activities, your snooping around, ever comes close to exposing this legation, which I head, to any negative scrutiny by the Swedish government, I personally will go to the Swedish Foreign Ministry and ask that they deport the lot of you. Am I getting through to you?" The closing question came with a light spray of spittle.

Homer stood and cleared his throat. "Of course, Minister. You have nothing to worry about. You'll have to excuse me. I have some people waiting for me. For us, actually." The three men turned and headed for the door.

Conor stopped and turned back to Ramsay, who was reseating

himself behind his desk. "Minister, that's quite an impressive painting you've got. Many people don't get it ... the unfinished look there. It's the *Athenaeum Portrait*, right?"

Ramsay beamed. "That's right, Mr. Thorn. You've got a good eye."

#

Outside Ramsay's office, Karlson started laughing. Homer had a small smile.

"Well, that was a smart move, Thorn. I think it surprised him. Maybe Minister Ramsay is your new friend," Homer said over his shoulder as they walked down the hall.

"It actually might lead to Ramsay backing off his heavy-handed monitoring of our activities," Karlson said.

"Of course it won't. You're dreaming," Homer said, entering an outer office toward the back of the building.

"Well, we can only hope," Karlson said. Homer didn't hear Karlson; he was talking to his secretary in hushed tones.

Conor turned to Karlson. "He has his head buried in the sand pretty deep. Just what does he think the OSS, the Abwehr, the SD, and the NKVD do anyway? Even the Swedes are reading mail and tapping phone lines, for God's sake."

"He's not alone. There are quite a few people in the State Department who aren't used to the ways of the world's second oldest profession."

Conor was shaking his head when Homer turned to him and Karlson. "They're here. So let's put our heads together before they come up." Homer led them into his office, and Conor headed over to look out the windows above the courtyard below. The statue of the naked lady straining to hear had her head tilted up toward Homer's office windows. "Exactly who are these guys?" he asked, turning back to the room.

Karlson started to open his mouth, but Homer waved him off. "Felix Kersten," Homer replied. "He's a Finish national with quite a few top contacts in the Swedish, Finish, and German governments. Kersten is also Heinrich Himmler's doctor or, well, physical therapist. His masseuse."

Conor jerked his head back. "You're meeting with that devil's masseuse?"

"And his lawyer, Carl Langbehn."

"Does Himmler know they're here? Hell, does Hitler know?"

"I doubt Hitler does. But Himmler does. And according to the letter I received asking for this meeting, so does Walter Schellenberg, Himmler's right-hand man and head of the SD," Karlson said.

"So they're here to pitch a peace plan? We haven't even opened a second front yet. It doesn't make sense," Conor said.

"They have their hands full with the eastern front. Convincing us to stand down now, before a second front opens up, does make sense. Then they can focus on beating the Soviet Union into the ground and not worry about their rear," Karlson said.

"That being said, Colonel Donovan has communicated to me that any deal with Himmler is a nonstarter. The news out of Germany makes it impossible to get in bed with them," Homer said.

"Well, time is ticking fast, as far as the second front is concerned," Conor said.

"That's why they're so eager to get their plan in front of us," Homer said. "And I'm sure that Gus told you that our German isn't up to par. Actually mine consists of three words: *sieg heil* and *nein*. I just don't want to screw up by not understanding what they have to say."

"Well, let's get on with this. We've got some people to locate. And fast."

#

By the time Kersten and Langbehn were shown into Homer's office, the sun had set, and the flickering light from gas lamps outside threw shadows against the far wall of the courtyard. After the introductions, made awkward by the shaking of too many hands, Conor moved from his position near a window and took a seat adjacent to Homer's desk. Homer fidgeted in his chair and stared at his guests, who, it seemed to Conor, weren't sure who should start the conversation.

"Thank you for coming such a long way, gentleman," Conor said, the pacing of his German a bit halting.

It was a way of announcing that Conor would do the speaking. Kersten and Langbehn angled themselves somewhat to face Conor. Kersten, a plump man with a large forehead created by a retreating hairline, sat with his legs crossed at his ankles. His right hand rested on top of a portfolio in his lap.

Kersten spoke first. "Thank you for receiving us. I shall get to the point. We, Herr Langbehn and myself, are here to bolster Reichsführer Himmler's proposal for the British and Americans to agree to peace terms with the German state and join forces with the reichsführer, as the new leader of the Germany, in … a joint effort to defeat the Soviet Union." A solemn-faced Langbehn nodded as he stared down at his spit-shined wingtips. "The reichsführer understands the gravity of his proposal. But he is a loyal German who has come to the realization that the Führer is … unfit to rule Germany."

This guy isn't just talking peace; he's talking high treason.

"Unfit? We have Republicans in the States that think President Roosevelt is unfit for office. On what basis, besides politics, is he 'unfit,' as you say?" Conor asked.

Kersten opened his mouth, but no words came.

"Adolf Hitler is physically ill," Langbehn said, still staring at his shoes. All eyes in the room turned to him. "The Führer deals, on a daily basis, with severe neuroses that make governing increasingly difficult." He raised his head and looked at Conor. "The reichsführer is convinced that these neuroses have greatly harmed the execution of the war."

"Himmler is prepared to move against him, but not without an agreement with the British and the Americans to join with him in defeating the Soviet Union," Kersten said.

Conor shifted to English and explained the proposal. He kept it brief and, thinking it safe since he was speaking English, ended by asking Homer if he wanted his two cents.

Homer paused and started to open his mouth.

Conor didn't wait for an answer. "I'm no fan of the Russians, and I know that feeling is shared with some top-level people in Britain and the States, but we're in bed with them. And they're"—Conor stopped and glanced at Kersten, who was studying him intently—"spilling a lot of blood on the eastern front."

Kersten frowned. "You can't tell me that your country, along with Great Britain, doesn't fear a postwar Soviet threat." Kersten's English was surprisingly good.

Homer and Karlson exchanged glances. Conor didn't telegraph his surprise.

"I have had personal conversations with the reichsführer," Kersten said. "He realizes now, with setbacks on the eastern front and America's entry into the war, there is no hope of eventual success. Unless—"

"We drop our dance partner and leave the party. That's what you want?"

Kersten smiled. "If I understand your metaphor, Mr. Thorn, indeed it is. I know the reichsführer. He confides in me on an almost daily basis. He is vehemently anti-Russian."

Langbehn nodded enthusiastically.

"He has a preference for the Anglo-Saxons," Kersten added.

Conor shot a glance at Homer and Karlson. "Is that so? Why is that, Doctor?" Conor asked.

"The reichsführer's thinking is based on shared racial characteristics with the German people. Similar bloodlines. None of which have any commonality with the Russians."

Homer placed his elbows on his desk and rested his chin in his hands. "Hitler and Himmler are cut from the same cloth. So you must know that what you are telling us about Himmler's intentions are very hard to believe."

Kersten glanced down at the portfolio in his lap. "I would like to show you some photographs, if I may."

"Of what?" Homer asked.

Without answering, Kersten opened the portfolio and extracted a stack of photos. He handed the first one to Conor. It was a color photo of Heinrich Himmler holding up a file that was stamped with the SS lightning bolts. Kersten was looking over Himmler's shoulder. "The reichsführer is holding a secret file he showed me mere days ago—a file that contains the medical records of the Führer dating back to his days in the hospital after suffering a poison gas attack during the Great War."

Conor handed the photo to Homer, and Kersten handed Conor the remaining photos. They appeared to be pages from a file detailing the medical condition of one *A. Hitler*. In several photos, a hand could be seen holding down one corner of a page. One photo clearly showed a right hand. On the ring finger was a ring with the *SS* lightning bolts with an eagle clutching a swastika in its talons on both sides. "The information in these photos will back up the reichsführer's claims."

Conor handed the stack to Homer. "Who, besides Himmler, knows you're here?" Conor asked.

"Only Brigadeführer Schellenberg," Langbehn said.

"Well, I've got to hand it to you, both of you," Conor said.

Kersten tilted his head and squinted.

"You have balls coming here with this plan. You might want to think about staying in Sweden for the duration. You'd be safer."

Homer stood quickly and held up a hand to stop any further comments from Conor. He had gone too far. Homer didn't like his toes being stepped on. He turned to Kersten. "I will report to my superiors. I seriously doubt that there will be a need for a follow-up, but if there is, how do we reach you?"

Kersten and Langbehn stood. "You can message Count Folke Bernadotte through the Swedish Red Cross. He is a close friend."

"Very well. Would you care to stay? We are screening a movie tonight for some of our Swedish friends. It's *The Great Dictator*. Charlie Chaplin plays—"

"No," Langbehn said sharply. "We have an engagement tonight at the Grand Hôtel. A dinner to honor Benjamin Andersson. A great friend of Germany."

The announcement caught Conor off guard. He knew where he was headed that evening.

When their guests left, Conor turned to Homer. "That was a nice touch, *The Great Dictator*."

Homer smiled and shrugged. "I have my moments."

Conor headed to the door. "So who's going to tell Donovan that Hitler has a traitor in his midst?"

CHAPTER THIRTY-SIX

"That might be one of the strangest situations I've ever been in," Conor said. "I'm not sure Colonel Donovan would believe any of it." He stood next to Karlson under a lamppost in the courtyard.

Karlson finished lighting a cigarette, and the sound of his Zippo snapping closed echoed off the courtyard walls. "Kersten, the doctor, he seems to be the real deal. You could hear it in his voice." He took a drag from his cigarette, then released the smoke through his nostrils. "Where are you headed?"

Given Conor's growing fondness for Karlson, he didn't want to mislead him. "I have a room at the Grand Hôtel. I think I'll freshen up and maybe drop by the Andersson dinner that Langbehn mentioned. Maybe I can pick up where I left off with Andersson earlier today."

Karlson took another drag from his cigarette. "I have a suite over there. So if you need any help, let me know. But be careful."

"It's a hotel, Gus."

"It's a hotel crawling with staff who work for the Swedish counterespionage unit. They go through your trash, and they have big ears. I've been able to turn a few by putting a few extra krona in their pockets, so now I get a few choice wastebaskets and some ink blotters from the rooms of key diplomats."

Conor chuckled at the image of Karlson going through wastebaskets. "Be careful yourself. Ramsay will have your ass kicked out of here pretty quick if he finds out about you going through people's trash, looking for secrets."

"Is that you, Karlson?"

Both men turned to the voice that came from the top of the stairs in the rear of the courtyard. The light from a nearby lamppost illuminated a man in a service dress blue US Navy uniform. The insignia on the jacket sleeves announced the rank of commander, his combination cap tucked under his right arm. As he trotted down the steps, his heels resounded in the cobblestone courtyard.

"Hey, Buster. Haven't seen you since you got back. How was England?" Karlson asked.

Typically, meeting old classmates, especially ones he played football or lacrosse with, was a welcome occurrence for Conor. It was different with Seaker, now that Conor had learned that Seaker was responsible for getting Bobby ousted from the academy—that and the arrogance that some pilots displayed.

"Gus, you have to be more careful about the people you hang around with," Seaker said, slapping Conor's back. "Hey, Conor. Staying out of trouble?"

"Doing my best."

Karlson was surprised by the camaraderie. "Where the hell did you guys meet?"

"The academy," Seaker said. "Played football together. Conor was one hell of a defensive back, I can tell you that." He looked at Conor. "So, hanging around an OSS man tells me that the navy's loss is the OSS's gain. Do I have that right?"

Conor nodded. "Afraid so."

"Buster, how about a quick drink over at the Grand?" Karlson asked.

"Can't, old man. I'm headed over to the Tattersall, where a dinner date named Greta awaits." He glanced at his watch. "And I'd better get going, seeing as I'm already late. Can't keep the pretty ones waiting too long, or some hungry reporter with a big expense account might get lucky." Seaker squeezed between Karlson and Conor and headed out of the courtyard. He stopped ten paces away and turned back. "Conor, you need any help, let me know. I have some connections with some ... friends that can get their hands on anything."

Both men watched Seaker turn the corner onto Strandvägen. "What do you know about Seaker?" Conor asked.

Karlson dropped his cigarette butt and crushed it beneath his shoe. "Not much. He seems to know plenty of people in town. His boss, Colonel Waddell, wasn't very welcoming when we arrived a few months ago. Didn't know why the OSS needed agents in country, thought the information they were sending back was sufficient. Buster was a good buffer, ran interference for us. He's a pretty good guy ..." Karlson trailed off.

"I hear a 'but,'" Conor said.

"Yeah, there's a but. Before I go on, just how close are you two?"

"Actually, not close at all. He knew my late wife. That and we shared a locker room."

Karlson raised an eyebrow. "So sorry to hear that ... about your wife." He coughed into his hand and looked down at the cobblestones. "Buster is a ladies' man, but he gets sloshed and acts like an ass. That's what I hear from the ladies who work with us."

Conor flinched. The picture emerging in his mind of Buster Seaker was troubling.

"There's one other thing. Word has it his father, a congressman from Massachusetts, was responsible for getting him this assignment, which, I have to admit, is pretty cushy. He told me he's going to run for his father's seat when the war is over."

"I imagine that happens all the time." Conor looked up into the dark sky and buttoned his suit coat. "Can I give you a lift?"

"Nah, I need the exercise." They walked to Conor's Ford. "Remember, be on your toes at the Grand. And don't pull the same stuff you did at the German Legation. The C Bureau should have men all over the place."

Conor extended a hand and they shook. "Deal. Could you open the gate for me?" He pointed at the tall wrought iron gate to the courtyard.

"Sure."

As they turned to go their separate ways, a taxi screeched to a stop on the other side of the gate. A short horn blast followed. Conor put a hand up to shield his eyes from the glare of the headlights and heard a familiar voice.

"As I live and breathe. I can't believe I found your sorry ass."
Bobby Heugle had arrived. Stockholm would never be the same.

CHAPTER THIRTY-SEVEN

1750 Hours, Wednesday, October 28, 1942
German Safe House, Stockholm

The smell of boiled eel made itself known well before the older guard brought Emily's meal down to her cell. She leaned against the wall and opened her mouth to ask him some questions, but the jolt of pain up the side of her head stopped her.

The guard noticed the untouched bowl of boiled cabbage from the morning beside Emily's mattress. "If you don't eat, you will only suffer more."

Emily opened her mouth slowly using the smallest amount of movement she could to speak. "I am nauseous all the time."

The guard shrugged. He was approaching his fifties, Emily guessed, given the thinning hair and middle-aged paunch. He limped on a leg that wouldn't bend at the knee. A veteran of the Great War presumably. "It's the best I can do," he said, pushing the bowl under the cell door. "Here is another cloth for your wound." He tossed a thin cotton cloth the size of a handkerchief between the bars. It was cool and damp. "If you have blisters, do not puncture them. The fluid will keep the skin underneath clean. Infections can be bad with burns. I know this from the war." A grimace fell over his face as he turned to leave.

"Thank you, but you might get in trouble with that woman for helping me."

He turned back to look at her. "Yes, I might. Maybe she'll shoot me and put me out of my misery. That would be fine with me." The older man made no move to leave. "I have a friend. A woman friend. She tells me she is sweet on me. I'm not sure I believe her. She works at the German Legation for Stuben." He reached into his back pants pocket, produced a flask, and took a sip, his hand trembling a bit as he did. "She also tells me an American man is looking for someone named Gunnar Lind."

Emily's expression froze.

He noted the reaction and took another drink before he continued. "This man … the American … he has big balls. He made a commotion in the legation. It seems he's looking for you also."

Emily smiled ever so slightly. *Conor.* She knew few who would be foolish and reckless enough to confront the Germans directly.

"He left a message with Stuben. He wants to know where you are." He put the flask back and continued gazing at Emily. She turned away, hiding her eyes as they slowly welled up with tears.

"I know no Americans," she said, her voice raspy and soft. She cursed herself for not sounding more emphatic.

"Ah. Of course. Neither do I." He turned to leave. When he reached the bottom of the stairs, he turned back to Emily. "Killed a few back in the day, though." He started up the stairs practically dragging his stiff right leg.

"Can I use the toilet?"

He stopped. "Ah, I'm sorry. I have been told you have to use the bucket. We can't be up and down these stairs all day."

"Would you please empty it? It's almost full."

"That's Willy's job. With my limp, I'd only spill and make a mess."

Emily watched as he slowly progressed up the stairs. She rubbed her jaw and wondered why Conor thought making a fool out of himself in the German Legation was a smart move. It seemed more like a desperate one. Her fears were mounting that his risk-taking and rule-breaking habits would someday lead to an early demise. But given the equally desperate situation involving Gunnar Lind, maybe that's what was called for. She shook her head and smiled, generating another jolt of pain.

CHAPTER THIRTY-EIGHT

1930 Hours, Wednesday, October 28, 1942
Grand Hôtel, Södra Blasieholmshammer 8, Stockholm

The Grand's street-level bar was filling up with guests dressed in their finery. Some of the men wore black tie, others had finely tailored dark suits. The women were in long dresses and sparkling jewelry that highlighted, in some cases, ample bosoms. The bar stretched nearly the length of the room. The chandeliers were blazing; bright light bounced off the alabaster ceiling that featured intricate bas-relief designs. The room was buzzing with indistinct chatter, the scent a fusion of various perfumes.

Bobby and Conor sat at the end of the bar closest to the double doors, giving Conor a clear line of sight to the front entrance of the hotel. Bobby had just finished instructing the bartender how to tell the kitchen to make a grilled cheese sandwich. He'd complained all the way over from the legation how he hadn't eaten for over twenty-four hours. Conor barely got a few words in, explaining they were going to ask the guest of honor, Benjamin Andersson, some questions. It was just as well, as Conor didn't really have a plan—Karlson wouldn't be pleased that Conor could very well be reprising his German Legation act.

The beer in front of Bobby was half-drained. The one in front of Conor was untouched. Bobby took another sip of his and looked around the room. "So, you have much contact with that snake Seaker?"

Conor kept his eyes on the front entrance. "Not really. But we did run into him just before you showed up. He was on his way out on a date."

Bobby grunted. "I hope she has a gun."

Conor looked at Bobby. "What are you talking about?"

"I told you—Simpson told me a story about Seaker."

"What about him?" Conor leaned in. It struck Conor that the subject of Seaker kept bubbling to the surface, like swamp gas to the surface of a pond. The connection to Grace wasn't fully clear, but Conor couldn't help but feel it was headed in that direction. He took in a deep breath; he didn't want to get ahead of himself.

"Simpson, the guy I was helping with his German, he liked this particular bar on Main Street in Annapolis. Actually, he liked a barmaid who worked there, so he went there whenever he could. So, one night, Seaker shows up with some guys from the football team after a game. They had a table in the back and were getting pretty rowdy. They were throwing peanuts at each other, spilling beer, breaking glasses."

"Bobby ..."

"Yeah, I'm getting to it. So the barmaid goes to the ladies' room. Simpson sees Seaker get up and follow her in. Simpson panicked. He didn't know what to do, Seaker being two years ahead of him and all. He knew that she didn't like Seaker and his buddies. She made that clear with comments she made under her breath when they started getting rowdy. About five minutes later, Simpson was about to get up and knock on the bathroom door when Seaker comes out, rejoins his buddies, and soon they're all laughing. A minute later, the barmaid comes out. She looked like she'd been crying. Simpson asked what happened." Bobby finished his beer.

"What'd she say?"

Bobby pushed the empty beer glass to the back edge of the bar. "Nothing. She wouldn't speak to him the rest of the night. He told me that she didn't even respond to Seaker and his buddies when they were pounding empty mugs on the table. She just ignored them. When Seaker came up to the bar, he slammed down a handful of mugs and yelled at her. Simpson said Seaker had a scratch along his jawline. She took one of the mugs and filled it from the tap, then tossed the beer in his face and ran into a back room. Seaker's buddies thought that was the funniest thing they'd ever seen. He made a beeline for the back room, but his buddies got up and stopped him."

Conor thought back to his time in the locker room during football season at the academy. He'd gotten to know some guys really well. Others kept to themselves and were just happy with being an audience for those who like to preen and tell stories about their sexual exploits. Most stories were funny. A few weren't. Conor couldn't remember Seaker telling a story about a barmaid on Main Street.

Bobby made a futile attempt to get the attention of the bartender. "On Seaker's way out of the bar, he whispered something to Simpson."

"What?"

"He said, 'No one will believe you or her.' It shook him up."

Conor stared at his glass of beer. *If he raped that woman, did he do that only once and never again?* It rattled him.

"That's the story I wanted to tell you at Leuchars. But … time ran out." Bobby eyed Conor's beer with interest. "You gonna drink that?"

"No, it's yours." Conor paused while Bobby took a swig.

A commotion near the front door caught Conor's attention. Hotel staff scurried about, and several photographers were taking pictures, flash bulbs popping. Conor glimpsed Andersson as the man took the short flight of stairs from the sidewalk into the lobby. An older woman trailed behind, walking arm in arm with Eve Lind.

#

After waiting for fifteen minutes to let the dinner guests settle in, Conor nudged Bobby.

"Come on, let's get going," he said just as the bartender emerged from the kitchen with a golden brown grilled cheese sandwich cut on a diagonal. Bobby looked like someone just told him his winning Irish Sweepstakes ticket was counterfeit. "Too late. We've got to get moving."

Bobby handed a krona to the bartender. "Hide that sandwich. And hide it good. I'll be back."

They headed to the ballroom, located toward the rear of the hotel. A line of guests was still waiting to be seated, so Conor and Bobby joined the line.

"Tell me again what we're doing here," Bobby said.

"I just want to ask some questions about his son-in-law. And—"

"I hate *ands.*"

"And depending on who I run into, maybe I'll get a chance to go fishing with a cherry bomb."

"What the hell does that mean?"

"You throw a cherry bomb into the pond and see what floats to the surface. Don't tell me you never did that."

"No, I'm a conventional rod-and-reel guy. Should I map out an escape route?"

"We'll be fine. Don't worry."

"Easy for you to say."

When they got to the head of the line, Conor flashed identification stating he was with the American Legation. He told the event security he needed to deliver a message to Minister William Ramsay. Security pointed at a table on a seating chart where Ramsay was to be seated and let them through.

Inside the ballroom, the waitstaff, wearing black waistcoats over white shirts, scrambled about filling wine and champagne glasses. Some guests were still standing, talking, as they settled in. Directly across from the entrance was the dais. Already seated were several dignitaries, along with the Andersson family. Conor and Bobby headed in the opposite direction of Ramsay's table, on a circuitous route toward the dais.

They were halfway across the room when he saw Andersson and Eve get up from their table. Conor stopped abruptly.

"What's up?" Bobby asked.

Conor pointed at Andersson. "See that old guy up ahead with Eve trailing behind? That's who I want to talk to—Eve's father." Conor watched as Andersson and Eve wove their way through the crowd, stopping several times to shake hands. Andersson seemed to be headed in the direction of a table of ten already seated. Conor recognized Kersten and Langbehn, and it was hard to miss

Lina Stuben with her short, silky blond hair, cut on a sharp angle, framing her face. She sat next to the stocky Kurt Eklof, whose silvery crew cut sparkled with a freshly applied dose of pomade. It looked like his eye patch was spit-shined, given that it reflected the candlelight.

When Kersten noticed Conor, he leaned over and spoke to Langbehn. Stuben noticed the men look away and tracked their gazes. She started to get up just as Andersson approached the table but sat back down. Conor and Bobby slowed their progress. As they got closer, he heard Andersson begin to introduce his daughter to the German guests. Eve hadn't noticed Conor's approach.

"Good evening, Mr. Andersson," Conor said, prompting a flash of surprise on Eve's face. "Congratulations on being honored this evening. It must be a special—"

Stuben sprang from her seat, knocking over her glass of wine. "What are you doing here?"

"Miss Stuben, I'm here to honor Mr. Andersson. Certainly nothing to get excited about."

Without saying a word, Eve grabbed her father's arm and pulled him away from the table—another helpful gesture from the woman who "desperately wanted to help locate her husband."

Kersten stood and opened his mouth, but Langbehn tugged firmly on his arm, pulling him back down into his seat.

Conor could feel Bobby pulling the back of his suit coat. "Actually, I have another reason for coming. On the chance that Lina would be here, I just wanted to let her see this photo up close." Conor pulled a photo of Roger McInnis from his breast pocket. "I just wasn't sure if she got a good look at it earlier today." Conor held up the photo for all to see. "Roger McInnis, a staff member from the British Legation, was killed, most likely in your legation. He was dumped into the harbor, most likely by Mr. Eye Patch."

That produced a reaction from everyone at the table. Not surprisingly, Eklof jumped out of his chair to stand nose to nose with Conor and attempted to snatch the photo from him, but he passed it over his shoulder to Bobby.

Eklof started to push Conor and thus Bobby, but Bobby pushed back, making Conor the meat in the human sandwich.

"Leave. Leave now," Eklof ordered.

"As soon as you tell me why you killed Roger McInnis. Then we'll leave."

Eklof's facial expression hardened as he planted both hands on Conor's chest and shoved. Both Conor and Bobby took a half step back, which gave Eklof the space to draw his right arm back across his chest.

A backhanded slap to the face coming your way. Conor raised his right arm, blocking Eklof's movement, then clamped down on the man's wrist. In one smooth motion, Conor spun Eklof and pinned his arm behind his back, pulling up on the wrist. Eklof's grunt was drowned out by the gasps from the dinner guests. Conor shoved Eklof back toward the table, just missing the advancing Stuben.

"Lina, you must keep better control of your goons," Conor said.

Stuben stopped two feet away, nostrils flaring.

Homer had told him that Colonel Donovan said a deal with Himmler was a nonstarter, so Conor decided to stir the pot even more. He took a step toward her and leaned in, his mouth inches from Stuben's ear.

She stiffened.

He could smell a strong scent of soap. "Here's something to chew on, Lina. Himmler is doing a little dealing behind Adolf's back, looking for a peace deal with the Brits and Americans."

Lina snapped her head back in alarm.

"I know. Pretty fantastic. But it's true. Just ask your table mates here, Kersten and Langbehn."

"Let's go, Conor," Bobby said. "You're out of cherry bombs."

CHAPTER THIRTY-NINE

2000 Hours, Wednesday, October 28, 1942
Grand Hôtel, Södra Blasieholmshammer 8, Stockholm

Moments after order had been restored, Minister Kleist asked Stuben if the scene with Thorn was really necessary. She made it clear that if not for her self-control, it would have been much worse. Couldn't Kleist see that Thorn initiated it with his provocative behavior? She wouldn't let anyone, including Kleist, make a fool of her. Reichsführer Himmler had taught her that.

Stuben turned to the red-faced Eklof, who was massaging his shoulder. "Come with me."

She headed for the ballroom's exit, found a vacant corner of the lobby, sat in a plush armchair, and lit a cigarette. The effects of her adrenaline rush from the encounter were beginning to wear off.

Once Eklof was settled across from her, Lina announced, "Thorn ... he's a persistent nuisance who must be dealt with."

Eklof nodded his agreement.

"But there is something that you must do first. Tonight. The woman, Andersson's daughter. Take her."

"Why? What reason could there—"

"I don't trust Andersson. He seems too casual ... too smug about this arrangement we have. Taking his daughter will give us leverage, insurance that he will live up to his side of the agreement. Watch her. If she leaves to go to the lavatory, intercept her. Take her to the safe house and let her join the Durs woman or whatever her real name is. Once our deal has been executed, she will be returned. Leave no marks on her. We don't want Andersson going to the authorities with a complaint afterward."

"And Thorn?"

"I am flying to Berlin tonight. We will deal with Thorn when I return."

"Should an opportunity arise to deal with him while you are away, should I proceed?"

"As long as the odds for success are overwhelmingly in your favor, yes. But taking the woman is your first priority. Do not fail."

CHAPTER FORTY

2000 Hours, Wednesday, October 28, 1942
Grand Hôtel, Södra Blasieholmshammer 8, Stockholm

Seeing the American engage with his German acquaintances un-
nerved Andersson—first an appearance at the German Legation
and now here. He assured himself the Germans would put a stop
to the behavior with a complaint to the American minister—yes,
he would have to make the suggestion to Lina Stuben to forestall
any further interruptions to their dealings.

He realized he needed to take another trip to the lavatory. His
doctor's diagnosis of an enlarged prostate explained his seemingly
incessant need to urinate. A condition, he was told, he would have
to live with for the rest of his life.

While washing his hands, another man entered, going straight
to the sink next to his. It was odd behavior, and it was obvious this
man was not attending his dinner—his trousers, made of a heavy gray
woolen fabric, were tucked into rubber galoshes, and he had a fishy
odor. *Herring,* Andersson thought. The man ignored the soap and just
used water, followed by a quick wipe with a towel from a stack on the
counter. He shoved the towel into his pocket and pulled out a folded
piece of paper, sliding it along the counter to Andersson.

"You will please read this note," the man said and promptly left.

The accent was unmistakably Russian, and the note was slightly wet from the man's hastily dried hands. It was brief, the scrawl
difficult to read.

You are selling something that we would like to pur-chase. We offer 2,000,000 krona for the documents and the person you are representing. Café Mona Lisa. Österlånggatan 17, Gamla Stan 0900

As Andersson stared at the note, his hand began to tremble—double what he'd asked of the Germans. He rushed to the door and flung it open, hitting the wall behind the door. He looked up and down the long hallway. A few dinner guests were stretching their legs nearby and chatting, but there was no poorly dressed Russian who smelled of herring in sight.

CHAPTER FORTY-ONE

When Conor and Bobby first retook their seats at the end of the bar, the bartender came over and told Bobby that the grilled cheese sandwich was the tastiest thing he'd eaten in quite a while and handed back a krona. Bobby's low, long groan made the bartender laugh. Each nursing a glass of beer, Conor and Bobby, who had ordered another grilled cheese sandwich, waited patiently in case Andersson exited early from his dinner. It was an hour and a half later when the first guests started leaving the dinner.

The guests poured out onto the wide street between the hotel and the quay. Lina Stuben led the German delegation out, but Conor noticed Eklof was not with the group. Conor had gotten the best of him tonight, but he knew when you poked someone hard enough, you needed to look over your shoulder—if you wanted to stay in one piece.

Conor gave Bobby a punch on the arm and slid off his stool, heading toward the lobby to get a closer look at the dwindling flow of exiting guests. Andersson and his wife appeared but no Eve. His wife was dabbing her eyes with a hankie as Andersson called someone over dressed in a dark suit and seemingly gave him a lecture. After some finger pointing, the dark suit ran off, and Andersson and his wife headed out the main entrance to their waiting Rolls-Royce. The Rolls didn't drive off right away; instead, it sat with the rear door open.

Waiting for their only child?

Conor led Bobby outside, where they watched Andersson and his wife having a heated discussion. "Let's get to the car," Conor said. "We need to follow him."

They sprinted to their car, parked around the corner, hopped in, and waited for the Rolls to start moving, which it did a minute later. It raced past them, executed a tight U-turn, and headed back toward the hotel. Conor followed but had trouble keeping pace. The cobblestone boulevard under their wheels made for a noisy ride. At least streetlights lit the way, an aid Conor wasn't used to after spending time in London. The distance between the Ford and the Rolls kept growing.

"That Rolls is flying. We're going to lose them," Conor said.

"There's a one-lane bridge up ahead. If we're lucky, they may have to stop."

They were at least two hundred yards behind when the Rolls's brake lights appeared, and Conor closed the distance between them.

"Bingo," Bobby said.

"Where are we?"

"The bridge takes you to a small island called Skeppsholmen. Some of the fat cats have second homes there so they can be close to their boats. I remember it being a busy place in the summer months but really quiet the rest of the year."

Three cars and one delivery truck drove past the line of waiting cars headed in the opposite direction. Conor, the Rolls, and several other cars took their turn going over the bridge with the Rolls having to contend with the traffic ahead of it, so keeping pace was no longer an issue. They had been on the island for less than a minute when the Rolls turned left into a gravel driveway. Conor turned opposite the driveway into a stand of trees, shut the engine off, and turned to watch Andersson climb the two steps to a porch that ran the width of a two-story building.

"What is going on to get that old guy moving that fast? And where the hell's Eve?" Conor said. "Bobby, the glove box. Hand me the binoculars."

"Maybe Eve got lucky and met someone at the dinner," Bobby joked, handing Conor the binoculars.

"I wouldn't put it past her."

With the help of the light from a half-moon, Conor could make out two men standing guard on either side of the house. The one on the left had a rifle slung over his shoulder and another had his rifle stock pinned under his arm. A third guard appeared and joined the one on the left, all of them lighting cigarettes.

"Andersson is loaded, so this is probably his house, right?" Bobby asked.

"Makes sense. But why the need for guards? What or who is he protecting?"

Through a large bay window, Conor saw three men: one was Andersson. Another man was at least a head taller. Andersson seemed to be doing all the talking, while the tall man scratched his head. The third man passively stood by.

"I count four guards, maybe five."

Conor didn't recognize the two men with Andersson, but he could only see their profiles. Their conversation continued for another few minutes, and then all three men disappeared from view. The tall man and Andersson appeared in the doorway, walking out onto the porch and facing Conor. A porch light finally gave Conor a better look at the tall man.

"Hey there, Gunnar," he said softly.

"What? Are you kidding me?"

Conor passed the binoculars to Bobby. "Tell me that isn't our man, Gunnar Lind," Conor said, a smile slowly growing on his face.

Bobby raised the binoculars to his eyes. "I'll be damned. Jackpot."

"Now we know why the guards are here. I wonder how many there are. That other guy in the house might be the head guard."

"Which would mean there are four. Maybe more in back," Bobby said. "Andersson is getting back in the car. Lind just went back into the house." He handed the binoculars back to Conor, who watched the Rolls drive off.

"I need you to stay here. Keep an eye on the house," Conor said. "I'll reach out to Karlson to send someone to relieve you. We need some reinforcements to help us deal with those guards." He looked at his watch. "And we need to move fast. We'll hit the house sometime after midnight."

CHAPTER FORTY-TWO

The quiet was broken by what Emily thought were the footfalls of more than one person. Someone was slowly coming down backward—the older guard—and another man she couldn't see yet was swearing at the older guard for moving so slowly. When the guards came into full view, she saw what they were carrying.

A body.

The older guard was holding the unconscious—hopefully not dead—woman under the armpits. The other guard held her ankles. As the guards reached the bottom, the old guard swayed slightly, struggling with his grip. When they pivoted toward the cell adjacent to Emily's, he lost his grip entirely, and the woman dropped to the floor. This brought an onslaught of condemnation from the man with the eye patch, who had followed them down—it was the man who had knocked her out.

"Pick her up, you idiot," he said. He seemed more annoyed at the pace than the possibility that any harm may have come to the woman. The guards dumped her on the mattress, where she landed on her back, at an angle, most of her left leg resting on the floor. A clump of blond hair obscured the side of her face closest to Emily.

The man with the eye patch drew a ladle from a water bucket and threw it on the woman's face. She didn't stir, but the wet clump of hair fell from her face, and Emily recognized her. What she didn't follow was why Eve Lind had been put in the cell next to hers. For that matter, she couldn't figure out why the woman wasn't still in England.

The two guards headed up the stairs, but the one with the eye patch remained. A smile spread across his face as he stared down at Emily. "We checked—your aunt is dead." His smile dissolved into a mocking frown. "But you won't be going to the funeral. You'll be going to Berlin for questioning by people with greater skills than Lina Stuben." He headed toward the stairs, then stopped at the bottom. "Enjoy getting to know your new friend."

CHAPTER FORTY-THREE

2300 Hours, Wednesday, October 28, 1942
Grand Hôtel, Södra Blasieholmshammer 8, Stockholm

Karlson's suite at the Grand was impressively spacious, as well as being neat and orderly, as if an army of maids had just left. A copy of the *New York Herald Tribune* lay neatly folded on a glass and brass coffee table. A small envelope lay on top of the paper. An ashtray, free from any ash, was placed alongside the newspaper and a pack of Chesterfield cigarettes, unopened.

Karlson peered up and down the corridor before letting Conor in. "I hear you've been a busy boy tonight. Your dustup is all over town."

"Thought it might be. What did Ramsay say?"

"Well, it didn't take him long to dictate a cable to Donovan in Washington."

"Let's hope he's still in London. I just need a few more days," Conor said.

Karlson motioned him to the couch, and Conor pointed to the ceiling with his index finger and spun it around the room.

"It was swept this evening. And I haven't left the suite since it was done."

Conor nodded and took a seat on the couch. His body ached from the long day. He was hungry and thirsty. "I think we've found Lind."

"Where is he?"

"Holed up at a house on Skeppsholmen Island. Bobby Heugle and I followed Andersson there after he left the dinner. Could be owned by Andersson. I'm not sure."

"What can I do?"

"You know those three friends of yours who were your backup at the German Legation today? Well, I could use them. Lind is guarded by at least four men with rifles. I need to send someone out there to relieve Bobby, and I need at least one other man to help Bobby and me take down the guards and grab Lind."

"Done."

"And I could use some hardware. A sidearm for me and Bobby."

"Shouldn't be a problem." Karlson went over to a sideboard and picked up the phone.

While he walked the person on the other end through the situation, Conor's thoughts turned to Emily. He hadn't checked in with Masterman at the British Legation since his first meeting, but if there was any news, Masterman knew he could leave a message at the US Legation.

Karlson finished his call and strode over to Conor. "Okay, two of our legation's Marine guards are heading out to Heugle in two cars. One will bring Heugle back to the legation. The other will take over watching the house. If Lind and his buddies take off, he'll tail them. As far as hardware goes, we'll have to get over to the legation. The gun room is in the basement. There shouldn't be anyone nosing around at this hour except for the one guard at the front desk, so the chances that you'll run into Ramsay are low."

Conor chuckled. He appreciated Karlson's dry sense of humor. "Gus, there's one other thing. I'm not sure it's a critical problem, but we lost track of Eve Lind. She arrived at the dinner with her parents but didn't leave with them. It could mean something ... or not."

"Could she have left the dinner to meet with her husband?"

"No. I'm sure we would have seen her as a part of the greeting party at the house we followed Andersson to. But, just to be sure, can you send someone out to the Andersson home and see if she's there?"

"I'll call in a favor from a detective with the local police. He'll be discreet."

"Good. Thank you."

"Oh, and Captain Masterman sent over a courier tonight with a message for you," Gus said. He snatched an envelope off the coffee table and handed it to Conor.

Conor read it, tore the note in half, and dropped in on the coffee table.

"What?"

He drew a deep breath and exhaled loudly. "I never mentioned it, but I'm also looking for an MI6 agent I've been working with— Emily Bright. She was sent here to track down Lind, but she turned up missing too. Masterman says he thinks the Germans have Emily in a safe house in the city. His men were calling in favors and spreading some money around to known informers."

"Have you worked with her long?"

"Not long enough."

The phone rang, and Gus rushed over to the sideboard to pick it up. The call lasted less than ten seconds. "One of the team says he'll meet us over in the gun room. He's prepping some firepower for us."

"Gus, you can't go. The colonel will have my ass."

"Try to stop me and you may get a bloody nose, Conor." If there was anyone who understood the deep need to get off the sidelines of this war, it was Conor. He would have tossed around a few threats of his own if someone had tried to keep him out of the game.

"How much training did you get back in the States?"

"Enough."

Conor began to shake his head.

"Listen, if I thought I was going to slow you down or screw up this operation, I'd beg off." Conor opened his mouth to speak, but Gus held up his hand. "Trust me."

"Okay. But I reserve the right to change my mind."

#

Crossing the lobby of the Grand, Conor could hear laughter and loud voices coming from the bar. Conor and Gus were twenty paces from the front entrance when someone shouted their names. Exiting the bar with a woman on his arm was Seaker. The woman—one could only assume Greta—had a flushed face.

"Hey, boys. Heading out for a nightcap?" Seaker asked with a thick tongue.

"Some late-night business," Karlson said.

"Ah, too bad. Gus, Conor, this is Greta. We're just going to call it a night, but if you want to change your mind, we'd be happy to join you."

"No, no, Buster. I can't," Greta said. "I'm feeling—"

"You just need a little fresh air, that's all," Seaker said.

"Buster, we have to get moving. Really," Conor said.

"I was telling Greta about running into you, Conor. Gave me a chance to tell some football stories."

Greta was directing her gaze all around the lobby, not locking on anything in particular.

"Greta, are you all right?" Conor asked.

Her head swiveled, and her red eyes landed on Conor. "Oh, yes. I just didn't eat enough … I think."

"So I was saying that telling some football stories reminded me that I know a friend of your wife—Sue Ryan. At least Sue said they were pretty close."

Conor's face slackened. The connection to Sue Ryan shook him. He took in a deep breath. Aftershave. Sweet-smelling aftershave.

"How do you know Sue?" Conor asked, his voice flat and emotionless.

"We dated some during my last year at the academy. We got together a couple of times after that. Didn't go anywhere. How is Grace, by the way?"

Conor gave no thought to softening the news. "She's dead. Died during childbirth."

It was like smelling salts to Seaker and Greta, who both flinched.

"Oh, I'm so sorry," Greta said, her reddened eyes welling with tears.

"Jesus Christ, Conor … that's horrible news. I—"

Karlson grabbed Conor by the arm. "Buster, I hate to break this up, but you guys can catch up some other time. We've some business to attend to."

Conor turned his head just as they went through the door. Greta was wiping a tear from her cheek. Seaker stood motionless, a blank look on his face.

CHAPTER FORTY-FOUR

0030 Hours, Thursday, October 29, 1942
United States Legation, Strandvägen 7A, Stockholm

Exiting the elevator in the basement of the legation, Karlson and Conor were met with an overpowering damp stink. The corridor that ran the length of the building was two-toned. Halfway down the weakly lit hallway, Conor noticed that the lower half was darker not because of a paint choice but because a dark green mold was creeping up the wall.

At the end of the hall, a metal door painted a glossy black stood open; an unlocked padlock hung on a U-bolt welded to the door, the bright light from the gun room spilling out into the hallway. Conor could hear a series of clicks and metal-on-metal clanks. Karlson entered first and slapped a man on the shoulder. On the far side of the room, a metal cabinet ran the length of the wall, displaying an array of weapons.

"Master Sergeant Lancer, thanks for rolling out of the sack for us. This is Conor Thorn, who I believe you have met ... sort of."

The broad-shouldered Marine's shaved head sported a bit of stubble. The six stripes of a Marine master sergeant normally required a service time of twenty years, which would put him around forty.

"Hello, Sergeant. As he said, thanks for helping out ... and that includes earlier today," Conor said, extending his hand to shake and surveying at least a dozen .30 semiautomatic M1 carbine rifles.

When the Master Sergeant let Conor's hand go, Conor slipped it into his coat pocket so his hand could recover in private. "When duty calls, Mr. Thorn. It was too quiet around here ... at least before you showed up. A local deployment to help out the OSS is just what the doctor ordered."

"Right. Hopefully, we can get you back in your rack in a couple hours. And call me Conor."

"Yes, sir, Mr. Thorn."

Lancer explained that the .30 caliber carbine, only in service for a few months, was shorter and lighter than the M1 Garand and provided greater mobility. Several were the M1A1 model that featured the spring-loaded folding paratrooper stock, making them easy to conceal under a coat or a pack. Three Colt M1911 semiautomatic pistols had been placed on a metal table in the middle of the room; one of them was completely disassembled. A can of Ballistol oil and a soft cloth lay nearby.

"Let me give you the lay of the land and how I see this coming down." Conor walked over to a chalkboard that listed the room's inventory and drew a rectangle and a circle to indicate the house and its driveway. "As of a couple of hours ago, we spotted three guards on the grounds." He placed Xs where he'd seen them. "They seemed to be patrolling the grounds. We think there is only one guard inside the house with our target."

Lancer scratched his head. "You *think*, sir?"

"Yes, hopefully we'll know more when Agent Heugle gets back here since he's been keeping watch. The guards we saw had rifles. No scopes. Couldn't make out types."

"Gunny Miller is at the house. Including Heugle, that makes five," Karlson said.

Conor and Lancer looked at Karlson. "Gus, before we go, I need you to track down Captain Masterman.," Conor said. "Tell him we're moving in on Lind. He has to get in touch with the motor gun boat in Lysekil to put them on alert. We're six hours away. That puts us there sometime mid to late morning. Get them to top off their tanks if they haven't already. And ask him if they are any closer to locating the German safe house and Emily Bright."

Karlson nodded and took off.

If Masterman wasn't successful, Conor's only option was to

beat it out of Eklof. Failing that, a gun to the head of Stuben would work.

Conor knew he was ready, but as far as he knew, Bobby hadn't seen much action since joining the OSS six months earlier. "Here's one problem, Master Sergeant—" Conor stopped and looked down the corridor when he heard the elevator doors open.

Strutting down the hall was Bobby. He was waving a hand under his nose. "Holy shit, it sure stinks down here. How can you stand it?"

"You get used to it." Conor introduced the two men. "So what's going on at the house?"

"Nothing. Very quiet. Lights went out inside just before I left."

"Still just the four guards?" Conor asked, shooting a glance at Lancer.

"Yeah. No change.

"You were saying something about a problem, sir?"

"Right, we don't know when the guards get relieved. If we move when the shift changes, that could get messy."

"Then we should get moving ... right, sir?" Lancer asked.

"Yes, but there's one more thing," Conor said.

"What's the problem?" Karlson asked.

Conor inhaled deeply and avoided looking at Lancer. "We shouldn't use our guns. We take the target without raising a ruckus." He looked at Lancer. "We can't have Stockholm police or the C Bureau on our tail. We take sidearms and some extra magazines and use them only as a last resort." Lancer didn't look fazed, but Conor was waiting for pushback. "Any issues with that?"

"Your show, sir. But I think we should take some of these." Lancer went over to a locker and swung open the door. Hanging on four hooks were leather sheaths holding knives with five-inch handles. Lancer collected all of them and slammed the door shut. He slid one knife out of its sheath. Conor recognized the acutely tapered and sharply pointed blade of the Fairbairn-Sikes fighting knife. It was designed exclusively for close-quarters fighting and surprise attacks. Both Conor and Bobby had trained at Area F back in the States with similar weapons. "Do you know how to handle these, sirs?"

"We've been through the training. A while back, but we'll be okay. Do you have any blackjacks?"

Lancer smirked and stroked his chin. "Well, they're not what you call an official part of the legation's weapons complement, sir."

"Sounds like there's a *but* floating around in there somewhere," Bobby said.

"There sure is. I can get my hands on few. We like how quietly they can short-circuit any bad situation."

"Nicely put, Master Sergeant," Conor said, looking at his watch. "As soon as Gus comes back, we move out."

#

0100 Hours, Thursday, October 29, 1942
Andersson Summer Home, Skeppsholmen, Stockholm

Conor doused the headlights and cut the engine on the Ford as they approached the house, letting it glide down a slight slope into the stand of trees a hundred yards from the house. The light from the half-moon was intermittent due to sporadic, low cloud cover.

"Keep it quiet. Don't even shut the doors," Conor said. They approached the Marine guard, Miller, who was lying prone behind a fallen tree, and took up positions on either side of him. He was surveying the house through binoculars.

"What's the sitrep, Gunny?" Lancer asked.

Miller continued to scan the property. "Nine."

"Nine?"

"Nine guards total. A car dropped off five more about an hour ago." Miller lowered his field glasses and turned to Conor. "What now?"

Conor raised his own binoculars and studied the scene. "Shit. Where did these guys get machine pistols?"

"Doesn't really matter. What does is they have them and we don't," Lancer said.

"I did a little reconnoitering about a half hour ago. Got a little closer. The pistols are Mausers with detachable magazines that look like they could hold twenty rounds," Miller said.

"Outmanned *and* outgunned. Not the—"

185

"Bobby, really?" Conor slumped to the ground with his back against the tree trunk. *Damn it. When do things start to beak our way for a change?*

"Do you guys want some good news?" Miller asked.

"Fire away," Conor said.

"When I was over there looking around, I noticed only one guard on the back side of the house, facing the water. There's a small garage and a boathouse at the water's edge that looks like it's closed up for the season. There's a steep path from the back door down to the boat house."

"So they think that if anyone is coming for this guy Lind, they're coming in the front door," Lancer said.

"Yep, given the way they're deployed. Not real smart if you ask me," Miller said.

"We need to regroup. We move now, we blow this whole operation. There's too much at stake for that to happen," Conor said.

"We need the cavalry," Bobby said.

"Well, maybe not the cavalry, but some help from our British friends might be just as good."

CHAPTER FORTY-FIVE

0230 Hours, Thursday, October 29, 1942
German Safe House, Stockholm

Eve had remained motionless since the guards left. Emily called out to wake her, but Eve was unresponsive. Three long hours after being dumped in the cell, Eve finally began to stir. When she opened her eyes, Emily heard her say one word: ether. She sat up and looked around at her surroundings. When her gaze fell on Emily, her look became hard.

"Oh God," Eve muttered.

"Hello, Eve."

Eve brushed the hair from her face. "Emily Bright," Eve said in a scornful voice.

Emily let that one go.

Eve shifted on her mattress and wrapped her arms around her knees. "When I think about it, it makes sense they would send you to look for my husband. You knew each other well."

"We did. That's why it was hard for me to believe that he would conspire with the Germans. Was it hard for you to believe that he would do that?"

Eve began to rock back and forth. "Why have the Germans taken you?" she asked, ignoring Emily's question.

"They didn't like me snooping around. Maybe they think I might know something about your husband."

"Do they know you work for the British?"

Emily paused. They don't. At least not yet. But Eve does. "They have their suspicions."

"Oh. That's interesting," Eve said finishing off with a crooked smile.

"But the more intriguing question is: Why have they taken you?"

"I don't know. Maybe because I am the daughter of Benjamin Andersson."

"Ahh, you're their leverage. And that comes into play when you're trying to do a deal with someone. Your father and the Germans are dealing. For what, Eve?"

Eve didn't respond, but she stopped rocking and stared at Emily.

Footsteps from above drew their attention. When the rush of water from a flushing toilet above them sounded, they both looked at each other.

"Has your father told his Nazi friends that you are Gunnar's loving wife?"

"Of course not." Eve struggled to her feet. Unsteady, she braced herself by gripping the bars of the cell door. "He wouldn't do that … put me in danger."

"Well, here you are. In danger." Emily decided she would hold off pressing Eve on what she knew about the Germans. She was more curious about other matters. "How did you get out of England?"

"I traveled with Conor Thorn. I am helping him find Gunnar."

Emily scoffed. "Can't be much help behind bars." Eve started to open her mouth, but Emily cut her off. "Do you know if Conor has made any progress?"

"None that I know of. He's more arrogant than effective." Eve squinted at Emily. "What happened to your face? It looks bruised. Did someone—"

"Hit me? Yes. Maybe you've run into him yourself. He wears an eye patch."

"Yes. The bastard with the ether."

Emily ran her hand down the side of her face. Her cheekbone was still tender, as was the memory of being knocked unconscious. "Speaking of the Nazis. You would think that knowing you're Gunner's wife would be valuable information. Wouldn't you say?"

Eve leaned against the cell door and made no attempt to respond; a look of concern overcame her face as Emily spoke. "To be able to threaten the safety, the life, of not only the daughter of the man they're dealing with but the wife of the—"

"Stop. It would seem that we both have information that we don't want revealed. My connection to Gunnar and yours to British intelligence." Eve pushed off the cell door toward the bars that divided the two cells. Her knuckles turned white as she squeezed the bars. "They would never let either of us go if they knew the truth about us."

Emily paused. Eve thought the Nazis didn't know she was Gunnar's wife. Emily thought the Nazis probably already knew who she was and whom Emily was working for. "All right, Eve. On the chance they don't already know, we'll keep each other's secret."

Eve exhaled and released her grip on the cell bars. She returned to her mattress and closed her eyes.

"So, Eve, where is your father hiding Gunnar?"

CHAPTER FORTY-SIX

0800 Hours, Thursday, October 29, 1942
German Legation, Södra Blasieholmshammer 2, Stockholm

Eklof offered Andersson a seat, but he declined. He wouldn't be there long. Eklof sat behind Lina Stuben's desk, his feet propped on top. He had just explained that Stuben had been called to Berlin but would be returning to complete their arrangement, so Andersson's only choice was to deal with the man who had most likely abducted his daughter. He thought about asking what the Germans hoped to accomplish by doing that, but he already knew the answer—to keep him in line.

"Where is my daughter?"

"What do you mean?"

"I understand why you took her. Have you harmed her?"

Eklof removed his feet from the desktop and fingered his eye patch, repositioning it slightly. "You seem very calm for someone who has misplaced his daughter."

"I am a businessman who has, on occasion, had to do certain things to protect my business, to make sure matters always turn out in my favor. You and Ms. Stuben seem to be like-minded. Am I correct?"

Eklof smiled. "She has not been harmed."

"That is very good news. Am I right to assume that once we have concluded our business she will be returned ... unharmed?"

"It is not that simple. We will make a judgment as to the value of the information you are selling. If the information is judged to have high value, then our dealings will conclude favorably and your daughter will be returned. If the information is disappointing … well then …"

Eve's abduction made it difficult to accept the offer from the Russian, but Andersson would find a way. "Your judgment seems rather subjective. I am not comfortable with that."

"Your comfort is not my concern," Eklof said with a dismissive wave of his hand. "Is there anything else you wish to discuss?"

Andersson abruptly took his leave. Ten paces down the hall, he could hear Eklof laughing.

CHAPTER FORTY-SEVEN

0800 Hours, Thursday, October 29, 1942
United States Legation, Strandvägen 7A, Stockholm, Sweden

Conor raced through an update on the situation at the summer house, while Karlson sat behind his desk and listened. He couldn't remember when he last slept. Conor rubbed his eyes with his fingertips. His beard stubble was getting out of control. His brain was slowing down.

"You made the right call. But the problem is, I can't come up with any more men. We are thinly staffed as it is."

"I think we need some help from Captain Masterman. Can you reach out and see if he has any manpower to lend us a hand? At least four men to match their numbers?"

"Sure, but I can't do that by phone. The Swedes tap most of the lines in and out of the legations. I'll have to go to his office."

A knock at the door was followed by the entrance of Bob Homer. "Good morning, gentlemen," he said, shutting the door. "What's the update?"

"We found Lind. That's the good news. We're doing some planning on how to grab him, but I think it's best that you don't know the rest. If you could just keep Ramsay out of our hair, that would be a help," Karlson said.

Homer nodded. "Are you keeping the Brits in the know?"

"Yes. I'll be seeing them inside of thirty minutes."

"Good. I want updates on the hour," Homer said.

After he left, Conor got up and headed for the door.

"Where are you going?" Karlson said.

"We need a boat. I'm going to ask Seaker to find one."

#

On the sixth floor, Conor found Seaker at his desk drinking a cup of coffee. He looked a little banged up from the previous night—his eyes were red, and good-sized bags now drooped from them. The scratch marks on the side of his neck, though—Conor hadn't expected those.

"Good morning, Buster. How was your night?"

Seaker saw Conor staring at his neck. "Oh ... these," Seaker said, touching the scratches with the tips of his fingers. "Yeah, what can I say? It got a little crazy last night."

"I can see that."

"You look like a man on a mission at this early hour. You also look like I feel."

"It's been a long few days," Conor said, noticing that Seaker hadn't forgotten to lay on the Brylcreem this morning. "I need a favor. I need to get my hands on a boat. Maybe a sixteen or eighteen footer. For tonight."

"Something tells me it's not for sightseeing."

"No. Not quite."

"I know someone that has one like that. He keeps it tied up just west of Beckholmen Island. It's in rough shape, but it runs."

"That works. Can you make the arrangements?"

"Sure. Glad to help. It'll just take a bottle of good bourbon. I'll take it out of my supply. You can owe me." Seaker took a sip of his coffee.

Conor didn't make a move to leave. He had some questions, and they had some time to kill before the mission launched.

"Buster, last night you said that you dated Sue Ryan your last year at the academy. That was thirty-six, right?"

Seaker tilted his head and gave Conor a quizzical look. "That's right."

"Then you said you got together a couple of times after that. When exactly?"

"Why all the questions, Conor?"

"I don't know. I was just thinking about her."

Seaker kept his eyes on Conor as he drained his coffee. "We saw each other a couple of times early last year. She was living in Washington, and I was flying out of Anacostia. She just got divorced and needed some company; she picked me. Go figure," he said with a smile.

Conor nodded. "My sister, Maggie, got a letter from her last week. Sue was diagnosed with heart disease and doesn't have long to live. I thought you'd want to know."

"No shit? That's rough. She's a sweet girl. Sad news. Say, by the way, speaking of your sister, I was at a dinner last year, and she was there. It was at Grace's father's place. I didn't get a chance to talk to her though."

Conor gave Seaker a long, hard look; he needed to back off asking questions. Conor needed a cooperative Seaker for the operation. He forced a smiled, then got up and reached for the doorknob. "By the way, where did you meet Greta? She seemed nice."

"Whoa, hold your horses there, Conor. You trying to muscle in on my territory?"

"No ... no. I'm a loner these days."

Seaker put his hands behind his head and stretched out in his chair. "Yeah, she's a real sweet thing. Quite taken with ol' Buster, if I may say. She's a secretary at the British Legation. Met her at some diplomatic welcoming party a while back. Lost touch but saw her one day over at the Strand Hotel, right across the bay."

Another forced smile and a nod of the head and Conor opened the door. "One more favor—I need a coxswain. You up for that?"

Seaker sat up. "Well, I ... I guess," Seaker said in a quiet uncertain voice.

"Good. I'll be in touch." Conor headed down the stairs to Karlson's office. He needed some time to put everything about Seaker together, but he pretty much knew what the picture was going to look like.

CHAPTER FORTY-EIGHT

0900 Hours, Thursday, October 29, 1942
Heinrich Himmler's Office, Prinz-Albrecht-Strasse 9, Berlin

Himmler never ceased to surprise Schellenberg. First, it was learning of Himmler's interest in astrology, then graphology. Then, one day, Himmler went on and on about his hatred of lawyers. But today's revelation about Himmler, the head of the quarter-million-man-strong SS, was astounding. He was a prolific gift giver, and as he explained the card index of his gift giving, Schellenberg heard in his voice the passion one would hear from a bird watcher who had just seen an extremely rare species.

"You see, Walter, first you always have to know whom you have given a present to so as not to give the same gift twice, and second, you ought not to give too much, or people become acquisitive. For example, my usual gifts are candlesticks, plates, SS calendars for male recipients and a half a pound of coffee or chocolate, bacon, or canned sardines for the women." Himmler, his head bowed, shuffled through the index cards in an olive-colored metal box, his wire-rimmed glasses slipping down his nose. "As you know, I have a great interest in graphology. Just from the way the letter of thanks is written, you can establish what sort of a person the writer is. This information is of great value to me."

"May I see the card you have for me?" Schellenberg asked.

A thin smile appeared. "If you like." Himmler pulled a card from the box, glanced at it, and pushed it across his desk.

As Schellenberg read the card, Himmler settled back in his chair, most likely watching for his reaction. The card was full of gift-giving details, a bookkeeper's work of art. It contained Schellenberg's birth date, rank, position in and Nazi Party number, number of children, wife's maiden name, address, and how he should be addressed. Schellenberg noticed that his second wife's maiden name was misspelled. He thought of pointing out the error but decided against it. Why put Himmler in a defensive mood? It would make the upcoming meeting with Lina Stuben more difficult than it had to be.

"Herr Himmler, I am truly amazed by the detail," Schellenberg said, making a mental note to be careful when writing anything to Himmler.

When Brandt escorted Stuben into the office, Himmler took the card from Schellenberg and refiled it.

"Hello, Lina. I trust you had a good flight?" Himmler said as he handed the file box to Brandt, then motioned for Stuben to take a seat. "Rudolf, please correct the spelling of Walter's wife's maiden name. You must be more careful in the future."

Schellenberg worked hard to suppress a smile.

"Yes, Reichsführer. I shall."

Stuben sat with a straight back on the edge of the chair and placed a small black leather satchel at her feet. She was dressed in a dark pantsuit that one moment looked black, then dark blue. The double-breasted jacket was tailored, hugging the curve of her waist. The ends of her straight blond hair were angled starting just below her ears and ending at her collarbone. The look resembled Cleopatra in schoolbooks. She was more attractive than Schellenberg remembered. He watched Himmler, looking for any signs of arousal at seeing his former mistress but saw none.

Schellenberg had read her file the night before and learned that her father was a fervent, loyal, and early member of the Nazi party who worked with Minister of Armaments and War Production Albert Speer. He was divorced from Stuben's mother, a Swede, after she was discovered bedding down with one of her husband's coworkers. Lina hadn't seen her mother in five years. She was her father's daughter.

"Reichsführer Himmler, I am honored to be in your presence

once again." Stuben rested her tightly clasped hands in her lap, the veins on the back of her hands clearly visible.

Himmler waved off the comment. "Give me a full report on this affair that will cost the Reich almost six hundred thousand Reichsmarks," Himmler said.

Lina Stuben did just that. The report told them nothing they didn't already know. Himmler looked at Schellenberg several times to check his reactions, especially to Stuben's growing distrust of Benjamin Andersson. When she finally reported something new—the abduction of Andersson's daughter—Himmler smiled and nodded rapidly.

"Do not harm her. Just return her safely when the arrangement concludes in our favor," Himmler said. "After all, we need the man's ball bearings to win the war."

"And if it does not end in our favor, Reichsführer? What are your orders then?"

"You are never to return to Berlin."

And watch your back, Schellenberg thought.

Stuben stayed silent.

"This intercept about my visit to Rome—do you have it?" Himmler asked.

"Yes, Reichsführer," Stuben said, reaching for her satchel. She flipped open the top flap and pulled out a file. Her hand was shaking as she handed over the paper. Himmler's threats, especially the calmly delivered ones, consistently produced such reactions.

Himmler, his brow furrowed deeply as his face paled, read the message and passed it to Schellenberg. The three short paragraphs, marked at the top in bold letters MOST SECRET, dryly laid out the time and place of the fete honoring Himmler. But the phrase in the last line of the intercept—OPPORTUNITY FOR TERMINATION—wasn't something he remembered being in the last report Stuben transmitted. Himmler sat staring at her.

Schellenberg's words cut through the silence. "Reichsführer, if I may?"

Himmler gave a curt nod.

"Stuben, have you received any specific information or indications as to what this intelligence would be?"

Stuben turned to him. The red flush to her cheeks didn't seem as vivid as when she'd walked in. "I can only surmise that, given his background, it has something to do with military codes."

"Ours or theirs?" Schellenberg asked.

"I do not know. Maybe both."

Himmler looked at his watch and stood. The two subordinates followed his lead. "Come back at one o'clock. The money will be here. I shouldn't have to say this, but I will nonetheless. Do not fail me."

"I swear that I shall not fail you, Reichsführer." Stuben didn't move.

The three of them stood there awkwardly.

"What?" Himmler said with a raised voice. "Do you have more to report?"

Stuben stiffened. "Yes, Reichsführer." She cleared her throat. "The Americans are spreading lies in Stockholm about back-channel peace agreements with the Western Allies. I have been told by an American from their legation that Herr Langbehn and Dr. Kersten are involved."

Himmler dropped back into his chair. Her delivery of the damning claim was weak voiced and questioning, as if what she wanted to say was *Please say this is untrue.*

Schellenberg retook his seat as well, his mind racing.

Stuben remained standing. "He told me that these … feelers have been put out by you. I thought it my duty to report these preposterous claims to you directly."

Himmler gave Schellenberg a hard look. Schellenberg could only think of the stress and consternation he harbored when he'd first broached the plan to Himmler at Zhytomyr. "Who exactly is spreading this trash?" Schellenberg asked.

"An agent named Thorn. He is newly arrived in Stockholm and has proved to be a nuisance."

"Thank you, Lina. Our enemies will do and say anything to divide us. But that will not happen, will it?"

"Of course not, Herr Reichsführer."

Himmler nodded slowly. "Give your written report to the brigadeführer, then, please, give us a moment."

Stuben nodded, grabbed her satchel, and exited the office with long strides.

"Walter, that woman should not live to see the morning sun." Himmler's pale face showed no emotion, but his eyes narrowed on the door she had just walked through. He was thinking. "It must be done quickly and thoroughly. To be sure she is not identified, remove her teeth. All of them. Before or after you shoot her in the head, I don't care."

Schellenberg realized he was holding his breath as Himmler rattled off his orders. The juxtaposition of the horrific nature of his orders and Himmler's calm state was uncomfortable to witness.

"Remove any jewelry. Make sure you check for the necklace I gave her. It is inscribed. You may keep any of it."

Schellenberg let out a long, slow breath. It struck him that Himmler sounded like he was ordering dinner at a restaurant—no emotion, precise, monotone.

Himmler's gaze snapped to Schellenberg. "Have all her records in Berlin and Stockholm concerning her service to the Reich destroyed. Her father will, in time, reach out to us. But make sure he is directed to you so you can adeptly deflect any questions as to her whereabouts. Maybe a story of her traitorous activities on behalf of the Soviets will be enough to make him stop his inquiries." Himmler stopped but did not unlock his gaze.

Schellenberg finally nodded.

"Lastly, Brandt's apartment building has an incinerator. He will tell you how to access it. It will serve our purposes well, as it has in the past."

"I understand, Reichsführer. It will take be taken care of." He got up to leave.

"And, Walter, as far as this matter regarding the purchase of intelligence—I want the intelligence *and* this traitor who is selling it. If it proves worthless, I may want to exact some revenge for making us look so foolish."

Schellenberg turned toward the door.

"Oh, one last thing. Take a camera. I want proof of her demise."

#

In Himmler's outer office, the reichsführer's assistant, Brandt, typed away while Lina sat straight backed, her satchel on her lap. Her hands were clasped tightly together to hide the tremors. The turn the meeting took was upsetting. But she felt strongly that she had no choice. The reichsführer had to be told there were people dragging his name into traitorous plots. Brigadeführer Schellenberg walked over to Brandt and had a short conversation. Brandt scribbled on a paper and handed it to him.

He patted the man on his shoulder and gave him a quick nod before he turned and approached her. She stood abruptly, her satchel nearly slipping from her lap. He was smiling, which relieved some of the angst that was building inside her.

"Lina, that was an excellent report. This arrangement with this man Andersson could have a major impact on the war. This could mean a significant promotion for you."

"Should that happen, I would be only too pleased to have contributed to our glorious cause. But, Brigadeführer, was I right to disclose the … other matter? I was torn as to what was expected of me." She hoped the quavering in her voice wasn't noticeable.

"Lina, Lina. Please do not worry. We hear of these types of ridiculous fantasies all the time. Come, walk with me." The brigadeführer headed to the door, Lina a pace behind him.

The hallway had marble floors with a high sheen that reflected the sunlight from a row of windows along one wall. Staff rushing in the opposite direction saw Schellenberg and gave them a wide berth. He leaned in as they walked, so he could be heard without speaking too loudly.

"My driver will take you to the Aldon Hotel. Wait there for me while I conclude some matters with the reichsführer. We will dine there, a late breakfast, to celebrate your stellar report and your looming success. Then we will return for your … shall we call it your package."

"Brigadeführer, I cannot impose upon you. I am sure you have many matters to attend to more important than me. I—"

"Nonsense, Lina. This morning, *this* is the most important item on my list," he said, smiling broadly.

She marveled at how white his teeth were. His reassuring words triggered a release of the tension that had gripped her since her arrival in Berlin.

Outside the RSHA building, dark clouds were rolling in. On Prinz-Albrecht-Strasse, a Mercedes was parked, which the brigadeführer approached. An untersturmführer, a burly man with the thick neck of a heavyweight boxer, sat in the front seat next to the driver, who started the engine as soon as Schellenberg made eye contact. Lina was shocked that the brigadeführer himself held the door open for her. As she slipped into the back seat, a cloud of cigarette smoke escaped from the open door. She thanked him, and he smiled again, his teeth gleaming.

Before he closed the door, he summoned his aide. "Untersturmführer Lindemann."

The man jumped from the car and hurried toward his superior officer.

Schellenberg talked for several moments with his back to the idling car, then handed Lindemann the note Brandt had given him earlier. While she watched, Lina's stomach growled, reminding her that she had not eaten since midday the day before. It was a high honor to dine with the brigadeführer—an honor that her father would be most proud of. The anticipation brought a smile to her face.

Lindemann saluted Brigadeführer Schellenberg and dashed around the back of the car. Lina's smile faded when Lindemann joined her in the back seat. As the Mercedes pulled from the curb, Lindemann reached over and locked her door. She looked out the window and saw Brigadeführer Schellenberg. His smile slowly faded into a sneer.

In that moment, she knew what Thorn said was true. "Where are you taking me?"

No answer.

"I asked you—"

"Somewhere deep in the woods, where no one will hear you scream."

CHAPTER FORTY-NINE

0930 Hours, Thursday, October 29, 1942
Café Mona Lisa, Österlånggatan 17, Gamla Stan, Stockholm

Benjamin Andersson had to demand the outside table after being told by the café staff they had closed the outside area for the season. They pointed at the sky as dark, angry clouds passed slowly overhead, but eventually, they scrambled to retrieve a table and place settings for two from the rear of the restaurant. He didn't want anyone to hear what was to be discussed at that table.

Andersson ordered a cup of coffee. "I am not interested in any of your ersatz coffee. Save that for ... others. I will pay whatever it costs. This morning, I am your best customer." He looked at his watch. It had been a little over thirteen hours since he had received the offer from the Russian. The morning was still early, the sun shielded by the café itself. The bronze statue of Saint George, an eight-foot sword raised above his head, a dragon below about to be slain, loomed over a granite water fountain across the narrow cobblestone street, water gurgled in a slow trickle into its three large stone basins.

Andersson wondered when the man sitting on the edge of the fountain—not the one who delivered the message at the Grand Hotel—would make the move to join him. This man was clearly better dressed. He wore a dark suit with an open-collared white shirt. An attaché case was resting between a pair of brown shoes. He had been smoking a cigarette and doing a poor job of pretending to read a newspaper while observing Andersson. Andersson thought he could just get up from his table, signaling that he was done waiting, or he could just wave the man over.

When the man looked his way, Andersson finally raised his hand and pointed in an exaggerated fashion to his watch. The man looked up and down Österlånggatan, tucked his newspaper under his arm, and sauntered over to Andersson's table. Before he sat, he snuffed out his cigarette in an ashtray.

Andersson's gaze was on the man's attaché case, leather and seemingly well used, as the leather bore several deep gouges. The area surrounding the two clasps was a deeper color, most likely having absorbed the oil from fingers that had opened the clasps many times.

"As you have observed—for quite some time, I must say—I was not followed," Andersson said.

A waiter approached and took the man's order—a glass of water.

"And your name?" Andersson asked.

"That's quite possibly the least important piece of information you could ask for this morning."

Andersson's raised eyebrows signaled his surprise. The man's accent was unmistakably Irish.

"Yes, I get that a lot. The look of complete shock is usually followed by questions of 'Why?' and 'For how long?' and sometimes 'Do you do it for the money?' if they are bolder than usual."

"The why is easy—the Irish have an abundance of hatred for the British. How long? Not important. As for whether you do it for money, I would hope so. It would be foolish not to." The pointed comments brought a look of annoyance. "Excuse my insolence. I usually do not annoy someone I am negotiating with. It's a bad strategy."

"Your words, Mr. Andersson. Now ... the intelligence?"

"Yes. Down to business. It's a shame I did not get a chance to explain to your messenger last night that I personally do not have this intelligence. I am merely an intermediary. What I can do is tell you the day and time when what you seek will have fallen into the hands of the Germans. You can take the intelligence from them."

The man's laughter drowned out the noise from the fountain

and spooked a flock of pigeons. "You double-dealing snake. I was told to be mindful of such a ploy. A consummate capitalist—my disdain for you has grown dramatically. You steal from both the Germans and the Soviet Union. Perhaps you are truly neutral in this conflict."

"We Swedes have friends everywhere."

"I hope they have your back because you are playing a very dangerous game, Mr. Andersson." The man lit another cigarette and tossed the packet of English Players on the table as he blew a stream of smoke across the table into Andersson's face. "And the location of this exchange with the Germans?"

"That will be communicated to the Soviet Legation thirty minutes before the information is in German hands. It will take you no more than thirty minutes to reach the location. I have checked the timing."

The man took another drag, squinting at Andersson through the smoke. "Well, what I can tell *you* is that, in our opinion, it's doubtful that the intelligence you are selling is worth the price you have set for it. You could say that we have come to our senses, overcome a moment of hysteria. In fact, we think it's worth a fraction of what we told you we'd pay."

"Then why offer what you did?"

"To get you to the table, of course."

Andersson started to squirm but then froze.

"And speaking of our offer, it was to cover the inclusion of the person you are representing ... *if* such a person exists."

"I cannot hand him over. It is not possible. That is why I am willing to compromise."

"Another reason why the intelligence is not worth what we initially offered. But tell me, compromise how?"

"I will take twenty-five percent of what you offered now. Once you have the intelligence in hand, you will deliver another twenty-five percent."

"You are very trusting, to say the least. Nothing would stop us from disappearing with the intelligence and the balance."

"You are right. But after you pass the first twenty-five percent to me, the person you seek and the intelligence could also quite possibly disappear. I am no more trusting than you need to be."

The man took a sip of his water, looking over the rim of the glass at Andersson all the while.

To give him time to consider the situation, Andersson turned to the bronze statue looming above their table. "Saint George and the dragon. One of several dragon slayers from Christian lore. Did you know that Saint George is the patron saint of Moscow?"

The man turned toward the statue.

"And did you know that the country of Georgia takes its name from Saint George?"

The man ground his cigarette in the ashtray. "It's the Republic of Georgia, and it is a part of the Soviet Union. Spare me the history lessons. I grew up drowning in history."

"I see."

"No. I don't believe you do. You see, matters have changed since we presented our offer, Mr. Andersson. We know the Germans have taken your daughter."

Andersson stifled his look of surprise, sat back, and folded his arms.

"Actually, I'm surprised you're even here trying to make a deal, knowing that if the Germans found out, your daughter would surely die. Just what were you thinking?"

Andersson's wife often told him that his penchant for always thinking he was the most intelligent man in the room would one day cause him great embarrassment and possibly harm. His plan to recover Eve was to simply demand she be returned to him before the planned exchange; if she wasn't, there would be no intelligence and ... no future deliveries of ball bearings, machine tools, and other items vital for waging war against the Allies. "I have that matter well in hand."

"I doubt that. Actually, I doubt you know how ruthless the Nazis can be at all."

"As ruthless as the Russians?"

The man chuckled. "Yes, maybe so. But once you hear my proposal, you'll agree that we ... you might say, have a heart."

"Go on."

"Once the intelligence has been taken from the Germans, we will pay five hundred thousand krona *and* give you the location of where your daughter is being held. You will need to move quickly to retrieve her before the Germans become aware of your back-stabbing as she is under guard. And here is a bit of advice for free: be prepared to fight to reclaim her. And while we don't appreciate you trying to cash in on both the Soviet Union's and Germany's needs, we don't mind killing a few Nazis to get what we want. Those are our terms." The man looked at his watch. "We'll play your game, Mr. Andersson, but only to a point. So, do you agree to proceed?"

The pigeons returned to the street, pecking away at the cobblestones. Andersson looked up at the statue once more and thought that he might not be Saint George in the events now playing out, but maybe the dragon being slain. This prospect did not sit well with him. "Yes."

"We are done here, Mr. Andersson." He picked up the weather-beaten attaché case and tucked it under his arm. Andersson wondered if there ever was any money inside it. "I'll leave you and Saint George to mull over our scintillating conversation."

CHAPTER FIFTY

1130 Hours, Thursday, October 29, 1942
Heinrich Himmler's Office, Prinz-Albrecht-Strasse 9, Berlin

Schellenberg stood at attention and fired off a Nazi Party salute. Himmler, without looking up, flipped his right hand toward the ceiling and continued to read a file. Schellenberg remained standing.

"Well?" Himmler asked, prompting his subordinate.

"It is done."

"And?"

"I will be on a flight to Stockholm in two hours to complete the transaction."

Himmler fell back in his chair and folded his arms. "Did she mention my name at any point? Did she plead for her life?"

"She ... Untersturmführer Lindemann said she said she had one regret, that she failed you." A lie, of course. "After saying that, she was ... inconsolable." In a way, she was. Her screams for leniency were quite loud, according to Lindemann.

Himmler considered his response in a brooding fashion. "But you guarantee it is done."

"I do."

"And the photos?"

"They will be developed in short order, Reichsführer."

Schellenberg saw that the details agonized Himmler. Rubbing the back of his neck, Himmler muttered something indistinguishable.

"Sir?"

"I said this plan—your plan—was a mistake. I should have never let you talk me into it."

"Respectfully, I don't—"

"The idea of discussions with the British and Americans was a fool's errand from the start." Himmler's body became rigid, as it often did when he experienced pain deep in his abdomen. His eyes closed tight.

"Reichsführer, shall I send for Dr. Kersten?"

Himmler waited for a full minute before responding. Then he said through clenched teeth, "No, it can wait until after he delivers his report to me."

Schellenberg knew he had to calm Himmler down, keep him from derailing the process to save Germany.

Himmler opened his eyes. "Getting rid of Ribbentrop by Christmas of this year, signaling to the British and Americans a change in policy on Germany's part, could have been accomplished. But getting Bormann on board with any plan to deal with the Western powers had little chance of happening."

Schellenberg agreed. "Sir, do not waver. You yourself have said that war between England and Germany was a war between brothers. They are not the true enemy of the Reich. Look to the east, you always said."

"Do you not realize that if any word of this peace plan were to reach Hitler, my life is over?" His last words were spoken in a tone that made Schellenberg think it wasn't the first time the realization hit him. A long stretch of quiet ensued. Schellenberg was gathering his thoughts for another run at boosting Himmler's resolve when Himmler pounded his open hand on the desk. It was loud enough to bring Brandt into the office to ask if the reichsführer needed anything. Himmler waved him off.

"That was the way I felt this morning, after Stuben's report about this man Thorn. But the news from Stalingrad is bleak. The counteroffensive you spoke of yesterday—sixty thousand troops, Germany's finest, and two tank divisions … two," Himmler said. His voice got harsher as he continued, "It has been stopped." He became sullen. "We are losing, Walter. And the Western Allies have yet to open a second front. America has been in the war for less than a year. Their factories are only now reaching full production. Even if our Luftwaffe could reach their shores, the outlook is bleak."

Schellenberg sat back. He need not add any arguments about continuing with their plan.

"We must press on in some way and save Germany," a spent Himmler mumbled.

#

Himmler kept Dr. Kersten and Carl Langbehn waiting for over thirty minutes while he retreated to his bathroom to rest and regain some energy. When the two emissaries started their report on their meeting at the American Legation, Himmler mostly listened, which allowed Schellenberg to ask carefully chosen questions that he'd developed after a chance meeting he had with Kersten earlier. Kersten delivered most of the report, which helped their peace-plan cause, given Himmler and Kersten's unusually strong relationship.

Kersten followed Schellenberg's suggestion to play down any overt negativity voiced by the Americans, and Himmler jumped in to ask how one of his SD agents came to learn of their meeting.

"There was an incident the evening after we met with the Americans. It involved a man named Conor Thorn, who also attended our meeting as an interpreter."

"What type of incident?" Himmler asked.

"That is not clear to me. There seems to be some bad blood between this Thorn and members of our legation's staff. He's quite an unpredictable individual. Strangely, he seemed to carry most of the Americans' side of the meeting."

"*Pfft*. He was utterly rude," Langbehn said. "We should have left once he started to insult ..." Langbehn looked at Kersten.

"Insult whom?" Himmler asked.

Schellenberg squirmed in his seat. He'd told Kersten not to mention too much about Thorn. Obviously, Kersten had failed to tell his cohort the same.

"Actually, I don't quite remember. But he was rude. He—"

"There were words between Thorn and Lina Stuben. He may have shared information about our meeting, Reichsführer," Kersten said.

Himmler removed his glasses and began to clean them with a handkerchief, something he often did while he pulled his thoughts together. "You both have failed me and mishandled this vital assignment. I believe you have misread our enemies. Maybe you have shared too much." Himmler rose, as did Kersten and Langbehn, both with pale, slack faces. "But hear me when I say, regardless of the fact that you are members of my inner circle, I will not hesitate to silence you both if I feel you have betrayed this discussion to Ribbentrop, Bormann, or Hitler in the slightest way. Now go."

Two minutes passed. Schellenberg watched Himmler pace behind his desk, which gave him time to process the fact that, should Himmler's plan succeed, Schellenberg's own stature would rise considerably as well. His determination would be rewarded with greater control and influence over German affairs, both internal and external. It would be smart to take bold risks to achieve that power, no matter the costs.

"Reichsführer, what are your orders?"

Himmler stopped and turned on his heel like a foot soldier on the parade ground. "My resolve has been compromised, but it has not been drained. When you go to Stockholm to complete the arrangement with Andersson, seek out the Americans. The British are too pigheaded. Tell them that time is running out."

CHAPTER FIFTY-ONE

1130 Hours, Thursday, October 29, 1942
United States Legation, Strandvägen 7A, Stockholm

Time is running out. Conor stared so intently at a calendar on the wall of the gun room he thought it would catch fire. The motor gun boat's ball bearing run to England was set for Friday night, he hadn't grabbed Lind, Emily was still missing, and they still had the six-hour trip to Lysekil ahead of them.

Your level of success is overwhelming.

The door was propped open to mitigate the damp stuffiness in the room, so Conor heard the elevator door squeal as it opened down the hall. Karlson emerged and hurried toward Conor, sporting a sly smile. Good—he needed some positive news.

Karlson flung his raincoat and hat clear across the table and onto the floor. "I found you four men. Or I should say, Masterman did."

Conor slapped him on his back. "You came through. Fantastic. Who are they?"

"Three of them are members of RAF aircrews. Two Halifax bombers were too damaged to get back to England after taking mine-laying runs at the Tirpitz in Norway this past spring."

"You're kidding. Aren't they in Swedish camps for the duration?"

"They were. But as the war has progressed, the Swedes have been a little more lenient. Some of the crews were actually in flats in towns close to the main internment camps. The Swedes

211

even repatriate crews back to England periodically, along with Luftwaffe crews, playing it down the middle."

"So what am I missing here?"

"They fly them out of Bromma, and they're already in Stockholm. Actually, they're at the British Legation. They're scheduled to leave tomorrow night for Scotland."

Conor looked at the calendar on the wall. "What did Masterman tell them?"

Karlson pulled out a metal chair and sat. "Just enough to convince the fly-boys that this was an extremely critical mission that would impact the future of the war—and that Churchill was being updated daily. They say they will do what they have to."

"You said four."

"Number four is Roper-Hastings. I believe you know him."

"Yeah, I do, but he didn't strike me as a 'storm the beach' kinda guy."

"Masterman said that he had orders that MI6 had to be a part of any operation to get Lind."

"Well, that settles that," Conor said. He looked at his watch. "Get them all here for a briefing at fifteen hundred." He paused and thought about his earlier conversation with Seaker. "I need a favor … a strange one. I can't give you all the reasons for this, but can you call Captain Masterman and have him check on a secretary who works there named Greta? I don't have her last name, but he probably knows her."

"That the Greta that was with Seaker last night?"

"The same."

"Okay. But I don't like the smell of this."

"Neither do—"

The squeal of the elevator door opening interrupted them. Bobby and Gunny Miller headed down the hall to the gun room. The third man who exited the elevator was Seaker himself, and as the three men entered the room, Bobby put as much distance between himself and Seaker as the small room allowed.

"Any changes at the house?" Conor said.

"Nope. Very quiet. Except for a delivery truck from a market, dropping off food, I guess. Master Sergeant Lancer is on watch," Bobby reported.

Conor nodded. "Seaker?"

"The deal for the boat is done. It's a thirty-three-foot Pettersson Backdecker. It can handle about ten people. Tight, but it should work. It cost me two bottles of the best bourbon from my stock."

"Your liver thanks you. Is it over on Beckholmen, like you said?"

"Yeah. Fuel topped off, ready to go."

Conor glanced at his watch. "Okay, I want our RAF friends and everybody in this room back here at fifteen hundred hours."

"RAF friends?" Bobby asked.

"I'll fill you in later. As I was saying, back here at fifteen hundred." Everyone nodded except Seaker. "Are you ready?" Conor asked, looking at the man.

"I'm not sure exactly what to get ready for," Seaker said.

"Just steer the boat and try not to get killed."

CHAPTER FIFTY-TWO

1500 Hours, Thursday, October 29, 1942
German Safe House, Stockholm

Emily would bargain with the devil for five minutes outside, breathing in lungfuls of fresh air. Added to the ever-present odor of rotten vegetables was the stench coming from the bucket in Eve Lind's cell. Earlier that morning, Eve had sat on her mattress, her back against the river rock wall with the bucket in her lap. Her vomiting lasted for a quarter hour. Emily had been curious; Eve hadn't eaten anything since she'd arrived. She'd ruled out a pregnancy, given that Gunnar revealed to Emily that he couldn't have children, but, Emily thought, that wouldn't stop a woman who was dead set on having them.

After Eve's wave of sickness passed that morning, Emily pressed her about her relationship with Gunnar. When Emily brought up her disbelief that Gunnar had a mistress and mentioned his previous declaration of his devotion to Eve and that it seemed deeply heartfelt, Eve had dismissed the comment with a wave of her hand.

"I know Gunnar too well, and he only confides in me. He is too shy a man to reveal anything private, especially to a woman he hardly knows."

"Oh? If that's right, he doesn't sound like a man who would have a mistress."

Eve glared at Emily, then yelled, "I have the letters. You saw them. And empty bank accounts. That's all the proof I need. All you have is a lie that he was devoted to me." She then retreated from the conversation.

Emily wanted to press her more about the letters and why Gunnar didn't take them with him, but Eve's overwrought response to her probing convinced her to back off. That had been over three hours ago.

The door to the basement opened, and the young guard came loping down the stairs. It was the time of day when they collected the morning meal plates. Before he reached the bottom of the stairs, Emily quickly reached for her cell bucket and began to dry heave into it. She planned on feigning sickness, but the odor of her own waste made the act very convincing.

The guard stopped at the bottom of the stairs and wouldn't get closer. He looked down at the floor of her cell. "You haven't touched your food. That is not good."

"The food is what is making us sick," Emily said in between heaves.

"Fine, then don't eat. Soon you will be someone else's trouble."

"Please, empty my bucket. It's full."

Ignoring the request with a half smile, he grabbed the two plates of cabbage and black bread and headed up the stairs.

"Are you all right?" Eve asked.

Emily wasn't going to tell Eve she was faking. "I could be better."

"What did he mean, 'someone else's problem'? Did he mean both of us?"

"You'd have to ask him that. But given what I know, my guess would be yes."

"Just what *do* you know?"

Emily answered with a question of her own. "How far along are you?"

The question brought an incredulous look from Eve, followed by the slow shaking of her head. "You are mistaken. I am not pregnant."

"Morning sickness, weight gain, a fuller bust line. You're a doctor. What would you tell a woman in such condition?"

"I would say to stop eating poorly."

"I'm not a doctor, but I would say, 'Congratulations to you ... and the father.'" *Whoever that might be.*

CHAPTER FIFTY-THREE

1515 Hours, Thursday, October 29, 1942
United States Legation, Strandvägen 7A, Stockholm

Bobby, Karlson, and Lancer had arrived first for the briefing, followed by Captain Masterman, three British airmen, and Roper-Hastings, all dressed in civilian work clothes. Introductions were made and several of the airmen and Lancer took the opportunity to light up while they waited for Seaker to arrive.

Conor joined Roper-Hastings and shook hands.

"Thanks for inviting this old man to your party," Roper-Hastings said.

"It could be a noisy and messy party, James."

"So be it. There needs to be someone there from British Intelligence along for the ride. It is our mess to clean up, isn't it?"

"I see where you're coming from. Just keep close to the ground. C is running out of agents."

Roper-Hastings laughed and rejoined the group of airmen.

Masterman came over to Conor and offered a cigarette, which Conor declined. Masterman slipped one out of his packet and lit up.

"Any news?" Conor asked.

Masterman reached into his breast pocket and handed him a note.

When Conor finished reading, he placed it in an ashtray, bummed a match from Masterman, and burned it.

"Anything you want to tell me?"

"Not yet. I need a little time to see how things play out."

Masterman nodded.

Just when Conor finally asked Karlson to head over to 7B and the attaché offices to find Seaker, the elevator door squealed open to reveal the man himself. All eyes turned to Seaker as he entered the gun room. He took up a position leaning against the wall just inside. Conor stared at Seaker, but Seaker wouldn't play. His gaze was locked on the chalkboard.

"First off, thanks to Captain Masterman for lending a hand in this operation. And to Pilot Officer Hammond and your men, an even bigger thanks for taking the trip with us tonight. I know that Captain Masterman shed some light on what this is all about earlier this afternoon ... at least what you need to know."

Conor pointed at the chalkboard, where he had redrawn the summer house with greater detail, including the water approach from the east. "There are, at last count, nine guards—at least eight outside and one inside the house." He added eight Xs to the board. "Most of the guards are focused on the front of the house. Our surveillance showed they are leaving the rear of the house relatively exposed."

"How well armed are the guards?" Pilot Officer Hammond asked.

"They're all armed with at least machine pistols," Conor said.

A low rumble from the airmen made Conor stop. Seaker ran his hand through his hair several times.

"Our original plan was to go in quietly and overcome the guards. We didn't want to deal with the Stockholm Police and Swedish security personnel. But that won't work now." He drew a large arrow heading from the bay to the house. "This time, we go in by boat." Conor looked at Seaker, who was biting the inside of his cheek. "Mr. Seaker here is in charge of the boat," he said.

An airman raised his hand. "Flight Engineer Danaher. What about weapons?"

Conor turned to Lancer. "Master Sergeant, would you do the honors?"

Lancer opened the metal gun cabinet along the back wall. He first pulled out a M1 carbine with the folding stock. Lancer held it up over his head. "Model M1A1 carbine. A lightweight semi-automatic rifle. Effective range maxes out at three hundred yards. It has a fifteen-round magazine. It has a spring-loaded folding stock"—Lancer demonstrated the folding mechanism— "which makes it real easy to hide it from prying eyes. It has a simple flip sight with two settings, one hundred fifty and three hundred yards. Plenty of range for our mission."

"Conor, one concern," Hammond said. "Most of us only received small arms training. Our air gunners received training and can handle the Vickers K .303 caliber machine guns."

"Don't worry, Lancer here will run your men through what they need to know. You each also get a Colt M1911A1 sidearm."

The airmen nodded.

"So it's obvious we aren't going to be very quiet."

Conor spent the next fifteen minutes going over the attack plan in detail, explaining that they were going to cut engine power on their approach and use oars to approach the dock. He assigned two teams, one with four men, one with three, to flank the house on the north and south sides. Lancer would lead one team, while Heugle would lead the other. Using the cover of darkness, Conor would first take out the guard at the back of the house.

"Gunny Miller will keep the guards busy from his post in front. He'll be armed with a M1 Garand rifle with a scope. Each team's main mission is to keep the men guarding the west from moving to the backside of the house." Conor looked around the room.

No one looked like they were ready to bail.

"If they do move to the rear for cover, though, you can take the guards out. That will help me. I'll enter the house from the rear and take our target. But I need to find him. It may take me a little time. Once I do, I'll signal with this." He held up a whistle. "This is the second of three days with a full moon. The skies are clear at this point, but that could change by the time we push off. I get that you Brits are on your way back home. So if any of you want to reconsider now that you've been given the lay of the land, let us know."

"We've already had that talk," Captain Masterman said. "These boys have an understanding of just how critical this operation is, and they want in, right, boys?"

Heads nodded. "Do we get to keep the carbines?" asked one airman.

"The answer to that is a big fat no and that goes for the sidearms too," Lancer said.

As the laughter was dying down, Conor looked at Seaker.

No smile. No laughter. Just glistening sweat on the forehead.

"All right, then. We shove off from the quay in front of the legation at midnight. Any questions?" No hands were raised. "We'll get some food and drink down here for you guys while the master sergeant does some quick weps training. And again, thanks."

Seaker quickly approached. "Conor, a word?"

"Sure, Buster. You feeling all right?"

"Well, now that you ask, I'm a bit queasy," Seaker said in a gravelly voice. "I may not be the right man for this. I've spent all but three months of my career tied to a desk. And those three months were spent as copilot on a C-47 flying out of Anacostia. Pretty different than any type of surface action you probably saw."

"Right. Until Congressman Seaker got you reassigned. I heard about that." Conor flashed a big toothy grin. "But don't worry. You know how to duck, don't you?"

CHAPTER FIFTY-FOUR

1630 Hours, Thursday, October 29, 1942
German Legation, Södra Blasieholmshammer 2, Stockholm

Walter Schellenberg looked across at Eklof, who had just arrived and was getting settled in his chair. The framed photograph on Lina Stuben's desk, of her with Himmler, caught his eye. An innocent-enough photo of a secretary and her superior. The inscription, citing Stuben's loyalty to Himmler, struck him as unfortunate in as much as the loyalty did not go both ways.

"When will Stuben return, Herr Brigadeführer?"

Schellenberg took the photograph and placed it in the upper right-hand desk drawer. He leaned back in the chair, steepled his fingers, and rested his chin on his fingertips. "That is no concern of yours. You should know better than to ask such a question."

Eklof straightened his spine and cleared his throat. "Yes, sir. I understand."

"Oh? Just what do you *understand?*"

"That Lina Stuben will not—"

Schellenberg held up his hand to stop Eklof. "The right response was 'Yes, sir. Please excuse the question.' Now let's get on with it." Schellenberg retrieved a smooth leather briefcase with three gussets that allowed the case to expand. The case made a soft thud when it hit the surface of the desk. "I believe you have the instructions for the exchange."

"Yes, Brigadeführer. I will take care of the arrangements." Eklof went on to relate, in a halting fashion, the details of his recent meeting with Andersson.

Schellenberg peppered him with a few questions and received satisfactory answers. "There is one change. By order of the reichsführer himself, what we want for this ridiculous sum of money is not only the classified intelligence but also the mystery man who is selling it. Nothing more, nothing less. This must be communicated to Andersson immediately. Any questions?"

"No, Brigadeführer."

"I have one question for you. Who is Conor Thorn?"

The question surprised Eklof, making him flinch. "An American. He just arrived this week asking questions about missing people."

"What missing people?"

"One we believe is a British agent, and the other might be the person who has the intelligence we are after."

"Does this mystery man have a name?"

"Gunnar Lind."

"I assume you and Stuben have looked for Lind's other family members in the area?"

"We have, Brigadeführer. But we have come up with no other family here except for Andersson."

"How are they related? Have you determined that?"

"We have attempted to but have no clear answer. Andersson has not been forthcoming."

"*Ach,*" Schellenberg spat. He slumped down into the chair and steepled his hands. He closed his eyes. Without opening them, he asked, "The daughter you are holding. How old is she?"

"I'm not sure exactly. Maybe twenty-five years."

Schellenberg open his eyes and sat up. "Is she married?"

"She … she had no wedding ring when we took her. I assume the answer is no."

Schellenberg frowned and began to rub his temples. "In Stuben's report, she mentioned that this Thorn had inquired about someone you are holding, a Mia Durs. What about her?"

Eklof shifted in his seat. "We know little about her. She has not divulged any useful information."

Schellenberg nodded. "What else do you know about Thorn?"

"We have monitored his comings and goings. He has evaded us

some of the time. But one of our men has reported that Thorn has just returned to the Grand Hotel."

"Would you recognize him?"

Eklof cleared his throat into his fist. "Yes, sir. I would."

Schellenberg looked at his watch. "I have some spare time. Let us go to the hotel. I must meet this person."

Eklof's mouth popped open. His lips moved but he said nothing.

"What is it, Eklof?"

"May I ask what you want with Thorn?"

Schellenberg shook his head slowly and started to rise. "Ah. Once again, an inappropriate question."

CHAPTER FIFTY-FIVE

1715 Hours, Thursday, October 29, 1942
Grand Hôtel, Södra Blasieholmshammer 8, Stockholm

Walter Schellenberg was glad he had changed into his blue double-breasted suit before going to the hotel. He had made the mistake of wearing his uniform on a previous trip and was the recipient of numerous cold and unwelcoming stares from Swedish citizens.

A string quartet dressed in formal wear was playing at the far end of the lobby, which was humming with activity. He sat on a cream-colored settee near the elevator while Eklof talked to his man, seated not far away reading a newspaper. When Eklof returned, he sat next to Schellenberg but gave the Brigadeführer ample space.

"And?"

"Thorn went to his room about thirty minutes ago. No one was with him."

"Do you have his room number?"

"Yes. It's 120."

"And what did you find when you searched the room?"

"Nothing that would shed any light on why he is here."

Schellenberg nodded. He'd expected to hear that they hadn't followed normal procedures. He was pleased he didn't have to reprimand Eklof. He was drained from his meetings with Himmler and the hastily arranged trip to Stockholm.

"You said 120?'

"Yes, sir."

"Wait here. I'm going to meet Mr. Thorn." Schellenberg rose, followed by Eklof. Schellenberg smoothed out his trousers and straightened his tie.

"Sir," Eklof said with a hushed voice. "There he is, by the elevator."

Schellenberg saw a man around six feet, dressed in dark clothes, a dark coat draped over his arm, and a wool cap in his hand. He was taking purposeful strides toward the exit.

Schellenberg rushed to cut him off. "A minute, Mr. Thorn?"

#

Conor stopped when someone behind him with a reedy voice called his name. A thinly built man in a dark suit was approaching. Conor picked up a sweet, boozy scent of ... aftershave? He had become more aware of men's cologne since the letter from Sue. The man before him was cleanly shaven, his hair cut close above the ears.

"Who are you?"

"I am Brigadeführer Walter Schellenberg. I work with Reichsführer Himmler. I believe you know of him?"

"Sure. The peacemaker. What do you want? I have somewhere I need to be."

"I'll get to the point, then."

Conor could see Kurt Eklof over Schellenberg's shoulder. He smiled and gave Eklof the one-finger salute, who returned the gesture with a stare that would make a weaker man shiver. Himmler's buddy noticed the silent exchange but chose not to address it.

"Could we step over there and find some privacy?" Schellenberg asked, pointing at a sitting room adjacent to the Grand's bar.

Schellenberg led the way. As Conor followed, he wondered if Schellenberg was going to defect or ask to become a double agent for the Allies—that would be worth his time—or take him to task for being rude to Himmler's messengers.

Conor took a seat on a couch along with Schellenberg. "You're on the clock, Walter." He noted the raised eyebrow at the use of his first name.

"I am here to vouch for Reichsführer Himmler's motives in seeking a peaceful arrangement with the Americans and British. He is displaying great courage in proposing his plans for peace with the West. He has put himself, and his family, at great risk."

"Sounds like a really good guy. Like a neighbor who would mow your lawn when you've broken your leg." Conor saw that Schellenberg couldn't make heads or tails out of that response. "Except that he's a butcher. Just like his boss." Schellenberg flinched at the word 'butcher.' "But before you go further, tell me: Why are you talking to me? I was just passing through when I got dragged into the discussion."

Schellenberg smiled like he was expecting the question. "Ahh, yes. It seems my associates, those you met with, were rather impressed with the way you engaged them. And ... very much unimpressed with Mr. Homer. That, and you have gotten the attention of certain people at the German Legation. People that, let's say ... work for me."

"So you're saying that because I'm a pain in your ass, you're bending my ear with this peace feeler nonsense? I don't buy it. And I'm running late." Conor started to rise. "So I'll just take—"

"Wilhelm Canaris."

Conor fell back onto the couch. Canaris. The head of the German Abwehr. The man he and Emily had had to free when they intercepted secret Operation Torch directives as they were being handed off to Canaris. "He is a friend. We see each other regularly. We share information."

Conor was anxious to get on with other matters, but Schellenberg had him hooked. "Get to the point, Walter."

"I don't give the Abwehr credit for much, but they do have quite an impressive catalogue of dossiers on Allied intelligence agents. The Abwehr had just started one on you. He wouldn't tell me why it was just started. In any case, it doesn't really matter. What does matter is it seems that your family is very well connected. Colonel Donovan is a close family friend. And your father is a friend of your president."

Conor's father, Jack, and FDR had been close since law school at Columbia. His father had turned down several positions in FDR's cabinet, claiming he could do more good for the war effort by running the Republic Broadcasting Company as its chairman.

"I believe you can help make a case for Reichsführer Himmler's peace plan by speaking directly to your president."

Conor looked at his watch. "You've got one more minute."

Schellenberg leaned closer to Conor. "You do not know the real Heinrich Himmler. He is a true leader who sees that the war is lost. He is more convinced of this than ever. He realizes that the manufacturing might of the United States, once at full production, will … well, let us just say that it is a matter of time. Which, for Germany, is running out. Terms for the West would be favorable if you allow Germany to continue its campaign against the Soviets—and they could be even more favorable if you would decide to join Germany in its campaign against them." Schellenberg had trouble keeping his high-pitched voice from carrying. Luckily for him, and probably for Conor, there wasn't anyone nearby.

"You sound desperate."

"No, but pragmatic and maybe a little opportunistic? Yes. As I said, now is the time to take action. News from the eastern front is demoralizing to our troops. We know that you and the British are about to mount a second front somewhere. If you would give us an indication that you would support Reichsführer Himmler's plans, we could convince the key leaders of the Wehrmacht and Luftwaffe to join with him. Most of these career military men realize they are being led by a madman."

"Just words. I'm not sure we can trust any of you people. It's clear to us, as it is to you, that any known cooperation with you and Himmler would lead to a breach in our relationship with Stalin. Something that you would love to see." Conor let that sink in.

"Excuse me? I don't understand. You forget the meeting with Dr. Kersten and Langbehn, both close friends of Reichsführer Himmler. And my involvement." Schellenberg sat up straight. "I am, after all, chief of the SS's SD, the reichsführer's most trusted ally." Schellenberg's voice grew louder. He was no longer trying to keep the conversation between the two of them. "Is this not enough of a signal of our honorable intentions?" Schellenberg sat back, crossed his legs, and folded his arms.

Conor could be as pragmatic as this Nazi. *Is there a deal to be made after all?*

"Maybe there is something you could do."

"I'm listening."

"I'll bet my monthly paycheck and yours that you have Mia Durs, a Swiss citizen, in custody. She is … important to me. Bring her here at nineteen hundred. When I get her to safety, I'll take your case to my family's friends."

Schellenberg's eyes lit up, and he began to squirm. "The president? Just to be clear."

Conor hesitated, just to witness Schellenberg's discomfort more. "Yes. But no Mia Durs, and all your back-channel peace efforts will go nowhere except, in some way we'll figure out with time, to Adolf. Maybe we'll convince the British to send Rudolf Hess back with the message. Mia Durs … nineteen hundred." Conor stood and marched out of the Grand Hotel.

#

Schellenberg watched the arrogant American exit the lobby. He looked over and found Eklof standing with the agent assigned to watch Thorn. Eklof approached Schellenberg.

"Just who *is* this Mia Durs?" Schellenberg asked.

"Durs?" Eklof looked away toward the exit.

"Yes. Mia Durs. Look at me."

Eklof turned back to Schellenberg.

"Who is she?"

"We believe she is a British agent. She was asking questions about …" Eklof's voice trailed off and he looked away again.

He reminded Schellenberg of someone being caught breaking a curfew. "Look at me when I speak to you. Asking questions about what?"

"About a dead British Legation staff member who was acting suspiciously around our legation. We thought he was looking for Gunnar Lind. We brought him into our legation and questioned him."

"Well, that was a dangerous thing to do. You and Stuben could have been deported if you were caught, and it isn't easy to get SD agents placed in this country. What happened to him?"

"He died while being questioned."

Schellenberg took a step toward Eklof, stopping inches away from his face. "What else are you not telling me?"

Eklof leaned back but did not move his feet. "We … we took Durs because she was asking too many questions, probably looking for Lind too. She had Swiss papers, but we don't believe she is a Swiss citizen."

Schellenberg thought Thorn's interest in Durs confirmed that belief. "Where is she?"

"At the safe house, the same place we took Andersson's daughter."

Schellenberg stepped back. "Tell me the house is guarded."

"Yes. Two men. Not our best, but they're just guarding two women."

Schellenberg mulled over what Durs meant to Thorn and whether it made sense to give her up to him. If it meant having their plan presented directly to the American president, he would make that happen. He looked at his watch. "Go retrieve this woman. Clean her up and have her here," Schellenberg looked at his watch, "in two hours. As for this Gunnar Lind matter, I will be at Andersson's home to make sure he holds up his end of our agreement."

#

Sitting in the legation's Ford, Conor watched the front entrance of the Grand Hotel from the far side of Södra Blasieholmshammer. If Schellenberg was going to take him up on his offer—Emily for a whisper in FDR's ear about a crazy peace deal—he expected them to make a move to get Emily to the hotel.

No less than a minute later, Kurt Eklof sprinted from the hotel, down the boulevard toward the German Legation, the next block down from the hotel. Conor coasted down the street and stopped the Ford fifty yards short of the four-story building. The roof-mounted Nazi flag fluttered against a darkening sky. Eklof disappeared inside the legation and came back out less than two minutes later with another man. Both jumped into a gray Mercedes and took a hard right onto Hovslagargatan.

Conor followed at a discreet distance.

CHAPTER FIFTY-SIX

1745 Hours, Thursday, October 29, 1942
German Safe House, Stockholm

Eve Lind hadn't spoken a word in several hours. Emily had prodded her with questions about Gunnar, but Eve had only turned her back and appeared to go to sleep. The only time she responded was when Emily asked who the father was. Eve had rolled over and thrown a shoe at the bars that separated their cells. The shoe bounced off and fell into the urine bucket. Her scream of frustration pierced the squalid air and brought a guard to the top of the stairs, who told them to shut up.

Emily had told Eve to take the shoe out of the bucket and let it dry.

Eve looked at Emily like she was speaking Greek.

"You're going to need that shoe."

Emily sat on her mattress, her back to the sleeping Eve. She shook her head at the growing list of unanswered questions. Who was the father of Eve's baby? What triggered the Nazi-hating softhearted man to turn against the country that saved him from falling into German hands? What part was Eve's father playing in the unfolding drama? There were too many questions without answers. Which never sat well with Emily.

Ten minutes later, the older guard slowly descended the stairs, struggling with his lame leg. He carried two bowls, a slice of black bread perched against the side of each. A whiff of boiled cabbage assaulted Emily's already pummeled olfactory nerves.

"Rest and eat up, Mia Durs. You're going on a trip tomorrow, and you must look your best."

The guard made slow progress across the basement floor. Today, he seemed to be dragging the lame leg more than just limping on it. Emily, now lying on her mattress, rolled over on her left hip to face him. The pain no longer jolted her, but it continued to make its presence known when direct pressure was applied. She accepted that as positive medical progress. "Where are they taking me?"

"They tell me nothing," he said, sliding her bowl under the cell door. "And I ask no questions." He shifted over to Eve's cell, the shoe on his lame leg scraping the floor. "But I would assume somewhere out of this country, to somewhere where they can do what they want, no questions asked—Germany, Norway, northern France. Who knows?" He grunted when he bent over to pass the bowl under Eve's cell door. When he straightened, he let out a belch, then reached for his flask, mumbled something incoherent, and headed for the stairs.

"Did they tell you when?" she asked, worried that her timetable would need to be pushed up.

He stopped and turned. "I told you they tell me nothing, woman." He resumed his slow march up the stairs. His mumbling waned with each step.

The time had come. Sitting on her mattress with her legs outstretched, she began to moan. She slowly ratcheted up the volume, until she was emitting a mix of squealing and groaning.

"What's wrong?" Eve asked.

Emily responded with another high-pitched groan. "Get down here. I'm sick," she called out.

The door at the top of the stairs opened. "What do you want?" the younger guard said from the top of the stairs. Just the man she wanted to see—the one with the pistol stuffed under his waistband, in the small of his back.

"I'm sick."

The guard sauntered down the stairs. "My God, why are you shrieking like that? You sound like a stuck pig."

"I told you, this food is making me sick. I need you to take me to the toilet."

"Use your bucket."

"It's full. Because you won't empty it or take us to the toilet." Emily shut her eyes and rocked back and forth, her arms wrapped around her torso.

The guard looked into the cell and saw the full bucket.

Emily opened her eyes to slits. The guard was looking at her.

"Take her to the toilet. Or you'll have a mess to clean up. Eklof won't like that," Eve said.

"Damn, woman," the guard muttered as he unlocked Emily's cell door. He stepped in and reached behind Emily, grabbing her under her armpits, and lifted. Emily let her feet drag, so the guard was carrying her full weight. He nearly dropped her to the floor when they reached the toilet. There were three inches of water at the bottom that gave off a rusty, brackish smell. Emily started dry heaving. Out of the corner of her eyes, she saw the guard, on her right side, turn away. She raised her left hand and shoved her finger down her throat. What was left of her stomach contents splashed into the bowl. She heard the guard gag.

Emily emitted a raspy groan as she reached for the nearby mop. The guard heard her move and turned back, but not fast enough. Emily already had two hands on the handle, and she rammed the end up into the guard's windpipe. Eve stifled a shriek with her hand as the guard flailed his arms, falling off-balance, and clutched his throat. He fell to his knees, then collapsed.

Emily had received hand-to-hand combat training at MI6. After a blow like that, the crushed windpipe blocked all airflow. In no more than three minutes, he should be brain dead—it only took two.

Emily wiped her mouth with her sleeve and snatched the gun, an Astra 400, small but heavy. She stood motionless, listening for the older guard. Hearing nothing, she took the keys from her cell door. Eve started to get up, but Emily raised the Astra and pointed it at the woman's chest.

Eve laughed and turned away. "You wouldn't shoot me."

A moment passed before Emily realized that she had tightened her grip on the pistol. Slowly, she released it. "No, Eve, not to kill you, but I would to send a message that I'm quite serious."

"That would just bring the other guard."

"I'm not worried. He's finished his afternoon flask by now and probably passed out. That, and I don't think he's up for a fight of any kind."

"What are you going to do?"

"I have two choices: take you or leave you."

"Why would you leave me?"

"Because when I asked you to tell me where Gunnar is, you said nothing. You are of no use to me."

A beat passed. Eve gave her a thin smile. "He's at my father's summer house."

"Location?"

"It's on Skeppsholmen. Just east of Gamla Stan."

"Eve, if you're lying to me, it won't be good for you."

"He's there. Or that's where I last saw him."

"All right, grab your shoes," Emily said as she unlocked Eve's cell.

At the top of the stairs, the door was open wide. Emily peered around the corner into a living area containing a couch and one overly stuffed armchair with cigarette burn holes. Sunk deep into the cushions, as if the chair were swallowing him, was the older guard. His flask rested on his lap, and his head was tilted back. Emily grabbed Eve by the upper arm and pointed toward the front door with the gun.

Outside the house, Emily sighed when she didn't see any form of transportation. Dense woodlands surrounded the house, and the front yard was comprised of weeds and loose gravel. Multiple sets of tire tracks led to and from the top of the driveway into the yard.

"Let's head to the back of the house. Maybe we'll get lucky and find a car in a garage or barn."

#

Eklof didn't waste any time getting to where he was going. The Ford had a difficult time keeping pace with the Mercedes. Ten minutes into the trip, the Mercedes pulled into a gravel drive, until the grille of the car almost touched a wooden gate. The driver got out, shoved the gate aside, and sped up the driveway without closing the gate.

Conor pulled the Ford onto the shoulder fifty yards farther up the road, got out, and jogged back to the gate. The wooden rails looked rotted and warped. A battered sign hung by a single nail from a nearby post with a warning about a dog. He started to hike up the driveway. The thick woods on each side of the gravel driveway appeared to be reclaiming the cleared land. The edges of the driveway had been eroded by water runoff. Soon enough, a small house emerged in the distance.

\#

Emily found the area behind the house completely overgrown with weeds and tall grass. Broken tree limbs were scattered about. A wooden swing set in the middle of the yard was fighting off an encroaching army of weeds. A rutted double track led directly to a detached single-bay garage; the weeds along the tracks had been tamped down. The garage doors hung at odd angles, leaving a widening gap toward the bottom.

"Eve, open the door."

The woman complied, opening the right side door, dragging the bottom of it across the gravel. The garage was empty inside.

"It looks like we're walking," Emily said. She turned, then froze at the sound of a racing engine and the crunching of tires on gravel.

\#

Conor crouched behind a tree and watched Eklof's Mercedes parked by the house. The driver was leaning on the front fender, smoking a cigarette. A window on either side of the front door shed a soft light out onto a front porch, as did the door, which was wide open. Conor saw Eklof talking to another man agitatedly. Eklof picked up a phone and talked for less than a minute, after which he slapped the man across the face with the back of his hand. Eklof hurried out the front door, the man a step behind him.

Conor noticed movement to the right of the house. Two people. One in a long dress, the other in a knee-length dress who was limping and holding a gun—Emily.

Conor leaned against the tree and closed his eyes. He let out a deep breath. He closed his eyes to make sure his mind wasn't playing tricks on him. When he reopened them, they locked onto the sight of Emily. *Damn nice to see you again, Em.* He recognized the other woman; Emily and Eve were moving slowly and about to turn the corner of the house, exposing themselves to Eklof and the driver.

Conor stepped from the edge of the woods, twenty yards away from them.

"Eklof, you sure do like slapping people around, don't you?" Conor held his gun out of sight behind his back.

As he'd intended, Emily and Eve stopped before they rounded the corner.

#

Emily wasn't surprised to know that Eklof had shown up, but she couldn't say the same about Conor, right on Eklof's heels. But Conor was alone. *That's so Conor Thorn*, Emily thought. She shoved Eve into the side of the house and placed her index finger on her lips signaling quiet. Emily pressed up against the house, gun at the ready, her eyes on Conor.

#

The man behind Eklof was older and looked disoriented.

"Thorn, you bastard. Shoot him," Eklof yelled to the driver. The driver reached for a gun under his coat, but before his hand reappeared, the round from Conor's M1AI Colt had already penetrated his chest. His body crumpled to the ground, and Eklof pulled a gun from his holster and grabbed the old man around the neck, positioning him as a shield. Conor no longer had a clear shot at Eklof unless he wanted to kill both of them, something he wouldn't lose any sleep over if that's what he had to do.

\#

Emily stepped around the corner of the house, the motion catching Eklof's attention. He reached around the old man's chest, aimed, and fired off two rounds. One of them ripped open the house's siding, showering Emily with wood splinters. She crouched, but before she could fire off a round, she heard another gun fire.

Eklof released the old guard, stumbled backward, and toppled onto the porch, clearly hit by Conor.

Emily heard a moan behind her. Eve was lying on the ground, holding the right side of her face. Several wood splinters had pierced her cheek and forehead. Blood was trickling down her cheek.

\#

As Conor squeezed off the shot that sent Eklof reeling backward, he heard a body hit the ground to his right. *No, not Emily.*

His eyes still locked on the front of the house, Conor yelled, "Emily, you in one piece?"

"Pretty much."

Conor sprinted toward the Mercedes, momentarily losing sight of Eklof, the car blocking his view, and as he rounded the back end of the car, he saw Eklof racing toward the woods, holding his right shoulder.

That's not gonna happen. Conor started to close the distance when he heard Emily call out: "No, Conor. Let him go."

He turned back to Emily. "No way. He's going—"

"He doesn't matter. Gunnar Lind does."

CHAPTER FIFTY-SEVEN

1810 Hours, Thursday, October 29, 1942
Home of Benjamin Andersson, Norrmalm, Stockholm

Schellenberg followed the woman into Andersson's study. She didn't question him when he said he was a dear friend of her husband, visiting from Germany, and wanted to surprise him, since they hadn't seen each other in years. She knocked on the study door and entered. From the doorway, Schellenberg saw Andersson putting a handset back in its cradle, but his wife's appearance startled him, and he nearly dropped it.

"Darling, your old friend Walter Schellenberg has come to visit. He wanted to surprise you."

Andersson brushed his hair back with his hand. "Thank you, Edith."

"What, dear?" she asked loudly.

Andersson dismissed her with a wave, and she left the study, quietly closing the door behind her.

Schellenberg moved to the desk, where Andersson took a seat. "My mother is also nearly deaf," the German said. "It can be ... frustrating at times."

"Excuse me, but I know no one by the name of Walter Schellenberg. I can only surmise that you are an associate of Lina Stuben's."

Schellenberg took a seat. "Impressive, but I have been told that you are a smart man, which I am counting on, actually."

"Really? How so?"

"We have an understanding about how events will unfold tomorrow. I am here to remind you that if you fail to live up to those arrangements, you put your own daughter in grave danger."

"Your brazen act has angered my relation very deeply. He says he may change his mind altogether and leave the country."

"Isn't that touching. Your 'relation' cares for your daughter. Is he a cousin ... a long-lost uncle?"

Andersson's posture sagged. Was he about to capitulate?

Schellenberg decided to elevate the pressure. "We want the intelligence *and* this person you represent. That is what we are paying for."

Andersson leaned forward. "That was not the agreement."

"And that is why we took your daughter. To convince you to agree to new terms if we determined the need to change them."

"I cannot agree to that." Andersson's voice faltered. It sounded as if it was choked by phlegm.

"Then your daughter—"

"He's my daughter's husband."

Schellenberg tilted his head and smiled. "Hmmm, yes. That makes so much sense. A dutiful father helping his daughter *and* husband. Quite honorable on your part." Schellenberg rose and looked down at Andersson. "It would be best if you told Gunnar Lind that if he doesn't turn himself over to us so that we can ... discuss the intelligence in greater detail, he won't see his wife ever again." Schellenberg pivoted and headed for the study door. "I'll show myself out. If I run into Edith, I'll tell her we had a very pleasant conversation. Good day, Mr. Andersson."

CHAPTER FIFTY-EIGHT

2000 Hours, Thursday, October 29, 1942
Andersson Summer Home, Skeppsholmen, Stockholm

Lind was not doing well. He ran through the growing list of his maladies: a racing heart, trembling hands, gastrointestinal issues, weakness coupled with fatigue, but a complete inability to sleep. His sense of impending doom was worrisome, but worst of all was his inability to connect with Andersson.

His last call to the man's home rang twenty times before he slammed the handset back into the cradle. He paced for several minutes after. His white cotton shirt was thoroughly damp from the sweat running down his chest and back. His scalp was moist, which mirrored the clamminess in his crotch. He called for the guard, who had been ensconced in the kitchen in the rear of the house for the past several hours.

"Grab your coat and the keys. We're going to Andersson's house."

"No. I have orders from Mr. Andersson to keep you here no matter what."

Lind looked at the guard and calculated the odds of overcoming him, a man in his late twenties built like a stevedore. When he factored in his weakness and fatigue, he came up with a zero. That left one choice. Lind reached for the m/1940 Husqvarna pistol from a nearby end table.

The guard recoiled when Lind brought the pistol into view.

"You're not going to shoot me. There are too many guards around. You're too smart for that."

"You're probably right. But I could shoot you in the knee. That would surely be unpleasant. And I'm sure my father-in-law would forgive me, given the stress I've been under."

The guard considered his options while staring at the pistol in Lind's hands. "Get in the car. I'll get the keys."

Lind waited beside the car for the guard. He tightly gripped the Husqvarna in his coat pocket. The moonlit night was cool. His damp clothes and the cool temperature made him shiver. The guard appeared. Before he hopped in the front seat, he called out to the guards in the front. "We'll be back soon. I will blink my headlights as we approach the house on our return, so no nervous trigger fingers."

Once inside, the guard started the engine and shoved the car into first gear. "Where is your gun?" he asked.

"Pointed at you. Let's get going."

The guard shook his head, released the clutch, and punched the accelerator, sending a rooster tail of gravel in the direction of the guards gathered at the front door. They drove down the circular driveway and toward the bridge, Lind catching a glimpse in the woods of a reflection deep within the trees. He twisted in his seat to peer out the rear window. It was a reflection off a shiny surface, but a second later it was gone.

"What?" the guard said.

"I ... saw something. A reflection from our headlights. Just for a second."

"Relax. The guards have been telling me there are plenty of raccoon dogs out in those woods. At night, their eyes light up like flashlights."

"Never heard of them."

"Sort of like a fox, not really a dog. Does resemble a raccoon though. Relax. And think about how you're going to explain to Mr. Andersson why you left his house after he ordered you to stay there. He won't be happy."

Neither am I, Lind added silently.

CHAPTER FIFTY-NINE

2015 Hours, Thursday, October 29, 1942
German Legation, Södra Blasieholmshammer 2, Stockholm

The three shots of vodka that Eklof consumed while the doctor dressed his upper arm wound had dulled the sharp edge of the pain. The black sling that now held his right arm chafed the back of his neck as he mulled the prospect of facing Schellenberg's wrath.

"He's sitting on a bench on the quay in front of the legation. You are to meet him there," the doctor told him.

Eklof offered no response but left Stuben's office and headed down the hallway.

"He is very angry," he heard the doctor call out.

He should be, Eklof thought.

As soon as he walked outside, he saw a lone figure sitting on a bench. A nearby streetlight suffused the area with light. People on bicycles rode up and down the quay, even though the temperature had dropped noticeably since Eklof had flagged down a delivery truck after his escape from the safe house. He crossed Södra Blasieholmshammer. With each step toward the man on the bench, the stiches where Thorn's round had taken a chunk of flesh tugged at his skin.

"Sir, you wanted to see me?" Eklof asked, grayish wisps of breath marking each word.

Schellenberg sat with his legs crossed. His hands were buried deep in the pockets of the heavy overcoat, the collar of which was pulled up around his neck. Schellenberg sat, unresponsive, gazing out at two passenger ferries passing each other in the bay. A horn blast from one of them seemed to be the signal he was waiting for.

"Where do I begin?" he asked. "We'll have to locate a new safe house, for one. Then there's the botched interrogation of the British agent. The investigation could still lead back to our legation … to you, actually. If you don't go to prison, you at least become persona non grata and get yourself shipped back to Germany." Schellenberg turned his gaze to Eklof. "Then you let Eve Lind escape. Leverage in our dealing with Andersson gone." His voice dripped with disdain. "The Durs woman, whoever she is, is not an issue for me. She was going to be released to Thorn anyway. But Eve Lind, that is another matter." He returned his gaze to the strait. "This man, Thorn, he got the better of you, just like he did at the dinner last night."

Hearing Thorn's name made Eklof grind his teeth. The hand of his uninjured arm balled into a fist. He had to track Thorn down. Best to let Schellenberg get on with it.

He straightened his posture and lifted his chin. "I have no excuses. I have failed you and Reichsführer Himmler. But—"

"Eklof? Be careful. 'But' always signals to me that I am about to hear an excuse. You said there are no excuses. I am confused."

"I was going to say … it will not happen again."

"I certainly hope not. For your sake and Germany's. And please do what you must to ensure that you do not make a mess out of tomorrow's exchange, or it will be your last opportunity to serve the Reich. Now leave me."

Eklof could feel his face flush. With long strides, he walked across the street. As he neared the legation, he removed the sling and flung it into a trash bin.

CHAPTER SIXTY

Down the hall from Karlson's office was a small kitchen where coffee and light meals were prepared for legation guests. Next to it was a small dispensary. When Conor opened the door to it, he was shaken—Emily was lying on a white table with an IV in her arm. A white sheet covered her from the waist down. Her eyes opened when she heard Conor suck in a quick breath.

"What's going on here? You okay? No, that's a dumb question. You're—"

"Fine. I'm fine. Just a little worn out. Hungry. A little sore."

"Sure doesn't look like you're fine. What's in the bottle?"

"It's a dextrose solution. Something to get me going." She paused and tugged on his sleeve. "Listen, there's something I have to tell you."

"Maybe you should rest, Em."

"Maybe you need to listen to me, Conor."

"Okay, okay. What is it?"

"Eve. She's pregnant. But it's not possible. At least not by Gunnar."

"What are you talking about?"

"The night the Linds landed in England, we took the train from Tempsford to Bletchley Park. Eve fell asleep while Gunnar and I shared a bottle of wine to celebrate their escape from France.

244

He got a little drunk and told me his biggest shame was that he couldn't have children of his own. The man is sterile. It was Eve who had an affair."

Conor shrugged. "I'm not shocked. I've had a bad feeling about her for quite some time." He placed his hand on her thigh.

Emily flinched at his touch.

"Shit. I'm sorry, Em. Did I hurt you?"

Emily's face turned a light shade of red. "I asked the doctor to take a look at … some burns. On my thighs."

"From what?" It took a second before Conor realized—the Germans wanted information, any way they could get it. His face hardened. "Who did it to you? Was it Eklof?"

"Stuben. It was Eklof who planted his fist in my face."

Conor's face softened and he closed his eyes. His breathing quickened. *There are scores to be settled.* He felt Emily grab his hand.

Emily's eyes welled with tears. "I'm okay, Conor."

"You are one hell of a brave woman. But I already knew that." He wiped the few tears that escaped from her vivid green eyes, then bent down and kissed her on the forehead, then on her lips, where he lingered for a long, light-headed moment. After pulling back, he brushed some stray hair from her face. "When we get back to London, how about I take you to my favorite place?"

"Which is where?"

"The Savoy. They're holding a room key for me." Conor felt Emily squeeze his hand. "I'll be back to check on you later. I need to talk with Karlson. I want to make sure he got a message to Masterman about you."

Emily nodded. "Come back soon."

#

Conor's body screamed for sleep and a shower as he sat in front of Karlson's desk, his elbows on his knees, holding a cup of something that smelled like coffee.

Karlson listened intently as Conor told the story of following Eklof after meeting with Schellenberg. His jaw dropped. "You're kidding? You winged him? Eklof?"

"Pretty sure. Took off like a bat outa hell."

"Ha. I guess we'll keep that tidbit from Minister Ramsay. Homer too. How's Bright?"

"She's getting medical attention downstairs. Eve Lind also." Conor took a sip from his cup, his thoughts turning to the operation ahead. "Speaking of medical attention, any chance we can keep that doctor around until after we make our move on Lind?"

"I think so. We send a lot of business his way. I'll ask."

"Thanks. What did Masterman say when you told him about finding Emily?"

"A little less excited than I thought he'd be. Maybe that's just the reserved Englishman for you. He said he was going to notify MI6." Karlson paused. "I sent a message to Colonel Donovan, letting him know as well. I told him we're moving on Lind tonight."

"Any response?"

"Not yet. Are you taking her on the operation?"

"She already told me that if I tried to stop her, she'd put a bullet in *my* shoulder."

"The Nazis losing Eve Lind takes a little pressure off Andersson, as far as following through with the deal. Right?"

"Maybe, but I'm counting on money being the big motivator for him."

Karlson raised his arms above his head and stretched. After a half-stifled yawn, he leaned forward in his chair. "Tell me more about Schellenberg."

"Just one of Himmler's henchmen making a case for his boss's plan to partner with us to kick some Russian ass."

"I'll be damned. He's Himmler's go-to guy. Has been for quite a while. What'd he say? Anything new?"

"Not really. Just played a violin while he told me how brave Himmler was and how he thinks the war is lost."

Karlson lit a cigarette and tossed the match in an ashtray. "Sending Schellenberg is a desperate move. But with all the news about the camps, it's just too much water under the bridge. Congress would run FDR out of town on a rail." He took a drag of his cigarette. "By the way, any idea where he's staying? If he's at the Grand, I might want to look though his trash or take a look at the ink blotter from his desk."

"No idea." Conor swiveled in his seat toward the sound of leather-soled shoes pounding the parquet floor toward Karlson's office.

Bobby burst into the office and bent over, hands on his knees, breathing heavily.

"What the hell, Bobby. You all right?"

His friend took in several deep breaths. "No. And you won't be either when you hear this."

Conor made a circular motion with his index finger to urge Bobby on.

"Lind is on the loose."

Conor's shoulders slumped.

"He left the house"—Bobby looked at his watch—"over half an hour ago. Just he and one guard. Miller couldn't follow because of a dead battery. A fucking ... dead ... battery."

Conor bolted out of his seat, his cup flying at the wall behind Karlson's desk. When it slammed into the plaster, Karlson was halfway under his desk. The brown dent resembled a deep dimple. "Come on, Bobby. We have to go see someone." Conor grabbed his peacoat. When Bobby shot him a puzzled look, he added, "Andersson. The guy who has been yanking our chain for too long."

CHAPTER SIXTY-ONE

2100 Hours, Thursday, October 29, 1942
Outside United States Legation, Strandvägen 7A, Stockholm

Eklof glided to a stop in front of Strandvägen 7C. The front tire bumped the curb hard before the Mercedes came to a complete stop. His sight line to the entrance of the American Legation was clear. He reached over to the passenger seat, his hand passing over his Walther P38 before it found his flask. He unscrewed the cap and took a long pull. He didn't miss the sweetness of his usual schnapps; in fact, he had grown quite fond of the Swedes' *brännvin*. His gunshot wound still throbbed but less so as the brännvin went down.

Three passenger ferries were tied up along the quay, sterns extending into the bay. Two small flatbed trucks were being loaded with crates stacked haphazardly along the quay. A street cleaner and his horse-drawn wagon were parked on the street. Eklof flashed his lights, then opened his window before turning off the engine. One of the men loading crates shuffled over, taking off his gloves as he approached the waiting Mercedes.

Eklof locked his gaze on the lone lit window on the fourth floor. When he first drove up, he'd spotted the piece-of-shit Ford that Thorn was reported to be driving around Stockholm parked in the building's courtyard. Between the half-moon and the gaslights in the courtyard and on the street, he could see well, but that worked two ways—if he could make out Thorn, he could be made also. But what did that matter as long as he did not fail? The cocky American would no longer humiliate him. He was a decorated Luftwaffe pilot with seven confirmed enemy kills on the verge of being given command of his squadron. Not a punching bag. Eklof softly stroked his eye patch.

"He's inside. Been there for at least five hours," the dockhand said as he took off his glasses, fogged the lenses with two deep exhales of warm breath, then wiped them clean with his gloves. "Someone else arrived about fifteen minutes ago. He was in a rush. Ran into the building."

Eklof saw the car parked next to the Ford. "Did you recognize him?"

"No. He was moving too fast."

Eklof took another drink from his flask, then laid it on the passenger seat. He noted the slight buzzing in his ears and thought if he was going to act, he might lay off the brännvin for the rest of the night.

"Keep watch. Report in when you're relieved." He picked up his Walther and ejected the magazine, confirmed the full load, and slammed it back into the grip. He chambered a round, then used the safety-decocking lever to lower the hammer without firing the round. He placed the Walther on his lap. After lighting a cigarette, he leaned back and folded his arms.

The street cleaner was done smoking and resumed his sweeping. The dockhands took a break and drank from metal canteens. A light breeze blew in Eklof's open window. His eyes were half-closed, but he would not sleep. He was too disciplined. He could easily fight his weariness off.

He jumped at the sound of the wood-and-glass door to the legation slamming into the limestone wall with a loud crack. His Walther slipped off his lap to the floor. Thorn and another man, his companion at the Andersson dinner the previous night, exited the legation and headed to the Ford. Thorn hopped in the driver's side and started the car. Eklof fished for his Walther, then flicked his cigarette out the window. Now he just needed the man to drive by. It wouldn't be long.

#

"How did Miller get word to you?" Conor asked.

"He ran off the island and called from the Grand, then headed back to the house."

"Shit. He could be anywhere within a ten-mile radius by now."

"Then why are we going to Andersson's house?"

"Because if he's not there, Andersson should know where he is. And I'll beat the old man until he tells us." Conor jammed the gearshift into reverse, turned in his seat to look out the rear window, and backed into the courtyard. When he shifted into first gear, he saw a light gray Mercedes sedan parked along Strandvägen. "We have company." He revved the engine and popped the clutch, the Ford lurching toward the iron gate.

The Ford had just cleared the gate when two shots rang out, followed by a muffled explosion. The steering wheel felt like he was reeling in a ship anchor—a blown tire. Their momentum carried them toward a tree in the median beside the sidewalk.

Before Conor could hit the brakes, the Ford smashed into the tree. The steering wheel stopped his forward momentum, while Bobby's head slammed into the dashboard.

Conor grabbed his Colt from a shoulder holster and kicked open his door. The Mercedes pulled a tight U-turn on Strandvägen, but midturn he slowed.

Conor saw an arm extended out the driver's-side window, and he took a wide stance, holding the Colt's grip with two hands. Two shots whizzed past him, slamming into the Ford's trunk. A horse tied to a wagon along the far curb began to rear up in panic, the man standing with it struggling to calm it by pulling on its reins. Conor squeezed off three shots at the Mercedes.

The rear driver's side window exploded as the Mercedes accelerated, fishtailing down Strandvägen. The man lost control of the horse, and it bolted into the street. The Mercedes's front right fender clipped the horse's front legs. The horse squealed, then collapsed to the cobblestones. Conor sprinted to the middle of the street and took his stance again and shot three more times. The last two shattered the rear window and blew out the left taillight.

It didn't take long for the speeding Mercedes to get out of range.

Lights were coming on up and down Strandvägen. Several men along the quay were coming out from behind stacks of wooden crates.

"Conor," someone called out. He turned and saw Karlson and Lancer running through the gate toward him. "What the hell? You okay?"

"Yeah." Conor felt his hand tremble as he slipped his Colt back in its holster. "But check on Bobby."

Lancer ran over to the Ford.

"I shot out the rear window and left rear taillight. Can you have someone check to see if it shows up at the German Legation?"

"We'll try. If they're smart, they'll find a warehouse somewhere and hide it."

"He's okay. A bit groggy," Lancer called out from the Ford. "He's got a bump the size of a goddamned walnut on his forehead."

Conor remembered when he and Emily had almost been killed on Victoria Embankment. It was less than three weeks ago, and it was hard to fathom that so much had happened since. His conclusion that day had been that they were making progress in their investigation into who had Ike's missing diary page with the directives for Operation Torch. This time, he didn't feel they were making progress—not with Gunnar Lind back among the missing.

CHAPTER SIXTY-TWO

2215 Hours, Thursday, October 29, 1942
Home of Benjamin Andersson, Norrmalm, Stockholm

Benjamin Andersson was in his nightclothes, but he wasn't sleeping when Gunnar rang the front doorbell. A body needs water, food, and sleep, but the latter had been elusive since the Germans took Eve. Food and water held no interest for him. But brandy did. He poured another from the decanter on his desk while Gunnar paced.

A sole desk lamp lit his study, so Gunnar was pacing in and out of the light, appearing, disappearing, appearing again. Andersson had moments when he had to tune out Gunnar's raving—usually when the irrationality became excessive. He fully appreciated that Gunnar loved his daughter, which made what would transpire in the coming hours that much more difficult to explain to Eve, but he would think of something. Gunnar's regret over the entire scheme also seemed believable but not welcome, as far as Andersson was concerned. He had already reprimanded Gunnar for coming to his house, knowing it was probably being watched.

"The end is near," Andersson said, then immediately regretted his choice of words.

Gunnar stopped in the middle of the desk lamp's light and stared at him.

"I mean, we are reaching the end of our dealings with the Germans. Soon, this will all be behind us."

His son-in-law's pacing resumed.

"Gunnar, please sit. You are making me nauseous."

Gunnar dropped into the armchair in front of Andersson's desk and crossed his legs, his left ankle over his right thigh, his left foot bouncing up and down.

"Are you ready for tomorrow?" Andersson said, pouring another splash of brandy in the snifter that he held between his middle and ring fingers. He swirled the caramel-colored liquid around in his glass and took in the warm, fruity scent. "Well?"

"What do you think? That's all I've been thinking about—the exchange and Eve."

"Don't worry about Eve. I'll take care of her."

Gunnar uncrossed his legs and leaned forward to put his forearms on the desk. "Why won't you tell me where they took her?"

"For one reason. I believe the more you know, the less safe she is."

"What the hell do you mean by that? I'm—"

The pounding on the front door could be heard in the study and made Gunnar spin in his chair—three loud knocks, a pause, three more knocks. The sequence grew louder each time it was repeated. "Head down the back staircase and wait in the wine cellar. And be quiet about it."

\#

Conor's pounding on the heavy oak door was hurting his knuckles. Either the house was empty or he was being ignored. He looked through the door's curtained side windows and made out nothing but a sliver of light underneath a door off the foyer. He headed to the back of the house. A single car was parked in the driveway in front of a garage. He felt the hood. Cold as a stare-down from Lina Stuben. He headed back to the front. As he reached the corner, he saw a beam of light from a flashlight moving back and forth like a metronome as it searched the ground. Conor turned to backtrack to the rear of the house, but he found himself face-to-face with a towering Stockholm policeman. He did not look happy.

CHAPTER SIXTY-THREE

1000 Hours, Friday, October 30, 1942
United States Legation, Strandvägen 7A, Stockholm

On the elevator ride down to the basement, Conor glanced at his image in the mirrored wall. His stubble could almost be called a short beard. His eyes were bloodshot and puffy in spite of getting a couple hours' sleep in the lockup before he'd been released. His teeth felt like they had cotton undershirts on.

Find a toothbrush and a bathroom.

Bobby was sitting at the metal table in the gun room, Emily across from him. The sight of her immediately improved Conor's state of mind. He smiled for the first time since Donovan told him she was missing. As for Bobby, Conor could see the walnut trying to punch through his forehead.

"Shit, Conor. Where have you been? We've got half the team out there looking for you."

Conor threw his blue peacoat on the table and took one of the metal chairs. "Lind?"

"He's back," Bobby reported, "as of about an hour ago."

Conor nodded, running through the extraction schedule in his head. They had to make the move. The details of the operation came and went, swallowed up in a fog of fatigue. Two hours of sleep wasn't enough to make up for the many long days he'd had in a row.

"So where were you?" Emily asked.

Conor buried his face in his hands. "In jail," he said, his words muffled.

"Did you say 'jail'?" Bobby asked.

Conor raised his head. "Yes. But no more questions about it."

"Who sprung you?"

Conor glared at Bobby.

"Sorry."

"Homer. And he's none too pleased about it. Says Ramsay might have me shipped out. Or 'recalled,' as he put it."

"Then we shouldn't hang around here."

"Just what I was thinking. We can't wait until tonight. We need to take Lind today."

"That's damn crazy, Conor, and you know it."

"No. It's not," Emily said. "Every minute he's not in our hands means he's closer to making a deal with the Germans. That can't happen."

"Emily's right. We have no choice if we plan to return him to England on the gun boat," Conor said.

Bobby rubbed his forehead.

"You up for this?"

"It's crazy, but hell yeah."

"I'm going too," Emily said. "And that's final. Right, Conor?"

"You heard the lady. Bobby, get everybody together for a rebrief in thirty minutes. No changes to the plan, but I want to give everyone another chance to back out."

Bobby nodded.

"A few other things. I need fishing gear for at least eight people. See if Gus can help out with that. I want to look like a bunch of guys on a fishing trip out on the Nybroviken. Then get someone to get a car here in the courtyard ready to go here in the courtyard for the trip west. Some extra gas would be great if you can find some."

"I'll have to get someone with black market contacts. Gas is pretty scarce. Hard to find even for legations," Bobby said.

"Do what you have to. Might be another issue Gus can help with. And one more thing—I saw someone from the legation driving a delivery truck. See if you can track it down. We could use it to get all of us to the boat."

Conor fought through the fatigue that sapped his brain. "Oh

yeah. Find Lancer and tell him I need another Colt. It seems I lost one somewhere last night. But tell him I have a special request. I need a suppressor. If I'm going to take out the guard at the back of the house without alerting the guards at the front, I've got to do it quietly."

"Got it." Bobby pushed his chair back, producing a metal-on-concrete rattle, the sound accompanying the squeal of the elevator door opening down the hall. As Bobby passed Buster Seaker, he made sure his shoulder made hard contact with Seaker's. "Oh, excuse me. Need to watch where I'm going."

Seaker looked peaked. His washed-out face was a strong contrast to the dark blue of his navy dress uniform he was wearing.

"This is Emily Bright," Conor said. "MI6. She and I ... we work together."

Emily sat up a bit straighter and cracked a smile.

"Listen, Buster, we're all meeting here in thirty. We're going to hit the Andersson house today."

Seaker sat in one of the metal chairs, looked at Conor's diagram on the chalkboard, and set his combination cap on the table. "I can't go."

Conor was ready for this. "Why is that?"

Seaker had beads of sweat on his upper lip. "I'm just not cut out for it. I admit it. I'd just screw up, and you don't want that, right?"

"No. So just reach down deep and find your balls and get the job done. You're just handling the boat on this mission. You can manage that."

"Conor—"

"Because if you don't, I will make sure that every voter in Massachusetts will know that you backed out of an operation because you just didn't feel up to the challenge. You felt—how did you put it—a little queasy. Your campaign to succeed your father in Congress will go up in smoke after *my* father's radio network digs into your naval background."

What color was left in Seaker's face drained away. He was betting Seaker, who didn't know the high-level urgency of the mission, didn't realize that Conor wouldn't be able to talk about this mission to anyone.

Seaker left in a hurry, forgetting his combination cap on the table.

"Well, that was strange ... and a bit embarrassing, I must say," Emily said.

"Yeah ... well, had to be done. There's a story there. A dark story. But it's coming to a fitting conclusion. Soon."

CHAPTER SIXTY-FOUR

1030 Hours, Friday, October 30, 1942
En Route to Beckholmen, Stockholm

The canvas that covered the sides and roof of the delivery truck snapped in the breeze as they sped down Strandvägen toward the islet of Beckholmen. The rumbles of thunder they had been hearing most of the morning could now only be heard sporadically over the truck. Conor sat on the floor, Emily on his left and Heugle on his right. His newly issued Colt M1911A1 was holstered. In his lap lay a .22 LR High Standard HDM. He had trained with it at Area F but never thought he'd have to use it. It was a semiautomatic pistol with an integrated suppressor that stretched its length to fourteen inches, which forced Conor to carry it in his waistband. It was a model based on a target pistol and adopted by the OSS for close-in operations. The story around Area F was that Colonel Donovan had demonstrated the weapon for President Roosevelt inside the White House. The First Lady must have been out of town.

Seaker sat directly across from Conor, his legs pulled up to his chest. Gus sat next to Seaker, just as Conor had asked him to. Master Sergeant Lancer sat next to Pilot Officer Hammond, and the rest of the British airmen lined the sides of the truck. Several wore wool hats; others wore flat caps. Dark-gray and blue wool coats over wool trousers or overalls gave the group the look of fishermen. Conor's last-minute idea to wrap their shoes and boots with burlap to quiet their arrival on the dock, however, would be hard to explain to anyone if they were stopped. The satchels and duffel bags with their weapons would also tell a different story. On top of the satchels were several fishing poles and a single tackle box. The driver seemed to be doing a great job of finding every rut and pothole.

The men were mostly quiet. Some smoked. Lancer pulled out a pack of cigarettes, tapped one out, offered it to Hammond, who accepted the offering.

"Thanks, I think I'll save it for later," Hammond said.

Conor smiled at the optimism. "Master Sergeant, do you have a lighter I can borrow?"

"Sure." Lancer tossed a lighter to Conor, who pocketed it in the breast pocket of his flannel shirt. "Uh, to borrow, Mr. Thorn, not keep."

Conor nodded. "I'll return it after."

He heard one of the airmen say to his friend that he had never fished before. "I wouldn't know what end of the pole to point to the water."

The ripple of laughter that followed the comment soon faded.

"Stand next to me, Lance Corporal. I'll show you some tricks," Roper-Hastings said.

Conor's thoughts drifted to Eklof and his attempt to put Conor in a pine box. He hoped he would have the chance to return the favor. He nudged Bobby in the ribs. "How's the head?"

Bobby touched the shrinking knot on his forehead gently. "Fine. Say, do I get a Purple Heart?"

Gus laughed. "Mr. Heugle, to most people, we don't even exist."

Gus looked calm, which made Conor feel like he made the right decision about taking him along. He'd put him on Lancer's team with instructions to stay close to Lancer and not be a hero.

Conor looked at his watch. They should be arriving in the next ten minutes. In his mind, he ran through the key points of the plan: hit the dock at 1100 hours. Conor and Emily would move out first toward the slope between the boathouse and the main house, while the two teams moved into position on the north and south sides of the house.

Conor and Emily would move up the slope to the back door, take out the rear guard, and move into the house to grab

Lind. Gunny Miller, with his scoped M1 Garand, would start a diversion from the woods across from the front of the house at 1110 hours sharp. Bobby's and Lancer's teams would take out any guards flushed out from the front of the house by Miller. Emily would signal the pull-out with a whistle, and they'd ride back to the legation. Simple—on a chalkboard and in his head, yes.

But it could start raining shit the minute we hit the dock.

A hush fell over the back of the truck. Conor looked over at Seaker and found him involved in a thousand-yard stare. He had considered having Seaker meet them at the boat, but he was too shaky, and Conor couldn't trust him to show up on his own.

Conor tapped Seaker's leg with his foot, jolting Seaker out of his trance. "The dinner at Grace's father's house ... I think my wife was there. Grace. You didn't mention that. Did you get a chance to talk to her?"

Emily shot a surprised look at Conor that melted into an *I understand now* look.

"What?" Seaker said.

Conor repeated the question a little louder, which caught the attention of the others. "Why didn't you mention her?"

"We chatted briefly. We were both pretty drunk. I'm not even sure what we talked about." Seaker wrapped his arms around his legs and pulled them into his chest. If he were lying on the floor, he'd have been in fetal position. "To be honest, I don't think she liked me much."

"Grace always did have good taste in men," Bobby commented.

Seaker jerked his attention to Bobby. "Shut up, Heugle."

Bobby snapped off a mocking salute in Seaker's direction.

That was enough for now, Conor thought. He detected a whiff of aftershave and noticed a shaving cut on Seaker's chin. Then the truck stopped abruptly.

"Time to move, boys," Conor called out.

#

The last of the fishing gear, satchels, and duffels had been loaded. Seaker had been running the engines for the last five minutes. Conor noticed an occasional misfire, but otherwise, the thirty-footer with a mahogany hull and teak deck looked like it was in decent shape. They wouldn't need the small fore and aft cabins for their short excursion to Skeppsholmen. Seaker, in position in the open-air pilothouse, reversed the engine and maneuvered the boat from the dock.

Conor estimated the trip would take fifteen minutes. They would have to be mindful of the steamship ferry traffic. As they headed into the bay, Emily organized several pieces of rope, cut into two-foot lengths for binding hands and feet, and three rags to be used for gagging Lind and any guards inside the house. She handed some of the materials to Conor, who shoved them into his pocket.

The men started to covertly do a weapons check, then each grabbed a fishing rod and began to play their parts. Nervous chatter ensued until they could see Skeppsholmen. Conor tapped Seaker on the shoulder and pointed at the Andersson boathouse as it came into view. Conor glanced at his watch. They were a little early. Fifty yards from the boathouse, Conor told Seaker to cut the engine and drift. The current slowly pushed them toward the shore. The cloud cover was darkening, the growls of thunder lasting longer.

"Get those poles in sight, boys," Conor said. "And last reminder: when we pull up to the dock, no talking. Absolute quiet."

#

1100 Hours, Friday, October 30, 1942
Andersson Summer Home, Skeppsholmen, Stockholm

After watching some of the most original demonstrations of casting he had ever seen, Conor nodded to Seaker, who restarted the engine. With as little throttle as possible, they headed toward the boat dock. Twenty yards out, Conor signaled Seaker to cut the engine. The breeze was in their face—*Good news*, Conor thought, as it had carried the sound of the boat's approach back out into the bay.

Pulling up to the short dock, Conor saw they were right on time: 1100 hours. The boathouse had two large doors on the bay side, which allowed for the storage of a large boat.

Conor stepped close to Seaker and cupped his hand around his mouth. "Keep your head down. I don't want you to take a stray round."

Conor, with Emily following, passed through the two teams and stepped onto the dock. They scuttled to the base of a short slope facing the house, low-growing shrubs providing some cover. The two teams headed toward their flanking positions. As soon as they looked settled, Conor tugged Emily's sleeve. "Ready, Em?"

"As ever. Just another Portela Airport."

Conor smiled, then jumped up and headed for an outdoor cooking pit framed with red brick. Once huddled behind it, he peered over it at the back of the house. There wasn't just one guard. Two of them were standing under a small overhang above the rear door. Emily crouched beside him. Conor held up two fingers, and she nodded. The two guards, their machine pistols slung over their shoulders, were engaged in an animated conversation, unaware of the ten-man team about to make their lives a noisy mess.

Conor lifted the nose of his suppressed HDM semiautomatic over the edge of the brick enclosure and let it rest there. He slowed his breathing, exhaled, then squeezed off two rounds. Both guards crumpled to the ground, falling into each other. Conor and Emily slipped around the cooking pit and headed for the back door. His boots temporarily lost their grip on the slope due to the burlap covering, but he regained his balance as they reached the house.

He listened for any movement inside. Hearing only Emily's labored breathing, he reached for the doorknob and gradually turned it. The door was unlocked. He pushed it open and entered a room with umbrellas, muddy shoes, and rain hats hung on hooks. Through an open doorway to the right, he saw that the next room was lit up. He shuffled close to the edge of the doorway and saw a man in a kitchen, sitting at a table, his back to Conor. He was broad shouldered and dressed in a sleeveless undershirt, pants, no shoes. His braces were off his shoulders and dangled at his sides. This man was bald. Not the wavy-haired Lind. There was no gun nearby, only the newspaper he was reading. Conor raised the

HDM Colt over his shoulder and brought it down hard on the back of the guard's head. His body fell forward, his head hitting the table loud enough to draw attention.

When Conor heard no movement, he scowled. *Either Lind is not here, or he's deaf or hiding.*

Conor left Emily to tie up and gag the guard so he could prowl through the house. Five minutes later, Conor returned to the kitchen. "No Gunnar."

"He's around here someplace. You check the closets and basement?"

"There's no basement that I can find. And yes. All the closets."

Emily shook her head. "What's this?" She was looking down at the floor along the edge of a baseboard. A copper wire ran from the living room through the kitchen.

Conor followed it back into the room they'd first entered and out a window no more than a foot square.

#

Gunnar took a breather. He was winded from his efforts to pry a floorboard free. A claw hammer rested in his lap. He thought he heard footsteps outside, but after stopping for a beat and hearing nothing, he went back to the task of freeing the floorboard so he could stash the documents. The pry bar that he had carelessly let fall into the water would have made the job so much easier. He looked at his watch. Five minutes after the hour. He glanced at the phone he had just hooked up to the wire he'd strung from the house earlier that morning. The call from Andersson, if the Germans followed their instructions, would be coming within minutes.

#

Conor and Emily retreated through the back door, stepped over the bodies of the two guards, and followed the wire to the boathouse. After slipping down the slope, Conor stopped and listened. The pounding of a hammer was immediately drowned out by the gunfire from Miller's Garand, followed by sporadic gunfire from the assault team's carbines. His watch read exactly 1110 hours.

#

1110 Hours, Friday, October 30, 1942
BI Maskineri Företag, Östermalm, Stockholm

When Andersson's office phone rang, he glanced at the wall clock. By the time he hung up, he was smiling. Just as he did upon seeing, ten minutes earlier, the second outside line on his phone light up. His secretary was following his order to call the Soviet legation with information as to the location of the exchange.

"The money has been deposited and verified."

Walter Schellenberg initially offered no response. His steely eyes didn't blink. Finally, he spoke. "Make the call."

Andersson picked up the phone and dialed. A beat passed. "Leave the documents as planned. But stay there. There seems to be a slight delay in the authentication process." He hung up. "You can find the documents under a floorboard in the center of the boathouse at my summer home." Andersson handed Schellenberg a note. "Here are directions. It will take you no more than fifteen minutes from here. If Gunnar follows my orders, he will be there."

Schellenberg stood up and handed the directions to a man in a leather coat, black hat, and gloves. "Eklof, take your men and leave at once. Bring the documents and Lind to the legation."

Eklof saluted crisply.

"And, Eklof ... do not fail me."

#

1113 Hours, Friday, October 30, 1942
Andersson Summer Home, Skeppsholmen, Stockholm

Conor and Emily, plastered against the boathouse door, heard a phone ring but no voice. A one-way conversation. Conor stepped back and kicked the doorknob. The dry wood of the door and doorjamb shattered and the door flung open. Standing by the phone was Gunnar Lind. A hammer lay on a loose floorboard close by.

"Hello, Gunnar," Emily said. "It's been a long time."

Lind, his face ashen, looked blankly at Emily, then at the opening where the floorboard had been pried free. Conor followed this gaze to the opening, bent down, and pulled a brown envelope from the hole. He handed it to Emily, who pocketed her Colt and slid the envelope open and began to thumb through the pages. "Notes, a lot of notes in long hand. It seems to detail code-breaking methods of wireless traffic for Lorenz teleprinters used by the Germans. There're mentions of *Fish* and *Tunny*." She looked at Lind. "What do *Fish* and *Tunny* refer to?" she asked as she passed a page to Gunnar.

He looked at the page and froze, his mouth agape. Emily snatched the paper from his hand and thumbed through more of the file. "There are also some detailed notes on dates of successes and failures at reading Nazi ciphers and names of those involved." She handed them to Conor. "This gives the Germans all they need to know to immediately change all their codes. It will set Bletchley back a year, probably more."

"We need to destroy these. Sound the recall of the teams, then tie his hands and gag him." Conor dropped the file on the floor and knelt. He kept his HDM trained on Lind as Emily blew three short blasts on the whistle.

"If we don't leave here soon, we'll run into German agents swarming the house, looking for those documents and me."

"Patience, Gunnar. First things first." Conor pulled the lighter from his shirt pocket and lit the documents. The pile smoldered at first but caught fully in seconds. As Emily bound Gunnar's hands and placed a gag in his mouth, Conor noted Lind's defeated look;

his entire body sagged. Emily took him by the arm and led him to the boat.

Bobby's team arrived first. One of the airmen, the one who had never gone fishing, had his arm wrapped around Roper-Hastings. The airman's right pant leg was soaked with blood. They headed for the boat. Lancer followed; Gus was assisting wounded RAF airman Pilot Officer Hammond. A round had grazed his head, taking with it a patch of hair. The whole left side of his face was awash with blood.

Only two wounded. Not bad, Conor thought. He looked up the slope behind the house and didn't see anyone following the two teams. He could still hear occasional shots from Miller's M1 Garand, and he hoped the man was going to follow instructions to drop the rifle and beat it out of there on foot at twenty after the hour no matter what.

Conor jumped into the bow deck and signaled, a circular motion of his raised index finger, to Seaker to hit the throttle. Lancer and Bobby hustled to get the weapons back in the satchels and duffel bags, while Gus kept an eye on a pale looking Lind.

Once out in the bay, Seaker mixed in with the ferries and other maritime traffic. The men that could grabbed their fishing poles and settled in for the trip back to the legation. Conor went over to Hammond, who was lying on top of the rear cabin's roof.

"You want me to light up that cigarette now, Pilot Officer?" Conor asked.

"That would be just stellar." Hammond dug the cigarette out of his breast pocket.

Conor cupped his hand around the lighter and lit the cigarette, then he headed to the pilothouse, flipping the lighter to Lancer as he passed him. "A borrow, not a keep."

Lancer smiled. "That's right. But you keep it. You may need it," Lancer said as he handed the lighter back. "Think of it as a thank-you gift for the fishing trip. I haven't had that much fun in quite a while. Not since Manila."

"Glad to oblige, Master Sergeant."

The thunder rumbled, and this time it sounded like it was right on top of them. As rain started to fall, the men groaned. Conor saw Emily in the pilothouse; she was watching him. He stepped toward her and Seaker, who looked like he had regained a spring to his step. Bobby was at Conor's heels as he slid between Emily and Seaker.

Now or never.

The rain was coming down hard. The wind whipped it into horizontal sheets, blowing right into their faces. Conor leaned in to Seaker. "Did you rape my wife?"

Seaker jerked his head toward Conor and then froze.

"Did you, on the night of the Maxwell dinner, rape my wife?"

Emily and Bobby exchanged looks. Bobby looked stunned. He crept a bit closer to Seaker, then pushed him aside, toward Conor, and took the wheel.

"Here's what I know," Conor said. "You raped a barmaid in Annapolis your last year."

"Sandy Evans," Bobby shouted.

"You raped Greta."

Seaker pulled back, but Bobby pushed him back toward Conor.

"I had it checked out. She's still not back to work. This is a pattern any police department would be interested in."

"Thorn, you are way off base. I never touched your wife. And Greta wouldn't be able to remember—"

"The dinner at the Maxwell house—you were there. You're the one who Grace told Sue that arrived late. You were already drinking, according to my sister. Grace laid out some other details about that night. You told Grace you just wanted to talk, and Grace, being the type of person she was, said sure. The library, that's where you raped her: the hand over the mouth, the slicked-back hair, the overpowering smell of aftershave. Aqua Velva. Your favorite going back to the Academy." Conor paused as a ferry passed them, some passengers waving at the group of fishermen. "Any of this making sense to you?"

Seaker's jaw muscles were flexing. He ran a hand through his hair.

Conor wiped the rain from his face.

"Did you rape Grace Thorn?" Emily asked, her voice harsh.

Lancer took a few steps toward the pilothouse.

Seaker stared straight ahead, blinking rapidly against the rain. Suddenly, he slumped against the bulkhead. "She was drunk. I was drunk."

"She wasn't drunk enough to forget the details, though."

"She didn't say no."

Conor stepped in and drew within an inch of Seaker's face. "She couldn't." A surge of rage was stripping Conor of his control.

"Because you had your hand over her mouth," Emily said.

"Say it, Seaker," Bobby said. "Say it, you bastard."

Seaker pushed off the bulkhead. "Yes. Yes, I did. She wanted it. I could tell."

Lancer held out a Colt. Conor reached for it, but Emily beat him to it.

"That's not going to happen, Conor," Emily said.

"Then let me do it," Bobby said. In a flash, Bobby had slapped the butt of his Colt across the back of Seaker's head and sent him to the deck in a heap.

CHAPTER SIXTY-FIVE

1128 Hours, Friday, October 30, 1942
Andersson Summer Home, Skeppsholmen, Stockholm

The rain began to fall heavily as the two cars drove across the narrow one-way bridge linking Skeppsholmen with the central part of Stockholm. There were few pedestrians and fewer vehicles to slow their transit. Eklof, driving the lead car with an agent beside him, approached the end of the bridge at high speed. The wipers flailed at the stream of water that flooded down the windshield, making Eklof strain to see what was up ahead. The agent, his arm extended to the dashboard to steady him, pointed ahead and gasped. Eklof swerved and slammed his fist on the horn, nearly colliding with a lone figure in dark clothing running across the bridge.

The trees in the patch of woods across from the house danced back and forth in the stiff wind as both cars skidded to a stop. A battered Volvo was parked near the front door. Before Eklof got out of the Mercedes, he had already counted five bodies. Pulling out his gun, he headed to the Volvo and placed his hand on the hood. It was warm. He made for the bay side of the house, three agents just steps behind. When he rounded the corner, he saw three men, their heads down. Wide-brimmed hats shielded their faces from the downpour as they made slow progress up the rain-soaked slope that led down to the boathouse, its door standing open. He had no time to ask questions, even if they were Stockholm police. But these men didn't dress like the plainclothes officers he had seen in and around Stockholm. These three men looked like they had just stepped off a soup line at a church mission.

He raised his Walther just as his other agents slid to a stop, their guns also raised. The lead man reached the top of the slope and raised his head as the crack of the Walther filled the air. He fell to the ground as the second man in line drew his gun and fired. The agent beside Eklof grunted and grabbed his chest. Eklof stood his ground and fired off two rounds. The second man in line dropped to his knees, then fell, sliding down the slope, stopping at the feet of the third man who stood frozen. Eklof's next shot found its target—the three men on the slope, all dead.

"One of you, search them. I want to know who they worked for. Someone search the house. You know who I want. Find him," Eklof said as he slithered down the slope to the door of the boathouse, carefully avoiding the human detritus.

Before he even walked through the door, he smelled smoke. His shoulders slumped when he saw the pile of ashes on the floor near a pried-up floorboard. He knelt and stirred the ashes with a finger to verify that whatever intelligence the documents once held had burned completely—nothing readable remained.

Eklof stood and looked around the boathouse. Smoke still lingered among the rafters above his head. Rain pelted the roof, producing a low roar.

An agent entered the boathouse, the rain sliding off his leather coat. Mud was smeared up and down his left side from an apparent fall on the slope. "Herr, Eklof. I found this," he said, holding up a folded piece of damp paper. "It was in a pocket of one of the dead men."

The paper had a phone number and details of an extraction plan for MI6 agents Thorn and Bright through the port of Lysekil on the west coast of Sweden that night. Eklof exhaled slowly.

"Herr Eklof?" the agent said.

"Nothing."

A second agent entered and reported a guard tied up in the kitchen, out cold. "I revived him and asked about Lind. He couldn't tell me anything. I searched the house ..." The agent just shook his head.

"Go collect the Mausers off the dead guards and get ready to leave." Eklof walked to the phone and dialed the number on the paper.

A woman with an Eastern European accent answered, "Red Star Import Export."

Eklof dropped the phone in the cradle. Pointing at the agent who found the extraction plans, he said, "You stay here and call Brigadeführer Schellenberg at Benjamin Andersson's office. Report our findings and the details laid out in this." He handed the paper over to the agent. "Tell him I request German E-boats and search planes from Skagen to monitor sea traffic out of Lysekil." Skagen, on the tip of Denmark's Jutland peninsula, was the closest German base to Lysekil. If Eklof couldn't stop Thorn from leaving Lysekil, he would need resources to keep them from reaching England. "And tell the Brigadeführer I am headed to Lysekil immediately. I will not stop until I have Thorn and Lind."

Eklof left the boathouse. Outside, he heard sirens, the shifting winds carrying the sound inland, then back toward the house, making them sound intermittent. He looked behind him and saw a police launch two hundred yards out in the bay headed for the house. Time to leave.

CHAPTER SIXTY-SIX

1200 Hours, Friday, October 30, 1942
White's Club, No. 37–38 St. James Street, London

Donovan hustled up the stairs to the first-floor Coffee Room. He was well aware of the reputation his lunch companion had for punctuality. Ian Fleming would be pleased if Donovan was already seated at the corner table, sipping his first cup of coffee when he arrived, but as Donovan reached the top of the stairs, he spotted Fleming through the doorway. He was dressed in a double-breasted dark-blue Royal Navy commander uniform, his back to the window overlooking St. James Street. He was focused on inserting a cigarette into a holder.

"Early as usual, I see."

"Never keep a good man waiting. And never, never keep a good woman waiting. How are you, Colonel?" Fleming asked, extending his hand over the table. The bright sunlight gave a backlit glow to Fleming, who looked very much at ease in the confines of his club. Donovan, who hadn't seen his longtime friend for several months, took note that Fleming's hairline had receded since their last meeting. They were the only guests in the south end of the Coffee Room. A club attendant was seating guests at the north end, and he assumed Fleming, a popular club member in good standing, had asked for some privacy.

"Fine, Ian. I must say, you look quite chipper today."

"Considering there's a war on, I'm surprised I'm so happy.

Nothing like opening a second front to pound the Germans to make one's outlook a bit rosier."

A waiter arrived with a pot of coffee, poured two cups, and left menus on the white linen tablecloth. Fleming lit his cigarette. "You must be pleased with the outcome of your man Thorn's efforts to secure the secrecy of Torch."

"Let's not forget Bright. I think she kept him from acting in his usual impetuous manner."

"Oh, I don't know, Bill. Impulsive and rash action can put the Nazis on their heels. I wish Montgomery had some of those qualities; if he did, we might be farther west along the coast of North Africa than we are."

Donovan smiled. He had heard from more than one source about General Montgomery's penchant for overanalysis and delayed action, a clear contrast to his chief adversary, Field Marshall Erwin Rommel. "Speaking of Bright, are you up to speed on her … situation?" Donovan asked.

"Yes. Not directly from Menzies, but word does get out. Mostly through patrons of MI6's bar—the most secret drinking establishment in the western hemisphere," Fleming said, smiling broadly. "Has Thorn made any progress on his current mission?"

Donovan wasn't surprised that Fleming knew about what were supposed to be eyes-only operations. He worked as personal assistant to Rear Admiral John Godfrey, the Director of Naval Intelligence, and operated as the abrasive Godfrey's liaison with MI6, among other branches of government. "No word since he arrived late Monday, I'm afraid. He's right up against his … their extraction window."

"Ah, yes. The motor gun boat ball bearing run. Great idea, that," Fleming said, his voice trailing off. Fleming looked away, stroked his eyebrow and then finished off half a cup of coffee.

"What, Ian? Something about the gun boat?"

"Yes. Well, it seems they've been having engine trouble. Parts are hard to come by where they are. And, on top of that, their lead motor mechanic is out of commission for a few days. There is some concern about their ability to outrun German E-boats with one of their four engines running poorly."

"Did you get that from Menzies?" Donovan asked, concerned that the chief of MI6 was keeping secrets from him.

"No. That's directly from the Admiralty."

"Hmm." Donovan stared out the window, looking past Fleming through a haze of cigarette smoke. He didn't like being out of the loop.

Fleming reached into his coat and pulled out a gun. "Bill, I want to thank you again for this." He brandished the .38 Police Positive Colt revolver given in appreciation for taking Donovan under his wing while he helped open doors to the British intelligence community. The wealth of information that followed came at a critical point in the establishment of the Office of the Coordinator of Information, later the Office of Strategic Services. "It is my full-time travel companion. Well, almost full-time." Fleming brought the two-and-a-half-inch barrel closer to his face. "And the inscription ... that is what I am most proud of: 'For Special Services.' I show this to almost everyone I meet."

"You deserve it. You were a great help to my country and me. But maybe you should put it away. It might scare off our waiter."

"Yes, of course."

At the sound of soft footfalls on the Persian rug, Donovan turned and saw his assistant, Duncan Lee, walk up to the table, his breathing a bit labored.

"Colonel, this message arrived from Karlson late last night. It must have been overlooked, as it only got to our office about forty-five minutes ago. I thought it couldn't wait."

Fleming stubbed out his cigarette as Donovan took the message, read it, and leaned back in his chair. "Emily is safe. She's a little banged up, but she's okay."

"Excellent news. And Lind?"

"It says they were closing in on him last night." He turned to Lee. "Did you check for any other messages from Gus?"

"I did, sir. Nothing else from Stockholm."

Donovan turned to Fleming. "No news is—"

"No news. Not bad, not good," Fleming said, slipping his .38 Colt into his jacket.

CHAPTER SIXTY-SEVEN

1200 Hours, Friday, October 30, 1942
United States Legation, Strandvägen 7A, Stockholm

Bobby tied the boat up to the quay in front of the legation. Homer and a fidgety Masterman were waiting next to the delivery truck along with Gunny Miller. The airmen and Roper-Hastings boarded the truck, while Lancer and Miller helped take the two wounded men into the legation for treatment.

Bobby escorted Lind off the boat, across the street, and into the legation. Homer and Masterman walked over to meet Conor and Emily, who were joined by Gus.

"Buster Seaker's in the pilothouse. You need to place him under house arrest or whatever you call it. He admitted, in front of witnesses that …" Conor's voice halted. His throat closed.

"He raped Conor's late wife. Back in the States," Emily finished.

Homer and Masterman exchanged looks, which seemed to lack the surprise Conor expected.

"Why don't you tell us that story when we get inside the legation?" Homer said. "I feel a little exposed out here, don't you?"

#

1205 Hours, Friday, October 30, 1942
BI Maskineri Företag, Östermalm, Stockholm

Schellenberg listened to the agent on the phone while he kept his eyes fixed on Benjamin Andersson, who tightly gripped the armrests of his chair. His roving eye moved more rapidly than in previous meetings. Schellenberg had no questions or comments about the report. When the agent finished by telling him Eklof was in pursuit of Thorn, and most likely Gunnar Lind, he, in a very deliberate fashion, hung up the phone.

Neither man spoke.

Neither man moved. Finally, Schellenberg broke the silence.

"What do you think that call was about?"

"I wouldn't ... I have no way of knowing that," Andersson said.

"It seems that we were too late. It seems that the Russians arrived before us." Schellenberg stopped to study Andersson's reaction. "Was it a coincidence that they were there?"

"I wouldn't know. You'd have to ask them that."

Schellenberg waited before replying. He had a decision to make. Quickly. "And we did just that. Before Eklof put a bullet in his head, one of the Russians said they had a deal with you for the same intelligence that we ... purchased ... for one million krona. Which, of course, you will return to me before the day is out."

The mention of returned money seemed to deflate the man. Andersson released the armrests and sank deeper into his chair.

"Your plan was to sell to us, we take possession of this supposedly invaluable intelligence, you give the Russians the information about when it's happening, and they steal both Lind and the intelligence from us."

Andersson pushed his chair away from his desk and started to get up.

"Sit down. Do not move unless I tell you to."

Schellenberg walked around the desk and sat on the corner inches away from the old man, glaring down at him. "Someone beat us to the house. And beat the Russians. By the way, the guards you had watching the house ..."

Andersson looked up at Schellenberg, his roving eye moving back and forth in his eye socket like a porch swing.

"They're all dead, I am told."

"All those men had families," Andersson said nearly inaudibly.

"That is on your head. Not mine." Schellenberg paused. "Now, where was I? Ah, yes. Of course we know who that someone is. And we will find him. And your son-in-law. And the intelligence." Schellenberg paused and stroked his chin. "Do you know Carl Tolberg, chief of the C Bureau?"

"Yes. I have met him once or twice. Why do you ask?" Andersson said haltingly, his voice uneasy.

"Good. Call him. Tell him that an American by the name of Conor Thorn has committed murder at your summer home and has kidnapped two Swedish citizens. He is on his way to Lysekil. And please make sure you mention that one of the citizens is your daughter." A beat passed. Then Schellenberg clapped his hands once, which sounded like a slap to a face.

Andersson flinched at the sound.

"I am done here … for the moment." He walked to the office door but stopped halfway there. "*Ach*, how could I forget?" In a low voice, he said, "Germany expects your company to double the amount of ball bearings you send to us and lower the price by fifty percent. On this, we demand immediate action." He exited the office, capping his conversation with Andersson with a sharp slam of the door.

In the outer office, Andersson's elderly assistant sat at her desk with a gaping mouth. "Leave," Schellenberg said.

"What did you—"

"Leave me. I need to make a call." Hurriedly, the woman gathered up a notepad and pencil and ducked into Andersson's office. Schellenberg picked up her phone and called the German military attaché. He gave instructions, in the name of Reichsführer Himmler and Brigadeführer Schellenberg, to have air and naval units dispatched from bases at Skagen and Aalborg to monitor and intercept any suspicious watercraft headed west.

On his way to the elevator, Schellenberg realized that, if his thinking was correct, Thorn had Lind, Eve, and the MI6 agent. And he'd destroyed the intelligence that Schellenberg paid for. Thorn was having a streak of good luck—but all streaks come to an end at some point.

CHAPTER SIXTY-EIGHT

1500 Hours, Friday, October 30, 1942
E18, West of Örebro, *Sweden*

Conor didn't like being on a main road. His plan had called for taking back roads and staying under the radar. But they didn't have enough time. The most direct route would barely get them to Lysekil in time as it was. Bobby, his M1A1 carbine and his Colt M1911A1 on the seat beside him, had taken over driving to give Conor a chance to sleep. But his sleep was fitful at best. He turned to look over his shoulder. Both Eve and Emily were asleep. Emily's head rested against the side window. Wisps of her light-brown hair covered her face. Conor was glad he hadn't pressed her for details about how Stuben tortured her. But maybe the details didn't really matter.

Eve was slumped down in the leather seat, her arms folded across her chest. A bandage covered the wounds to her cheek. Emily had told Conor that he couldn't put Eve in the trunk with her husband. He let Emily win that one.

"Did I ask you where you got this car?" Conor said.

"You did. A while back. But I think you were half-asleep when you did," Bobby said. "She's a beaut, isn't she? Volvo PV54, eighty-six horses under that hood. She even looks fast parked in the lot."

"I miss the Ford. Too bad about hitting that tree."

"What about my head hitting the dash?"

"Yeah, that too," Conor said, prompting a slow, disgusted shake of Bobby's head.

"So who owns it?"

"Well, the US government does. But it's assigned to Minister Ramsay."

Conor's eyes widened and he turned to Bobby. "No way he let you use it." He looked at his friend for a few seconds. "You didn't ask, did you?"

"Like you said, no way he'd let us use it."

Conor shook his head. "What did the extra gas cost on the black market?"

"Two pounds of coffee and two bottles of Johnny Walker."

"Ah, let me guess ... compliments of Ramsay?"

"Sort of. His secretary. She really likes me."

Conor snorted.

They drove in silence, cutting through large expanses of fallow farmland interspersed with tracts of land carpeted with bright yellow flowers.

"You know, I'm not just a little pissed that you never mentioned Grace and Seaker. I thought we were friends."

Conor was surprised it took Bobby as long as it did before he brought the subject up. He was actually relieved. "We are. You know that. But I didn't have the whole picture until just before we left to get Lind. Plus, I worried what you might do to Seaker if I told you I suspected him. You two aren't exactly pen pals."

Bobby swore under his breath.

"I'm sorry I didn't—"

"No, no. It's not that. You hear that hissing? I think we have a radiator problem."

Puffs of steam were coming from the seams of the front hood. "Pull over as soon as you can. We don't want to lose too much water."

Bobby pulled onto a rough single-track dirt road with ruts that seemed to fit the narrow base of farm tractors. The road cut through two fields of the bright yellow flower he had seen earlier. Emily and Eve stirred.

"Did that secretary give you any tools?"

"No. I'll look in the trunk," Bobby said, hopping out of the car.

"What's going on?" Emily asked.

"Engine issues. We're taking a look. Let's get Lind out of the trunk and let him take a bathroom break. But keep your gun on him. We don't want to lose him again."

Conor poked his head under the hood and saw the clamp on the rubber hose at the base of the radiator had come loose. Bobby found a canvas bag with a set of common tools and a pair of leather gloves in the trunk. "I'll take care of this. You keep an eye on Eve."

#

Emily untied the rope around Gunnar's feet and hands and removed his gag. Eve helped him as he struggled to get out of the trunk. "You all have guns. I don't. Is it really necessary to keep me in the trunk?"

"Can't trust you. A shout to a passing policeman would not be good. We're not taking any chances. Now take a walk over there, keep your back to me, and go to the bathroom. Eve, this is the best we can do."

"I'm fine. But I'm thirsty."

Bobby came up behind Emily. "He should have it fixed in a few minutes. Nothing major. And there's water in the basket on the floor in the back seat."

"Any chance we have time to take some back roads? I feel we're a little exposed on a main road," Emily said as she kept her eye on Gunnar, who was buttoning his fly.

"Conor says there's not enough time. And this delay isn't helping much." Bobby looked around. "What is it with all these yellow flowers … in late October?"

Emily started to speak, but Eve interrupted. "They're winter rapeseed plants. They mostly make a vegetable oil from it." She took a step toward Emily and Bobby. "Can I talk to my husband … alone, please?"

Emily was slow to respond. She didn't trust either of them but decided there was no harm. "I'll give you thirty seconds." Bobby walked around the rear of the car and pulled out a three-gallon can of gas and topped off the tank. Emily watched Eve and Gunnar huddle in the shade of the tall rapeseed plants. Eve touched her stomach as she spoke. Gunnar listened until he grabbed Eve by the shoulders and shook her. Eve slapped him across the face and stomped back to the car.

"Something he said?" Bobby asked.

Eve jumped into the back seat and slammed the door behind her.

CHAPTER SIXTY-NINE

1630 Hours, Friday, October 30, 1942
En route to Lysekil, Sweden

Conor peeked at the gas gauge. The needle seemed to be dropping more quickly the closer it got to empty. The stretch of road they were on ran between more farms and fields. An occasional house set far off the road would appear, but the farther west they traveled, few commercial buildings or options for fuel were evident. Eve had fallen asleep a few minutes after they'd resumed their journey. Emily sat next to Conor to give Bobby a chance to catch some sleep in the back seat. He had been asleep for thirty minutes when Lind started kicking the trunk lid, waking both Bobby and Eve.

"Shut up, Gunnar," Eve called out.

Lind stopped kicking ... for ten seconds.

"We can't listen to that for the rest of the trip," Emily said.

"No, we can't." Conor pulled the Volvo onto the shoulder, grabbed his Colt, and got out. Bobby and Emily joined him. He opened the trunk lid and was hit with the overpowering smell of gas, the intestinal kind. All three took a step back. Lind laid on his right side with his feet bound and his hands tied behind his back. He was trying to talk; Conor thought about taking the gag out but decided that he didn't need to do him any favors.

"Okay, so we need a bathroom." Conor looked at his companions. "And we need gas. We won't make it on what we have left."

"We might need to take one of these side roads to a town nearby," Bobby said.

Conor looked at his watch. Forty minutes after the hour. They needed to get to Lysekil Harbor no later than sunset. "That detour could really set us back … but we have no other choice." He grabbed the trunk lid and looked at Lind. "We'll stop as soon as we can." Then he slammed it shut.

Fifteen minutes later, they passed a battered wooden sign advertising a roadhouse that featured fresh fish and steaks five miles ahead. More importantly, in the corner of the sign for the Tivoli Restaurant was the phrase "Petrol Available."

"Whoever was saying prayers, thank you," Conor said.

Five minutes later, they drove past a gravel parking lot. The weathered clapboard building looked as battered as the road sign. Conor pulled into a small stand of trees to avoid anyone looking out the windows at the restaurant, and he and Bobby got out, untied Lind, and pulled him from the trunk. "We're heading to a gas station and restaurant. I am going to ungag you. I will be right behind you when we go inside. And in my hand will be this," Conor said, pushing his Colt under Lind's chin. "I will use this and make a mess of the place if you step out of line. You get what I'm saying?"

"Yes. Of course. Can we please hurry?"

"Get in the back with Eve."

Conor pulled the car up to a single gas pump in the middle of a gravel parking lot that hosted two cars and one tractor. Bobby got out and started pumping gas.

"Ladies first," Conor said.

Lind groaned.

Emily, gun in her coat pocket, followed Eve into the building. Conor and Lind waited until they returned.

"Any issues?"

"No. The bathroom is in the back before you enter the restaurant. There's an attendant at a counter on the left when you first go in. Busy reading the newspaper."

"Got it." Conor turned to Gunnar. "Let's move. And remember what I have in my pocket."

Lind took off at a brisk pace.

"Easy, boy. Don't look so desperate."

They walked past the middle-aged attendant who was folding

up his newspaper. He didn't pay either of them any attention. But that was not the case when they came out. He was standing behind the counter with his arms folded; a potbelly hung well below his belt. He watched Lind pass and then Conor, who smiled as he strode passed.

"*Vill du ha mat?*"

Lind stopped abruptly and turned to the man. "*Ja.*"

Conor bumped into Lind and poked the nose of the Colt into his ribs. "Move, Gunnar."

Lind headed for the door.

Back at the car, Emily and Eve were already in the back seat. Bobby came running out of the woods as he zipped up. When Gunnar slid into the seat next to Eve, he took her hand. Eve jerked her hand free.

They stopped at the same place as before and loaded Lind back into the trunk. Before Conor shoved in the gag, he asked, "What did that guy say?"

"He asked if we wanted some food."

"And you said yes. So now he thinks we're a couple of idiots for not grabbing some food. Not helpful," he said, before shoving the gag deep into his mouth.

#

The parking lot of the Tivoli Restaurant was empty except for a man bent over, working on the engine of a farm tractor and a flatbed delivery truck at the lone gas pump. The driver pulled the Mercedes up behind the truck. Eklof got out, stretched for a moment, then looked at his watch. Forty-five minutes after five. He tamped down any hope that this stop would yield useful information about his prey. The previous three stops had produced no such information. He marched across the lot and entered the building. A portly older man, the corner of a white napkin tucked into the collar of his flannel shirt, sat at a desk behind the counter, picking at the bones of a small fish. Eklof looked into the restaurant beyond and saw nothing but empty tables. The man wiped his hands on his napkin and approached the counter.

"Have you seen this man?" Eklof asked, holding up a photo of Gunnar Lind.

The man motioned to have the picture brought closer. *"Ja."*

Eklof froze. He hadn't expected an affirmative answer. "You are sure?"

"As sure as I am standing here." He looked at an antique carved wood clock on the wall behind the counter. "Thirty minutes ago."

"Who was he with?"

"An American or Englishman, I am not sure, but he spoke English. There were three others in the same car. One man said he was hungry, but he didn't buy any food."

Eklof spent five minutes going over a verbal description of Thorn, the woman called Durs, and Eve Lind. The old man confirmed that they all used the facilities a little less than thirty minutes prior. Eklof looked out the window and saw that his agent had pulled up to the gas pump.

"What type of car were they driving?" Eklof asked as he watched his man begin filling their tank.

"Ah, I believe it was a Volvo. A dark color. I think one of the PV models."

He turned to the old man and nodded. "How much farther is Lysekil?"

The old man looked up to the ceiling. "About two hours. That's if the ferry isn't broken down, like it usually is."

News of a ferry surprised him. He realized he hadn't looked at the map closely enough. "Isn't Lysekil on the coast?"

"Yes, but the road you're on crosses the Gullmarsfjorden."

Eklof nodded. "Can I use your phone?"

The man pointed at a closet-size office tucked in a corner behind the counter. "You can leave a krona or two?"

Eklof reached in his pocket for three krona. "An extra one for privacy."

#

1800 Hours, Friday, October 30, 1942
German Legation, Södra Blasieholmshammer 2, Stockholm

The satchel of money was placed in the middle of the desktop. Schellenberg didn't offer Andersson a chair. He stood, hat in hands, stoop shouldered. He now had no German money and no daughter.

"Is it all there?"

"Yes. Every krona."

"And did you reach out to Tolberg at the C Bureau like I asked?"

"Yes. And he said that he would call the Lysekil Police."

Schellenberg nodded.

"Can I see my daughter now?"

"No. As I said, not until we have Gunnar Lind in our hands."

Andersson reached into his breast pocket and pulled out an envelope, which he presented to Schellenberg. "Would you at least give this to her?"

Schellenberg took the envelope and saw penmanship that could have only been done by a woman's hand. "Ah, a note of encouragement from a loving mother."

"Yes. She is worried about Eve terribly. She says I am to blame."

Schellenberg smiled. "Well, of course you are." He ripped the envelope in half. Andersson's jaw dropped. "Good-bye, Mr. Andersson. And remember: double the ball bearing shipments and make sure you apply our discount."

Andersson shuffled to the door just as the secretary entered the office. "Herr Eklof is on the phone. He says it's urgent."

Schellenberg watched Andersson leave, then picked up the handset. There was a low hum on the line. "Yes, Eklof, speak."

"We are thirty minutes behind them. They do not know that. We are two hours from Lysekil. Have the police been notified?"

"Yes. Of course, a small town will have a small force. They may be of no help."

"I understand. And the Luftwaffe and Kriegsmarine units?"

"Notified." There was a long pause. "Eklof, are you still there?"

"Yes. Sir, excuse me for asking. I know you have an … interest in Thorn. When I find him, what do you want me to do?"

Schellenberg thought the chances of Thorn actually presenting Himmler's peace offer to Roosevelt were slim. There were other channels Schellenberg could explore to sell the peace plan, which was as much his as it was Himmler's.

"Kill him. He has caused enough trouble for us."

"And the women?'

"*Ach*, kill them too. I just want Gunnar Lind."

CHAPTER SEVENTY

1800 Hours, Friday, October 30, 1942
Holy Trinity Church, Knightsbridge, London

The prior night, when Kim Philby signaled that he wanted to meet with Shapak—placing his bicycle along the iron fence in front of his home, then locking it in place—he had taken the time to smoke a cigarette. He needed the extra few minutes away from his wife and children to calm himself. He had received no word from Shapak since he'd handed off the details of the extraction plan for Thorn and Bright. It was not like Shapak to go so long without communicating in some manner.

Today, being an even-numbered day, he went to Holy Trinity Church and walked to the corner below the mezzanine, featuring a bank of three confessional booths. The booths had narrow stalls on each side with a heavy felt curtain across their thresholds. Philby entered the dark confines of the left stall, per instructions. The mustiness was familiar to him from previous meetings, as was the extreme firmness of the kneeler. Philby always thought it was the first phase of a sinner's penance.

He had no sooner knelt than the glass window separating the booth and the stall slid open. A black semi-sheer gauze covered the opening. As Philby lit a cigarette he could still make out the familiar profile of his handler.

"I told you, no smoking."

Philby shook his head and stubbed it out against the dark wood framework of the window. "So, tell me, why are you fascinated with churches?"

Philby heard Shapak take a deep breath and exhale slowly. "It's not churches. It's priests. Somehow they think they are closer to God, yet the priests I knew before the Revolution were not to be trusted—with money or children."

Philby chuckled.

"They think they are closer to God than other people because they read the Bible, pray, and wear a collar. It's just another manipulation by the few to control the many."

Philby couldn't help but think that was what many capitalists thought the root problem of Communism was. He let Shapak's comments pass. "I've not heard from you since I passed the extraction plans to you," he said, careful not to sound too annoyed.

"I have been busy. You are not our only asset."

"Yes, yes, as you remind me all too often. What about Lind and his intelligence?"

The pause lasted for several seconds. The only sound was of one man breathing rapidly—Philby.

"Lind cannot be found, nor his intelligence."

Philby sat back on his haunches, defeated.

"Someone unknown to us interceded before we or the Germans were able to secure Lind or his intelligence."

"Did they report anything useful at all?"

"How could they? They are all dead," Shapak said in a tone that said he was done talking.

With a crack, the glass window slid shut.

CHAPTER SEVENTY-ONE

1830 Hours, Friday, October 30, 1942
Ferry Embarkation, Gullmarsfjorden, West Coast of Sweden

The ferry was a surprise. Twenty minutes ago, when Bobby turned off Route 444 onto Route 161, Conor had taken another look at the map. He'd followed Route 161 with his finger and came to a large body of water—the Gullmarn fjord. There wasn't a solid line crossing the fjord, just a dotted one.

"Tell me if I'm wrong: a dotted line across the water means a ferry, right?"

"Yep. Why? Something wrong?" Bobby asked.

"I didn't notice it before. I guess I didn't focus on that end of the trip as much as the start."

"What's your worry?"

"Well, for one, that gas station attendant. I'm sure he heard me speak English. That's one red flag. And he saw what we're driving. That's two. And don't forget, we didn't exactly leave Stockholm on a quiet note. I'm sure Swedish authorities have bulletins out to police that we are—"

"Armed and dangerous," Emily said.

"Yes. But the ferry is a choke point. If anyone is onto us, maybe we can slow them down some. Keep driving while I think."

Thinking time was now over. Conor was only somewhat confident that he had an idea to slow down any pursuers. They started to drive down the ramp and stopped behind a truck that had a canvas cover over the bed. They were the last vehicle in the line. The vehicles ahead of them were ready to pull aboard the ferry, which had finished off-loading the cars that had come from Lysekil. Conor counted the vehicles that came off. Twenty. All short-wheelbase cars. He got out of the car and walked up the line about twenty feet and counted the cars about to board. Their car was the eighteenth in line, but three trucks with double the wheelbase of an average car were lined up ahead of them. A quick calculation said that their car wouldn't make this run. On his way back to the car, he peeked around the canvas flap into the bed of the truck directly in front of them. It was empty except for a couple of wooden crates, looked wet, and smelled strongly of fish.

Conor jumped into the Volvo. "How's your Swedish?"

"Not so good when I first got back here, but I knocked some rust off in the last few days. Why? What are you up to?"

Emily leaned on the back of the front seat. "Remember, we have another passenger in the trunk, Conor."

Conor turned to face Emily and noticed Eve watching him. "How could I forget?" He turned back and looked at the truck in front of them. He could hear cars up ahead turning their engines over. "Bobby, go ask the driver if he could take us into Lysekil ... to the waterfront. Offer him some money. I checked; he's going back to town empty."

"And when he asks what happened to our car?"

"Tell him it just died and we have to leave it alongside the ramp and come back with a mechanic later."

"All right. Be right back."

As Bobby got out, Conor found the screwdriver he'd used to fix the radiator hose and pocketed it. While Bobby dealt with the driver, Conor busied himself by sticking his head under the hood on the driver's side so the truck driver could see him in his side mirror. The darkness forced him to feel for the gas line. The engine made cracking and hissing sounds as the engine block began to cool. He took the screwdriver and punctured three holes in the gas line. It started to drip onto the hot engine block. He shut the hood.

"All set. Cost us one hundred krona. I think he took advantage of us," Bobby said.

"Okay, get Lind out of the trunk. Untie his feet and get him on the truck." Conor moved to the back of the Volvo. "Emily, gotta move quickly. Get Eve aboard the truck, then help Bobby."

Without responding, Emily grabbed her gun and motioned Eve out of the car. Bobby had Lind halfway into the back of the truck, pushing on his rear end like Lind was a sack of potatoes, as the truck started up. Conor reached in through the Volvo's open driver's-side window and began to push while steering the car to the right side of the ramp. Bobby joined him. Once it was sufficiently out of the way, he told Bobby to sit up front with the driver. Conor lifted the hood again and pulled Lancer's lighter from his coat pocket, flicked the flint wheel, and tossed it onto the engine block. The sprint to the back of the now-moving truck took five seconds. In another ten seconds, the fire fed by the leaked fuel was visible from a distance.

By the time the truck was driving off the ramp on the far side of the fjord, Minister Ramsay's Volvo PV54, all eighty-six horses, was fully engulfed in flames.

CHAPTER SEVENTY-TWO

1915 Hours, Friday, October 30, 1942
Lysekil Harbor, Lysekil, Sweden

Conor and Emily shared a wooden crate in the back of the truck. Eve and Gunnar did the same. They had been on the road for ten minutes when the truck made a right turn and pulled to a stop. Conor pushed the rear canvas flap aside and saw that they had arrived at a gas station. Bobby came to the back of the truck.

"The driver said that he has to fill up for his deliveries tomorrow morning. That's his routine. It won't take long."

"Long enough for a phone call?"

"I guess."

Conor hopped down and headed inside the station's office. There wasn't anyone inside, so he laid a few krona on the desk, dialed the Grand Hotel, and asked for Gus Karlson.

"Are you there yet?" Karlson asked.

"Close. Maybe another fifteen, twenty minutes. Any fallout from our fishing trip?"

"Quite a lot. Tolberg visited us. The C Bureau is pretty grumpy. The body count at the Andersson house was out of hand, as far as they're concerned. They say that quite a few people from all three legations are going to be sent home. I might be one of them."

"Wait, you said three legations?"

"There were three dead Russians at the house, along with one German."

"How did the Russians get involved?"

"They have eyes and ears everywhere, Conor."

A man in a grease-smeared coverall walked into the office through a rear door. He held his hands up as if to say, *What the hell?*

Conor pointed at the coins on the desk.

The man shrugged and sat down.

"Could they have been a competing buyer for Lind's intelligence?" Conor believed that, once the war was over, the shotgun marriage that was the relationship between the Americans, Brits, and Soviets wouldn't last long.

"Wouldn't put it past them."

"Any sign of Eklof or Stuben?"

"Actually, they have been noticeably absent of late."

"That's not necessarily good news." Conor saw Bobby waving at him from the cab of the truck. "Gotta get going, Gus. Keep your head down."

"I could say the same thing to you. By the way, you taking good care of Ramsay's Volvo?"

Conor dropped the phone in the cradle, gave the man a quick nod, and walked out to the truck. Conor stepped up into the cab and sat next to Bobby. He wanted to study the lay of the land as they made their approach to the harbor area.

Less than fifteen minutes later, they were driving along a road that ran beside a long wharf. The dockside was lit by a sparse number of streetlights. Three fishing trawlers were tied up along the wharf, all of their pilothouses lit up and their navigation lights on. Conor could see a few men washing down the decks with hoses. The driver pulled into a dirt lot adjacent to a long, three-story warehouse. At the near end was a sign for a fishmonger, most likely the driver's boss. Farther down the quay, Conor could make out the shape of a motor gun boat tied up close to a single railcar. According to the extraction plan, it was motor gun boat 622, the Fairmile D. The Dog Boat. The same one that he and Donovan saw demonstrating high-speed maneuvers in the Thames. All armaments were removed from sight, and extra fuel was supposed to be on board. It was to fly the red ensign of a merchantman, crewed by trawler men from Hull. The captain, a man called Peter

Scott, was former Royal Navy.

A sedan parked near the gun boat caught his attention. Conor couldn't make out who or how many people were inside, but he knew they were enjoying cigarettes given the smoke drifting out the open windows.

The driver of the truck cut the engine, placed the keys in the visor, and said something to Bobby.

"What's up?" Conor asked.

"Our friend here is going home to his family. He says we can stay in the truck as long as we like."

Conor looked at his watch: 1934 hours. "Tell him we'll be moving on in a few minutes. And thank him for the ride."

The driver jumped down from the cab and headed up a sloping road toward the center of town.

"What now?" Bobby asked.

"Do you see that car parked down near the railcar and the gun boat?"

"Yeah."

"Not sure who they are, but the chances that they're keeping an eye on our transportation out of Sweden is good. The problem is, they can't see us board or we'll never get out of here."

"So do we wait them out?"

"No time for that." Conor got out and went to the rear of the truck.

Emily was sitting on the crate, gun held loosely in her lap. Eve and Gunnar were dozing. Gunnar's hands were still bound behind his back.

"Emily, I'm going to drive us down to the dock where the gun boat is tied up. As soon as I stop, get moving and board."

"Understood." At that moment, Eve and Gunnar woke up.

"And for good measure, get the gag back in Gunnar's mouth."

Conor walked around to the driver's-side door, jumped up, started the truck, and pulled out of the lot.

"You going to tell me what your plan is at any point?" Bobby asked.

"Once I get rid of our visitors, we board the boat. Not complicated."

Bobby said something, but Conor couldn't make it out over the sound of the truck's engine. He kept the truck in first gear as he set it on a direct path to the rear of the sedan. The truck's headlights revealed two men turning around in their seats to watch the truck coming toward them. Conor glanced over at the motor gun boat and saw someone in the pilothouse, as well as a plume of dark exhaust spouting from the boat's stern.

Ten feet from the sedan, the passenger-side door opened, and he punched the gas. The force of metal on metal closed the door. The truck picked up some speed as it began to push the sedan toward the end of the wharf, but progress slowed as it fought the braking power of the car. More gas and the sedan and truck neared the end of the quay. The sedan balanced on the wharf's edge momentarily before tumbling into the harbor.

"Let's go."

Conor jumped out of the cab and rushed to the back of the truck. Emily was on the ground, helping Eve jump down. Gunnar was right behind her. With the truck engine silent, the throaty sound of the motor gun boat's engines filled the night. Conor was last to board.

"Get them below, Emily. Bobby, tell the captain that now would be a good time to shove off. Those two guys might be good swimmers."

Conor heard the car before he saw it, but the headlights quickly found him on the aft section of the deck. The car skidded to a stop under a streetlight. The driver got out, then the passenger. Eklof.

Conor reached for his Colt, but before he could raise it, Eklof fired off two rounds. A deckhand on the foredeck tossed the last line into the water and took cover behind the craft's superstructure. As the gun boat started to drift from the quay, Conor fired two rounds, shattering the window of the door that Eklof was using as cover. The driver began firing as well, rounds whizzing over Conor's head. Bobby and Emily started firing from the bridge, and soon the driver fell to the ground behind his door.

As the gun boat pulled forward, Eklof sprinted toward the stern. Conor pulled the trigger of his Colt, but the gun's slide snapped back, signaling an empty magazine. He dropped the gun on the deck as Eklof leaped and landed on the aft deck, losing his balance due to the accelerating boat, which, luckily, kept him from firing accurately. Before he could regain his balance, Conor raced toward him. Jumping, he planted both feet into Eklof's chest. Eklof's pistol flew into the air and landed in the boat's prop wash, while Conor landed on his back, knocking the air from his lungs.

Eklof struggled to his feet, also gasping for air. He charged Conor, who had barely gotten to his feet, and landed on him. Eklof wrapped his arms around his chest, pinning Conor's upper arms against his body. Eklof landed one headbutt, then another. Conor's vision blurred. He raised his right arm and, before Eklof could launch another headbutt, grabbed the man's ear and ripped it from his head; blood gushed, covering Conor's hand, and Eklof let out a scream as he rolled off Conor and grabbed the side of his head. Conor, his head pounding from the headbutts, rolled on top of Eklof, grabbed his hair, and started pounding his head on the deck.

"You. Don't. Ever. Hit. A. Woman," Conor screamed. Each word was punctuated with Eklof's head slamming into the deck. Blood pooled under it, and his eye patch had come loose. The eye socket looked like a dried peach pit.

Conor heard Eklof's short, hoarse breaths, and he rolled off the man, grabbed his legs, and dragged him toward the stern, letting his body slip into the churning water with no fanfare, no emotion.

When Conor turned, he noticed a commotion on the port side of the wheelhouse. Emily was bent over a body. He ran forward, the motor gun boat picking up speed. When he reached Emily, he saw that she was tending to a wounded man. Bobby Heugle.

#

Below, they laid Bobby on top of wooden crates that were marked "Ball Bearings." The crates were set on top of two lower berths on the port side, with three more crates on the two lower berths on the starboard side, and more crates on the deck in the forward crew quarters. The cramped space also accommodated a two-burner stove and small sink on one side of the hatch that lead to the wardroom, where Emily had dumped Gunnar.

Eve Lind leaned over Bobby, who was in pain but conscious.

His shirt was blood soaked. Conor tore the shirt open, buttons flying across the cramped space. Eve began to mop up the blood to examine the entry wound.

"The bullet is in his upper chest, right side. The path of the bullet suggests a right lung injury. And look at his neck," Eve said. The veins in Bobby's neck were engorged. "Tension pneumothorax … it looks like his right lung has collapsed completely."

"But he can still breathe with his other lung, right?" Conor said.

"You don't understand. Air inside the right chest cavity is pushing the collapsed lung along with his blood vessels, heart, and windpipe to the other side. You can see his windpipe … it's not in the center of his neck. It's been shifted to his left side. The bullet is not the prime concern." Eve, her brow furrowed, her speech pattern quickened, was engaged. Not aloof. Not pouty. Not vengeful. She was energized. "The prime concern is once the air has collected in the negative-pressure pleural space, it quickly becomes high-pressure air that cannot escape."

Bobby's breathing was labored; he began coughing up blood-tinged sputum. Each cough triggered a spasm of pain that registered on his contorted face. When he wasn't coughing, his breathing came with gurgling sounds. His eyes were open to mere slits.

"I need time to release the pressure in the chest cavity, to eliminate the impact on the other organs. If we don't do this soon, he won't make it."

"How do you do that?" asked Emily.

Eve exhaled loudly. "I need a sharp knife to make a small incision. Then I need to insert a tube of some sort into his chest."

"That's it?" Conor said.

"Stop interrupting me," Eve snapped. "Just listen. Once the air is released, we … I need to make sure that air can only escape, not come back into the chest through the tube. So I need something … something to attach to the end of the tube that will allow air to escape but not reenter when he takes a breath. Something that would collapse onto itself and seal when he breathes in."

"What about a patch of canvas? I saw some top side. It's probably waterproof and airproof," Emily said.

Eve took a moment to consider it. "Yes … that could work. I'll also need a small piece to cover the entry point, so air won't get back into the chest cavity. And tape. I need some medical tape. I don't have my kit, and even if I did, the rocking of this boat wouldn't allow me to do this procedure properly. If you want this man to live, you must tell the captain that we have to stop."

Conor knew that the captain would be dead set against stopping. In the heavily patrolled Skagerrak Strait, that would be like sending a flare up to the Germans.

"How much time do you need?" Conor asked.

"With makeshift materials … twenty minutes for the collapsed lung. The bullet can wait until he's back on land."

Conor knew that twenty minutes drifting in the strait would be suicide. "I'll be back. Make him as comfortable as possible. Emily, keep an eye on her."

Emily nodded, but Eve sneered and muttered in Swedish. He was sure it was something along the line of *And fuck you too.*

He went topside to give it a try, passing two thirty-gallon drums with petrol lashed to the port side of the deckhouse. He saw two more drums tied down on the starboard side. The half-moon was playing hide-and-seek behind a partly cloudy sky. He approached the pilothouse and saw Scott and his first officer standing next to each other. The first officer was at the helm. Both men had unlit pipes in their mouths.

"Captain Scott," Conor said, extending a hand. "Thanks for the ride. Sorry for all the commotion back there."

Scott shook his hand. "They told me that trouble has a tendency to follow you around—you *and* Miss Bright."

"Can't argue that, Captain. How's she running?"

"Well, that'd be a sore point. Number 622 has been acting up as of late. We beat it out of Lysekil with one of the starboard engines off-line."

"What's the problem, as far as you know?"

"I'm told the engine status panel says that there's no oil pressure. And the two stokers below don't have the expertise my lead motor mechanic had. They've done what they can. I need that engine back online if we ever hope to outrun anyone."

"Where is your lead man?"

"He came down with appendicitis. Had to leave him behind."

"I'm pretty good with engines, Captain." His father still brought up the story of Conor swapping out the engine in the family's Chris Craft with the Packard engine from his car. He had been so mad that he made Conor put it back that same day, then claimed to his friends it never ran better. "I'd be happy to take a look and see if we can get it back online."

Scott looked at his first officer. "What do you think, Chapman?"

Chapman looked at Conor. "You ever been in the engine room of a gun boat, Mr. Thorn?" he asked.

"Can't say I have. Been in one on a four-stack destroyer though."

"Hah, a big difference. Both are hot and noisy, but there's little room down below," Scott said.

"Still willing to give it a try. But we need to stop for a while. If we don't, all I could probably do is figure out what's wrong, but given this chop and our current speed, I know I wouldn't be able to make repairs. And full disclosure, Captain, I have a man down there who needs some serious medical attention or he may not make it. That blond woman ... she's a doctor. She can do it but not with the boat bouncing around. She says she needs twenty minutes."

Scott scratched his eyebrow with his thumbnail. "You're pulling my leg, right? Twenty minutes drifting in the strait?"

"We have darkness on our side, Captain," Conor said. When Scott didn't reply, he added, "What about fifteen? I'll need at least that much time to troubleshoot and repair, as long as it's not a major fix."

"Sounds like you're negotiating a swap."

"I guess I am."

Scott looked at his first officer, who leaned toward him and said something indecipherable.

"Once we get a little farther out into the Skagerrak, we'll need all the knots we can get. But I can't sit in the water like a toy in the tub for long. I'll give you fifteen minutes. Not one more. If you can't fix it and get the procedure done in that time, well, then we play the cards we're dealt." Scott paused. "Deal, Mr. Thorn?"

"Deal, Captain Scott."

Scott looked at his watch; its radium face glowed slightly. "We'll come to a full stop at twenty thirty hours. Get your doctor ready. And you might want to put on some coveralls; it's grimy down there."

CHAPTER SEVENTY-THREE

2005 Hours, Friday, October 30, 1942
Skagerrak Strait, 170 Miles West of Lysekil, Sweden

Conor delivered the news to Eve; the fifteen-minute window was not received well.

"You don't understand. I'm not treating a paper cut."

"Listen, I get that you need more time. But we could have an Me 109 or an E-boat halfway down our throat anytime. We just can't sit for that long. The captain is right. Do what you can. If it's not enough time, just do the best you can to make him comfortable until we get back to England." Conor added, "Don't think I don't care … he's my best friend. But he's pretty tough." Conor looked at Emily. "Give her a hand, Em. The captain said the boat's radioman would help out too."

#

"We need something to help manage the pain," Eve said.

"There's got to be some alcohol on this boat."

The radioman came through the hatch, rolling up the sleeves of his wool shirt; the bottoms of his blue pants were tucked into calf-high rubber boots. "Tony's my name. Skipper says I'm to do what I can for you. Now, what do you need, ladies?"

Eve ran down the list of items. Tony told her and Emily that there was a small amount of brännvin on board. "It's got quite a kick to it."

"Get it," Emily said.

"But," Tony said, scratching his bald head, "those other items ... sharp knife, canvas, no problem. A tube of some sort, I don't know ... and what's an occlusive bandage?"

"That's where the canvas comes in. I need something to seal the opening in his chest, and it needs to be airtight. I need to do that before I release the air in his chest with the tube," Eve said.

"Tony, do you have some petroleum jelly?" Emily asked. "My brother said that they had some on his merchant ship for sunburns."

Tony's eyes lit up. "Ahh, right you are, miss. Last assignment for the line was out of the Rock. They called the stuff Red Vet Pet. I brought some on board when I shipped in with these boys. The lads laughed. Said there wasn't enough sun in the North Sea to worry about."

Eve nodded. "And I need some tape. Do you have a small medical kit aboard?"

"Sure do, ma'am. It's small. Some gauze, iodine, but that's it. We run out of medical tape."

Emily and Eve looked at each other.

Tony scratched the same spot on his head. "Well, how about some duct tape? Sticks like glue. Amazing stuff, that tape is."

Emily smiled. "Great, Tony. And the tube?"

Tony's scrunched-up face was a study in bafflement. "I think that's a dead end, ladies. I can't think of anything."

Emily quickly plucked a pen from Tony's shirt pocket.

"Hey, that's my favorite pen. My dad gave that to me on my eighteenth birthday. Never been without it since."

Emily unscrewed the barrel from the cap, then the nib from the barrel. "Tony, can you poke a hole in the end of the barrel?"

He scratched his head again. "I can, but I don't want to."

"I'll make sure you get another one; that's my promise to you. With a note of thanks from the prime minister." Emily turned to Eve. "This would work, right?"

"Yes. It's not perfect, but it will do."

#

Conor went aft, found a pair of overalls, and slipped into them. When he stepped down the short ladder into the engine room, all his senses overloaded. The sound of just the three working Packards was deafening; his lungs seemed to vibrate inside his rib cage. The smell of fuel, grease, and oil mixed with sweat made his eyes water. He started to open his mouth to yell a greeting, but the port and starboard engines throttling back made him pause. The engines shut down, and right on cue, the first officer poked his head through the topside hatch. "You're on the clock."

Conor turned to the older of the two stokers, thinking he had the most experience. "Have you narrowed down the problem any further?"

The stoker shrugged and looked at the other one, who couldn't have been twenty.

"No oil pressure in number three. The dry sump oiling system looks fine, but she's still not getting enough oil," he said.

Conor breathed through his mouth to mitigate the overpowering smell of the compartment's fumes. "And you checked the oil filter?" The filter was made up of thin screen segments and was mounted underneath the supercharger next to the oil pump.

"First thing. No worries there," the younger stoker said.

Conor rubbed his chin. *What are these guys missing?*

#

Bobby couldn't stop coughing. His eyes were closed tight, his face awash with pain. He coughed up some of the brännvin Emily had given him. While she finished sterilizing the small pocketknife by heating it with a flame, then pouring a small amount of brännvin over the blade, Eve wiped bloody sputum from around Bobby's mouth.

Emily handed the knife to Eve, both women struggling to maintain their balance; the rocking didn't lessen as much as Emily had thought it would. Eve hesitated.

"What's wrong?"

"It's … it's just that I haven't actually done this procedure before. I know it sounded like I did, but I've only seen it done."

"You're joking. Why didn't you mention that before?"

"I just didn't think it was that important. It's a simple procedure, really."

"Then I suggest you get on with it. He's in severe pain and we have limited time."

Eve bent over Bobby, the knife in her right hand, the barrel of the fountain pen in her left. Tony had cut the tip of the barrel to create a tube that she would insert into the incision. "Hold him. Keep him from moving."

Emily spread her feet wide for balance, grabbed Bobby by the arms, and held tight. Her face was inches away from his, and just as Eve lowered the knife to his chest, Bobby coughed again, spraying Emily's face with blood.

Eve made a two-inch incision and a pool of blood started to form around the cut. She placed the knife on Bobby's chest and jabbed the fountain pen tube into the incision. Bobby's eyes opened wide, then closed. At first, a misty, blood-tinged fluid flowed from the tube, followed by a rush of pure air. Less than ten seconds later, just as the stream of air stopped, Bobby opened his eyes again.

"Ohhh … that's so much better," he said, his voice slow. He opened his eyes and saw Emily's face mere inches away. "Do you have any more of that rotgut?"

#

"Did you check the oil pressure relief valve on the oil and freshwater pump assembly?"

The stokers looked at each other, then back to Conor.

"I'll take that as a no. It can sometimes become stuck open or closed if foreign material got through the filter. It sounds like it could be stuck open because the oil pressure has dropped to zero."

Conor bent down to where the supercharger was located on engine three. Next to it was the oil filter, and next to that was the oil and water pump assembly. The oil pressure relief value was located next to one of the two freshwater outlets. Conor felt for the valve and located it. "I need an adjustable wrench," he said.

The older stoker passed it to him. After five turns with the wrench, he freed the valve and handed it to the young stoker. Conor looked at his watch. Five minutes had passed since the engine shut down.

"Blow it out and wipe it down with a clean cloth."

The younger stoker started to follow Conor's instructions but fumbled, dropping the valve through a metal grate.

Conor told the two stokers to remove the grate. He, along with the younger stoker, dropped down into the recesses of the engine room floor. Their feet were in three inches of murky seawater, oil, and fuel. He fished for the valve directly below where the younger stoker had stood. His fingers passed over a large metal object, and he snatched it from the bilge. It was an open-end wrench. He went fishing again. Nothing.

He looked at the stoker. "Anything?" His reply was a shake of his head. Thinking that the valve might have rolled in the bilge as the boat rocked with the swells, he widened his search. His fingers brushed by another hard object, but it seemed to roll away. He plied the surface of the deck with his fingers spread wide. While he searched, he glanced again at his watch. Another five minutes gone.

Just then Conor's fingertips passed over what felt more like the size of the valve; he scooped the object out. The valve, covered with an oily sheen, rested in his hand. He motioned for the stoker's cloth—another minute gone. Conor wiped it off and did a quick visual inspection. Satisfied, he reset the valve into the pump assembly, careful not to overtighten and strip the valve's threads. Another glance at his watch; they had three minutes left to finish up. He gave the younger stoker a thumbs-up, and the kid smiled, his white teeth a stark contrast to his grease-and-oil-stained face.

"Turn her over," Conor said.

The older stoker went to the engine status panel and punched the green starter button. The initial engine turns were slow. The stoker released the button. "She's always a little stubborn. Don't you worry, sir." He punched the starter button again, and the 1,250-horsepower Packard engine roared to life.

\#

Conor went topside, walked up the starboard side of the deckhouse, and gave Scott a thumbs-up, then dropped down the foredeck hatch ladder into the confined space of the crew quarters. Before his feet hit the deck, the sound of the three other Packards turning over rattled his eardrums.

Emily and Eve were huddled over Bobby. A square piece of canvas was slathered with some goo and secured with olive drab tape over his bullet wound. A few inches below, a short brown tube protruded from his chest, a roll of canvas taped to the end of it. The sight, even though it had been explained earlier, was jarring. But a more comforting sight was Bobby's chest expanding and contracting more easily.

"Is he all right?"

Eve nodded.

"Eve says the tube will have to stay inserted for three to four days," Emily said. "The bullet is still in his chest. He's still in pain, but he's breathing normally." She turned to Conor. "It's the best we could do."

Conor let out a huge breath and then hugged Emily. "Thanks. I owe you. Both of you."

"Just don't let me forget that I owe Tony a new fountain pen."

\#

A half hour later, Conor, still in his coveralls, took in a report about Bobby from Emily.

If fixing one of the starboard side engines was a double, hearing that Bobby was resting comfortably and asking for more brännvin was a triple. A home run would be getting back to England with no further blood loss.

"He's weak, but he's going to be fine. Eve says that he'll need to have an X-ray when we get back to see where the bullet is and determine if it can be removed or left in his chest."

"Oh dear God, if they leave it, I'll never hear the end of it."

He and Emily met with Captain Scott in the boat's inappropriately named chart house, located just behind the wheelhouse. It was just as cramped as any other space aboard the motor gun boat. The crew complement, normally two officers and ten ratings, had been whittled down to five in addition to the two officers in order to maximize the ball bearing load and accommodate Conor, Emily, and the Linds. Bobby was an unplanned add-on.

"You didn't oversell yourself, Mr. Thorn. You did a right good job down there. My hat's off to you," Scott said as he passed around two heavy ceramic mugs of tepid coffee.

"Two birds with one stone, as they say, Captain. Glad it worked out." All of them drank from their mugs.

"Glad our German friend didn't put a round into one of those extra drums of fuel you have lashed against your deckhouse. Sure would have woken up a few people in Lysekil," Emily said.

"That would have been a disaster. We'd be adrift just west of the Broad Fourteens and a sitting duck without that extra fuel."

"The Broad Fourteens?" Conor asked.

"It's a large area in the southern North Sea off the coast of the Netherlands that stretches toward the English coast. Its depth is a pretty constant fourteen fathoms. We see a lot of German E-boat activity there."

"Speaking of Germans, if we do make contact with them, do you have any weapons? I noticed gun mounts but no guns," Emily said.

"We're not Royal Navy. We're British Merchant Navy. We fly the red ensign. We couldn't just sail into Lysekil with a complement of weapons, or we'd be interned for the duration."

Conor's shoulders slumped. "So, no weapons."

"Didn't say that, Mr. Thorn. As far as the Ministry of Supply is concerned, we have no weapons. But the Admiralty and MI6 felt some weapons were needed to protect our cargo, which includes all of you." Scott leaned closer, like he was about to divulge a secret.

Conor winked at Emily and got a smile in return.

"Well-hidden below in the forepeak storage space, we have two single 20 mm Oerlikons and two twin .303 in Vickers machine guns. Not close to the full complement for this motor gun boat, but we have a limited crew. And we can make smoke, which may help us get out of trouble."

"Can you outrun an E-boat if you have to?" Conor asked.

"Well, if it's an S-100 class, they have a bit of an edge. They can sustain forty-three to forty-four knots, but they can push it to forty-eight knots for a brief period."

"How brief?"

"Not brief enough, I'm afraid. Their diesels also give them much greater range."

"What's your top speed?" Conor said.

"With moderate seas, thirty-one to thirty-three knots."

Conor frowned. The boat speed differential was a problem that might bite them in the ass.

"The plan was that we'd be left alone, acting like a merchantman, not a gun boat, Mr. Thorn. Get our cargo close to the English coast and call for help if needed."

The odds against them were stacking up. "There's no guarantee that the red ensign of the Merchant Marine will protect you if the Germans know that Gunnar Lind is aboard."

"So who is this precious cargo you've brought on my boat?"

"He's been working at a high level in German code breaking," Emily said. "He was attempting to sell secrets to the Germans— we're talking something that would put the Germans at a great advantage. He can't fall into their hands," Emily said.

"Why not shoot the bugger?" Scott blushed. "Excuse my language, miss."

Emily waved him off. "We haven't had the right circumstances to interrogate him. We need to know the extent of his dealings with the Germans."

"But don't worry. If it comes to that, I'll take care that he won't see another Nazi," Conor said.

"How would the Germans know that he's on this boat?"

"Well, that would be my fault. The German that attempted to board … he's not dead. He's most likely already communicated to the Luftwaffe and the naval bases along the Danish coast what to look for. That's what I would have done."

"You're probably right. But those two men in the car that you shoved into the harbor—they said they were from the Swedish Security Intelligence Service. They boarded and said they were looking for your man Lind. They did a search and came up empty.

They also described another man they were looking for—you, Mr. Thorn. So someone told *them* that Lind and you were headed here, and it wasn't your German friend you threw in the drink."

The news jarred Conor. Of all the port towns on the west coast, how did the C Bureau know their destination was Lysekil? And how did Eklof know? The real question of course being, how the extraction plans had been leaked.

"We have more questions than answers at this point. But getting back to the Germans, they want Lind and what he knows about British code-breaking efforts. So we need to be prepared, especially if they attempt to board, which is the only way they can take Lind alive," Conor said.

"I see. Well, we have what we have. We need to make do."

"Can I make a suggestion, Captain?" Emily asked.

"All ears, miss."

"If we can make several petrol bombs using bottles, they could prove to be quite useful, should an E-boat or two get too close."

Scott pulled back as if Emily had told a rude joke. "Miss, we need every drop of petrol to ensure we get back with our cargo, including you."

"We need to surprise them, Captain. Surprise is our only advantage, given that they outgun us," Emily said. "They won't expect we'd use explosives at close range."

Scott tried to drink from his mug, but it was empty. He put it down on the felt surface of the table with a thud. "All right. Explosives at close range ... it's risky, but I get your point. We'll make it happen."

Conor and Emily exchanged glances. "How quick can you get the guns up from below and mounted?" Conor asked.

"Inside three minutes. But hearing all that you've told me, I need to think about pulling the red ensign down and hoisting the Union Jack. I don't like getting surprised."

"Up to you, Captain. No arguments here though. Since we'll be outgunned by any E-boat we run in to, I'll work on a plan for when they try to board."

"You do that, and I think I'll send a message out to the Admiralty that we could use some assistance from a motor torpedo boat squadron out of Yarmouth."

CHAPTER SEVENTY-FOUR

1000 Hours, Saturday, October 31, 1942
Heinrich Himmler's Office, Prinz-Albrecht-Strasse 9, Berlin

On the flight to Berlin, Schellenberg rehearsed. While he couldn't predict with complete accuracy what Himmler would question him about, he was certain he knew two subjects: his peace plan and the matter of Gunnar Lind's intelligence. But in the approximately two days he had been away from Berlin, the list of topics could now be fraught with mines both large and small.

When he entered Himmler's office, he found him sitting at his desk studying a file. "Good morning, Reichsführer."

Himmler initially didn't make any effort to acknowledge Schellenberg's arrival or greeting. He slapped the file shut and looked up. "Your report?"

"May I take a seat, Reichsführer? It has been a long few days."

Himmler sat stone-faced.

His cold reception threw Schellenberg, but it gave him an idea how his report would be received.

"The peace plan. Were the Americans receptive to your persuasion?"

"No. They were not." Schellenberg determined that due to Himmler's black mood, embellishments regarding his outreach to the Americans were called for if he was to remain in Himmler's good graces. To be marginalized by Himmler could lead to a series of unfortunate events. "Not at first, Reichsführer."

"Just whom did you reach out to?"

Schellenberg cleared his throat. And cleared it again. He pulled a handkerchief from his breast pocket and blew his nose. "Excuse me, Reichsführer. I engaged members of their legation who met with Dr. Kersten. They were very impressed with the higher level of outreach. I believe we may have made some progress."

Himmler sat up; his eyebrows raised. "Go on."

"I made the case … your case for your plan. They were not interested at first, but I pressed further. They had many questions and concerns about the impact on their relationship with Stalin. I was able to convince them of your … sincerity. And that you are most concerned with the future of the German people. And … most willing to … negotiate."

Himmler nodded and leaned forward. "But can they be trusted to properly represent my plan?"

"Yes," Schellenberg said emphatically in spite of Eklof's report of the escape of Thorn's associate Mia Durs. "They can be trusted."

Himmler sat back without any sign that Schellenberg's report was satisfactory. "And the other matter? The Swede. What has come of that?"

"That, Reichsführer, is a different story. It seems that Lind deceived us and destroyed the intelligence before escaping."

Himmler shot forward and slapped his desk with an open hand. "I knew it. I knew this was nothing but a diversion, a British trick to redirect our attention away from other more important matters. Why did I listen to you and that woman?"

Schellenberg waited for more, but Himmler's rage seemed to be spent. "I have not given up hope. My … our man Eklof has chased him across Sweden, and I expect that he, along with the help of elements of the Swedish Security Intelligence Service that are sympathetic to our cause, will bring him to us."

"And what of this man Andersson? It would seem that he deceived us. Did he not?"

"I must admit that he did indeed."

"And is he still alive?"

"Yes. Yes, he is."

A second slap on the desk. Followed quickly by a third. "Why?" Himmler asked in a guttural voice.

"Reichsführer, the simple reason is that Germany needs his ball bearings. I convinced him to double his shipments and charge us half."

"That is not enough. When you leave here, put the name Benjamin Andersson on our list of people to be dealt with when we have won the war."

CHAPTER SEVENTY-FIVE

Philby had come to know Menzies well since his first encounter with the chief of MI6 in the lift at No. 54. Actually, that first time, Philby didn't know who the pale-faced man was. The extent of their engagement was a quick glance from Menzies followed by … nothing. When he got out on the fourth floor, Philby asked the lift operator who he was.

"Why, sir, that's the chief," he'd answered in a tone that seemed to call into question Philby's level of intelligence.

Philby liked Menzies. And he respected Menzies for those characteristics that Philby held in high regard, such as secrecy, calm in the face of calamity, and loyalty to a cause.

The intercom on Menzies's desk buzzed, but Menzies, with a wave of his hand, motioned for Philby to continue his report on German Abwehr activities on the Iberian Peninsula. It buzzed once more, and Menzies blew out a stream of air through his nostrils in exasperation as he reached for the intercom box and picked up the Bakelite handset.

"Miss Pettigrew, I believe I said I wanted no interruptions … Well, can't he wait? … Send him in," Menzies said as he replaced the handset. "Commander Fleming. Won't take a minute." Philby started to rise, but Menzies raised a hand. "No, don't run. I'm sure it's some outlandish request from Admiral Godfrey."

Philby knew Fleming through a common friend, Nicholas Elliott, who knew him from his time with MI6 before the outbreak of war. When Fleming came in, he acknowledged Philby with a quick nod. Menzies pointed at a chair, but Fleming declined.

"This will be short. The Admiralty received a request from a motor gun boat out of Lysekil for ... assistance. The request came in overnight."

"Any news as to cargo?"

Cargo in the name of Gunnar Lind? Philby wondered. And the person possibly responsible for wiping out the NKVD's team of agents?

"Unfortunately, no. And no information as to whether they have been detected."

"Did we try—"

"To contact them? Yes," Fleming said. Philby picked up on Menzies's annoyance at being interrupted. Deference was not Fleming's strong suit. "We had no success getting through. Could be due to weather in the Broad Fourteens."

"Has assistance been dispatched?"

"Yes, a patrol of four motor torpedo boats is headed west out of Yarmouth as we speak."

Menzies mulled over Fleming's report, running his hand through his thinning silvery blond hair. "Commander, please make sure our OSS friend is aware of the news."

Fleming turned to leave.

"Wait, remind me where they're headed."

"To Harwich, sir."

CHAPTER SEVENTY-SIX

1030 Hours, Saturday, October 31, 1942
Eastern Edge of the Broad Fourteens, Southwest of Lysekil, Sweden

Conor stood alongside the pipe-smoking Scott on the bridge, filling in for First Officer Chapman while he supervised three ratings as they hauled their weapons topside. The vibration from the four supercharged Packards ran up his legs. He had never experienced such a feeling before. Destroyer duty was a far cry from speeding across a choppy sea with over five thousand horses under your feet. He looked up to the tormented sky. Conor spied a thick bank of fog stretching for at least a mile across the horizon.

"Captain, not sure you know, but I am former navy. Never got past executive officer on a destroyer, but mind if I take a turn at the helm? Wouldn't mind getting a feel for the wheel."

"Mr. Thorn, I do know a little bit about you. I was wondering when you were going to ask." Scott stepped away from the wheel, and Conor stepped into his place. The oak wheel didn't dampen the vibration from the Packards. The instrument display was simple—oil pressure, fuel, RPMs for each engine; the needle indicators inside the gauges quivered. Nothing on board escaped the impact of the boat's engine power.

"Maybe now is a good time to let me in on your plan," Scott said.

Conor nodded. "Let me just say there is no perfect plan."

"Well, there's a vote of confidence for you. I'll let you know if it's crazy or not. Get on with it."

316

"The petrol bombs. Emily and your radioman, Tony, are down in the chart house prepping some of the bombs. That's what we're going to use to take down any E-boats we run into."

Scott started to say something, a protest most likely. That's what Conor would do if the roles were reversed, so he held up his finger to short-circuit the protest.

Conor went on. The Germans needed to take Lind alive and beat the intelligence that Conor burned at the boathouse out of him, which meant they would most likely attempt to board or at least stop the motor gun boat. When they demanded Lind be handed over, they would be told that Lind had suffered injuries and was dead. Not believing this, they would ask for the body because they would need to prove to their superiors that they completed their mission one way or another. Scott would agree to hand over Lind.

"But we both know that once they get the body, they would waste no time in sinking us," Conor said.

"Words right out of my mouth," Scott said.

Conor continued. The body on the stretcher would be Conor, his head heavily bandaged. Under a blanket he would have six petrol bombs. Since they would most likely have a description of Lind, Conor would need to act quickly. Once aboard, he would toss three of his bottle bombs fore and three aft. From the bridge of the gun boat, two flares would be fired fore and aft as near as possible to the hatches to start fires. Then the four gun mounts would open up.

"We have to draw them in and hit them first. Hit them hard and fast. Do the unexpected. Then we fight our way out while they deal with any damage and chaos we cause. I'll make my way back to the gun boat. Hopefully, they'd be too busy keeping their boat from blowing up to worry about me."

Scott shook his head. "Yes, it's far from a perfect plan. In fact, it's just plain crazy. The Germans aren't that stupid."

"We need them to be just a little stupid."

"You might want to take a more serious approach to this matter, Mr. Thorn."

"I am, Captain. We just don't have a lot of options, at least not until we get some help from that squadron of motor torpedo boats.

I'm just counting on the Germans taking some … crazy risks to complete their mission. I suspect that they know their orders have been issued from some highly placed Nazis in Berlin. Possibly Himmler himself."

They were a hundred yards from entering the fog bank. Scott played with his pipe for a long moment and stepped in to take over the helm. "It will probably be an S-100 class E-boat. It's about 114 feet long. Four diesel engines are amidships with fuel cells aft of the engines. Make one of your tosses amidships, where one of the flak guns are located. There's some deck venting for the engine room. You might get lucky. God knows I hope you do … for our sake."

Chapman popped out of the forward hatch with one of the twin Vickers machine guns in one hand and a drum magazine in the other and laid both on the deck. Someone from below pushed up the other Vickers. The fog surrounding them was thinning. A moment later, the gun boat found itself in the clear. Conor was about to head below when Chapman called out, "Captain, starboard side."

A three-engine seaplane was approaching, and less than thirty seconds later, the Luftwaffe black-and-white cross on the fuselage and the Nazi swastika on the tail were clearly visible. It circled the speeding gun boat. Chapman quickly mounted one of the twin Vickers on the port side of the chart house, but before he could load a drum magazine, the plane banked sharply and headed east, probably back toward its base somewhere in Denmark.

"It won't be long before we have company," Scott said.

"How much longer before we see the MTB squadron?"

"Not soon enough. Better get ready. I'll have Chapman get the flare gun ready after they finish bringing the Oerlikons topside."

#

Conor stopped in the wardroom to check on Lind. He tugged at the man's restraints. Satisfied, he turned to leave.

"When do we get back to England?" Lind asked.

"Soon. But what's your hurry? You're going directly to the Tower of London."

"I won't be the only one."

"What does that mean?"

Gunnar looked past Conor into the forward crew quarters. Eve stood there scowling at Gunnar.

"Something you wanted to say?" Conor asked her.

"Emily wants to see you."

Conor followed Eve to where Bobby was still resting. Emily had finished working with Tony on the petrol bombs and was sitting on a nearby crate, dabbing at Bobby's chest wound with a soft cloth. His face was pinched; deep creases ran across his forehead. "How's he doing?"

"He's in pain. The constant pounding of the boat is keeping the wound from clotting. Eve wants to pull the bullet out," Emily said.

Eve's hair was a tangled mess. She rubbed her eyes with the palms of her hands. The bags beneath them betrayed her fatigue. It had been long days and nights for all of them, but Eve looked like she was paying a higher toll than the rest of them.

"Can we stop again? I'm worried about infection setting in," Eve said.

"No chance. Is there any brännvin left to give him?" Conor asked.

"No," Emily said.

"He's tough. Do what you can about the infection issue. Keep the wound as clean and dry as possible," Conor said to Eve. "Em, let's go talk to Gunnar."

Eve bit her lower lip and started to say something.

"What?" Conor said.

"Could I talk to Gunnar too?"

"No. Take care of Bobby."

#

The wardroom was bereft of any personal touches except for a small photograph of a woman in her twenties. The photo, with saw-toothed edges, was creased; the top edge looked like tape had stripped away some of the emulsion. The woman's head was cocked at an alluring angle. Gunnar sat at the felt-covered table, his back against the bulkhead. His eyes were closed; he didn't hear Conor or Emily enter because of the steady whine of the Packards.

Conor rapped on the table and Gunnar jerked, his head hitting the bulkhead with a thud. "Tell me exactly why you thought you'd get away with selling top secret intelligence to the Nazis. Did you think we wouldn't find you?"

Gunnar craned his neck to see behind Conor and Emily. "Where's Eve?"

"She's busy being a doctor. Why?" Emily asked.

Gunnar took a deep breath and let it out slowly. "I did it for her."

"She told you to do it?" Emily asked.

"She did. She said that we'd—"

The sound of a machine gun cut through the low roar of the Packards.

Conor shot a look at Emily. "The curtain is going up. Let's go."

#

Tracers from a fast moving boat were flying high overhead when he and Emily emerged from the foredeck hatch. Warning shots. Conor saw that the two Oerlikons and the Vickers were manned and ready. Conor had never seen an E-boat and was impressed with its low, menacing superstructure, giving it a sleek profile to hide behind waves. Painted on the side below the bridge was a large black panther, its jaws open. The E-boat and the motor gun boat were circling each other, neither firing, taking the measure of each other. A distance of approximately three hundred feet separated the two boats.

Conor and Emily headed to the bridge and joined Captain Scott. "They came out of that fog bank to the east like a cat with its tail on fire. No way to outrun her. We held return fire, hoping your plan of a surprise hit-and-run works. Oh, and in case you didn't notice, their torpedo tube hatches are open."

Conor grabbed a set of binoculars and zeroed in on the port side torpedo tube. It bulged out from the side of the foredeck, its hatch open. "It's a bluff. They won't fire off any torpedoes. At least not until they have Lind."

"Well, there's a cheery thought."

"Have they hailed you?" Emily asked.

"Not yet," Scott said as he looked through his own binoculars. "Belay that. Someone on the bridge is raising a megaphone."

The E-boat came to a full stop but kept their engines idling. Scott mirrored the action. "Royal Navy gun boat ... you have a passenger ... a Gunnar Lind. Release him to us and we will let you proceed."

Scott turned to Conor. "You're up, Mr. Thorn."

"Tell them you'd be happy to hand over Lind but he's deceased. And if this is just a hand over, tell them to unman their guns and close the torpedo hatches. Otherwise, Lind will be sent to the bottom."

"What if they demand the same thing?"

"No deal. Stand firm. They'll agree. They want Lind."

As Scott started the negotiation with the E-boat captain, Conor and Emily headed below. A stretcher was laid across two crates of ball bearings on the starboard side. Tony had several rolls of gauze and two blankets stacked on another crate.

"When you wrap my head, cover my eyes with a thin layer of gauze. I'll need to able to see without them noticing my eyes are open." Conor took off his peacoat, and Emily and Tony started the bandaging process.

"Conor, I know we don't have many options but ... the chances—"

"That this will work are low. I know. Which is why I saved this last piece of the plan for you. If I don't make it back ... if we can't put that boat out of commission," Conor said in a hushed voice, "you can't let them get Lind. You have to shoot him. Can you do that?"

Emily nodded. "Yes." Her eyes became glassy, the pupils shimmering like precious stones.

"Another thing." Conor grabbed her hand and pulled her closer to his mouth. "They can't take you alive. You need to take one of these." He handed her the jeweler's box containing the cyanide capsules Donovan had given him. "Put one in your mouth and bite down." She took the box and gave him a slow nod. "Don't worry," he said as he brushed her cheek with the back of his fingers. "I have a good feeling about this."

Emily started to say something, but Tony interrupted. "We're not worried, Mr. Thorn. Emily here has been telling me all about you. You seem to be quite a capable fellow. And a good kisser, she told me."

Conor laughed as Emily playfully slapped Tony on the arm. "Let's get me looking like a truck hit me. Then, Tony, you and one of the snipes are going to have to hoist me up through the hatch to the deck on the stretcher. We need to make this look good, so you'll need to strap me to the stretcher so I don't fall out, but you need to pull the straps off once I'm topside. Just make sure they don't see you do it. I need to be able to move fast as soon as I hit the deck of the E-boat."

"I think we can pull that off. No worries on my end."

"Good. Let's get to it."

#

Conor was on the stretcher, wrapped loosely with a blanket, as Emily, Tony, and the younger snipe stood nearby. Only the upper half of Conor's head could be seen. The six bottles of petrol were tucked between his legs. Electrical tape held three bottles each together, so he wouldn't have to make six tosses, just two. More tape had been used to form a handle that he could quickly grab to fling the bottles. His Colt was tucked in his front waistband, a round chambered. Beside him was Bobby's M1 carbine with the stock folded.

"What do you see, Emily?"

She knelt beside the stretcher. "The E-boat is closer, about fifty yards off our starboard side, putting an inflatable into the water. There are only two men in it."

"Okay. I forgot to tell you something."

"Me too, but tell me later. When you're back safe."

He gave her an odd look. "'Keep your head down' won't be as relevant later," Conor said.

Emily blushed. "Oh. Of course I'll do that."

Conor felt moisture between his legs that was quickly followed by a waft of petrol fumes. A leaking bottle was a concern.

More than one was a serious problem. He counted on a breeze to disperse the fumes.

A minute later, Emily whispered, "They're here."

Chapman and Tony picked up the stretcher, placed it on the deck, and slid it out toward the two men in the inflatable.

Conor counted the seconds until they reached the E-boat. It took the two E-boat crew members two minutes to cover the distance. He would need at least an extra minute to swim back.

The stretcher was lifted by the men in the inflatable and passed on to two other crew members, then immediately laid down on the deck just behind the portside torpedo tube, next to a spare torpedo. The captain, wearing a black officer's cap and a leather waistcoat over a heavy turtleneck sweater, burst between the two deckhands. He leaned over, but before he could lift the blanket and bandages to check his identity, Conor raised his right leg and, like a piston, rammed his boot into the man's chest, sending him crashing into the E-boat's superstructure. Conor sat up, grabbed a taped petrol bomb in each hand, and heaved one toward the foredeck hatch and the other toward the amidships location of the engine room. From the kick to the bomb tosses, less than three seconds elapsed. Two more seconds and Conor had fired the first rounds from the M1 into his first target—the captain—then the two crew members that brought him over. The four gun mounts on the gun boat opened fire.

#

Emily, on the bridge next to Chapman and Scott, saw the kick that sent the E-boat captain flying backward. The petrol bombs followed. Some of the E-boat crew ran for cover while some raced to man their guns; then the M1 carbine started firing. Chapman had the flare gun at his side, but as he lifted to fire, the gun boat was hit by a strong swell and the gun hit a handrail and dropped to the deck. The gun boat's Oerlikons and Vickers ringing in her ears, Emily scooped up the flare gun and fired off two rounds, fore then aft. The boat's gun mounts pounded the length of the E-boat's deck and superstructure. The gun crew of the E-boat's foredeck flak gun was cut down. The rear flak gun fired; a rear section of the sloping superstructure of the gun boat was hit. The amidships flak gun ceased firing when the flare hit the petrol that had the aft deck awash. Flames shot up from the deck; the loader of the two-man gun crew found his pants were on fire. About four feet forward of the aft flak gun, Emily saw smoke pour from an open hatch. Chapman yelled something about the engine room.

"Where's Thorn?" Scott called out. Emily turned toward the bridge, where the shout had come from. One moment, Scott was standing there, searching the sea with his binoculars. The next, he was slumped over the gunwale.

#

Conor saw the white-hot trail of one of the flare gun's rounds as it hit the amidships deck and ignite the petrol. He felt the vibration of the E-boat's engines as they were throttled up. Time to go. He dropped the M1 and rolled off the deck. He swam underwater for as long as he could. In the academy swim test, he had gone twenty-five yards underwater without surfacing—when he was a younger man; with that and the currents factored in, twenty-five yards would be a challenge. Small-caliber rounds were landing all around him. He knew that rounds fired into the ocean lost their speed about one yard into the water, so he swam deeper. An explosion assaulted his eardrums like two massive sucker punches to the sides of his head. Thirty seconds later, with his lungs about to rupture, he slowly released his breath and made it to the surface. A glance over his shoulder revealed that the E-boat's midsection was engulfed in flames and it was drifting.

He went under again and surfaced fifteen seconds later alongside the gun boat. He could barely hear the boat's deck guns for the ringing in his ears. Emily tossed a rope down to him. He grabbed it and started to climb, but his arms were weakened by the underwater swim, and halfway up the side, Emily had to reach down and pull him up with both hands. They rushed to find cover from the increasingly sporadic gunfire.

They flopped to the deck behind the superstructure as another explosion roared. Conor craned his neck and saw the area near the foredeck flak gun burst into a raging fire. There were ammunition storage boxes near the gun mounts, and it didn't take the metal boxes long to cook before they lit off. The E-boat was down in the stern. What was left of the crew was trying to suppress the fires and save the boat.

Let them have at it, Conor thought as he felt the four Packards come to life in all their supercharged glory. He grabbed Emily to steady her as the four propellers bit into the cold waters of the North Sea.

CHAPTER SEVENTY-SEVEN

1300 Hours, Saturday, October 31, 1942
Mid-way through the Broad Fourteens, England

They had taken their share of loses. Along the sides of the gun boat's mangled superstructure were the bodies of Captain Scott, Tony, and the younger engine room snipe. Tony's death hit Emily hard. She had lingered over his body for at least fifteen minutes, primping his uniform and smoothing his hair. What was left of the crew had come by earlier and paid their respects to their crewmates. The older snipe said some kind words about Captain Scott and before he returned to the engine room, he slipped a pound note into the pocket of his engine room mate and mumbled something about paying his debts.

Conor was at the helm, while Chapman and Emily topped off the gun boat's fuel tanks. He scanned the horizon and the skies for unwanted guests. He spotted several seagulls circling and diving into the swells and took it as a sign that they were near land.

Chapman and Emily joined him, Chapman taking over the helm, and Emily picked up a pair of binoculars and started to search the sea ahead of them.

Conor put a hand on Chapman's shoulder. "Sorry about your men. I wish the outcome was better."

"They knew what they were getting into. We all did when we volunteered for this mission," Chapman said. "Don't take this the wrong way, Mr. Thorn, but those ball bearings down there are just as important to us as the lot of you people. Of course, we probably didn't get the whole rundown on this Lind fellow."

"Maybe someday you'll get the full story," Emily said. "I sincerely hope you do."

Chapman, his eyes on his instrument panel, nodded.

"I have something to ask of you. I know that we're supposed to head for Harwich," Conor said.

"That's right," Chapman said.

"Emily and I think we need to divert to a different port: Southend-on-Sea."

"For what reason?"

"Leaks."

Chapman's brow furrowed. "Leaks?"

"Only two people in Stockholm were supposed to know we were headed for Lysekil—one person in the US Legation, one in the British, both of whom Emily and I trust completely. Yet that SD agent made his way to Lysekil. He was responsible for that E-boat showing up. And those C Bureau gents—how did they know to visit you while you were docked at Lysekil?"

Chapman looked at Conor quizzically.

"Someone leaked our extraction plan. I don't know who, and at this point, it doesn't matter."

"It's Harwich, Mr. Thorn. Not Hamburg."

"Yeah, I know. But—"

"Gunnar Lind must not fall into the wrong hands. Not after all we and your crew have been through," Emily said. "My mother has a home in Southend-on-Sea. It will be safer, and your ball bearings can be shipped as easily from there as Harwich."

The gun boat plowed through the North Sea for another minute before Chapman responded. "I'll have to take your word that this diversion is necessary. Southend-on-Sea it is. Take over the helm, and I'll plot us a change of course."

Emily saw the plane before the sound of the engines could be heard. She pointed into the sky toward the stern. Chapman and Conor looked up.

"It's a Messerschmitt 110 ... he's alone," Chapman said. "I'll take over." He took the helm and began a tight zigzag pattern.

Conor and Emily took up positions at the two twin Vickers.

The Me 110 was at least a mile out, well beyond the range of the Vickers, but the twin-engine fighter plane was closing the distance rapidly. The 20 mm Oerlikons opened up. Conor pulled back on the Vickers's bolt handle as the Me 110's nose cannons started firing; rounds from the cannons ripped through the water along the gun boat's starboard side. As he and Emily started firing, tracers to the left and right of the gun boat filled the air around the Me 110. They were coming from the direction the gun boat was heading.

Two lines of two motor torpedo boats appeared, bracketing the gun boat's course. They laid on a steady stream of fire. The Me 110's port engine started trailing black smoke. Just as Conor and Emily added to the fusillade from the torpedo boats, the Me 110 banked hard left and headed back east, toward the Netherlands.

Chapman ceased his zigzagging and throttled back the Packards. Conor looked up to the sky and let out a whoop so loud that a startled Emily almost slipped and fell to the deck. The four torpedo boats took up positions off the gun boat's port and starboard sides.

"So, do you think we can get a good meal at your mother's place?" Conor asked.

"I suspect so. As long as you behave yourself."

"I'll be on my best behavior." Conor secured his Vickers. "I'll go check on Bobby."

"No, I'll do it. You spell Chapman so he can plot the course for Southend-on-Sea. The sooner we get there, the better off Bobby will be."

#

Ever since the battle with the German boat, Eve and Gunnar had been left alone. She had tended to Heugle, hoping to get in Thorn's good graces, but all the while, she worried about Gunnar, about what he might have said to Thorn earlier.

She left Heugle's side and walked through the hatchway to the wardroom. Gunnar was fast asleep, his head resting on his folded arms atop the table. She shook him. He woke and stared at her for a long moment as if he didn't recognize her.

"What were you and Thorn talking about?"

"What?"

"A few hours ago. You and he were talking. I interrupted you, then he and Emily came to see you. What did you say?"

Gunnar yawned. "I told them I was selling the intelligence for you. I said I did it for you."

Eve narrowed her eyes. "What else?" she asked, her tone accusatory.

"Nothing." Gunnar looked annoyed. "You know, I didn't hate him as much as you did."

"So what? It's done. Don't tell them anything."

"This is over, Eve. Nothing worked out as you planned. Nothing."

The sound of something heavy hitting the deck just outside the cabin startled them both. Heugle was lying on the deck on his back, his face white as a sheet. He was mumbling something she couldn't understand. The bandage over the bullet wound was soaked with blood, which was starting to pool on the deck. What had he heard? How long had he been standing there? She had no way of knowing.

As she stared at Heugle, the boat started taking tight turns. Gunfire from above told her another battle had erupted. She reached under Heugle's armpits and dragged him back to his berth, struggling to get him up on the bed.

The gunfire from above ceased abruptly, the boat staying steady on its course and engines quieting again. Her mind raced. If she was going to remove the potential threat that was Heugle, she needed to do it now. She took the pillow from under the man's head.

"What happened here?" Eve jumped at the sound of Emily's voice. Emily was standing next to Gunnar's cabin, staring at the pool of blood on the deck.

"He ... he got up. I was talking to Gunnar, and he must have followed me. But he's weak from blood loss and he collapsed, and it opened the wound."

Emily walked over to them. Heugle was taking short, shallow breaths. "Put the pillow under his head, Eve. Now."

"I was just going to—"

"Do what, Eve?"

Eve didn't respond. She replaced the pillow, not making eye contact. A long moment of silence followed. Eve busied herself gathering some bandages. "I'll help you change the dressing. But let's be quick about it," Emily said.

"If I had the proper instruments, I might be able to get the bullet out."

"We'll be ashore soon. He'll get what he needs then."

CHAPTER SEVENTY-EIGHT

2045 Hours, Sunday, November 1, 1942
Bright Residence, Southend-on-Sea, England

The ambulance bounced along the road from Southend-on-Sea's small dock to Emily's family home. She sat in the cab to give directions to the driver. The space in the back of the ambulance was even more limited than in the gun boat. Conor sat between Eve and Gunnar, Emily's family doctor across from him. He was cleaning Bobby's chest wound. Between the rough North Sea transit and the bouncing ambulance, Bobby couldn't catch a break. He let out an occasional groan while Eve explained how she was limited with what she could do. The doctor, a thin man somewhere north of seventy, said little. He had asked no questions when Conor loaded the restrained Gunnar in the back of the ambulance, which suited Conor just fine.

When the fifteen-minute drive came to an end, Conor and Eve piled out of the ambulance. The driver came around to the rear and started to pull the stretcher out. Conor lent a hand while Emily knocked on the front door. The air was filled with the smell of brackish water from the Thames estuary no more than a hundred yards away. A light went on in a room just above the front entrance, and a delicate woman in her sixties opened the door. The scene she found left her speechless.

"Hello, Mum." Emily hugged her mother, who was too startled or too sleepy to hug her back. "Sorry to disturb your sleep, but I have some friends who need a place to stay for a bit. I told them you would love the company. And I believe you know Doc Mathews."

Emily's mother placed her hand over her mouth and mumbled something Conor couldn't make out.

"Oh my, indeed," Emily said. "Conor, this is Bertie, my mother. Mum, this is Conor Thorn. I am sure you two will get along just fine."

Bertie stood on her tiptoes and hugged Emily again. "You could have called. I look a sight."

"So sorry. We had our hands quite full." Emily turned to Conor. "Shall we?"

He and the driver picked up the stretcher and led the group into the foyer.

"Up the stairs, second room on the right. And do be careful. That boy looks like he's had quite enough trouble. Dr. Mathews, what do you need?"

Conor liked Bertie already.

#

Bertie told Conor he could use the room that once housed her husband's hunting rifles, located next to the kitchen in the back of the house, to secure Gunnar. Eve asked to stay with Gunnar, and Conor agreed. It didn't matter now; they'd already had so much time together below during the action topside. Leaving them, he found the study off the foyer and pulled Bobby's Colt from his waistband. Putting it on a small table, he dropped into a leather wing-back chair. Above the fireplace hung a painting of a young woman and a man who looked slightly older. Conor rose and approached the painting to study it—it was of Emily, somewhere in her late teens, standing next to her brother, Richard, given the resemblance. Whoever painted it captured an element of mischievousness in their faces. He sat back down and checked his watch and decided to phone Donovan with his report.

As he reached for a nearby phone, voices from the foyer startled Conor. It was a little over an hour since they'd arrived. Emily and Bertie, who had assisted Mathews, were chatting. Conor grabbed the Colt and joined them. Bertie flinched when she saw the gun in his hand.

"The shot of morphine will last several hours. He needs a deep sleep," Dr. Mathews said. Conor heard fatigue in his soft voice. "Change the dressings again as needed. But we must leave the tube in his chest for another two days. We'll need an X-ray to see just where the bullet is lodged. Only then can we determine if we need to remove it. I'll be back around midday to check on him. Call me if problems arise."

"Thank you, Doctor. I'll have the kettle on for you," Bertie said.

When Dr. Mathews closed the door, Bertie turned to Emily and Conor. "There are bedrooms upstairs. They're a little dusty, but given the looks on your faces, I am sure you won't mind."

"Thanks for the offer, but I have to keep an eye on our two traveling companions," Conor said.

"We'll do shifts. I'll take the first and you can relieve me in three hours," Emily said.

"And I'll take the second shift so you can both can rest. I can handle a gun, don't you worry," Bertie said.

"I'll just grab some sleep in the study so I'm close by," Conor said.

"So, either one of you going to tell me what this is all about?" Bertie asked.

Conor and Emily looked at each other and shook their heads.

"I thought as much."

Conor returned to the study to call Donovan.

"Where are you? Do you have Lind?" he asked, rapid-fire.

"We're east of London. At the mouth of the Thames. It's called Southend-on-Sea. And yes."

Conor heard Donovan exhale.

"The body count was high," Conor added.

"We heard. You were supposed to go to Harwich. What happened?"

"Exactly what happened isn't clear. What is clear is that our extraction plans were leaked. People who shouldn't have known about our leaving from Lysekil did. And it caused some big problems for us. I decided to avoid going to Harwich."

"What about any documents?"

"Documentation was destroyed. As far as Lind is concerned, we've learned very little. He hasn't bared his soul, but—"

"But what?" Conor detected a hint of annoyance.

"Colonel, from the moment we grabbed Lind and destroyed the intelligence, we've been on the run, trying to stay alive. We hadn't had time to grill him yet."

"All right. I understand," Donovan said, his tone less sharp. "You did a good job. And thanks for finding Emily. Is she okay?"

"She is now. The SD wasn't too kind to her."

"Bastards." His sympathy lasted only a second before he said, "Tell me about Eve Lind. I hear she wasn't much help."

"No. I see no signs of the woman who wanted to wring her husband's neck a few days ago. Something's not right. And Gunnar … he doesn't come across as the brilliant guy Alan Turing said he was. I have some time before a MI6 team gets here to take him back to London. I'll spend some quality time with him and get some answers."

"Whether you're successful or not, Conor, he's going away for quite a while."

"Right."

"Oh, where's Heugle?"

"Convalescing."

"Okay, fill me in later. Get back here as soon as you can. Torch landings are looming. We may need you back in Tangier if Heugle is down for the count."

Conor sat for ten minutes after he hung up. He ran the Gunnar Lind file through his head, looking for contradictions. He recalled his conversations with Turing, Eve, and Maisie Buckmaster.

#

Conor woke up as the clock on the mantel struck midnight. Bertie came into the study carrying a tray with a small pot of hot water, a cup and saucer, a tin of biscuits, and a tea infuser loaded with tea leaves.

"You look like you could use this … before you take your bath. I've laid some of Richard's clothes out for you." Conor knew of the death of her son, Emily's brother, a Merchant Marine officer, in the Med the prior month when his convoy, headed to Malta, was attacked by Luftwaffe fighters.

"Thanks so much ... ah, can I call you Bertie?"

"That depends. If you're planning on becoming a fixture around here, yes. But if you don't, stick with Mrs. Bright."

"Okay ... Bertie," Conor said, which prompted a smile and a wink from the diminutive woman. "Where's Emily?"

"She's almost done with the first shift. And you should get some sleep. You look beaten down, Conor Thorn."

Conor nodded. "Thanks for the tea."

"You're welcome," Bertie said as she shuffled out of the room.

Conor took a bite out of a biscuit as he reached for the phone, then realized what time it was. The call to Bletchley Park would have to wait till morning.

CHAPTER SEVENTY-NINE

0900 Hours, Monday, November 2, 1942
Bright Residence, Southend-on-Sea, England

The phone connection to Turing at Bletchley Park was of poor quality and lasted under ten minutes. When Conor placed the handset back in its cradle, he sat and went over notes he had taken. Satisfied, he stood and headed to the kitchen. Mother and daughter were standing side by side in front of a massive black iron stove. The aroma of cooking eggs and frying bacon almost knocked him over, but eating had to wait.

"Emily," Conor said, startling both women. "We need to talk to the Linds. Can Bertie finish up?"

"Yes, of course I can. Been doing it since before you both were born. Now go."

Conor filled in Emily on his conversation with Turing and his conclusions. As they approached the old gun room, they could hear Eve yelling at Gunnar—that sounded like the Eve Lind he first met, full of disdain for her philandering husband. Conor waited for a response from Gunnar, but none was forthcoming.

He unlocked the door, and he and Emily went in. Several blankets and two pillows lay in the corner of the room. Eve was seated in a straight-backed chair. Gunnar lay prone on the oak floor, his arms behind his head. He seemed unfazed by the tongue-lashing Eve was doling out, which, from the scowl on Eve's red face, incensed her.

Conor leaned against the wall directly opposite Eve. Emily stood next to him. "So I heard a joke a while back. See if you like it," Conor said.

Gunnar sat up; a slight, bemused smile appeared.

"You see, there's this guy, his name is Pi. He and his wife have a troubled marriage—maybe like the two of you do. So they go to a marriage counselor to try to work things out." Conor looked at Emily, who cocked her head. Conor turned back to Gunnar. "So Pi's wife opens up with a complaint. She says, 'He's irrational and goes on and on.'"

Gunnar, silent, looked at Eve. No one laughed.

"I called a friend of yours this morning: Alan Turing."

Gunnar nodded slowly.

"He says that you always … *always*, without fail, laugh at that joke."

Gunnar looked at Eve, then back at Conor. "I guess after what you've put me through, I'm not in a laughing mood."

"Yeah. That could be. Here's another thing: when we showed you the documents that you were going to sell to the Germans, you reacted like it was written in some unknown language."

"He knew what they were," Eve said, scowling at Conor.

"Really, Eve? I don't think so."

"I don't either," Emily added.

"Here's something else that bothers me, Gunnar. Your friend Turing told me about a letter that you wrote to Alastair Denniston. You remember him, he was the head of Bletchley Park when you arrived from France." Conor looked at Eve.

Her scowl was gone. She now looked confused.

"The letter came back because it was addressed wrong. When he mentioned the letter, it reminded me that Maisie Buckmaster said that one night, close to when you disappeared, you went out to mail a letter. It was a nasty, rainy night. So I asked Turing to open it and read it to me." He turned to Eve. "Do you know what it said, Eve?"

"I have no idea," Eve said as she stroked the cross around her neck.

"It said that Gunnar wanted to give back the money that MI6 paid him for the help he gave them when you both were in France … before war broke out."

Eve's mouth opened slightly and she turned to look at Gunnar.

"It seems your husband was upset at the news of what the Nazis were doing to innocent people in France and Eastern Europe. He confessed his hatred for the Nazis. He used the word 'subhuman.'" Conor paused to make sure he wasn't missing any signs from either of them. "I think it was the letter that Maisie Buckmaster told me about."

"She is a very nosy woman, never minds her own business," Eve said.

"And Maisie's mother. Maybe she didn't mind her own business either. Maybe you were jealous of the long walks that Gunnar took with her. Gunnar thought so, didn't you, Gunnar?" Conor looked for any reaction from Gunnar. None. "Maybe Gunnar told her too much. That's why you killed her."

Eve let the accusation go unanswered.

"And then there are the letters from Rubie to Gunnar. You had someone write them for you, didn't you? Maybe a friend or neighbor? Slip them a pound note for their trouble and a promise to keep it quiet. All bases covered."

Eve sat silent, stroking her belly.

"Emily, your turn."

"When it became obvious that you were pregnant, you said it was Gunnar, but I know that's impossible. The night we took the train from Tempsford to Bletchley Park, you were asleep. We shared a bottle of wine, and he told me that his biggest shame was that he couldn't have children of his own."

Eve slumped in her chair. Her hands dropped to her sides.

"He felt that you never forgave him for that. I thought you just had an affair to get back at him," Emily said, then paused for a moment. "I really feel that the Gunnar I knew wouldn't have cared, as long as it made you happy."

Conor turned to the mystery man. "You're not Gunnar Lind. You certainly look enough like him that you fooled Emily and Eve's father, which … makes you his brother."

The room fell silent. The only sound was the rushing of water through pipes under their feet.

"And the father of Eve's baby," Emily said.

The man seated on the floor let out a long breath. "My name

is Lars. I am Gunnar's twin. And I have allowed myself to be controlled by this crazy, greedy woman."

"Where's Gunnar?" Conor asked.

Lars looked directly at Eve, who kicked him on the shin. He grunted sharply in pain. "Search the woods behind the Crown Inn in Fenny Stratford."

"Shut your mouth, Lars," Eve screamed.

"That's where she buried Gunnar."

Conor shook his head in disgust.

It took Lars five minutes to unravel the rest of the story. Gunnar had brought home notes from Bletchley Park that detailed his contributions to the British efforts to break the German naval codes. He said he was going to use them for a book he hoped to publish someday. Eve convinced Lars they could sell the notes to the Germans, but they needed to go to Stockholm to get her father to help them.

"I was a pilot looking for a job when I heard the Norwegians were looking for pilots to fly the route to Stockholm from Scotland. My Norwegian was passable, and a last name change to Nilsen was all it took. So, I started to fly the route between Leuchars and Stockholm somewhat regularly. Eve and I have been meeting at Leuchars, in my down time, having an affair for the past year." It now clicked for Conor. The BOAC pilot at Leuchars recognized Eve but didn't pick-up on the Lind surname. "She worked on me for months to agree to her plan. My brother and I ... we were never close. When our mother died, I learned that she cut me out of her will. Eve told me that Gunnar talked her into it—I was so angry at him." Lars paused. "She most likely lied about that too." His gaze was fixed on nothing in particular. "Eve passed my brother's notes to me during one of her visits to Leuchars, and I took them with me on my last run to Stockholm."

"And you never planned to go back to England," Emily said.

"No," Lars said. "Eve never wanted to go back. We were going to stay in Stockholm, raise a family. I was going to work for her father."

Conor looked at Eve. Her head fell back against the chair; her eyes closed. Tears began rolling down her cheeks.

"So you knew that she was going to kill your brother, and you didn't stop her?" Conor asked Lars as he stared at Eve.

"I didn't know. The original plan was for her to find a way to get to Stockholm with the help of her father and just leave Gunnar, but I didn't think it through. I didn't realize she couldn't pull off her plan if Gunnar was still around."

"You do realize that if those notes had fallen into the hands of the Germans, many lives would have been lost because of it," Emily said.

"Listen, I don't know anything about codes and code breaking. My brother had most of the brains between us. Eve said that the Germans would just change their codes and the British would just break them again. And I bought into it."

"Well, by buying into Eve's plan, you all but pulled the trigger on your brother," Conor said. "Let that rattle around your brain for the rest of your life."

EPILOGUE

1830 Hours, Tuesday, November 3, 1942
Home of Ian Fleming, 116 Piccadilly, London

Conor and Emily slept most of the way on the train from Southend-on-Sea back to London that morning. Between the calls to and from MI6 and OSS Headquarters; taking turns watching over Bobby, who was on the mend; and their last parting words with Eve and Lars Lind as they were taken into custody by MI6, Conor hadn't had much of a chance to catch his breath, let alone sleep. The previous night, Bertie had peppered him with a litany of questions about his parents, place of birth—which Emily was surprised to learn was Dublin during the Easter Rebellion—siblings, and even his middle name—Capability. Emily had a tough time stifling her laughter when she heard that admission.

Conor told Bertie that his mother, Bridgett, was a historian who specialized in Irish and English landscape architects. One of her favorites was an Englishman named Capability Brown, who had designed over 170 parks. Conor didn't mention anything about his mother drowning while saving him from a riptide when he was ten years old. They were having too much fun, even if it was at his expense. And he loved hearing Emily laugh.

They were about to retire for the night when Bertie brought up Grace's rape. Emily didn't look too happy she did. She shushed her mother, but Conor said it was okay. He could tell Bertie was nervous. She stammered through her statements of horror, sadness, and grief. Conor just nodded. As she got up to leave, she patted his cheek softly and said good night. The sense of justice that came with the arrest of Seaker had weakened. It no longer was the salve that lessened his sadness. Grace will always have been raped. Always have been dealing with the dark memories alone. Always have felt vulnerable ... because Conor wasn't there. That would rattle around *his* brain for the rest of his life.

After Emily met with Menzies and Conor met with Colonel Donovan and David Bruce, she talked him into attending a party at Ian Fleming's apartment to celebrate Montgomery's successes against Rommel's Afrika Korps in the second major battle at El Alamein.

Conor eyed her on the elevator ride up to the fifth floor. She was glowing, amazingly showing no ill effects of the Lind affair.

She must have known Conor was staring because she asked, "How do I look?"

He laughed. "Caught me."

When Conor agreed to go, he had made her promise they wouldn't stay long. He had other ideas about how they should spend most of their evening.

The party was in full swing when they arrived. A cloud of cigarette smoke hung above the heads of the guests like bad weather over the North Sea. When Conor glimpsed Maggie in the corner of the living room, she was talking to his godfather, Ed Murrow. Conor headed over to say hello as Emily responded to Fleming calling out her name.

Maggie saw him making his way over, shrieked, and spilled some of her drink. The hug lasted a full minute without any words being exchanged. Murrow smiled, patted Conor on his shoulder, and excused himself.

"I won't ask because I know you can't tell me anything," Maggie said.

"That's right. But can I ask you a question? Did Donovan reel you in?" Conor knew that Maggie was bored with journalism and wanted to contribute to the war effort in a more meaningful way. So, Maggie being Maggie, she thought the best way was to join the ranks of the OSS instead of joining the International Red Cross, as he'd suggested.

Murrow returned with a new drink for Maggie. "Let's talk before you leave, Conor. I have questions for you—maybe some you can actually answer." Murrow winked and withdrew.

Maggie turned to Conor. "He did, not that I like the image of being 'reeled in.' I'm heading back to the States for training in three days. He says I'll probably get dropped in France. I just hope it's after we take it back from Hitler," Maggie said, smirking.

"Very funny." The news didn't surprise him. She never had been the type to sit and watch others, sort of like him.

Emily joined them, and the two women greeted each other warmly. Conor saw a tear rolling down Maggie's cheek.

"I'm so happy you two are together. You are together, aren't you? Please tell me you are." Emily looked at Conor, who made a *She's had a few* signal with his hand.

From across the room, Conor heard Fleming's voice, and someone clinking a glass to silence the crowd. "Quiet down, everyone." As Fleming waited for people to simmer down, he caught Conor's eye and nodded, which Conor returned. "A toast is in order, ladies and gentlemen. To the valiant soldiers of the Eighth Army and their intrepid leader, Lieutenant-General Bernard Montgomery, in their efforts to oust Rommel from North Africa. The Hun is on the run!"

A chorus of cheers from the crowd was followed by raised glasses.

"And, lastly, to the men *and* women who toil in anonymity for the Allied cause." Fleming raised his glass in the direction of Conor and Emily. Several people turned to see whom Fleming was acknowledging.

Fifteen minutes passed as Conor and Emily mingled a bit. Ed Murrow had cornered them both at the bar but was quickly pulled away by Fleming. Conor looked at Emily. "Can we go now?"

"Yes, of course."

"Take me with you, will you?" Maggie asked.

"Sorry, Mags, not where we're going. We'll get together before you ship out."

Conor gave her a kiss on the cheek, Emily did the same, and they both wound their way through the crowd, Emily leading the way. Just steps from the door, it opened, and Kim Philby appeared, dressed in a tailored blue pinstripe suit. It was clear Fleming's wasn't his first stop for the evening.

"Ahh, the intrepid duo. I see you're back from another spectacular success. How would we win this war without the two of you?" Sarcasm dripped from his words.

Conor's dislike of Philby swelled up. Their initial encounter, four weeks prior in the MI6 basement pub, had been the first time he'd felt like decking the man. But he was prepared to give Philby's attitude a pass for the night.

Philby leaned in to the couple. His eyes were bloodshot. "Emily, I must say you look exhausted. It couldn't be due to excessive shagging with your American friend would it?"

The sharp right jab to Philby's face sent him reeling against the door and, of course, quieted the crowd so quickly you'd have thought the queen had just walked into the room.

#

Conor got into the driver's seat of the Buick Roadmaster, and Emily got in beside him.

"I know I shouldn't have done that. Sorry."

"It wasn't fair, Conor. He was drunk."

"He was being an ass," Conor said as he turned over the engine.

"I'm sure we'll both hear about it. But he was a bit of an ass, wasn't he?" Emily said, smiling.

Conor chuckled and followed it with a wry smile.

"So, any ideas about how and where to spend the night?" she asked.

"Well, I'm not sure if you remember, but on our last visit to the Savoy, I left you high and dry."

"Oh, I remember."

"After I met with Colonel Donovan in his suite at Claridge's today, I made a call to the Savoy."

Emily tilted her head as she took him in.

"They're holding a key for me. Room 118. I'm told the decor is something to marvel at."

DID YOU ENJOY
THE ULTRA BETRAYAL?

You can keep reading by grabbing a free short story that pits Winston Churchill against Joseph Stalin, when you join my newsletter. You'll also get the Prologue and Chapter One of *The Torch Betrayal*, the first book in the Conor Thorn Series, and notice of upcoming releases, promotions, and personal updates.

Sign up today at:
WWW.GLENNDYER.NET/SUBSCRIBE

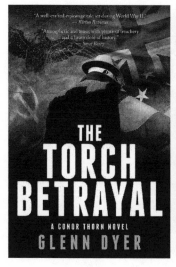
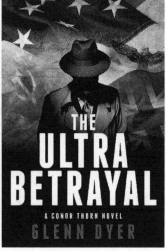

You can help other readers (and this author) by leaving a review for *The Torch Betrayal* and *The Ultra Betrayal* on Goodreads or Amazon. Don't worry—it can be short and to the point. Thanks!

And if you didn't get a chance to read the first book in the Conor Thorn Series, *The Torch Betrayal*, you'll find it at Amazon, Apple Books, Kobo, !ndigo, and Barnes & Noble.
Use this link: books2read.com/TheTorchBetrayal

AUTHOR'S NOTE

As was the case with *The Torch Betrayal*, the first book in the Conor Thorn Series, *The Ultra Betrayal*, while a work of fiction, incorporates a number of real people and references to actual events and places. Readers of *The Torch Betrayal* have told me that the added details regarding these people, places, and events that were provided in that book's Author's Notes were a satisfying end to the overall reading experience.

A good place to start is the inspiration for *The Ultra Betrayal*. Given my general interest in history, specifically World War II, I have countless books, fiction and nonfiction, that delve into various aspects of the conflict—aspects that are broad and some that are much narrower in scope. It was one such story that was briefly mentioned in Anthony Cave Brown's book *Bodyguard of Lies* that inspired *The Ultra Betrayal*.

The story starts in June of 1938. Stewart Menzies (pronounced *Mingiz*), then a deputy to the head of Britain's MI6, Admiral Hugh Sinclair, received word from Major Harold Lehrs Gibson, head of station for MI6 in Prague, that he had, with the help of the Polish intelligence service, met a Polish Jew who was a mathematician and engineer that worked in a Berlin factory where Enigma machines were built. (Cave Brown assigned the name *Richard Lewinski* to this person but noted that it was a pseudonym.) Being Jewish, he had been fired and expelled from German, and most importantly, he was willing to sell his knowledge of the Enigma machine to the British.

The engineer set his price: £10,000, a British passport, and a resident's permit for France, where he wanted to settle—not England as he didn't have any family or friends there. In exchange, he offered to build a replica of the Enigma machine and draw up diagrams of the internal wiring system.

After the engineer's knowledge was vetted in person by Alfred Dilly Knox, a highly skilled cryptologist whose experience in code breaking went back to World War I, and his assistant, Alan Turing—both assigned to Bletchley Park—they recommended to Menzies that he agree to the engineer's terms.

Lewinski, along with his wife, traveled on British laissez-passer documents from Poland to Sweden, then to Paris, France. There, in an apartment on the Left Bank of the Seine River, he fulfilled his end of the agreement and built an imitation of the Enigma machine. Cave Brown writes, "It was about 24 inches square and 18 inches high, and was enclosed in a wooden box. It was connected to two electric typewriters, and to transform a plain-language signal into a cipher text, all the operator had to do was consult the book of keys, select the key for the time of day, the day of the month, and the month of the quarter, plug in accordingly, and type the signal on the left-hand typewriter." After transmission of electrical impulses through the complex wiring of the machine's rotors, the message was enciphered and then transmitted to the right-hand typewriter. Following some additional steps, the enciphered signal was delivered in plain text.

Fast-forward to May of 1940. The German Wehrmacht swept through Belgium, the Netherlands, and France, employing "lightning war" or Blitzkrieg tactics. With the use of coordinated air and ground attacks aided by the use of Panzer tank divisions, the Wehrmacht raced through northern France toward the English Channel. With the Germans drawing close to Paris, causing the ultimate collapse of the British Expeditionary Force and French forces, Menzies, along with Frederick Winterbotham, who was charged with the overall security of Ultra, realized that they needed to evacuate all personnel from France who had any involvement in Ultra, along with any equipment and documentation. Among those evacuated were Lewinski and his wife.

Cave Brown went on to state that Lewinski was given lodgings by MI6 and put under police guard when they arrived in London.

"Then he disappeared . . . Whatever happened, Lewinski left no trace."

After Lewinski's disappearance, speculation as to what happened to him began. One theory had MI6 whisking him to Canada; another theory had Lewinski sent to Australia and given a farm; yet another had him joining a religious settlement somewhere in the Northern Territory of Australia.

Cave Brown does not report any further findings as to the whereabouts or fate of Lewinski. This anecdote, one of many that concern Ultra, intrigued me. Here was a man—who had already sold coveted knowledge of German Enigma machines to one of the belligerents in the conflict—unaccounted for, roaming unchecked around Great Britain or beyond. Did Lewinski have an idea of the level of success the British had achieved in breaking German military codes? To me, it seemed plausible that he did. And once I accepted that it was possible, it gave rise to an interesting what-if.

What if Lewinski escaped and attempted to reach out to once again sell what he knew, this time about British code-breaking efforts? But, of course, a Polish Jew would never turn to the Germans and negotiate a deal for his top-secret information. That assumption necessitated a change of nationalities and a believable way to exit the island of Great Britain. That's where the story of *The Ultra Betrayal* kicks off.

Before I delve deeper into the novel to note additional details behind some of the places, people, and events that are mentioned, I want to address the veracity of Cave Brown's reporting of Lewinski's involvement with the British in 1938. When I researched this particular story further, looking for corroboration, all I could find was a mention of a Polish mechanic who worked at a factory in eastern Germany in F. W. Winterbotham's book, *The Ultra Secret*, which was the first official account written about British code-breaking efforts during World War II. He also states that the mechanic built a replica of the Enigma machine after he was hustled out of Warsaw to Paris. Winterbotham makes no further mention of the Polish mechanic. That said, Cave Brown's story of the disappearance of a mathematician/engineer, with knowledge of British code breaking and who had a history of trading on his knowledge, was an inspiring set circumstances.

Chapter 1 introduces the character of Alan Turing, a mathe-matician and cryptologist who worked at the Government Code & Cypher School at Bletchley Park. He was a brilliant man whose life story was brought into wide public view with the release in 2014 of the film *The Imitation Game*. The film, which won an Oscar for Best Adapted Screenplay, was based on the biography *Alan Turing: The Enigma* by Andrew Hodges. His book was a rich source of information on Turing and his enormous contribution to British code breaking during World War II. In 1999, *Time* magazine named Turing one of the 100 Most Important People of the Twentieth Century. Yes, Turing did lock his mug to the radiator and wear a gas mask.

Also in chapter 1, background information is presented regarding exactly what the fictional character Gunnar Lind was working on. Needless to say, the process of intercepting and breaking German codes was extremely complicated. There are countless resources that thoroughly explain the intricacies of these code-breaking efforts and the discoveries that came from those efforts. One book I found helpful was written by Hugh Sebag-Montefiore called *Enigma*. Sebag-Montefiore tells the stories of the heroic actions taken by the Royal Navy in securing German naval code books, Enigma machine parts, as well as complete Enigma machines. These actions contributed immensely to the success of Ultra.

David Inches, Churchill's valet, makes an appearance in chap-ter 3. Inches was a Scotsman who faithfully served Churchill for many years. One reported exchange between the two men displays the personality of both: While Churchill was in his office in his Chartwell residence, Inches enters to tell him he has a call. After Churchill asks for the call to be sent to his office, Inches explains that he doesn't have the expertise to do so because he isn't "familiar with the mechanism." Churchill responds angrily calling him out for being rude. Inches, who, according to Churchill's chief secre-tary, Grace Hamblin, was known to consume an alcoholic bever-age on the job, responds by calling out Churchill for *his* rudeness. Churchill does own up to his rudeness, but adds, "but I am a great man." Game, set, match.

In chapter 3, Sir George Binney and his Motor Gun Boat

622, a Fairmile D model, 115-foot boat powered by four Packard marine engines, is mentioned by Conor Thorn.

From October 1943 to March 1944, Operation Bridford was mounted by the British at the suggestion of Sir George Binney, who in 1940 was responsible for bringing out of Sweden a number of interned Norwegian ships to the Britain. It entailed using high-speed merchant ships to sail to Sweden and bring back ball bearings and machine tools that were desperately needed for Britain's war production efforts. The ships were manned by nonmilitary crewmen and sailed under the red ensign, the flag flown by merchant ships. This tactic was necessary because warships would have been interned by the Swedes once in Swedish waters. The loading port in Sweden was Lysekil. For purposes of my story, I devised the need for a test run, or runs, to be taken in late 1942 to determine the potential success of such future missions. The boat in *The Ultra Betrayal* was a smaller boat—the Fairmile "Dog Boat"—than the boats that were ultimately used. During the five-month period of Operation Bridford, nine round trips were completed and a total of 347.5 tons of ball bearings, and machine tools and parts were brought back to Britain. It's as good an example of a little-known story of World War II as there is. If you have any interest in learning more, please read Ralph Baker's book *The Blockade Busters: Cheating Hitler's Reich of Vital War Supplies.*

Chapter 5 sees Kim Philby, a longtime Soviet spy, meet with his handler, Shapak. Philby laments not being trusted by Moscow, who seems to downplay the veracity of his intelligence. It brings up the issue of what Stalin knew of Ultra. In my research, I cannot find a definitive declaration that the Soviets knew about Ultra. Philip Knightly, the only western journalist to interview Philby after his defection to Moscow in 1963, states in his book *The Master Spy*, "My own belief, after talking to Philby and others, is that the Russians knew all along that Britain had Ultra...... It is inconceivable that three such highly motivated Soviet spies as Philby, Blunt, and Cairncross could know about Ultra and not tell their Soviet controllers about it." However, in F. W. Winterbotham's book, *Top Secret Ultra*, he writes, "There was never any question of divulging the Ultra secret: the fact that we were able to read German high-grade cyphers. Russian signals security was very bad and the Germans read a good deal of Russian traffic, as we knew from reading German traffic. That being so, to tell the Russians that we were reading Enigma would be tantamount to telling the Germans too." He goes on to state, "In general, Churchill himself, while he never considered telling Stalin whence Ultra came, was temperamentally in favor of giving more information rather than less." Facing these contradictions, I decided to run with the conclusion of Philip Knightly, that it was "inconceivable" that the Soviets didn't know about Ultra. Yes, Churchill did not divulge the Ultra secret, as he was aware that there were many Russophobes in the British military hierarchy, so he was careful about how forthcoming he was with his friend Stalin. To explain Philby's frustrations with Moscow, I made clear that Moscow was wary and hesitant to trust Philby—I assume they were of all agents spying for them, due to Stalin's deep distrust of his British and American allies.

In chapter 6, Benjamin Andersson asks Gunnar Lind: "And how did you travel here from England?" Also, chapter 23 depicts a scene at Leuchars airfield when Conor Thorn, Bobby Heugle, and Eve Lind head to Stockholm with other passengers and cargo. Travel from belligerent nations to neutral countries like Sweden did occur, but it was difficult to arrange and was often limited to people with high-level clearances. British Overseas Airways Corporation established service from Leuchars, Scotland, to Bromma Airport, Stockholm, in 1941. Lockheed Hudsons and Lodestars, owned by the Norwegian Purchasing Commission, were used to ferry high-ranking military personnel, diplomats, diplomatic pouches, as well as shipments of ball bearings. The planes were painted in BOAC colors and crewed by Norwegians. In late 1942, BOAC asked the British government for faster planes to replace the Lockheeds, which were slow and very venerable to German attack during the long days of the Northern summer. BOAC received their first de Havilland Mosquito, a fast two-engine plane that filled many roles for the RAF during World War II, on December 15, 1942. Making Gunnar Lind, or more accurately his brother, a BOAC pilot solved the problem of how to get him to Stockholm.

Fictional characters Lina Stuben and Kurt Eklof of the Sicherheitsdienst (SD) are introduced in chapter 9. The Germans maintained a large presence in Stockholm, just as they did in

Lisbon and Geneva, the capitals of other major neutral countries. This fact did not surprise me given my prior research for *The Torch Betrayal*. But what did surprise me somewhat was that legation staffs, military personnel, and members of intelligence-gathering organizations—such as the OSS, Britain's Secret Intelligence Service, the German Abwehr, SD, and the Gestapo—operated in proximity to one another in Stockholm, often sharing the same restaurant, bar, or coffee shop. A valuable resource covering what life was like in war-time Stockholm was the well-researched and touching *Lady Liberty: A True Story of Love and Espionage in WWII Sweden* by Pat DiGeorge, whose parents met and were married in Stockholm during the war. Pat's father, Herman Allen, was a bombardier and a lieutenant in the US Army Air Force who had been forced to land his B-17 in Sweden in April of 1944 after it was damaged on a bombing run over Berlin. Her book details her father's time in Stockholm, as he went from being interred after his B-17, *Lady Liberty*, crash-landed; his recruitment by the US military attaché to work at the US Legation; to his courtship of his future wife, Hedvig.

In chapter 18, the reader is introduced to three people, two of whom are key characters in the story as well as actual major figures in the Nazi Party. Let's start with Rudolf Brandt, who was the ever-faithful personal administrative officer to Heinrich Himmler. A lawyer by profession, he worked alongside Himmler from December of 1933 until the end of the war. Brandt was acquitted of charges of conspiracy to commit war crimes, crimes against humanity by the US Military Tribunal. He was indicted and found guilty of charges including performing medical experiments on German nationals and concentration camp internees, and membership in a criminal organization (SS). At the age of thirty-nine, he was hanged on June 2, 1948.

Walter Schellenberg headed the Sicherheitsdienst (SD) of the Schutzstaffel (SS), which was led by Himmler. The SS was the primary organization concerned with security, surveillance, and intelligence gathering within Germany and throughout German-occupied Europe. Schellenberg rose through the ranks of the SS from the time he joined in 1933 until he assumed the position of head of the SD, tasked with all foreign intelligence gathering.

As described in *The Ultra Betrayal*, as early as August 1942, Schellenberg was deeply engaged in discussions with Himmler about reaching out to the British and Americans in order to come to peace terms. The proposal included Himmler taking over leadership of Germany from Hitler, who Himmler felt was not fit to continue in his role as leader of Nazi Germany. A fascinating book that provides a comprehensive study of Himmler's peace campaign and the involvement of Schellenberg and Himmler's doctor Felix Kersten is John H. Waller's *The Devil's Doctor: Felix Kersten and the Secret Plot to Turn Himmler Against Hitler*. Schellenberg goes into some detail about the outreach to the Allies in his book *The Labyrinth: Memoirs of Walter Schellenberg, Hitler's Chief of Counterintelligence*. In June 1945, Schellenberg was in Denmark making attempts to surrender to the Allies when the British arrested him. He stood trial at Nuremberg, and on November 4, 1949, he was sentenced to six years in prison for his role in the murder of Soviet POWs. After serving two years, he was released from prison due to a liver condition. He died in 1952 in Turin, Italy.

There are few people who are interested in history or historical fiction who haven't heard of Heinrich Himmler, the Reichsführer of the SS. It can be argued that he was the second most powerful man in Nazi Germany. But, few would disagree with the view that he was one of the main architects of the Holocaust and the man who oversaw the building and operation of concentration camps. Torn between his loyalty to Hitler and his fear for the future of Germany, he vacillated in his desire to wrest control of Germany from Hitler. Yet there is a great deal of evidence that he saw early on that the chances of Nazi Germany winning a conflict with the Allies were fading. In Roger Manvell and Heinrich Frankel's book *Heinrich Himmler: The Sinister Life of the Head of the SS and Gestapo*, the authors note that Himmler's nascent thoughts of pursuing a separate peace with Britain is mentioned in Ulrich von Hassell's diaries as early as May 1941. Hassell had been the German ambassador to Italy from 1932 to 1937 and was a diplomat who held a strong belief in the friendship with Britain and America.

Himmler fell out of favor with Hitler when he learned of Himmler's efforts to negotiate with the Allies in April of 1945.

Hitler ordered Himmler's arrest, calling his secret negotiations the highest form of treachery. Himmler fled with some aids, and they were detained at a checkpoint by former Soviet POWs on May 21. Himmler eventually was taken to the headquarters of the Second British Army in Lüneburg and examined by a doctor. During the exam, Himmler bit into potassium cyanide capsule. Fifteen minutes later, he was dead.

On a lighter note, in chapter 20, the scene takes place at White's Club, the oldest gentleman's club for the rich and privileged in London, established in 1693. A notable current member includes Charles, Prince of Wales, who held his bachelor party there before his marriage to Lady Diana Spencer. Notable former members were the writer Evelyn Waugh; Randolph Churchill, only son of Winston and Clementine Churchill; Stewart Menzies; and the actor David Niven, who along with Menzies and Bill Donovan, makes a brief appearance in the scene.

Niven stared in the movie *The First of the Few*, which was the story of R. J. Mitchell, the designer of the Supermarine Spitfire, the British fighter that proved itself in the Battle of Britain. Leslie Howard directed the film and starred as Mitchell. David Niven, who rejoined the British Army as a lieutenant after Germany declared war on Britain in 1939, was cast as a composite character representing several of Mitchell's test pilots. The movie was released in Great Britain in September of 1942. American producer Samuel Goldwyn gave permission for the studio that produced *The First of the Few* to cast David Niven. But when Goldwyn saw the prints of the film, he became furious that Niven was not in the lead role and cut forty minutes from the US release of the film, which happened in June of 1943. He also changed the film's title to *Spitfire*. As far as Churchill recommending the film to his friend President Roosevelt to screen in the White House, it seemed to me quite possible, and it gave Bill Donovan something to talk about.

Lina Stuben mentions a Frenchman named Pierre Brossolette in chapter 24 while interrogating Emily Bright. Brossolette was quite accomplished. He was a journalist, popular broadcaster, politician, captain in the French Army, and leading member of the French Resistance. Brossolette was recalled to Britain to meet with Charles de Gaulle but the winter weather grounded many Lysander flights, forcing Brossolette to attempt the trip by boat from Brittany in February 1944. When their vessel was besieged by a storm, Brossolette and a companion managed to reach safety with the help of the Resistance. Not long after, they were betrayed by a local woman and jailed in Rennes for a period of two weeks. The Gestapo only knew him as a man called Boutet. He was later transferred to the Gestapo's headquarters in Paris, and eventually, it become known to them that the man identified as Boutet was a leader of the Resistance. Brossolette was tortured at Gestapo headquarters over a two-and-a-half-day period. He withstood severe beatings and waterboarding until, on March 22, left alone after an interrogation session, he jumped out of a sixth-floor window of Gestapo's headquarters. It was a commonly held belief among members of the Resistance that once captured and subjected to torture, it was nearly impossible to not reveal vital information. This belief must have led Brossolette to take such a horrific action. The leap did not kill him instantly, but he died later that day. I took liberty with the timeframe of this tragic event by moving it up to late 1942. I did so because the story of his life and the courage displayed by Brossolette was so moving that I wanted to expose his story to readers of *The Ultra Betrayal*. It is just one more story of bravery and sacrifice that, unfortunately, few people are aware of. His tombstone reads: *His mouth has remained shut. His example speaks to us. His sacrifice commands us.*

The second scene in chapter 27 takes place in the Grand Hotel, Stockholm. The five-star hotel, opened in 1874, is located on the Södra Blasieholmshammer overlooking the Blasieholmen Quay across from the Royal Palace. Being a neutral nation, many countries established legations there, as they did in other capitals of neutral countries. Besides the legation mention in *The Ultra Betrayal*, the list of legations included the Soviet Union, Poland, Norway, Italy, Japan, China, and France. Swedish newspapers had offices in Berlin, and as a result, news from inside Germany came through Stockholm. I mentioned briefly that Stockholm was a hotbed of espionage during the war, and the Grand was at the center of it all.

One factor that contributed to the Grand's reputation as

ground zero for espionage was the fact that many members of the international press set up their operations there when war broke out in 1939, as did some legation staff. There were so many journalists plying their trade at the hotel that the area that housed the correspondents from the United States, Britain, and France was known as "Fleet Street," after the London street famous for hosting most British national newspapers. Popular places where spies could gather intelligence were the hotel's barbershop and its opulent bar. In Pat DiGeorge's book, *Lady Liberty: A True Story of Love and Espionage in WWII Sweden,* she writes that many of the hotel's staff worked for Swedish authorities and that rooms were regularly searched by Swedish police and the Gestapo. In *The Ultra Betrayal,* I mention that Gus Karlson had a suite at the hotel and had convinced some of the staff to provide him with wastebasket contents. This, indeed, did happen. Wilho Tikander, the actual OSS mission chief, received ink blotters, names of arriving guests, and wastebasket contents. After my visit to the hotel in 2019, I can attest that the hotel hasn't lost its sense of grandness and style.

Felix Kersten, who I mentioned briefly when discussing chapter 18, makes an appearance in chapter 30, along with Himmler and Schellenberg. Kersten, a Finnish national, was a fascinating man. He was a gifted masseuse, according to Himmler, who was able to relieve much of Himmler's colic, a condition that involves fluctuating pain in the abdomen. Himmler was so impressed with the gifted Kersten, he convinced Schellenberg and Foreign Minister Ribbentrop to partake of his services. But what truly made Kersten remarkable was his ability to manipulate and reason with the likes of Himmler, which led to the pardons and release of thousands of individuals persecuted by the Nazis. Of particular note is Kersten's involvement as an intermediary between Himmler and a member of the Swedish branch of the World Jewish Congress, Norbert Masur, that led to Himmler agreeing to the release of thousands of concentration camp internees that were marked for extermination, by order of Hitler, toward the end of the war. I firmly recommend John H. Waller's book *The Devil's Doctor: Felix Kersten and the Secret Plot to Turn Himmler Against Hitler* for the full story about this remarkable man.

The issue of how OSS agents conducted themselves while in

Sweden comes up in chapter 35. The head of the US Legation was Hershel V. Johnson, who served in the role of American Minister from December 12, 1941, to April 28, 1946. The minister in *The Ultra Betrayal*, William Howard, also had a framed unfinished portrait of George Washington by Gilbert Stewart hanging behind his desk. And Howard also held the same views about Americans engaging in illegal activities, which covers most of what the OSS was engaged in. Minister Johnson once said to a pilot named Bernt Balchen, with orders from Bill Donovan to set up an operation to fly two thousand Norwegian trainees from Stockholm to England: "If I ever catch you doing anything illegal here, I'll have you deported." To which Balchen replied, "Don't worry, Mr. Minister. You'll never catch me."

Howard's attitude about intelligence gathering and other tasks undertaken by the OSS was consistent with the attitudes held by many longtime officers of the State Department. These officers were, to say the least, extremely naïve and didn't realize that the major powers of the time, minus the United States, had a long head start on what is called the world's second oldest profession.

In chapter 35, Kersten shows photos of a file that Himmler kept on the health of Hitler. In Felix Kersten's memoir, he writes about an encounter with Himmler on December 12, 1942, where Himmler takes a portfolio out of his office safe and presents a manuscript. Kersten reports Himmler saying, "Read this. Here are the secret documents with the report on the führer's illness." The report went on to say that at the beginning of 1942, symptoms indicated that Hitler was suffering from progressive paralysis. For plot purposes, I had Kersten say that the meeting with Himmler took place just days before the October 28, 1942, meeting at the US Legation.

Toward the end of chapter 35, Bob Homer cheekily invites Kersten and Langbehn to a movie screening at the legation of an anti-Nazi film, *The Great Dictator*, which featured an unflattering take on Hitler. According to Pat DiGeorge's book, *Lady Liberty*, movies were privately screened at the legation, such as Billy Wilder's *Five Graves to Cairo*. *The Great Dictator* was shown to Swedish trade unions by Attaché R. Taylor Cole, who was also the OSS Director of Secret Intelligence in Sweden.

A few quick comments. The beginning of chapter 48, the reader is given a little insight into the personality of Heinrich Himmler through his card index of presents. According to Felix Kersten's memoirs, he was given a short lesson on why and how Himmler kept a file on his gift giving.

In chapter 64, Conor is given a .22 LR High Standard HDM, a semiautomatic pistol with a suppressor. I mentioned that Bill Donovan demonstrated the weapon for FDR inside the White House. This did, in fact, take place, but according to Wikipedia, it actually occurred in the Oval Office.

Ian Fleming thanks Bill Donovan, in chapter 66, for the gift of a .38 Police Positive Colt, inscribed with *For Special Services*. According to Andrew Lycett's book, *Ian Fleming: The Man Behind James Bond*, it was one of Fleming's prized possessions.

In chapter 51, the repatriation of air crews from Britain, the US, and Germany is mentioned. At the close of World War II in 1945, more than 300 planes from various waring nations had landed, forced or crashed, in Sweden. All aircraft were interred until war's end, according to Sweden's declaration of neutrality. German crews were housed separately from Allied crews, and as the war progressed, the crews were given an amazing amount of freedom; Allied crews more so. The legations of each country did what they could to add to the care given by the Swedish for their crews. By the end of the war, 126 German planes had landed in Sweden. The first American crew, from the B-17 *Georgia Rebel*, landed in Sweden in July 24, 1943. The crew had bombed a factory in Norway and was badly damaged by flak. Early in the war, repatriation was done on a one-for-one basis: one German for one Allied crew member. But as the war progressed, there were fewer and fewer German crew members to repatriate.

I hope these notes were helpful in coloring in some additional background behind some of the story elements of *The Ultra Betrayal*.

ACKNOWLEDGMENTS

This is the best part of writing a novel—thanking those who provided the much-needed assistance in hammering out a, hopefully, compelling story.

First up are fellow authors JJ Toner and Susanne Lakin. Their help with the initial outline of the story was impactful and put me on the right path.

The Ultra Betrayal benefited greatly from comments from early readers who had to suffer through a very rough draft: Larry Moffit; Wayne Rommel; my brother Mike Dyer; and my son Tom Dyer. Apologies. I owe you all.

John Paine, as with *The Torch Betrayal*, was very helpful in guiding me toward a more solid story in the early drafts.

Gretchen Stelter, an editor with a highly skillful touch, held my feet to the fire on a several key plot points, and for that I am grateful. Her mastery of the editorial process is second to none. Thanks, Gretchen. If not for you, this novel would be so shallow. Sorry for all the emails.

I am blessed to have many great friends. That includes Krista and Craig Lauer, both doctors who helped me with the scenes involving Bobby Heugle and his battle wounds. Again, please excuse my repeated questions and requests for diagrams.

Another thank-you to Chris Grall at Tactiquill, who, as in *The Torch Betrayal*, was a great resource in fine-tuning the fight scenes and any scene that involved weapons. Chris is not only an expert in weapons and action, he also has a great sense as to what makes a good story great. I hope I didn't disappoint, Chris.

I apologize to a gentleman that I pestered relentlessly via email over issues of a problematic Packard maritime engine: John Gulbankian from J & M Machine Company, in Massachusetts. Thanks, John.

To Jane Dixon Smith, a thank-you for another eye-catching cover and a flawless interior design. You are so easy to work with and a fount of information on the publishing process. Thanks, Jane.

Thanks to Will Tyler for a thorough final proofread. A sharp eye and some thoughtful comments.

You can write a good novel, but when it helps to getting it noticed, I owe a great deal to Sue Campbell at Pages and Platforms, for their efforts in the launch of book two in the Conor Thorn Series. Sue, your knowledge can, oftentimes, make my head spin. Thanks for getting me to slow down and enjoy the ride.

A round of applause for Rob Stevens, an old colleague from my broadcasting days, who produced an amazing book trailer. He's a magician of the visual arts. Thanks. And sorry for all the emails about changes. So, what's new about that?

This is a good point to list some—just some—of the writers that have inspired me in this crazy journey: Lee Child, Steve Berry, Daniel Silva, W. E. B. Griffin, Brad Thor, Jack Carr, P. T. Deutermann, Elizabeth Wein, David Poyer, C. J. Box, James R. Benn, Steven Hartov, Jack Higgins, Ken Follett, Kate Quinn, Alan Furst, Anthony Franze, Thomas Kelly, Robert Dugoni, Phillip Kerr, John Lawton, Harlan Coben, John Altman, and Anton Myrer.

I want to mention the OSS Society, which honors the accomplishments and sacrifices made by members of the OSS during World War II. The OSS Society was established by then General William Donovan, in 1947, as the Veterans of the OSS. Please take a look at their website osssocity.org and think about making a donation to their efforts to establish a National Museum of Intelligence and Special Operations. So many stories that can now be told, so many stories that should not be forgotten.

Lastly, to my family: my wife, Christine, and children, Thomas, Michael, and Riley, for never saying anything that doubted I could do this. They did say a few times, "Are you done yet?"

PRAISE FOR THE TORCH BETRAYAL

"The disappearance in 1942 of a page from a secret document concerning Operation Torch . . . drives Dyer's suspenseful espionage thriller . . . Jack Higgins fans will find a lot to like."
— *BookLife/Publishers Weekly*

"Atmospheric and tense, with plenty of treachery and a heavy dose of history. What more could you ask for in a thriller? Take a walk on the perilous side and check this one out."
—Steve Berry *New York Times, USA Today* & Internationally Bestselling Author

". . . what sets Dyer's book apart from the others in the genre is his unfailing attention to historical detail and great writing."
—The BookLife Prize

". . . a classic spy story in the vein of John Le Carré or Daniel Silva . . ."
—BlueInk Stared Review

"*The Torch Betrayal* is the best mix of genre standards from a fresh voice."
—Foreword Reviews

Made in the USA
San Bernardino, CA
05 July 2020